"A classic, breathtaking adventure brimful of dangerous magic and clever politics. This is a book that will thrill and delight any fantasy fan"
Tasha Suri, author of *Empire of Sand*

"Full of magical and political intrigue, Caruso's latest novel will surprise and delight fans and new readers alike. With rich worldbuilding, nuanced characters, and ratcheting tension, *The Obsidian Tower* is a fulfilling read from start to finish"
Tara Sim, author of *Scavenge the Stars*

"Brimming with delights: gripping suspense, bombastic magic, political scheming, fascinating creatures, and ill-advised romance. Yet what I love most is that at its heart, it is simply the story of a young woman opening herself up to the world and embracing her own potential"
Jon Skovron, author of *The Ranger of Marzanna*

"Melissa Caruso's sparkling *The Obsidian Tower* combines a fresh fantasy world with resonant characters and sweeps them into a plot full of political intrigue and magical chaos"
Rowenna Miller, author of *Torn*

THE QUICKSILVER COURT

Rooks and Ruin:
Book Two

MELISSA CARUSO

orbitbooks.net

ORBIT

First published in Great Britain in 2021 by Orbit

1 3 5 7 9 10 8 6 4 2

A CIP catalogue record for this book
is available from the British Library.

ISBN 978-0-356-51320-1

Printed and bound in Great Britain by Clays Ltd, Elcograf S.p.A.

Papers used by Orbit are from well-managed forests
and other responsible sources.

Orbit
An imprint of
Little, Brown Book Group
Carmelite House
50 Victoria Embankment
London EC4Y 0DZ

An Hachette UK Company
www.hachette.co.uk

www.orbitbooks.net

In memory of Freya
The goodest girl, best doggo
Made of love and butter
And Ninja
Soft as a cloud, sharper than starlight
Ever a mama's girl, sometimes a diva, always a lady

Nine I name the darkest powers:
One for Hunger, who devours.
Two for Discord, sowing strife.
Three's Corruption, twisting life.
Four's Disaster, fire and flood.
Five for Carnage, steeped in blood.
Six is Madness, minds laid bare.
Seven's cold and bleak Despair.
Eight for Nightmare, dreaming dread;
Nine is Death, and now you're dead.

ONE

"Anything coming to kill us yet?"

Ashe tossed the question to me from her perch on a low stone column at the near end of the bridge. The cold light of the luminaries caught sparks in her eyes.

I shook my head, lips pressed together.

"Only because it's been two hours, and my rear is freezing off."

I tore my eyes away from the rough black edge of forest beyond the bridge. "Do you want to go up to the castle and get a coat?"

Ashe shrugged. "I hate fighting in a coat."

"I'm really hoping there won't be any fighting."

Ashe gave the restless, hissing trees on the far side of the bridge a dubious glance. "You go on hoping."

I couldn't blame her for being skeptical. The wind shook whispers and creaks from the night-hoarding boughs, a language I could almost understand. The tops of the pines swayed, seeming ready to march toward us with slow arboreal menace.

They might do exactly that, if my grandmother got angry enough.

I didn't feel anger surging through the link that bound us, or much of anything for that matter. My grandmother kept herself remote these days—for which I should be thankful, given circumstances. Instead it worried at my mind like an itch, not knowing what she was up to.

"This isn't like her," I muttered. "We always welcomed trade and visitors from the Empire." I'd built an entire diplomatic strategy on it. Now my grandmother was driving imperial citizens from her domain, and I had to watch all my work crumble with each frightened refugee crossing the border.

Ashe didn't answer. Either she hadn't heard me, or she didn't feel the need to point out the obvious: my grandmother had a reason for not acting like herself.

We stood on the imperial side of the graceful stone bridge the Serene Empire had built across the river, with its carvings of fruitful vines and twin lines of bright luminaries on tall poles. Well-laid paving stones continued the road behind us as it wound off through the hills into the Empire, a branch climbing to Castle Ilseine above us. On the far side, beyond the pooling brilliance of the luminaries, a rocky dirt road passed between two rough and ancient boundary stones into the darkness of the forest and vanished.

Home. I was close enough to feel it, through my magical link to the land of Morgrain: the life running strong through the pine-scented shadows, the birds sleeping in the boughs, the tiny creatures crawling in the earth.

It would be so easy to cross the bridge, to pass between the stones, to enter the forest. Every piece of me yearned to take that first step forward, to plunge back into Morgrain as if I were returning to my grandmother's welcoming arms. Even if what I was feeling from the land didn't exactly qualify as welcome. Slitted eyes watched us from the darkness, and behind sharp fangs rumbled a growl too low for human ears to hear—the same song the trees whispered, the words resonating in the earth: *You can't go home.*

"Hey," Ashe said, her voice low and rough. "Don't do it. She kicked you out, remember?"

"How could you tell I was thinking about it?" I asked ruefully.

"You had this glazed look." She lifted her head, keen as a dog pricking its ears at distant voices. "Wind makes it hard to hear if they're coming. You sure you can't feel anything?"

"Maybe if I were closer."

Ashe knew as well as I did that we were supposed to stay on this side of the bridge. The last thing the Empire wanted to do right now was rile up the living border to wrath by a perceived display of aggression. She chewed her cheek a moment, thinking.

At last, she let out a puff of breath. "All right. I hate standing in the light anyway. Makes us a target."

We crossed the bridge, pacing its stones between overlapping pools of light as the river rushed in darkness beneath us. There was no point trying to be stealthy in our approach; my grandmother could sense my presence. As both a demon and a Witch Lord, she could kill us in the blink of an eye if she chose.

Once, I would have said she'd never do that. Now, I couldn't be sure, and that uncertainty was like a ragged hole that let the bitter wind in through a favorite old coat.

"You realize they could all be dead," Ashe said conversationally. "We could be waiting here for nothing while the wolves eat them."

"The last batch of refugees made it through all right," I pointed out.

Ashe snorted. "Bit scratched and dented, and that was *without* an ominous warning first."

The warning was why we were here. My mother's note—just a scrap of paper, a torn-off corner dropped in my lap by a sparrow this afternoon—had said simply, *Expect trouble*. So we'd come down to watch at the bridge instead of waiting for the refugees in the warm castle. Ashe because she was adept at trouble herself, and me to try to pacify my grandmother if necessary. The rest of the Rookery were stuck in a meeting consulting with the imperial Falcons on potential anti-demon enchantments; there'd been a lot of those lately, peppered between outings to investigate fruitless tips on the location of the Demon of Hunger and the occasional quick jaunt to deal with an alchemical accident or a forgotten artifice trap leftover from centuries-old border wars.

"I just hope we're enough," I muttered.

"If we're not, then numbers wouldn't matter anyway."

She had a point. If my grandmother truly wanted to kill the fleeing imperials, they'd already be dead.

Ashe fell a step or two behind me as I passed beyond the light of the bridge and crossed the brief open expanse of weedy grass to the looming edge of the forest. The boundary stones stood so close I could almost touch them, vibrant with power, marked with my grandmother's blood to close the circle of her grasp around Morgrain. The forest exhaled its soft breath over me, scented with pine and decaying leaves and the soft musk of living things. I closed my eyes and breathed it in, almost weak with longing.

Something was coming.

A shiver of anticipation ran through the forest at the very edge of my senses. The trees rustled as if the wind surged, but the air lay still. An owl stretched its wings, staring down the road; small creatures woke from sleep and lifted wary heads to blink around them.

"Here they come," I whispered.

Ashe rolled her neck. "Time to find out if this is going to be a mortal danger sort of evening, or a drinks by the fire sort of evening."

Far down the road, someone cried out in fear.

"Sounds like mortal danger," I replied, my pulse quickening.

"No reason it can't be both."

Travelers *should* be safe on the road. The Conclave of Witch

Lords had decreed the trade roads neutral territory and prohibited assaulting those who stayed on the path; it was one of Vaskandar's oldest and most important rules. But those rules got bent or broken sometimes even under normal circumstances—and since she had merged with the Demon of Discord, we had no reason to expect my grandmother would hold much respect for them.

Another shriek sounded from the forest, rising with the sharp edge of terror in the darkness. An encouraging voice shouted "We're almost there! Hurry!" in response.

A voice I recognized. *Sweet Grace of Mercy.*

"I'm going in," I snapped to Ashe, throwing myself into a heart-lurching run without waiting for a response.

"What? Wait, Ryx, don't—"

"That's my *mother!*"

I plunged between the boundary stones, caution forgotten. Morgrain unfolded around me at once, painting my senses with a thousand colors of life.

The packed dirt beneath my pounding feet resonated at my touch, watered with the blood of my ancestors, linked to my very soul. The trees had known me before I was born; the creatures that prowled the darkness were my brothers and sisters by the bonds of magic, bound inextricably to my family line, part of the great web of life that ran through Morgrain like the blood in my grandmother's veins—and in mine.

For as long as I could remember, I'd lived with the comfort of knowing in my bones that every living thing in Morgrain would protect me. That everything from the smallest insect to the most towering tree was my ally, my friend.

Now something was different, colder, darker, *wrong.*

No, Ryx. You can't come home.

I pelted down the road in the moonlight-mottled darkness, breath seizing in my chest, following the sound of running feet and crying voices and chiming steel. Branches leaned down over the road, reaching for me. Twigs caught at my hair, and I had to leap over a root that buckled up from the earth to grab me.

My domain had turned against me. It hurt as if a member of my own family had stabbed me in the back. *Curse it, Grandmother.*

A handful of figures approached on the road ahead, three of them running and stumbling toward me, at least one clutching an injury. The fourth stood with her back to me, grounded in a graceful fencer's stance, the thin silver gleam of her blade leveled at a hulking, green-eyed shadow in the road before her.

My mother, facing down one of our battle chimeras by herself.

I threw a breathless "Keep going, the border's just ahead" at the fleeing people and passed them by without another glance; Ashe would ensure they made it. Heart pounding, I skidded to a halt beside my mother.

A shaft of moonlight fell full on her through the trees, catching the jeweled pins that held up her rippling black hair and the elegant swept coils of her rapier guard. Her vestcoat barely nodded at Vaskandran style, with a fitted Raverran bodice, fine Raverran brocade, and a fullness of fabric sweeping behind her that made the skirt look more like the back half of a gown than the bottom half of a coat. Her stance was pure poise and control, as always, and she regarded the battle chimera crouched before her as if it were some churl who had rudely interrupted a private conversation.

She didn't seem injured, thank the Graces. The battle chimera growled low in its throat, hackles up, teeth showing in a snarl; it had the bulk of a bear and the face of a wolf, with patches of scaly armor on its sides. A couple dozen of them always patrolled the border, but they normally had strict orders to never so much as come in sight of the road.

"Ryx," my mother greeted me, without taking her eyes off the chimera. "Good to see you."

I couldn't keep my own voice nearly so level and calm. "Mamma, get out of here. I'll hold it off."

"We'll hold it off together."

"You get the others to safety," I urged her. Whatever I had to say to get her out of danger. "Grandmother won't hurt me. *Please.*"

The chimera threw back its head as if it were in pain. A strange sound came from its throat, twisted and almost unrecognizable, starting as a gurgle and turning into something closer to a bark.

Laughter.

"*Won't I, Ryx?*" it hissed.

A chill walked down my spine. The battle chimeras weren't intelligent; their throats weren't formed for speech. The Lady of Owls must have seized control of this one from afar and shaped its tongue to suit her needs.

"Grandmother?" I whispered.

The beast leveled the flat green glow of its stare at me, reflecting the distant light seeping through the trees from the bridge.

"*I told you not to come home,*" it said, in a voice scraped up from deep in its animal chest.

Grief and anger stung my eyes. "Don't worry. I'll be leaving in a moment."

"Start backing away," my mother whispered. She took a smooth and careful step back herself, sword still pointed at the chimera's eye.

I tried to follow her, but something caught my ankle. I glanced down in alarm to find a root crooked up from the earth and around my boot, winding tighter like a snake with prey in its coils.

My heartbeat lurched faster. She was taking this personally. I was in trouble.

That horrid chuckle rumbled up from the beast's belly again. "*I didn't warn you to stay away because I wanted you gone, Ryx. I warned you not to return to Morgrain because I knew that if you did, I wouldn't let you leave.*"

The root coiled up my leg; a second one wrapped my other

calf. *Oh, holy Hells.* I managed to wrench that foot out of my boot, leaving it prisoned and empty on the road, but my trapped leg wouldn't come free.

My mother stepped up by my side again. "You've made your point, Most Exalted. Let her go."

This was no good. I had to get my mother out of here. "Ashe?" I called over my shoulder.

"All clear!" Ashe's voice floated distantly through the trees. "Got them past the border. You can come back now!"

"I'd love to!" This time, I couldn't keep the edge of panic from my voice.

The chimera paced closer, until its hot breath warmed my face and its fierce eyes stared directly into mine. "*I've missed you, Ryx. Time to come home.*"

A hard lump formed in my throat, and I stopped struggling to get free. I could almost hear my grandmother's resonant voice below the chimera's growling one, almost see the orange rings of her mage mark gleaming in the chimera's eyes.

"I miss you, too," I said hoarsely. "But last time I was home, you wanted to half kill me to see if it would get me to release my power. So forgive me if I'm reluctant to return to Gloamingard."

The chimera's lips drew back from its knife-sharp teeth in a wicked grin. "*Oh, you don't have to come to Gloamingard for that. I can do it right here.*"

The chimera's grin widened to a snarl, fangs bared, and its shoulders bunched to spring. A white-hot lance of fear ran through me. "Wait, don't—"

A hiss of steel sliced the air, and the chimera's head fell with a heavy *thunk* at my feet.

I couldn't suppress a yelp. My mother stared in shock, frozen halfway through a lunge; she wasn't the one who had killed it.

Ashe straightened from her landing crouch, magical energy crackling up her sword from the wire-wrapped orb at the pommel. She might as well have dropped from the sky. Her spiky near-white hair was even more disheveled than usual, and her eyes shone with intense focus.

"We need to run, *now*," she said, as the chimera's body toppled to the ground.

Before I could protest, her sword whipped around in a low, clean arc, slicing through the root that wrapped my leg. Its edge sizzled with magic. I shook the severed wood off, fear rising as the trees thrashed into life and angry animal cries rose up from the forest around us.

"Wise woman," my mother agreed. The three of us sprinted as fast as we could for the border.

Branches reached for us; wings beat at the air. My atheling's senses swarmed with all the life converging on us, roused at my grandmother's command. The air came into my lungs sharp as a knife, and the rough road jabbed at my bootless foot with each uneven step. Ashe paced me easily, slashing at anything that got too close; my mother kept up well enough, her long-skirted coat flowing behind her.

It was only a short dash to the border, and we dove between the boundary stones in a matter of seconds. The lights of the bridge blazed in our eyes.

The open ground felt dead beneath my feet again. The loss of that connection hit me like stepping into cold water.

I collapsed to my knees on the stony road, gasping. Ashe continued toward a cluster of people waiting nervously on the far side of the bridge, huddled together with fear—the refugees my mother had brought to safety, in person this time.

She could have told me she was coming herself.

"Ryx. Are you all right?" My mother hovered over me, not quite touching.

Expect trouble, she'd said. She was trouble, all right. I laughed, breathless. "I'm fine. Mamma, I know you like dramatic entrances, but this is too much."

She smiled, a strange hesitancy in her eyes, her hands caught empty halfway through some gesture I didn't recognize. "Are you . . . That is, can I . . ."

A hug. She was offering me a hug.

My chest constricted. I held up my wrist; the golden jess encircling it shone in the lamplight.

"It's safe," I said, my voice ragged with emotion.

My mother let out a low cry. For the first time since I was two years old, she threw her arms around me.

I knew her scent so well, from years of being wrapped in her scarf in place of her arms. But this—this warmth, this closeness—this was new. Hells, what I wouldn't have given for this when I was small and afraid and just beginning to learn all the ways I could ruin the world around me, all the lonely consequences of a killing touch.

I hugged her back, fiercely, and buried my face in her shoulder to hide my stinging eyes.

"I'm so glad you came," I muttered into the fine brocade of her collar. Her enfolding warmth promised I could let go of everything I held clenched in my middle, all the worry and responsibility and fear, and surrender it trustingly to her supporting embrace, like I dimly remembered doing when I was very, very small.

But that was a luxury of innocence, and one I'd lost long ago.

I drew in a deep, perfume-laden breath. "We have work to do."

TWO

I keep thinking I'm going to die." My mother laughed at herself, letting go of another quick hug and settling beside me on the velvet-cushioned sofa we shared in the sumptuously furnished Rookery sitting room. She seemed entirely at home among its brocade curtains and glittering luminary crystals, in a way I couldn't be—this place was too formal, too imperial, too unlike Gloamingard's ancient gloomy halls. "It's hard to break almost two decades of instincts."

I could feel those instincts in the tension that pulled her muscles taut beside me. It might have been nice to pretend it was left over from our brush with the chimera, but I knew better. It had always been a simple fact of my life that my mother was afraid of me, and for good reason.

"I'm glad you're all right. I was worried, after your note." *Expect trouble.* It summed up my mental state for the past few weeks rather nicely. The familiar knot in my gut tightened, an anxious snarl of everyone and everything I loved that I'd had to leave behind in Morgrain under a demon's power.

"Yes, sorry if that was a bit dramatic. I was short on time and paper." She scooped up her wineglass for a quick sip, as if gathering strength. "And we've had . . . communication problems."

"What kind of problems?" I asked, wary.

She grimaced. "As it turns out, when your primary method of sending messages is via bird, and all living creatures in the domain bow to the authority of the Witch Lord, there's no such thing as a secret plan. Every bird we sent trying to organize a coup stopped at Gloamingard on the way."

My chest tightened. I'd put my frail hopes and no small amount of organizational effort into the family attempt to usurp my grandmother's power; the implications of its failure were dire.

"Is Da all right?" Surely she would have mentioned it first if he weren't. "And the others? Did she—is she angry?"

"Oh, everyone's fine." My mother sighed, with a note of frustration. "She doesn't *need* to hurt us. She froze us in place for an hour to make it clear how disappointed she was. Every single one of us who'd started to put the plan into action, scattered across the domain." She fluttered her free hand distastefully, as if my grandmother's magic were clinging cobwebs she could shake off. "I'd hoped she couldn't control me, but alas, I've lived in Morgrain long enough to be part of it. I had the most terrible itch on my nose that I couldn't scratch. No, we can't challenge her from within Morgrain, I'm afraid. Much as I hate to say it, we're going to need outside help."

My heart sank as if I'd dropped it into a murky pond. "No one is going to help Morgrain."

Her sculpted brows drew together. "Surely the Empire—"

"They're moving Falcons and weapons to the border." I hated the words as they crossed my tongue, bitter and hard in their truth. "They're trying to hide it from me, but I've seen and heard enough. The Serene Empire isn't preparing to help us. It's preparing to attack."

"I see." My mother took another long sip of her wine. "That's...unfortunate."

I didn't mention what else I'd learned, something that set my stomach to churning with anger: the Serene Empire had dispatched assassins to kill my grandmother with a powerful magical trap. She'd sent what was left of them back to Raverra in a small box via Imperial Post.

"So it's just me, then," I muttered, half to myself.

It was a grim realization—not even my family could help me. I had no retainers, no soldiers, no mages, no chimeras at my command. I was one person, my magic sealed and useless, without any exceptional skills or strength that might let me protect an entire domain by myself. Even the Rookery couldn't help; their job was to find a way to *defeat* my grandmother.

I'd better come up with a damned good plan.

"You don't need to take it all on yourself, Ryx," my mother said softly. She clasped my hand, a deliberate gesture she visibly steeled herself to make. Her hand was warm and unfamiliar; I'd never learned the shape of it.

She frowned suddenly and flipped mine over, tracing a gentle finger across my palm. "Blisters? You *have* been hard on yourself! Where'd you get these?"

It was difficult not to pull away. "Sparring. Ashe has been teaching me to be a bit better with a rapier, so I'll have a way to defend myself with my power sealed."

"Good," my mother approved. "It always irked me that I couldn't teach you more myself, but there's only so much you can do without risking physical contact."

I curled my hand closed. "Forget about my blisters. Have you seen Grandmother? How... how is she?" *Is she herself, or has she become utterly a demon?*

"She's not seeing anyone but Odan. She's locked up in Gloamingard, and he comes out to meet people at the gates and pass along her words." My mother let out an exasperated sigh. "Your father went to see her, of course. The man is stubborn as an ox, but she wouldn't come out."

"She must be so lonely," I murmured, despite myself. "With only Odan in the castle, and the whole world turned against her."

I knew worrying about my grandmother was ridiculous; as a Witch Lord, she'd been nigh invulnerable even before the Demon of Discord fused with her spirit. And yet I still thought of her as the fierce-eyed woman who brought me lavender tea when I had nightmares, who shrugged it off with a laugh when I broke things, who stroked my hair and held me when I sobbed as a child over whatever poor soul I'd nearly killed this time. As a human, who needed human things.

My mother lifted incredulous eyebrows. "The Lady of Owls is stronger than the mountains. She's fine."

"How is Odan then, living alone in the castle with a demon? Have you heard anything about anyone else from Gloamingard? Gaven or Jannah or—"

The door banged open. I whirled in my seat as Ardith of Kar sauntered into the room, hands stuffed into the pockets of their vestcoat of butter-soft russet leather, grin plastered across their face.

"Evening, Valeria, Ryx. Heard you were talking politics without me, after I came all the way here from Kar."

I narrowed my eyes. "You were eavesdropping, you mean. Otherwise how could you know we weren't having a tender family reunion?"

"Oh, please. Valeria's Raverran. Family reunions *are* politics." They nodded graciously to my mother. "Good to see you, by the way."

My mother rose and curtsied. "Always a pleasure, Honored Ardith."

"Same, same." They turned back to me. "And of *course* I was eavesdropping. My father would be disappointed with me if I didn't."

"Ardith arrived here yesterday to consult with the Rookery about Grandmother on the Fox Lord's behalf," I told my mother, "since apparently we're the global experts on demons right now."

My mother blinked. "I suppose you are. How odd."

"About that." Ardith cocked a ginger eyebrow at her. "I don't suppose you've come with any handy secret news about what the Lady of Owls will do next? The leaders of Eruvia are all peeing themselves wondering."

"They'll need to change their breeches and get on with it, I'm afraid," my mother said. "Though I can tell you she's much less likely to take steps they won't like if they stop antagonizing her."

"Bunch of twits, playing poke the bear in the eye." Ardith shook their head.

"I'm glad your father has more sense, at least." My mother inclined her head to Ardith. "The Fox Lord has been entirely civil. Acting as if nothing is wrong is the best strategy right now."

"No sense picking a fight with an actual demon if you're not ready for it," Ardith agreed. "Speaking of which, I have a question for you. My father may have some friends who want to call a Conclave, to figure out what to do about this whole demon situation."

"I'm surprised they haven't already," I said, my gut tightening at the thought. It was bound to be bad news for Morgrain— I had trouble envisioning any scenario where the Witch Lords didn't unite against the demon in their midst.

"Yes, well, there's one little issue." Ardith grimaced. "The Lady of Owls is a Witch Lord. So either they invite her to the Conclave—literally inviting the Demon of Discord to a diplomatic meeting, which is proverbially a bad idea if kind of a neat trick—or they fail to invite her. Which is also, the stories tell us, a spectacularly bad plan."

They had a point. I thought it over, playing out one scenario after another in my mind; none of them ended well.

"If she's not invited, she's going to show up anyway," I concluded.

"Ah." Ardith rubbed the back of their head. "That was my question. Well. That's awkward."

My mother frowned. "Between this and the chaos in the Serene City, it'll be rather hard for Eruvia to muster any kind of coordinated response to the demons."

Uneasy suspicions churned into motion in my mind. "What chaos in Raverra?"

"Apparently when your Rookery reported that the Demon of Hunger had allied with the Zenith Society, it set off something of a . . . scuffle." She eyed her mostly empty wineglass as if considering whether to refill it. "To make a complex situation simple, the Council is trying to thoroughly purge Zenith Society members from the government—but as they'd worked their way into a lot of high positions, it's rather a mess. There's blood on the floor."

"If Raverra's distracted cleaning its own house, maybe that'll buy Morgrain some time," I said grimly. And then I heard my own words, and swore.

Ardith and my mother looked at me. "What?"

"Chaos in Raverra." I waved a hand northward. "Uncertainty blocking the Conclave from coming together. You might even call it *discord*."

Ardith whistled. "You think she's doing this on purpose somehow, to keep the wolves away from Morgrain?"

"I suppose it's arguably kinder than murdering them all," my mother murmured.

My fingers flicked out instinctively from my chest in the warding sign. "Avert."

Ardith turned to me. "Right, that reminds me! Speaking of things that might make your grandmother kill us all, what's this I accidentally heard through your super thin door—should get that looked at, by the way—about the Empire moving Falcons and such to the Vaskandran border? Seems less than neighborly."

"Are you asking as a random gossip, or as your father's emissary?" I countered.

Ardith made a flourishing gesture. "I'll have you know that

over my strenuous protestations, I've been promoted to an emissary not only of my father, but of a certain unofficial association of which he's a member. Or would be, if they existed, which they don't."

"The same international one that's behind the Rookery?" I guessed.

"Maybe. Perhaps. Who can say? I'm terribly mysterious." Ardith plucked a pastry off a plate Kessa had left out for my mother. "So spill, Ryx. What's the Empire up to?"

My mother watched me over the rim of her wineglass with interest. She could hardly urge me to reveal potential imperial secrets given her long years of service to the Serene Empire, but her eyes did it for her.

"I don't know as much as I wish I did." That was an understatement. The sheer frustration of no longer being at the epicenter of information was enough to turn my shoulders into a mass of knots. "Oddly enough, they don't want an atheling of Morgrain in meetings about preparations for an attack on the domain. But I can tell you there's an imperial emissary visiting tonight to talk to Foxglove about a secret weapon of some kind."

My mother lifted an eyebrow. "That doesn't sound like something they'd casually mention to the Warden of Gloamingard."

"They didn't," I admitted. "I overheard an officer setting up the consultation with Foxglove."

"Hmm." Ardith swallowed a chunk of pastry and licked their lips. "Has this remarkably informative consultation occurred yet? Do you know where they're doing it? Does that room also have thin doors?"

"I can't eavesdrop on *Foxglove*," I objected. "Tempting though it might be, I'm still trying to build trust with the Rookery."

Ardith waved an airy hand. "Yes, yes. And the Rookery works for the Crow Lord—"

"They *report* to the Crow Lord *and* Lady Cornaro, which is hardly the same thing."

"And the Crow Lord practically sent me here himself." Ardith shrugged off any further concerns I might harbor. "We're just sparing Foxglove the trouble of reporting the conversation."

"I don't think that's how this works," I said.

"It works how we make it work." Ardith lifted a finger. "Besides, you want to protect Morgrain, right? You're an atheling, and this is a threat to your domain. You *have* to know about it. It's your duty."

Ardith wasn't wrong, despite their flippant tone. I liked Foxglove and the Rookery; they were friends and comrades. But I'd told them from the beginning that my domain would always be my first priority.

"Fine," I said. "It's later this evening, in Foxglove's office. Meet me in half an hour, and we'll do this."

"Well, this is awkward," Ardith muttered.

I stared in disbelief at the supply closet that shared a back wall with Foxglove's office, where we'd intended to hide and eavesdrop. Or rather, I stared at the closet's current unexpected occupant.

The Exalted Atheling Severin of Alevar, heir to the Shrike Lord, attempted to look regal as he glared at us from between shelves stacked with spare linens and a bucket full of mops. He almost managed it, but the sheer absurdity of the situation was too great for even his impeccable tailoring and aura of power to overcome.

"What are you doing here?" I demanded.

"The same thing you are, I imagine. I heard that officer talk to Foxglove, too." The look he slid toward Ardith, who hadn't been there, suggested doubts as to my judgment in bringing them in. "I'm not enamored of the idea of the Empire pointing weapons at Vaskandar, either."

"Well, budge over before someone sees us," Ardith hissed, making shooing motions as if Severin were an annoying insect instead of a royal mage. "Ryx, squeeze in. He'll murder me if I stand next to him."

Every muscle in my body went rigid. Years of drilled-in instincts screamed that sharing such a small space with others would be fatal. But Ardith was right; we couldn't be seen. I held my breath and stepped into the closet with Severin, who pressed back against the linen shelf to make room for me, scowling. Ardith hustled in behind me and closed the door, plunging us into near darkness.

Severin's warmth pressed against me on one side, Ardith's on the other. Ardith's lean body practically buzzed with barely suppressed energy, while Severin stood stiff and still as if pretending to be a statue might spare him from the indignity of being crammed in with us. Every inch of my body strove desperately not to touch anyone and failed.

"Please take a moment to marvel at my restraint in not making an inappropriate joke," Ardith whispered. "I've thought of half a dozen already."

"We appreciate your sacrifice," Severin said.

For the next several minutes, only the sound of our breathing filled the dark, stuffy space. My nerves screamed at how close Severin and Ardith were; I almost wanted to lean into one of them just to prove to my ragged instincts that I could, that the jess made all this panic unnecessary. Preferably Severin.

Two sets of footfalls sounded in the hallway; an impossibly loud silence filled our hiding place as we all went absolutely still. Foxglove's voice, low and controlled, sounded over the latch as he unlocked his office door.

"I'm surprised Lady Cornaro sent you instead of discussing this over the courier lamps."

A fluid tenor responded, "Some matters require a delicacy best not disturbed by lamp clerks."

I pressed my ear to the cold boards of the wall, aware of Severin's face inches from mine in the darkness as he did the same.

"Fine." Foxglove's voice grew muffled as they passed into the room, but I could still make out most of his words. "I'm also surprised that Lady Cornaro would ask my counsel on a weapon. The Rookery is strictly forbidden from being used for military purposes."

You tell him, Foxglove, I thought silently at him.

"That's true." The other man's tone was respectful, almost deferential, but strength underlaid it like stones beneath water. "However, it is with regret and concern that I must admit the weapon is not currently under control of the imperial military."

I had to stop my breath from hissing between my teeth. The only thing worse than a dangerous magical artifact in the hands of the Serene Empire was a dangerous magical artifact on the loose somewhere.

A long moment of silence suggested Foxglove was chewing that over. At last, he said, "Tell me, Gaetano."

"The artifact in question was considered a failed experiment," Gaetano said, his voice calm and collected. "But one with enough potential for destruction that it was kept under high security in the imperial arsenal vault."

"I know about that vault." A soft impact reverberated against the wall by my ear, as if Foxglove had just leaned against it. "I wouldn't want to have to try to crack its wards, and I've taken down a few in my career. What happened?"

"Perhaps you are aware of the..." Gaetano paused, holding the space for his next word open while he considered precisely which one to drop into it. "...disturbance in Raverra, over the Zenith Society and their alliance with the Demon of Hunger?"

Ardith poked me, as if somehow I might have forgotten Aurelio, my cursed wretch of a former friend, and the terrible ways he'd betrayed me to become Hunger's host. I clenched my teeth until my jaw hurt and missed Foxglove's response.

"Precisely," Gaetano said. "The Council and the doge are arresting everyone who might remotely be involved. Unfortunately, some of them fled before they could be caught, and a few of those were highly placed. They didn't have time to do much on their way out, but one of them abused their access to the arsenal vault to steal this artifact, and managed to hand it off to an accomplice before they were arrested. Lady Cornaro is hoping that with your expertise in dangerous devices, experimental magic, and the Zenith Society, the Rookery might be uniquely suited to help us understand what purpose they have in mind for it and how to stop them."

I didn't like the sound of this at all. The Zenith Society's overarching goal was to obtain a military magical advantage over Vaskandar for the Serene Empire by any means, and I had little doubt which Vaskandran domain they considered the greatest threat right now. I pressed my palms against the smooth wood, wishing I could burst through it into the room and demand answers.

"Hard to say without seeing it." Foxglove's voice remained guarded. "Harder without knowing what it does."

Paper rustled. "Lady Cornaro provided me with these sketches of it from imperial records—though they're just drawings, not accurate schematics. My understanding is that it's an artifice device developed as an experimental weapon against Witch Lords about a hundred years ago."

Foxglove shifted off the wall; his next word was a muffled oath. "What the Hells is this? It's like a plate of dropped spaghetti. The wirework is denser than I've ever seen, and it's total chaos. Except for this part..." Foxglove paused. "This section looks like death magic. A killing enchantment that sends a pulse to stop a heart."

"Yes," Gaetano agreed softly. "Even the Master Artificer couldn't fully understand the device, but from the creator's notes, it seems the intent was to use it against a Witch Lord's domain. To touch it to a boundary stone and send that killing pulse along the link that connects every living thing in a domain to its Witch Lord, like lightning through wire. Stripping the Witch Lord of their power by destroying all life in the domain."

Beside me, Severin's whole body tensed with rage; the same fury surged through my veins. I might be a destroyer of life, but I mourned every blade of grass that died beneath my feet. This was an abomination. Even the most cruel of the Witch Lords would never have contemplated such a thing.

"Setting aside the complete moral abhorrence of the idea," Foxglove said, painstakingly neutral, "I don't see how you'd power that. There's a reason the Empire doesn't use killing enchantments much in warfare; they're inefficient. To kill every living creature in a domain, you'd need a chunk of obsidian the size of a continent."

"Sixteen times the size of Eruvia, actually," Gaetano corrected. "They did the calculations. It's why the project was abandoned; it's impossible."

"But the Zenith Society stole this, of all the artifacts in the arsenal vault."

"Yes. My lady wishes me to ask you how worried we should be."

Foxglove grunted. "I'd need to see it. If they've figured out a way to make it work as designed? Very worried. But more likely they're going to adapt it to take out a much smaller target."

Pieces clicked together in my mind, and I barely swallowed an exclamation. I knew of one source of limitless energy the Zenith Society already wanted access to: the gate to the Nine Hells.

"Do you know where they took it?" Foxglove asked.

"Intelligence traced it as far as northern Loreice, where the accomplice joined a larger Zenith Society group moving in the direction of the Summer Palace," Gaetano said. "We have reason to believe some of the fleeing Zenith Society members plan to seek refuge in the Loreician court, so they may be headed there."

"Are you assigning this mission to the Rookery, then?" Foxglove asked. "Track down this weapon, get it back from the Zenith Society, and disable it?"

Gaetano was silent for a moment. When he spoke again, it was with slow care, as if the words he handled were dangerous. "There is a difficulty. The Rookery is an international organization."

"I'd say this concerns Vaskandar as well as the Empire, given that it's a weapon that only works on Witch Lord domains," Foxglove pointed out.

"Lady Cornaro is only one of the Council of Nine. And the Council has forbidden sharing knowledge of this artifact with Vaskandar."

This time, it was Severin whose jaw clamped down tight on an unvoiced curse. On my other side, Ardith jammed their hands into their pockets so hard I heard a seam tear.

I had no doubt they were thinking the same thing I was: there was one obvious reason the Empire wouldn't want Vaskandar to know about the artifact.

"They're still thinking about using it," Foxglove concluded bluntly.

"I could not presume to guess the minds of the Council." That was decidedly not a no. "But the Serene Empire is not requesting the Rookery's direct aid with this matter at this time. Only for your personal consultation."

"I see." Foxglove fell silent; for a while, all we heard beyond the wall was the soft thud of his pacing. Finally, that too stopped. "Let me think on this."

"Of course. I return to Raverra tomorrow morning, and I can communicate with my lady over the courier lamps in our private cipher in the meantime if you have any questions."

"Thank you."

Footsteps sounded, and Foxglove's door opened and shut again. The three of us stared at each other, pressed together, whites of our eyes shining in what dim light trickled in from the hallway. Unspoken words hung between us, dire and urgent.

The door flew open, dazzling light pouring in on us. Foxglove stood there, taking us in unblinking.

"What in the Nine Hells do you think you're doing?"

THREE

There was a time I might have considered myself a diplomat, but explaining my presence in a closet with Ardith and Severin was beyond my skill.

Luckily, Ardith faced no such limitations. They grinned and sauntered out into the hallway as if this were the most natural situation in the world. "Exactly what you think we're doing, most likely. Unless your mind's more twisted than I expect, in which case please do share your ideas."

Severin stepped out of the closet next, brushing cobwebs off his fine embroidered vestcoat. "There's no need to speak of this. I think we'll all be happier if we forget it ever happened."

The few seconds of time they bought me were enough. Enough to move past my mortification at being caught. Enough for a great wave of anger to surge up at the thought of the Zenith Society having a weapon they might use to destroy all of Morgrain, and the Serene Empire prioritizing keeping the weapon over preventing atrocity. Hot words burned my tongue, but I forced them down, swallowing them like boiling tea. None of this was Foxglove's fault; he didn't deserve my wrath.

"Let's drop the pretense." I managed to sound far more confident than anyone standing in a closet had a right to be. I stepped out into the hall, catching and holding Foxglove's dark eyes. "We heard everything you said. We know about this horrific artifact designed to murder thousands of innocent civilians and destroy the land itself."

"Of course you do," Foxglove said. "Did you think we didn't know you were listening?"

The three of us stared at him, taken aback.

"Gaetano is Lady Cornaro's personal aide." Foxglove straightened his modest lace cuffs. "He's highly trained and competent. He certainly has access to anti-eavesdropping devices and knows how and when to use them—as do I, for that matter. The only reason he wouldn't use one would be if he were *hoping* to be overheard."

Well. I quickly reframed the whole conversation in my head. "So Lady Cornaro can't send us after the artifact, since the Council's forbidden it. But she sent her aide to consult with you as a way of…what? Giving you the mission anyway in an underhanded fashion? Warning Vaskandar?"

"I'm certain she would never do any such thing," Foxglove said. "Any more than I would contemplate undermining the trust the Serene Empire places in the Rookery by taking on a mission we are expressly forbidden."

Ardith snorted. "Forbidden by Raverra. Let me go find a bird, and I can have orders from the Crow Lord to send you after that artifact within half a day."

"That would cause conflict with the Empire and put Lady Cornaro in a difficult position," Foxglove warned.

Severin slashed the air with his hand. "I don't give a rat's ear about the Empire or Lady Cornaro. We're talking about a device designed to *wipe out an entire domain*."

"If it worked," Foxglove said. "Which it doesn't."

"But it could," I said, the bleak possibility like an open pit at my feet. "The Hells contain limitless magical energy; demons must have tremendous power as well, given that nine of them were enough to plunge the entire continent into a dark age. And we know the Zenith Society is working with the Demon of Hunger."

Ardith grimaced. "I don't like it when you make sense, Ryx. Next time you have a really depressing theory, please make it less plausible."

Foxglove rubbed his forehead. "We'd still need a mission to go after the weapon. If the Rookery tried to seize a secret war artifact on our own, we'd be disbanded for insubordination."

"Let's be clear," Severin said. "I'm not part of the Rookery, and I'm not letting worries about your little band being broken up stop me from preventing a massive slaughter of my own people." He gave a deliberately casual shrug. "If you can find some way to make it your mission as well, fine. I'm all for doing this without an international incident."

"No reason not to try for both," I agreed, before Foxglove could reply. The two of them stared at each other with the borderline hostility of a pair of cats who haven't quite decided yet if they're going to fight. "Here's an idea. How about if instead of going after the artifact, we go after the Zenith Society?"

"Believe me, I'd love to." Old grudges sharpened Foxglove's voice. "But our mandate is to deal with dangerous magical problems, not arrest fugitive traitors. We don't have the authority."

"Oh, come on," Ardith protested, "they're the Dangerous Magical Problems club. Surely you can come up with an excuse."

"Do we know why members of the Zenith Society are heading for the Loreician court?" I asked, looking for an angle. "They could probably hide better in a more low-profile place. What do they want in the Summer Palace?"

Foxglove frowned. "It's the seat of government of one of the most powerful and independent client states of the Serene Empire—but also one that's split by severe internal divisions. The Zenith Society could exploit those divisions to find backers in the court even if they're on the run from the Empire, and Raverra would have a hard time coming after them without causing a major incident."

"Politics are all very nice," Severin said with a touch of acid, "but I find it far more worrisome that Loreice sits on the border with Vaskandar and bristles with every magical weapon and defense the Serene Empire can provide. If they mean to use this artifact against us, it's the perfect place for them to launch their attack from."

"That all makes sense, but it doesn't give us an excuse to go there." I chewed my lip. "What about Hunger? The Rookery has already been tasked with finding ways to deal with him, right?"

"Yes, and with demons in general," Foxglove said slowly, "but I'm not sure how that helps us, when we have no reason to believe Hunger is at the Loreician court."

"On the contrary." I spread my hands. "Hunger is the Zenith Society's most powerful ally; maybe they're running to the Summer Palace because he's already infiltrated it. We'll never know if we don't investigate."

"That's a stretch," Ardith said admiringly, "but it's a stretch we can work with. It's a good enough excuse for my father and his friends, anyway."

Foxglove rubbed his chin. "After that conversation with Gaetano, I suspect it'll be good enough for Lady Cornaro, too." A spark kindled in his eyes. "Very well, then. I have a hunch that the Rookery will have a new mission by morning."

In anticipation of our departure for the Summer Palace, the Rookery gathered for an impromptu late-night dinner party, prepared and hosted by Foxglove's family.

I'd been surprised to learn Foxglove was part of a devoted triad with a married couple stationed at Castle Ilseine, Lia and

Teodor—I'd imagined him as a kind of solitary driving force, existing for the Rookery alone. I couldn't help watching their loving exchanges with a touch of wondering envy: the way Foxglove smiled, relaxed and free of all care, as he poured wine for Teodor, or the quick affectionate kisses he stole with Lia, familiar and comfortable with years of warmth behind them. The very idea of a healthy, complete, loving family existing at all seemed strange; my own family experience was made up of missing pieces and the sort of complex ties that hurt when they drew tight.

He was like a different person, all the shadows gone from his eyes and the tension from his spine. As if with them, he could put his burdens down.

I tore my eyes away from them and returned to the delicious lemon soup Teodor had made. I had enough going on in my own life right now without pining after someone else's.

My mother sat down beside me, back from chatting with Teodor to see who they might both know from his time traveling the Empire as a senior logistics officer and hers in the Raverran foreign service. She flashed me a smile.

"They're all lovely people, Ryx. I almost wish I wasn't going back to Morgrain in the morning—but if I left your father for too long right now, he'd do something impulsive and stubborn and land himself in more trouble than he could handle." She straightened suddenly, as if she'd remembered something. "Speaking of trouble! What's this I hear about you courting the Shrike Lord's heir?"

I nearly choked on a mouthful of soup at the sudden change of topic. Every vein in my face on fire, I forced myself *not* to glance at where Severin sat answering Bastian's questions about Alevaran stories of the Dark Days. "We're not courting! Where did you—"

"I have my sources." She raised a sculpted eyebrow. "Not courting? Ah, wait, I see. Of course." She nodded. "Courtship is an outdated custom of previous generations. These days the young folk just get to the kissing, without making a formal fuss about it first. I approve."

"Mamma! We haven't—That is, it's only been three weeks since I got exiled by my demon grandmother, and kissing hasn't precisely been on my mind!" That was less than entirely true, but I wasn't about to discuss it with my mother.

She sighed. "More's the pity."

Kessa leaned in from across the table before that line of conversation could go any further, thankfully. By the smile dancing around her mouth, I suspected she knew exactly what she was rescuing me from.

"So, Ryx! I hear we have to scrape together a court wardrobe for you on short notice. I've sent a message ahead to the Serene Envoy at the Summer Palace to see if they can get you anything, but I'm scouring the castle as well." Her eyes sparkled with anticipation.

Ashe plopped down beside me as if Kessa had summoned her. "Here—have your first accessory."

She thrust a long bundle at me, held vertical between our chairs: a rapier with an elegant swept hilt in a fancy gold-chased scabbard. It looked a bit more serviceable than the toys I'd seen imperial diplomats wear as unwieldy jewelry, but not by much.

"What's this?" I asked, surprised.

"The imperial who gave it to me claimed it was a sword, but I'm skeptical, too." Ashe made a contemptuous noise. "I'm told rapiers are in high fashion in Loreice right now, so you should have one to carry around. Apparently it has to be showy instead of practical. I drew the line at one with ornamentation on the grip that would rip the skin off your hand if you actually used it."

I eased the sword an inch or two from its sheath, exposing the clean, bright blade, then slid it back home. "Thanks. Hopefully I won't have a reason to draw it."

Ashe grunted. "Don't count on it."

"Do you need anything from the castle alchemists for the trip?" Kessa put in. "I've got the basics—pain elixirs, common remedies, stopping your menses—plus Foxglove's joint potion, and my melancholia elixir in case I have a bad stretch, but I realized I don't know what you need."

The idea of alchemy being so readily and casually available still seemed incredible to me, after all the work I'd done as the Warden of Gloamingard to import everything from cancer potions to gender elixirs for the people of my castle. It was yet another reminder that this place was utterly unlike home.

"I'm fine," I said. "Really, you don't have to go to any trouble for me."

Kessa waved a hand. "Nonsense. You're one of us now. We've got to make sure the Rookery is well equipped!"

"And that means pretty dresses and swords," Ashe concluded, with a wise nod.

Lia, a radiantly beautiful Ostan woman with a cloud of dark hair, nudged Kessa with a friendly elbow. "Listen, will you do me a favor and look out for Foxglove while you're at the Summer Palace?" She shot a covert glance over her shoulder after Foxglove, who was out of the room helping Teodor bring in the next dish. "He's so bad at taking care of himself."

Kessa gave her an impulsive hug. "Don't worry. I'll make sure he sleeps occasionally."

To my surprise, Lia turned to me next, with a stern expression. "And you, Ryx. You're as bad as he is. I've seen you two miss meals together, planning and scheming until all hours of the night." She gave my mother a commiserating look. "I'm sure you must have had to follow her around with a plate when she was young."

My mother and I exchanged awkward glances. She hadn't been sufficiently involved in raising me to do any such thing. "Ah . . ."

Kessa swooped in to the rescue once more. "Don't you worry, Lia, I'll take care of her, too."

I tried not to stare at her in shock. Nobody had *taken care of* me since I was very small, with the occasional exception of my grandmother when she could spare time from running her domain. I was the Warden, and I was dangerous; nobody thought of me as the sort of person who needed to be taken care of.

Kessa was looking out for me, Ashe had gotten me a sword—which had to be the paramount gesture of friendship, coming from her—and even Lia, who I barely knew, hadn't forgotten me. All around the table, the Rookery were laughing and eating and drinking and teasing each other—and here I was, among them. One of them. I could have a future here, with my friends. My throat tightened at the thought.

But my real future was with Morgrain. I was an atheling; my home was a part of me, inescapable. Whatever place I had with the Rookery was one more thing I had to be willing to sacrifice to protect it.

I stumbled to my bed exhausted after a long, lovely evening, the scent of my mother's perfume and the warmth of her good-night hug still clinging to my skin. Anxious thoughts about the various threats to Morgrain buzzed like hornets in my mind, now that the distraction of company was gone; despite how tired my body was, I had no idea how I was going to sleep.

I didn't realize until I was about to flop onto my bed that a sleek black shadow already occupied it.

"So you're going to the royal court of Loreice," Whisper greeted me, his voice smooth as silk.

He sat in the exact center of my bed with regal poise. His catlike yellow eyes watched me with intent curiosity, and his fox ears pricked to catch my answer.

"I am," I agreed warily. "I can't risk them using that thing on Morgrain."

I'd never wondered before how he always seemed to know everything; I'd vaguely assumed he slinked around Gloamingard spying on people. Now that I knew he was a demon, every detail about him had the potential for sinister significance, from the way he came and went through locked rooms and wards to the fact that I could never quite tell if he spoke his words aloud or only in my head.

It was a truth like a vast dark cloud, too big to fully see or understand. I couldn't grapple with it. I hadn't told the Rookery yet; maybe that made me a fool, but a lifetime of friendship weighed heavier on my loyalty than a few weeks.

Whisper's tail swished across the bedspread. "You've picked a poor time to go gallivanting about the Empire."

"It's precisely because it's a poor time that I *am* gallivanting around the Empire." I sank down on the bed beside him, which felt strange and familiar at once. "Setting aside the fact that I don't want everyone in my domain to die, this is all part of the mess I made, and I've got to clean it up. No one would be pointing such devastating weapons at Morgrain if I hadn't unleashed the demons."

Well, unleashed two of them, anyway. Whisper's presence in this world wasn't my fault.

He had to be one of the Nine. Discord and Hunger were accounted for; I couldn't imagine him as one of the more flamboyantly destructive demons like Carnage, Corruption, or Disaster. That left Nightmare, Madness, Despair, or Death. I'd been trying the options on him in my head for weeks as if looking for a coat that fit, but each seemed equally impossible. He was too familiar to be something so terrible.

My oldest and truest friend, a demon. Between him and Aurelio, my record suggested I was a terrible judge of character.

Whisper's ear flicked in disgust. "Assigning fault is a foolish human notion. It's irrelevant. The past is unchangeable; it's what you do now that matters."

"All right, fine." I crossed my arms. "What I'm going to do is recover this artifact and destroy it, then find Hunger and send him back to the Hells he came from."

"No." His voice softened wearily. "What you're going to do is make everything worse."

He didn't add *like you always do*; he didn't have to. Curse it, he knew how to get under my skin. I unclenched my jaw; I couldn't let him distract me.

"You don't care if I make things worse," I said. "You've got some reason to want me not to look into this, don't you?"

He washed a paw, avoiding my gaze. "Of course not. You're welcome to play with all the artifice weapons you want. It hardly matters."

He wouldn't dig at my sore spots without a reason. Whisper could be callous, but he was never petty. "All right, then. You don't want me to go to the Summer Palace."

He ignored me, his grooming growing more vigorous. That could mean anything.

It probably came back to his promise again—the promise he wouldn't talk about, but which he'd used as an excuse for everything from not telling me pertinent information to saving my life. "You're too wrapped in your own secrets to tell me. That's fine; I'm going regardless. What will you do about it?"

It wasn't until after the question left my tongue that I realized how much I cared about the answer. Somewhere in the back of my mind, I'd been assuming he'd come with me; he'd followed me here from Gloamingard, after all. But he had his own priorities, and he might abandon me for them. It made no sense, but I found that a more frightening prospect than a demon having attached himself to my shadow for unknown reasons.

Whisper examined a paw for a while. I held my breath.

At last, he sighed. "If you're set on this, I suppose I'll have to come with you."

Relief flooded me. Which was foolish; much as I might prefer to believe he solely wanted my company, he'd made it exquisitely clear that his own secret goals wouldn't always align with my own.

I analyzed his lean, elegant form as if his true name might be written in his shining black fur. A cold settled into my bones that didn't come from the early autumn breeze rolling down off the hills. *Nightmare, Madness, Despair, or Death.*

"Well, I can't stop you." I extended a hand for him to sniff; he bumped it with his forehead, and I succumbed to his demand, digging my fingers into the soft fur behind his ears.

"No, you can't," he agreed.

He leaned his head into my hand, eyes half closing.

Graces help me, I had no idea how I was going to explain this to the Rookery.

Good-byes consumed the next morning.

First my mother: we managed one last hug, awkward and full of the hard press of bones and corset stays and hair pins. She waved cheerily as she passed between the boundary stones—the same parting wave she'd given me a hundred times, a dashing and glamorous figure sweeping off to exciting and unimaginable imperial cities, to return months later with strange presents. Morgrain accepted her back without so much as a rustle; the forest swallowed her, and she was gone.

Next a friendly good-bye for Ardith, who headed back to Kar to report to their father and his allies with no clear answers, but a double handful of grim news and warnings. And finally came all the interminable lingering in the stable yard as the Rookery took their leave from everyone they knew at Castle Ilseine. Bastian's gaggle of scholar friends from the Falcons pressed last-minute books onto him to add to the trunks he hefted onto our waiting coach with apparent ease. Kessa seemed to know every single person in the entire castle, and even Ashe had at least a dozen sparring partners to give a final jostle and exchange bits of advice. Lia stood earnestly close to Foxglove, who held her crutches for her as she pinned something small and gleaming on his cravat; then Teodor swept both of them into a hug.

I lit a candle at the little shrine to the Grace of Luck against the wall of the old keep, since that was better than standing around awkwardly by myself. Every shrine in the row hung thick with fat bunches of fresh bright ribbons and a mass of melted candle stubs—offerings from a castle population that wasn't supposed to know demons had returned to the world, except for the Rookery and half a handful of senior officers, but there was no keeping a secret like that.

When I rose from my half-hearted prayer, everyone was still hugging, curse it. This was taking forever. I'd rather rip the bandage and get out of here. I climbed into the coach.

Severin was already there.

He gave me an ironic smile. "What, no lengthy heartfelt fare-wells for you, either?"

"Somehow, no."

I caught myself on the brink of choosing the seat farthest away from him out of habit. With six of us in here, the coach would be full, and my jess meant I didn't have to keep my distance regardless. I steeled myself and eased down on the bench beside him instead.

Severin glanced out the window to make sure no one was standing too close and lowered his voice. "I didn't think there was much left that could appall me. After you murder your own father, it's mostly downhill from there. But with this artifact, the Serene Empire has managed it."

"Oh, the Empire loves collecting horrible weapons they tell themselves they have no intention of ever using. But destroying *all life in an entire domain* is a lot even for them." The thought of Morgrain transformed to a lifeless desert turned my stomach.

The fact that I personally wouldn't survive such an attack due to my own link to the land wasn't much consolation. "We'll get it back and destroy it, no matter what it takes."

Severin shook his head. "Please tell me you're not trusting the Rookery to destroy it."

"Of course they will! Their entire purpose is to deal with dangerous magic."

"It's adorable that you have such faith in them, but be realistic." He gestured out at the castle surrounding us. "Do you think for a minute the Serene Empire would allow the Rookery to keep existing if they stole one of their secret war artifacts without permission from Raverra? You heard the man yesterday; they want it back. They're probably keeping it as an ace in their pocket against your grandmother."

"I'm well aware of that," I snapped. "That's why we have to destroy it, whether the Rookery approves or not."

"Then we agree for once." Half a smile pulled at Severin's mouth. "I'm surprised at you, Ryx. Using the Rookery to spy on and steal from the Empire, then leaving them to take the consequences once you have what you want? There may be hope for you yet."

"That's not what I'm doing," I protested.

He lifted an eyebrow. "Oh?"

I could argue that I wasn't using them, or that this was what they'd want me to do, but it would sound hollow in my own ears. I lifted my chin. "I'll face the consequences myself."

"No, no, claiming responsibility defeats the entire purpose of doing something underhanded." He rubbed his temple. "I suppose it's a work in progress. We'll corrupt you yet."

"I'm serious!"

"It's a deadly serious situation." No mirth shone in his eyes, and the piece of a smile slid from his face. His eyes slipped inexorably to the window, looking north, as if he could see through the castle walls all the way to Alevar. A sigh escaped him, faint and strangely wistful. "I must admit that this isn't what I expected to be doing a month ago."

"What, your career plans as the Shrike Lord's heir didn't involve infiltrating the Loreician court to retrieve a stolen weapon?" I chuckled. "I can't imagine why not."

"I meant that I shouldn't be here. *We* shouldn't be here." His voice dropped even lower, rough with frustration, and he gestured out at Castle Ilseine's stone courtyard with all its bustling, uniformed activity. "This land feels as dead to you as it does to me. We're athelings, Ryx. We belong in our own domains."

He had the same trapped longing in his dark eyes that I felt every day. To go back to where everything felt *alive* again, and we had the power to fix the problems around us.

"We do. But we have to protect them." Should I squeeze his hand? Would that be comforting or appropriate? I still had no sense of these things, curse it. "No matter how strange the Summer Palace is, we have to navigate it." I grimaced. "Though I wish I knew more about Loreician protocol, beyond general imperial etiquette."

Severin flashed me a wry smile. "We're close kin to Witch Lords, and this is the Empire. They probably expect us to bathe in blood and eat children. If you don't lay a curse on their lineage, they'll consider it a surprisingly lovely conversation."

Tentatively, I let my hand rest next to his on the bench between us, so that our little fingers were almost touching. "I'm glad we get to be on the same side this time, at least. It'll be a nice change."

He laughed. "I'm not sure I know how to work with someone without secretly trying to undermine them. What a novel idea."

"Yes, well, it's been a while since I didn't have to worry about my supposed allies ruining all my diplomatic efforts through sheer excess of drama, so we'll make a fine pair," I said dryly.

Severin let out a theatrical sigh. "It's easier to prepare to meet with foreign dignitaries when you're there to insult them, though. You don't have to worry so much when the worst that can happen is that they're insufficiently offended."

"It's nice to know that you cared enough to prepare for our early conversations," I replied tartly. "And here I thought you'd simply improvised off the cuff."

"Only the best for my enemies." He gave me a mocking bow from his seat.

I smiled, but even with him so close beside me on the bench— even knowing he was the only one in this entire country who truly understood what I was feeling now—I kept a hard little seed of wariness in my heart.

No matter how deeply I believed he was better than his brother, I had to remember that the people of Alevar might have reason to fear Severin as well. I didn't know what he'd done in his own domain, in his brother's name. After Aurelio's betrayal, I couldn't trust my own judgment; the fact that I liked Severin didn't mean he hadn't done terrible things.

Hells, I liked Whisper, too, and he was a literal demon.

Every foot we traveled away from Morgrain ached as if I left a blood trail behind me. The smooth imperial road ahead of our carriage led to political danger, if nothing more sinister; Morgrain and Loreice already had a history of bloody conflict to put a strain on our relations, even without the looming threat of a demon Witch Lord poised at their border, and the last thing I needed was to set off an international incident. *Again*. Still, the other side of this knife-edge was opportunity, if I could tip the balance toward peace.

"Hey, Ryx," Ashe said, looking up from her conversation with Kessa. Over half a dozen obsidian orbs lay spread out on her lap, each wound with a delicate pattern of golden artifice wire strung with colored beads. "Tell her I need my cleaving pommel, so that when we fight the Zenith Society I can take them down before they activate any magical trinkets. They're bound to be loaded with them."

"Stick to the stunning one, for blood's sake," Kessa insisted, pointing firmly to the orb with green crystals strung through its golden wire. "The entire Curia will be there, as well as the queen. Can't be too careful when you're swinging that thing around in the middle of a national government."

Ashe looked at me imploringly. I lifted an apologetic palm. "Sorry, but I agree with Kessa."

"Oh, fine." Ashe sighed. "Spoilsport."

Kessa, snuggled a little closer beside her than the bench strictly required, made a noise of triumph.

The straight swath of road passed through green rolling hills and charming towns, marked along its length by the tall spires of courier lamp relay poles topped with their flashing mirrors. The Grace of Beauty was the patron of Loreice, and art appeared everywhere: mosaics and murals on the walls of houses, field laborers with embroidered caps and sleeves, roadside shrines to the Nine Graces embellished with bright painted designs and lively carvings.

We stopped briefly at one of these to water the horses, and Foxglove knelt to tie a ribbon on the shrine; this one was to the Grace of Bounty, out here in the country. Only a handful of the other ribbons were bright and new, the others faded and tattered with weather. The news about the demons hadn't reached the general population yet, it seemed. Once it did, we'd likely have a panic on our hands, and another set of problems to deal with.

As Foxglove rose, his hand went to a gleam of gold at his throat: Lia's parting gift. It was a more elegant version of the sort of charm my mother had brought me once, a Raverran folk ward against demons and ill fortune: a chunk of sea glass crossed by the sword of the Grace of Victory. Except the sword on Foxglove's charm was gold where mine had been a cleverly hammered nail, and his sea glass gleamed bloodred, rare and highly prized as most effective—never mind that it had no more magic to it than the finger-flick gesture we used in Vaskandar.

He saw where my gaze fell, and his face softened. "Lia's too good for me." He straightened the sword, which hung slightly akilter—but he didn't repin it, as if he didn't want to undo the work of Lia's hands. "Teodor, too. He sent me with a batch of lemon cakes." He let out a rueful laugh. "I don't know how I'm going to make myself sharp for this mission, with them softening me up like this."

"Maybe that's why they did it," I suggested, with a tentative smile. "You seem happier when they're around."

Something shuttered in his eyes. "Like a different person. I know."

Hells, I'd offended him. "Sorry, I didn't mean—"

"No, it's all right." He shook his head. "I have to keep my lives separate. Because one of them has sharper teeth, and if they meet, I know which will devour the other."

Bastian looked up from the pile of books strewn across his lap and on the seat beside him. His eyes nested in pools of shadow; he'd been up late night after night, researching every story or record of the Dark Days he could find. His long fingers fiddled with the cover of a book in his lap, opening and closing it.

"So," he said, his voice higher than usual over the rumbling of the coach. "We're expecting to run into the Zenith Society on this mission, I gather."

The atmosphere in the coach changed. Foxglove's face went grim, and Kessa's lips pressed tight. I shifted with the discomfort of suddenly sitting practically in the lap of someone else's private pain.

"Yes," Foxglove said heavily.

Bastian bit his lip. "Do you know…Did they say who, specifically?"

Foxglove shook his head. "I don't know. I'm sorry."

"Oh, that's all right. It's foolish, I just—every time I know we're going to face them, I wonder whether we'll run into my old mentor." He let out a sound that wasn't truly a laugh. "But we never do."

"I'm sure we won't this time, either," Kessa reassured him.

"I actually sort of hope we do." Bastian smoothed the cover of his book. "It's the anticipation that's so awful. The not knowing. Meeting him would be upsetting, certainly, but if it resulted in him being arrested instead of at large, that would be well worth it."

Ashe frowned, looking from Bastian to Foxglove. "Wait, I thought everyone involved in that mess wound up in prison."

"Not all of them." An old anger hardened Foxglove's face. "Some of them got tipped off and ran before they could be arrested. Others never went to prison because all we had against them was Bastian's word."

"Bastian's word wasn't enough?" Ashe scowled.

Bastian shot Foxglove a panicked look. I could guess why they hadn't trusted his word alone—he was a chimera. But Ashe and Severin didn't know that.

"They were from powerful patrician families with high government positions, and Bastian was a poor scholar," Kessa said smoothly, which was probably also true.

Severin narrowed his eyes. "I know what bitter blood grievances look like—I'm from Vaskandar, after all. What am I walking into?"

A haunted silence fell. No one would meet his gaze.

At last, Ashe let out a loud sigh. "All right, mage boy. This was before my time, but I can see everyone else is still too messed up to talk about it after all these years, so I'll give it a go."

"Ashe," Kessa protested weakly.

"No. He's right. He's coming into this with us; if he's going to get stabbed over the old feud, he deserves to know why." Ashe pointed a finger at Severin. "Don't get cocky, though."

Severin inclined his head as gracefully as if he were conceding a point of protocol at a Witch Lord's dinner table. "I assure you, I appreciate your explanation for the spirit in which it's given and not as any sign of affection or goodwill."

"Damned right." Ashe stretched, as if limbering up for her story. "So five years ago, the Zenith Society used to have a good reputation. Part fancy social club, part magic research club, and all political, because everything in Raverra is political." She rolled her eyes. "They had members in high places, they threw obscene barrels of money at research, they paid for the education of promising poor young scholars! What could go wrong?"

Bastian winced. "Quite a bit, as it turns out," he murmured.

Ashe gestured dramatically toward Bastian as if he'd won a prize. "Why, yes. They were rotten to the core. They wanted a magical advantage over Vaskandar, and they'd do anything to get it: creepy illegal experiments, stealing magical stuff, kidnapping mages—and eventually, when the doge and the Council didn't fall in line with their agenda, planning a coup."

"That doesn't explain why everyone here hates them," Severin pointed out. "Unless you take treachery *very* personally."

"Oh, it gets much more personal than that," Ashe assured him. "Bastian's old mentor who betrayed him was Zenith Society; Foxglove ran afoul of them back when he worked for the Empire; and worst of all, they killed Kessa's brother."

"And would have killed me, too, if it weren't for Foxglove," Kessa put in, shooting Foxglove a grateful look, which he glanced away from with apparent discomfort.

"Right." Ashe's jaw flexed as if she'd like to stab them all personally for trying. "*But* in the process of getting done dirty by the Zenith Society, the three of them learned inside information, and they teamed up to bring them down and stop the coup.

So it's a mutual loathing—we hate them for what they did to Bastian and Kessa, but the Zenith Society hates us even more for basically destroying them. Twice now, given that we're the ones who found out they were dealing with a demon!" Ashe grinned triumphantly.

Severin exchanged a glance with me, and I knew what he was thinking: it was common Vaskandran wisdom not to get mixed up with other people's grievances. I had grievances of my own against the Zenith Society, though—or at least against Aurelio.

"Very well then, you have ample reason to despise each other," Severin concluded. "What does that mean for the mission?"

"It means bring a bucket," Ashe said, "because things could get messy."

FOUR

After a long half day on bumpy roads, our coach crested a saddle in the hills, and the elaborate confection that was the Summer Palace appeared out the carriage windows. It perched atop a grand sweep of green hillside, spreading its stony wings in imperial glory. A thousand luminaries twinkled from its dusky face, as if the stars themselves had fallen scattered across it. Smoke rose busily from many of the palace's innumerable chimneys, hazing a sky warmed at the edges by sunset.

It was nothing like Gloamingard. Its sweeping facade celebrated order and symmetry; it glittered with light instead of gathering shadows. The hundreds of windows suggested a bustling city's worth of people inside, more than I'd met in my entire life.

Our coach rolled up to the wide cobbled circle before the palace gates, pulling up in a line with other carriages that picked up and dropped off courtiers with feathered hats and dripping cascades of lace and jewels at the grand main entrance. As we approached, strains of music sounded as if from the stones of the palace itself; I couldn't guess whether they had discreet musicians tucked away somewhere or if it was some clever work of artifice. A boy in silver livery scurried around with a little spear and a velvet bag, picking up any trash blown from the carts or dropped by the guests, keeping the stones pristine.

The courtiers descending from carriages presented an even more spectacular display than the palace itself. Some wore gowns or coats with shimmering alchemical dyes that flowed with iridescent colors; tiny lights gleamed at throats and wrists, or nestled in elaborately styled hair. My own braid suddenly seemed painfully simple by comparison. Others seemed to have sewn a treasure chest's worth of jewels into the fabric of their bodices or waistcoats, or wore cascades of ostentatiously intricate artifice wirework as jewelry. I found myself having to tear my eyes away from the startlingly low necklines on gowns with far more *structure* than anything we wore in Vaskandar.

"Look at those hats!" Kessa crowed. "I always wanted a hat with a feather."

"You might want to wait on that," Foxglove warned. "My briefing tells me hats are a fashion of the merchant class this season; the nobility prefer elaborate coiffures instead. There's a lot of tension between the Common Council and the Noble Council in the Loreician court, and your fashion choices could be seen as picking a side."

"Bah," Kessa said. "I can plead ignorant foreigner. Besides, I see the nobles are also wearing pastels, and I look terrible in pastels, so I'm afraid my allegiance is firmly with the commoners regardless."

"The palace seems very, ah, populated," I said apprehensively.

"It is!" Kessa practically bounced in her seat. "It's got six ballrooms, a theater, a temple, a series of lovely art galleries, conservatories, bathing pools, extensive gardens—you never run out of people to meet or things to do."

Severin gave me a sympathetic glance. "I'm sure there are also places one can hole up and immerse oneself in one's disdain for humanity, when the mood strikes."

"Oh, absolutely," Kessa agreed, with no less cheerfulness. "It's so huge, there's plenty of space for privacy."

No matter how much I might yearn to slip into my own secret dusty spaces hidden between the walls of Gloamingard right now, that wasn't what I was here to do. I'd search this glittering place one end to the other and talk to every single person inside it if that would help me find the artifact before anyone could use it against Morgrain.

Formidable and intricate runework arched over the great open doors and bordered each window: the powerful wards that defended the Summer Palace, allowing the entire Loreician government to safely retreat to the northern hills for three months a year when the capital grew too hot. Dozens of guards in showy silver-caped uniforms stood about, some with rapiers and pistols and others with long muskets or pikes, all wearing hats trailing glorious plumes. I wondered whether that said anything about their allegiance, but surely even in a place like this, the uniform didn't change with the fashion seasons.

One guard with a spray of freckles across her nose straightened from slipping a tidbit to a scruffy-looking cat to greet us as our carriage pulled up before the entrance.

"Welcome to the Summer Palace," she said cheerfully. "The Rookery, I'm guessing, by the Castle Ilseine crest on your carriage? We're expecting you." She swept into a florid bow. "Elia of the palace guard, at your service. Come with me—don't worry about your luggage, the servants will take it—and I'll bring you to the Serene Envoy."

"Is that your cat?" Kessa asked, delighted.

"Oh, no," Elia laughed. "The guard can't have pets in the palace, more's the pity. There are strays all over the grounds, though, and I feed them. Follow me!"

As we approached the wide, towering doors and caught glimpses of a vast marble entry hall beyond them, I braced myself for the odd pressure-shift feeling I still hadn't quite gotten used to when passing through Castle Ilseine's wards.

Even so, when we stepped through, I gasped.

It wasn't because of the imposing marble columns, their outermost thickness cut into an elaborate filigree over colored glass with embedded luminaries, so that the massive stone supports seemed made of air and vibrant light. Nor was it due to the dramatic frescoes on the ceiling, cunningly painted so that the tinted light from the columns would highlight some key feature of a scene from Loreician history, the water glowing blue in a naval scene or the bright scarlet uniforms of Falconers shining red. I hadn't even gasped at all the brilliantly garbed people passing through the space, an overwhelming crowd decked out in scents and music and light as much as fine glorious fabrics and embroidery, their voices echoing in pattering laughter from the marble around us.

Magic hung in the air, thick and oppressive, like the musk of a beast in its den. I hadn't felt anything like this in Castle Ilseine, the only other imperial building I'd ever been in.

"Do you feel that?" Severin whispered beside me, the whites showing in his eyes. No one else seemed to notice. "It's like a Witch Lord's castle."

Not *my* Witch Lord's castle. My grandmother's magical presence might be powerful and pervasive, but it had a fresh clean feel to it, not this queasy, skin-prickling miasma.

"Why aren't the others reacting?" I rubbed my arms. "Is this normal for an imperial palace?" Surely it couldn't be.

"I don't think they can feel it." Severin glanced around at not only the Rookery, who were admiring the architecture and fashion around us, but all the crowd moving through the spectacular entry hall. "They're not mage-marked; they're less sensitive to magic."

Even as he spoke, the sensation faded, like a scent that seems overpowering when you first enter a room but vanishes quickly as you adapt to it. If Severin hadn't said anything, I'd already be sure I'd imagined it. Perhaps we were just overreacting to the artifice wards, since we didn't have them in Vaskandar. Or perhaps we weren't, and the Summer Palace hid a powerful and disquieting magical secret—the artifact we sought, or something worse.

Given everything that had been happening, I wished I could believe it was the wards.

"Thank the Graces you're here." Lord Elford, the Serene Envoy from Raverra and the most powerful man in Loreice, ran a lace-trimmed handkerchief across his high forehead. Jewels wrapped in golden artifice wire gleamed on his chest, and cinnamon-scented perfume teased the air. "The situation has escalated since we talked over the courier lamps this morning, Foxglove, and I'm hoping you can help me."

It would be a nice change if the situation could stop escalating for a while. I settled in a gilt-and-brocade chair, bracing myself for whatever new catastrophe awaited us.

I didn't know what to call this opulent room—a salon? Drawing room? Parlor? The imperials had so many names for rooms you received guests in, and I couldn't fathom the distinctions. Whatever it was called, it was small enough to be private. The Serene Envoy had shooed out aides and servants as soon as the wine was poured.

He and his staff occupied an entire small wing that protruded between the spreading arms of the palace, complete with public audience chambers and ballrooms, lavish private and guest quarters, independent kitchens, and a wide assortment of rooms that seemed designed for having conversations of different sizes and levels of formality. All of them burst with lush fabrics, breathtakingly delicate goldwork, and dramatic oil paintings in which the Graces smiled benevolently over key moments in imperial history. The imperial wing seemed almost in aesthetic argument with the rest of the palace; its warm palettes and antiques asserted

Raverran tradition over the jewel colors and exuberantly experimental architecture we'd seen on the way in. I'd known Loreicians revered art, but I hadn't realized that all forms of it, from fashion to architecture to the pointed scenes of Raverran military victories in the oil paintings, would be so political. Clearly I'd have to tread carefully here.

"Oh, I love exciting surprise developments," Kessa said, making a show of collecting her own glass and taking a long fortifying sip.

The Serene Envoy laughed, a bit nervously. "I was appointed to this post precisely because I'm *not* one for exciting surprise developments. The Empire is still trying to keep a light hand in Loreice to reassure them of their sovereignty after it intervened in the Festival Uprising fifty years ago. Frankly, I usually just go to parties and sign trade agreements; I'm not prepared for this level of..." He waved a hand toward the rest of the palace, distastefully. "Drama."

I nodded sympathetically. "And now you're caught in the middle of it."

"Under normal circumstances, my primary responsibility is keeping the delicate balance between the Serene Empire and the two chambers of the Curia—the Common Council and the Noble Council—who not only despise each other, but resent Raverra for forcing them to share power. Now after ten years of reassuring them that Raverra will keep its hands off Loreice, I may need to make arrests in the middle of their court." He produced a silk fan and began waving it vigorously, as if he could blow the idea away.

Just political troubles, then. Serious, to be sure, but still a relief. After what Severin and I had sensed in the entry hall, I'd half expected Lord Elford to tell us the palace was under some malign enchantment—though when I'd mentioned it to the rest of the Rookery, they'd confirmed they hadn't noticed anything.

Bastian clasped his hands tightly together in his lap. "So are they here already, Your Excellency? The Zenith Society?"

"This is why I'm glad you've come. I'm not sure." The fan whirred faster. "You see, a week ago, all the factions were equally terrified of the demon sitting right over the border in Morgrain, and we had a common enemy." *Well, pox.* That didn't bode well for my diplomatic ambitions. "Then Lady Silene showed up— the queen's new adviser."

Severin sighed. "So many problems start with a new adviser. I take it she has the queen's ear?"

"They're inseparable." Elford didn't hide his grimace. "Worse, Silene brought in a new crowd of favorites. On the surface, they're just offering solutions to the Morgrain problem— you know, taking advantage of the fear to come in acting like they could fix everything as a play for power. Given what I've learned from Raverra, however, I suspect they might be Zenith Society."

If they were, I didn't like the sound of them *offering solutions to the Morgrain problem* with that artifact in their hands. Not at all.

"We need to move quickly." The words tumbled out on instinct, before I remembered that we weren't supposed to know about the artifact.

"First I need to be sure that they're actually Zenith Society traitors." Elford flipped his fan shut. "I can't afford to make a mistake here. Lady Cornaro told me over the courier lamps that the Rookery might recognize one or two of the group we're seeking; I'm hoping you can identify them for me."

The incessant scratching of Bastian's pencil stopped.

"Do you have names?" Foxglove asked, his face still and guarded.

"No, but I can ask for them." The Serene Envoy glanced to the windows; night had fallen, and it was velvety dark outside. "You should be able to get a look at them tomorrow. The queen has taken to holding a sort of informal court in the gardens every morning," he said. "Lady Silene and her associates are bound to be there."

Bastian's pencil snapped in his hand. "We'll look forward to it," he said.

"Good, good." Elford smiled, oblivious to the tension in the room. "If you can identify them tomorrow morning, hopefully we can clear things swiftly with the Loreician government, arrest them, and have the whole thing wrapped up by dinnertime."

By the looks on everyone's faces, I doubted any of us thought it would be that easy.

"Hey," I asked Kessa quietly, "are you all right?"

The Serene Envoy's staff had whisked us through a hospitality gauntlet: first perfumed baths overflowing with iridescent alchemical foam, accompanied by echoing strains of string music that issued from an artificed conch shell; then a dinner with far too many rich courses, with delicate aromatic sauces and dishes arranged to look like little gardens so that I was never quite sure what I was eating. We were heading to our guest quarters at last, stuffed and smelling like flowers. Kessa, who had maintained a bright patter of conversation about everything from culinary techniques to the season's new plays in an obvious attempt to bolster Bastian's spirits, had lagged behind the rest of the group, her shoulders slumping from apparent exhaustion.

She picked her head up at once and flashed me a smile. "Oh, I'm fine! I was just thinking."

I raised an eyebrow. "I may have grown up socially isolated, but I'm not *completely* oblivious. You're all worried about this Zenith Society person who might be familiar."

Kessa looked for a moment as if she might try to laugh it off, but then she sighed. "Bastian's got it worse, worrying about whether it might be his old mentor. I don't have anyone specific to dread—I never found out which of them killed my brother. I don't know if they're alive or dead, free or in prison."

A frustrated edge came into her voice at that, no matter how she tried to keep it light.

"I'm not sure you have it better," I said, my chest heavy with sympathy. "I think not knowing who murdered my aunt and tried to kill me was even worse than knowing it was Aurelio. But Hells, it's all terrible."

"That's for certain," Kessa agreed, with feeling.

"Would you..." I hesitated; it was a personal question. But then, Kessa asked personal questions all the time. "If you had the choice, would you want to know who killed him?"

"Yes," Kessa said, without hesitation. "Seasons, yes. I've spent all these years hating this faceless figure." She waved a vague hand in front of her. "If I had a name, a face, anything—then I could..." She trailed off.

"Yes?" I prompted her.

She let out a rueful laugh. "Then I'd have someone specific to hate for killing Loren, I suppose."

I heard what she didn't say: *Someone besides myself.*

"You didn't kill him," I said softly.

"Didn't I?" She caught my eyes, her gaze weary and knowing and deeply honest. "You know better than anyone how complicated that question can be sometimes."

I thought of the mass of feelings bottled up in my stomach over everything I could have done differently—all the myriad paths that wouldn't have led to Lamiel lying dead at my hands and the Hells themselves unleashed.

"I understand," I said hoarsely.

We caught up to the others as we passed through the imperial wing's grand ballroom; massive crystal chandeliers hung dark overhead, like spiderwebs dangling heavy with prey. The only light came from pale and flickering night luminaries spaced at broad intervals between the oil paintings adorning the walls, and from their reflections in the glassy-smooth floor below. It was late, and the ballroom lay silent save for our own echoing footsteps.

Bastian suddenly froze, the color draining from his face.

"What is it?" I asked him, alarmed. The others paused as well; Ashe pivoted outward, scanning for enemies.

"Do you..." He swallowed. "Do you hear singing?"

No one moved. We strained our ears against the silence; I caught the slight whispering rustle of clothing, the distant muffled ticking of a clock. Nothing more.

"No," Severin said cautiously.

I shook my head. "Me either."

Kessa raised her eyebrows. "Just how little sleep have you been getting, Bastian?"

Foxglove flipped open one of the pouches at his belt and pulled out a loop of wire-wrapped metal—an artifice amplifier. He held it to his ear for a moment, then shook his head. "There's nothing."

"It's *her*," Bastian said, a shudder wracking him. A green cast crept up his neck, spreading toward his face. "I know that voice. Holy Graces."

Foxglove and Kessa exchanged alarmed looks.

I hesitated for an instant, gathering my courage, and touched his shoulder in what I hoped was a reassuring fashion. "Bastian, there's no one singing. We should—"

Grace of Mercy. Now I could hear it, too.

Echoing down the marble halls, from some unknowable point in the distance, came a woman's rich alto voice: "*Oh my love came up to meet me, and he wore a coat of gold...*"

I glanced sharply at Foxglove and Ashe, but they still frowned as if they couldn't hear it.

"*...But it couldn't keep him warm against the bitter mountain cold...*"

I released Bastian's shoulder, and the voice faded into silence.

He pressed his hands over his ears, squeezing his eyes shut. "It can't be her. It can't be. She's been dead for years. How can she be *here*?"

Cold horror crawled up from my belly. I didn't believe in ghosts, but at night in a strange palace, suddenly they seemed a lot more plausible.

"Oh. *Her*." Foxglove let out a breath. "Yes, she's very dead. I saw them do it; they burned the body to be sure. Cortissa can't hurt you, Bastian. She's gone."

Well, *that* didn't make it any less creepy. But Bastian seemed inexplicably relieved.

"I suppose you're right," he said, exhausted. "I need sleep, and I'm worried about the Zenith Society having that weapon in their hands, and I'm imagining things."

I could think of one reason they might feel the need to burn a body to make certain someone was truly dead—if they were a Skinwitch. A vivomancer whose magic could work on humans because they felt no sense of kinship with them. That complete lack of basic empathy meant they often did terrible things.

Like turning humans into chimeras against their will. *Oh, Bastian.*

Foxglove put away his listening device with a careful pat to the pouch it had come from. "Come on. There's a soft bed waiting for you." He laid a hand on Bastian's back—and froze, his face going still.

He must hear it, too.

Bastian didn't seem to notice. "Yes, I think that'll help. It's fading already anyway." He looked sick and pale, as if he might faint any minute.

Foxglove let his hand drop; Kessa moved up to take his place, throwing an arm around Bastian's shoulders. "Let's get you tucked in, you goose. I should give you one of your own sleep potions."

We started forward again, continuing through the shadowy palace. Foxglove caught my eye and jerked his head, his message clear: *Fall back and talk with me.*

"What in the Nine Hells was that?" I whispered fiercely to him, as soon as I was sure Bastian was far enough ahead not to hear.

Foxglove shook his head, a light of alarm in his dark amber eyes. "I heard it, too. I don't know."

"Could it be alchemy?" It was the only type of magic I knew of that could play with your perceptions. "Something in our food, or in the air?"

"Maybe." His jaw flexed. "Don't tell Bastian you heard it. Not yet. I wasn't lying to him—she really is dead. But he's got enough to be upset about right now."

"What in the four seasons does it mean that we heard a dead woman's voice when we touched him?" I couldn't help but think of the power Severin and I had felt when we entered the palace, hanging over everything like the scent of poison. As if the whole place were cursed.

Foxglove shook his head. "Speaking as a professional investigator of strange magic—I have no idea."

The bed in my guest chamber was soft and sumptuous as a Loreician pastry, but I couldn't fall asleep. What kept me awake wasn't only bone-deep worry that the Zenith Society would unleash a wave of death across Morgrain if we couldn't retrieve the weapon in time, though that certainly didn't help.

Alone in the dark, that sense of pervasive, smothering power teased at my senses again.

Every time my eyes began to drift closed, the dancing shepherds I could barely make out in the pastoral frescoes on the ceiling seemed to move, or the shadows to creep across their painted fields like spreading blood. Magic made insect tracks along my skin, raising gooseflesh in its wake.

Something was *wrong* in this palace, and none of the explanations my imagination came up with, lying there in the dark, made sleep any easier.

Where in the Nine Hells was Whisper? He said he'd come

with me. I could use his company now; I missed our familiar dance, him trying to withhold knowledge and me seeking to coax it out of him, and the comfort of his soft black fur. Maybe he'd even grudgingly dole out some useful information. Perhaps traveling by fast coach had been too much for even his unknown powers to keep up—or maybe he simply had better things to do than tag along after some foolish lonely human after all.

I must have drifted off for a few moments at last, because I awoke to a muffled cry from the next room.

I sat up in bed, heart pounding, the first gray hint of twilight falling across my lap. In a moment, it came again, faint through the walls: Severin.

First the singing, now this—was I under so much strain from everything that had happened that I was hallucinating? But he really was in the next room, and there had been so much fear and pain in that wordless cry.

I threw back my covers and ran for the door in the nightgown the palace servants had provided, trailing fine Loreician lace. Severin's voice came again as I hesitated outside his door, this time with words: "*No, I'm sorry, I'm sorry, don't kill me, please—*"

Pox take propriety and caution. I flung open the door.

FIVE

Severin curled on his side, fists clenched in the tangle of his sheets, glorious dark hair spread across the bed. In any other circumstances I might have been struck breathless by the twilight-softened angles and curves of his bare shoulders and chest—but his face twisted in pain, eyes squeezed shut.

A nightmare. I'd thought he was being murdered.

"Hey!" I dropped to my knees beside him. It was hard to force myself to touch that naked shoulder, the smooth warmth of his skin, even with the cold clasp of the jess on my wrist making it safe. I gave him a gentle shake, peering into his face. "Severin, wake up! It's just a dream."

He lunged at me, sudden as a snake, seizing my arm in a painful grip. I stared into wide dark eyes ringed with stormy gray—vague, wild, and clearly not seeing me.

"You won't kill us," he snarled. "I'll cut you apart again first."

Again. Who did he think I was? I tried to pull away. "Severin—"

His other hand shot out and grabbed my throat, chokingly tight.

Pox take it. I jabbed my thumb into his eye.

He reeled back, crying out in surprise and alarm; I scrambled to the other side of the room. The blankets tangled in his lap. Did he sleep completely naked? I couldn't quite tell, but suddenly it was all I could think about.

He blinked his vision clear. "Ryx! Hells, did I just try to kill you?"

"No harm done. You're not so dangerous when you're asleep." I rubbed my neck and came cautiously closer, pulse still racing, trying to keep my gaze on his face and not the bare sweep from his chest down to his abdomen. "Who did you think I was?"

His shadowed face looked lean and haunted, his silky hair falling all around him like black wings. "I..." He shuddered. "My father."

"Oh? *Oh.*" I swallowed. "So you, ah, cut him into pieces?" I should have guessed; Witch Lords were nearly impossible to kill.

Severin turned his face away, his tone deceptively light. "Collapsing a stone building on him and dumping powerful alchemical vitriol over him wasn't enough. He was cursing and threatening us while he regrew his flesh and knit his bones, so we had to do *something.*"

I tried to imagine that—two desperate teenagers hacking apart their father's raw, half-dissolved form while the ragged hole of his mouth cursed them and his ruined body struggled to rise.

"I'm sorry." My mouth had gone dry; the words came out rough and scratchy. "No child should have to do that to survive."

"I'll bet you say that to all the murderers you're trapped in a room with." He still wouldn't look at me, curse him, the line of his neck taut in the silvery light.

"I'm not going to run away in horror because you defended yourself the only way you could. My own hands are far from clean," I reminded him. "I've killed, too."

"But not like *that.*"

"I wasn't aware it was a contest," I snapped.

That got him. He faced me at last, faint shining tracks crossing the sharp lines of his cheekbones. He hovered on the edge of a moment of softness, of truth—of finally allowing himself to show weakness.

His mouth twisted. "Well, if it is, I'm winning."

"You're hopeless." I shook my head in frustration. "You're allowed to be upset, you know."

The barest whisper of something like a laugh huffed through his lips. "I...That's a novel idea. I'll have to consider whether it's true."

"I give up." I rose, ready to leave. But he grabbed my wrist—lightly, so that I could pull away without any real resistance.

"Thank you," he said, as subdued as I'd ever heard him. "For waking me."

I froze. The moment teetered on the brink of possibility; if I dared, I could nudge it over the edge into something new and dizzyingly unknown.

But inscrutable and hostile magic teased at my senses—and Severin had just awakened from a nightmare about the father he'd gruesomely murdered, for blood's sake. Whatever I might feel, seeing him with his chest bare and his eyes huge and vulnerable in the darkness, he couldn't possibly be feeling the same.

Or maybe I was just afraid.

"I like you better awake," I said at last, a bit gruffly. "Somehow, you're even more intolerably dramatic when you're asleep."

I gave his hand a brief, warm squeeze before heading for the door.

I stared about in a mix of wonder and dismay. "This...wasn't what I expected when the Serene Envoy mentioned the palace gardens."

Severin shook his head in disgust. "Imperials. It's always about control."

I was used to Vaskandran gardens shaped by magic, organic and strange and wild. *Garden* meant twisting branches and climbing vines, trees with faces, flowers blooming year-round in unearthly colors, mosses and lichens forming textural maps around and over tumbled boulders. It meant glowing insects and bushes teased into fantastical shapes with leaves that made chiming music in the wind.

The vast Summer Palace gardens stretched down from the back of the palace in descending terraces, like a neatly stitched carpet unrolled over broad, shallow stairs before us. On the first terrace, marble fountains sprayed contrived arcs and fans of water tinted vibrant colors by alchemical solvents. On the level below it, a great pool rectangular as a tabletop reflected the sky; courtiers dressed in skirts like blossoms and coats with leaf-shaped tails strolled around it, between ornamental trees clipped into neat cubes and topiary bushes trimmed to form fat, round rabbits or bears. Below that, straight paths of crushed white shells crisscrossed orderly flower beds in geometric patterns, sectioned by hedges cut with borders so clean and sharp they might as well have been furniture. Dramatic statuary and architecturally fanciful outbuildings scattered about the gardens like punctuation.

These artificial shapes cut by metal shears seemed wrong, and all the more so since I had no link to this land to feel the life within them. Everything that was real and organic had been made to seem false, and everything inorganic mimicked life.

"They've even warded it in," I murmured. A high stone wall surmounted with the same formidably complicated runes I'd seen around the doors ran from the edges of the palace off into the distance, encircling the vast acres of garden that unfolded dramatically before us. On the lowest terrace I spied artfully groomed groves, miniature mockeries of a forest. "Are they worried the flowers will try to escape?"

Foxglove gave me an odd look. "No, they're worried your grandmother and her peers will invade with an army of chimeras. We're not that far from the border."

Ashe tapped her temple. "This is the Empire, remember? Their gardens can't murder people. They need wards for defense."

The idea that a ruler could feel unsafe in their own land was utterly foreign. But then, this palace made me feel unsafe, too.

Not to mention that from the perspective of the mission, these sprawling grounds were a nightmare; it was that much more area to search for the stolen weapon. If the Zenith Society didn't want to get caught with it in their rooms, they could bury it in some flower bed or strap it up under an ornamental bridge, and we'd have Nine Hells of a time finding it.

Foxglove gazed analytically out over the expanse of gardens, marking the paths of strolling courtiers pretending to be merely taking in the bright sunshine while they circled and maneuvered to get closer to the center of power.

"Let's go find out what rats have gotten in through those wards," he said grimly. "Then we can search their nests for any trinkets they've stolen."

We strolled down from the first terrace into the gardens. My borrowed gown rustled around me with unaccustomed layers— deep sapphire blue, but with my hair pinned up in a simple coiled braid to avoid any unintended declaration of a side in Loreice's political struggles. Between that and the sword hanging on a silver belt at my hip, the simple act of walking had become as strange as my surroundings.

Once we got down among the hedges and fountains and carefully trimmed trees, the gardens felt less wide open, as if we wandered through rooms of a second palace cut out of leaves and flowers. I only knew one member of the Zenith Society, so

I scanned every figure we glimpsed for Aurelio's auburn hair—though if he were here, we'd have a whole new set of problems, given that so far as we knew he was still hosting the Demon of Hunger.

"Strange," Kessa murmured beside me. She looked especially jaunty this morning in one of the feathered hats she'd coveted, with a trailing scarlet plume and bright gold trim, but her expression was more subdued than usual.

"What is it?"

She was frowning at a pair of swordsmen in the silver uniform of the palace guard, standing unobtrusively by a statue of a man weeping with both hands over his face. I'd seen guards sprinkled around the garden, little splashes of silver, and thought nothing of it; presumably the Loreician court needed guards in the same way it needed wards, since its leaders were mortal and fragile in a way that Witch Lords were not.

"Their eyes," she said quietly. "Bastian, is that a potion you're familiar with?"

I took a closer look. A strange silver sheen covered their eyes from lid to lid, as if a thin wash of some metallic substance mixed with their tears. The guards stared straight ahead, unmoving. A shiver crawled across my shoulders.

Bastian squinted in their direction. "I can't say that it is. I suppose it could be some kind of sight-enhancing potion," he said dubiously. "Or an ill-advised fashion trend. You know how Loreice is about fashion. I read a study about a time eighty years ago when they decided it was dreadfully attractive to take poison to make their pupils dilate."

The guards' eyes didn't move to track us as we walked past them. They simply stared into space as if their minds were elsewhere.

"Creepy," Ashe muttered.

I couldn't help but agree. Combined with the oppressive magic Severin and I had felt and the dead woman's voice singing, we were well past the point where I could wave the strange magical phenomena off as side effects or imperial oddities. I ran through theories in my head, each more horrible than the last, as we descended onto the third terrace. A vast sunny lawn dominated it, anchored by a strange building and a great spreading tree. Smaller gardens surrounded the lawn, creating more intimate conversational spaces.

"And there's the heart of the web," Foxglove said. "Just the place to look for spiders."

The building at the far end of the lawn had no windows, but it flashed with thousands of chips of mirror glass in the bright sun, arranged in geometric patterns to form intricate mosaics across its surface. It looked like a discarded heap of cheap jewelry, gaudy and jarring against the carefully manicured gardens. Worse, whoever had built this eyesore had placed it directly behind the glorious tree that majestically presided over the lawn, huge enough that vivomancers must have enhanced its growth, its crown casting a wide circle of shade around it.

Beneath that tree, amid a cluster of courtiers, two women stood resplendent. Queen Mirthaine, a pale wisp of a girl, nearly vanished into astonishingly wide skirts of exquisite silver brocade and intricately layered lace. The one who I took to be Lady Silene towered over her, pleased as a well-fed cat at her side in a buttercup-yellow gown, her silver-streaked brown hair pinned up with pearls. The people flocked around them seemed mostly to wear the pale colors and elaborate coiffures of the nobility; knots of commoners in fanciful plumed hats and gorgeously embroidered earth and jewel tones watched from a skeptical distance.

"Recognize anyone?" Kessa asked Foxglove and Bastian, as we strolled closer along the edges of the conversation gardens to get a better look.

Bastian shook his head, his expression hovering between relief and disappointment. Foxglove casually lifted a rune-ringed monocle to his eye, which I suspected doubled as a spyglass.

"If this Lady Silene is associated with the Zenith Society, she's no one I know," he said. "And none of the other—" He broke off, sucking in a sharp breath between his teeth.

"What?" Bastian asked anxiously. "Who did you see?"

"No one." Foxglove lowered the monocle, his face tense and strained, and rubbed his eye. "My mind playing tricks on me." He lifted it again, scanning the faces in the crowd, a muscle working in his jaw.

"Who did you *think* you saw?" Kessa pressed, stepping protectively close to Bastian. "Someone from the Zenith Society?"

Foxglove stared at her as if she might be an illusion herself, shadows of whatever he'd seen clinging to his face. At last, he shook his head. "No. No, it was someone from long ago. Someone I wronged, who's dead now. It's impossible he could be here."

The back of my neck prickled. "Like the song Bastian heard," I murmured.

Kessa put an arm around Bastian's shoulders, but he frowned with curiosity, not dread. Apparently the prospect of seeing a ghost was less alarming than spotting someone he knew from the Zenith Society.

"How odd," he said. "There are potions that cause hallucinations, and a few that bring up old memories. I suppose someone in the palace could be dosing people as a prank, but of course I can't help but speculate on more sinister possibilities."

"Magic can't reverse death," Severin said, his brows creasing. "I should know; my brother's life magic is as powerful as it gets, and he couldn't do it." He glanced toward me, the reason his brother had needed to look into raising the dead; I winced.

"I just imagined it," Foxglove said firmly, though lines of strain lingered around his mouth. "He's gone now. Let's not get distracted. Time to settle in and watch what company this Lady Silene keeps."

"I know a lot of stories about people who go to a big old castle and start hearing and seeing dead people," Ashe offered. "They all end pretty horribly for everyone involved."

"Ashe," Kessa said firmly, "sit down and stop making things worse."

"Oh, fine."

Foxglove hadn't imagined it any more than Bastian had, and we all knew it. I gave him my best *We'll talk about this later* stare; he grimaced acknowledgment.

We picked a conversation garden with a good view of the tree, settling on a couple of marble benches beside a small bronze fountain ringed with the leaping dolphins that symbolized the Loreician royal house. An uneasy mood had descended on our group. I didn't believe in ghosts, but still... This place had better not be haunted on top of everything else.

"What's the building?" I asked, to try to lighten the mood.

"A folly." Kessa gestured expansively, seeming glad of the opening. "From before the Festival Uprising, when the monarchs of Loreice had absolute power to indulge their whims and far too much wealth. The king had visited a carnival mirror maze as a boy and was deeply impressed by the experience, so he had this oversized and rather gaudy one built on the palace grounds."

"I suppose it doesn't make any more or less sense than having rooms made out of bones," I granted.

Bastian's brows rose. "One might argue that bones are a less normal building material than mirrors," he suggested.

I shrugged. "Not in Vaskandar." I made a mental note to search the maze building if we didn't find the artifact when they arrested the Zenith Society members. It seemed exactly the sort of place a person with a flair for the dramatic would hide something.

From this far away, I couldn't make out many details of the queen and her adviser, but Queen Mirthaine looked young—

barely an adult. She gazed around her as if she found the garden and especially the courtiers fascinating; wherever her attention landed, a flurry of bowing and curtsying broke out. It was Lady Silene who determined who the queen would speak to, gesturing people forward with a surety of command in every line of her body that didn't match the story that she was merely a friend of the royal family who had only been in court for a few days.

"Where are her usual advisers?" I murmured. "The queen should have people she turns to as a matter of course to get things done, like I do with Odan and Gaven and Jannah. I only see Silene, plus guards and servants. The rest of this crowd is just currying favor."

Kessa frowned. "That's a good point. The last time I was here, you never saw the queen without her advisers. If these new favorites have ousted them already, this has gone further than we thought."

A handful of the silver-clad palace guard approached Queen Mirthaine at Silene's command and knelt in the grass before her, making dashing figures with their plumed hats. I thought I recognized the guard who'd met us at the gate yesterday among them; she craned her neck up to stare at the queen as if she couldn't believe the honor she was receiving. After a brief exchange, the queen and her adviser drifted off toward the entrance to the mirror maze, the cluster of guards following—not with the protective stance I'd expect, but with the more casual, excited stroll of invited guests. The courtiers left milling alone under the tree seemed disappointed to be left behind, but not surprised, as if they'd seen this before.

"That's odd." I frowned. "Why would she want to have a private conversation with a handful of guards in a mirror maze?"

"Why do athelings and royalty want to do anything?" Ashe retorted.

"Granted, but still—"

I broke off. Bastian was staring past me, his eyes intent.

"Is everything all right?" I asked.

"Grace of Mercy," he breathed. "Is he another phantom? Foxglove, look and tell me if he's really there. Just *standing* there like that."

Bastian was staring at the crowd of courtiers milling under and around the tree, his whole body trembling. At first I thought it was with fear—but no. His liquid brown eyes had gone hard, his face transformed with an emotion I'd never seen on it before: anger.

Foxglove followed his gaze and swore. His hand dropped to the pistol at his hip.

"What is it?" Ashe asked, scanning the distant group with keen eyes. "Do I need to stab someone?"

"Maybe later." Foxglove stepped in front of Bastian, as if to block him from view. "I see him, too, Bastian. *Damnation*."

Kessa's eyes narrowed. "I can guess who. The rotten stingroach."

I could, too: the mentor who'd given him over to a Skin-witch. Anger stoked a fire in my belly. Never take up other people's grievances, the wisdom went—except to avenge your friends and family.

At the near edge of the mingling courtiers, an older man with deep-set eyes and iron-gray hair was staring at us. He nudged the man next to him, and suddenly a whole cluster of people detached from the group by the tree and made their way across the gardens toward us with rather unwelcoming expressions.

"What should we expect?" Severin asked sharply. "They look like they're planning to start a fight."

Foxglove kept his eyes fixed on their leader. "Be ready for anything."

That was unhelpfully vague. Where I came from, *anything* could mean half an hour of dramatic grandstanding or hundreds of deadly poisonous chimerical bees exploding out of their pockets.

"I never asked to be part of your quarrels," Severin hissed.

Foxglove didn't so much as glance at him. "Then be ready to get out of our way."

Frustration tightened Severin's features, but we were out of time to do anything about it. The Zenith Society group had arrived.

Nothing unified the handful of people standing before us beyond a hard gleam of animosity in their eyes. Most of them looked Raverran, like Bastian and my mother, with olive-bronze skin and dark eyes and hair; one was paler, and could have been Callamornish or from the Vaskandran highlands, and another had the deep brown skin of Osta, like Foxglove. All of them were dressed for the royal court, in elegant embroidered coats and sumptuous gowns, bedecked with jewels and artifice wirework, and the obligatory rapiers or pistols.

"It could have been any of them," Kessa whispered, so softly I doubted I was meant to hear, something akin to desperation in her eyes.

"Well, if it isn't the Rookery," said the gentleman with the iron-gray hair, in a dry and gravelly voice. A humorless smile pulled at the corner of his mouth.

"You've got nerve turning up here, Moreni," Foxglove said, his voice cold as a year of winter.

"I could say the same to you." Moreni's eyes slid to Bastian, the bitter gleam in them turning almost eager. "Hello, Bastian. Are your studies coming along well?"

Bastian managed nothing more than a strangled sound; his glare should have melted Moreni on the spot.

Ashe must have come to the same conclusion about Moreni's identity that I had. A faint metallic scrape cut short as Kessa grabbed her shoulder. "Rule Four, Ashe," she murmured. "Talk first."

"Oh, come *on*," Ashe protested.

"I know," Kessa whispered, more vitriol in her voice than I'd realized she was capable of. "Believe me, *I know*."

Foxglove stepped closer to Moreni, his hand resting casually on his pistol belt. His voice went deadly soft. "You lost the right to talk to Bastian five years ago."

"That's rather judgmental, coming from an assassin." Moreni's lip curled. "Do your little friends know who you are, Foxglove? Do they know what you've done?"

Foxglove's temple twitched, but his tone remained icy calm. "You're still wanted for treason. I could take you down right now and be well within the law."

"Oh, let's," Ashe agreed, a sharp grin stretching over her teeth.

"This isn't the time." I tried to speak too softly for Moreni to understand.

"Try it," Moreni breathed, spreading his arms wide. The coiled wirework and sparkling crystal beads of artifice jewelry gleamed at his throat, his wrists, his fingers. "Go ahead. See what happens."

His companions dropped hands to swords and pistols; one clutched a rune-carved pendant. All of them held the wary readiness of people familiar with violence.

I let out a soft curse; all I had was my rapier, which I'd only ever used in practice, but that wasn't what I was worried about. If a fight broke out, not only would we have betrayed the Serene Envoy's trust in us, but the dozens of guards stationed around the gardens would probably assume we were murderers and join in on the other side. Even now, the closest bystanders strolling the garden drew back with muttered exclamations.

"Ah, Foxglove, there you are!" Lord Elford's voice rang out loud as a bell.

He approached quickly along a garden path, trailing aides and retainers who wore rapiers like everyone else. What fool had decided that deadly weapons made good fashion accessories? Any gathering of the elite in Loreice could break out into a pitched battle at a moment's notice.

Annoyance twitched across Moreni's brows. He lowered his arms, transforming in one graceful instant to a genteel courtier who couldn't possibly have been about to erupt into murder a moment earlier. The others around him took his cue, somewhat less smoothly, the tension muted but far from gone.

"You were saying?" Foxglove asked Moreni coolly, his hand still resting on his belt.

"We'll have to continue our intriguing conversation another time." Moreni gave Foxglove and Bastian a shallow, mocking bow. "I look forward to it."

He jerked his head to signal the others; they sauntered slowly off, as if they had all the time in the world and no reason to worry about trivial things like getting arrested. *That* was worrisome. If they'd gotten the queen's protection, this could escalate into a major incident, making it harder for us to get our hands on the artifact.

Elford caught up to us just as Moreni and his crew left. He glanced after them, looked at Foxglove's face, and let out a long, nervous sigh.

"I take it you recognized them, then?"

"Just one of them," Foxglove said, his voice flat. "But yes."

"I see." Elford drew his handkerchief from his pocket and patted his high brow. "Tell me everything. And then I'd best talk to the Curia leaders and the queen, to warn them I'll be arresting their guests."

"You should've let me kill him," Ashe growled. "Hells, you still should—it's not too late."

I half turned to Kessa, expecting her to remind Ashe about Rule Three—but she stayed silent, lips pressed together, patting Bastian's shoulder as he hunched in his chair with his face in his hands.

We were gathered in the Serene Envoy's own sitting room, where he'd asked us to wait while he spoke with the queen. It was less grand and more comfortable than the audience chamber he'd used yesterday, with tasteful sage-green draperies, a calm pastoral fresco framed in sculpted gold on the high ceiling, seven different artifice clocks displaying everything from the time to the tide to the phases of the moon, an impressively ornate wine cabinet, and a comforting fire. It should have been a calm and welcoming room, but we were all more than a little on edge.

Foxglove gave Ashe a long, absent stare, as if he saw something else when he looked at her. "Tempting," he muttered.

I couldn't believe what I was hearing. "Are you seriously considering doing this, after everything Lord Elford told us about the delicate situation here?"

Foxglove sighed. "No. No, of course not. It's what the me of six years ago would have wanted to do." He rubbed his temple. "Seeing Moreni takes me back. No, we have to let the Serene Envoy arrest him. That's his job. Ours is to make sure we get to the artifact before they can spirit it away or use it."

"Not to mention that we might need them alive to locate the thing," I added pointedly. "Getting that weapon is more important than capturing criminals, even if you have a grievance against them."

"Exactly." Severin, who'd been leaning against the mantel with his arms crossed, straightened. "All right, Foxglove, I'm going to come out and say it. I know there's old blood here, but you can't lose perspective like this. Out in the gardens you nearly turned it into a killing fight, and you would have stuck me in the middle of it. Aside from that being inconsiderate, please bear in mind I'm still the heir to Alevar, and Ryx is an atheling of Morgrain. If either of us gets killed in an imperial court, it's an enormous diplomatic incident that could easily start a war."

He was right, and I knew it too well, given everything I'd

gone through after I'd accidentally killed Lamiel. The entire Conclave might get involved. And I wasn't sure whether my grandmother still cared enough about me to attack a neighboring country over my death—but if she did, Eldest help them.

Foxglove grimaced. "That's a fair point. I hadn't considered that."

"You should have," Severin said bluntly. "Diplomacy is part of your job. Who is this man who's got you so rattled you're casually forgetting not to start the war your organization exists to prevent?"

"A monster," Bastian said suddenly, his fingers muffling his words. "This is so much worse than I expected."

"It's all right," Kessa said soothingly. "We won't let that wretch get near you. He'll be arrested within the hour, and then it's off to prison for him, if they don't execute him on the spot."

Bastian lifted his head from his hands, and it was determination on his face, not fear. "I'm not talking about my feelings. Not that I'm happy about this, mind you—I feel like I've eaten bad clams. I practiced in my head for five years what I'd say if I saw him again, but all I could make were animal noises." He shook his head. "But no, it's Moreni. I know him too well; he's a planner, with all sorts of contingencies always lined up. He'd never let us identify him like that unless there were some reason he thought it was safe."

"Maybe he thinks the threat of using the artifice weapon is enough blackmail to hold over our heads that he's untouchable," Kessa suggested.

Severin snorted. "That wouldn't make the Serene Empire hesitate more than about five seconds. They'd shed no tears over a Vaskandran domain."

"It's got to have something to do with the strangeness going on here," I said, with sudden conviction. "The song Bastian heard, the face Foxglove saw, the guards with the silver eyes, the power Severin and I felt when we entered the castle. He's got some magical ace up his sleeve."

"It would certainly be in keeping with the way the Zenith Society operates," Bastian agreed, his fingers wandering as if they could gather thoughts or reference materials from the space around his chair. "It's seeming more and more like the whole palace might have fallen under some kind of alchemical influence, although I'm not sure..." He broke off, cocking his head and lifting a hand to signal silence.

A heartbeat later, I heard it, too: the Serene Envoy had returned. He was heading our way, and he didn't sound happy.

He burst into the room, fanning himself furiously as if he could cool off the rage that reddened his face.

"Turned away," he snapped, before we could ask any questions. "I was *turned away* from the royal wing by Lady Silene."

Foxglove frowned, rising. "Can she *do* that?"

"She most certainly does not have the authority." Elford drew in a deep breath, clearly trying to steady himself and not quite succeeding. "I can't imagine the queen was aware. Mirthaine may be young, but she's never been rash enough to deliver a careless insult to the Serene City. This is some ill-considered attempt to seize power."

It seemed like a particularly foolish one, given that in Loreice the Curia had more power than the queen, so even with her ear, Silene was a long way from controlling the government. I frowned. "Or to cover something up. Could the queen be in some kind of duress? Under alchemical influence, perhaps?" I glanced at Bastian.

Elford blinked. "That's a good question. I—"

A shift in magical pressure stirred the hair on my arms. All around the windows, the ward runes blazed with sudden blue light.

I wasn't the only one to jump to my feet. Ashe had Answer half out of its sheath, swearing. Reflected blue light shivered on the exposed blade, on the gold ornamentation around the room, in the window glass.

"What in the Nine Hells just happened?" Severin demanded.

Lord Elford's fan slipped from his fingers as he stared at the glowing runes. "The wards," he said, stunned. "She's raised the palace wards and sealed us in."

SIX

An anxious crowd had gathered at the main palace gates, packing the grand entry hall between its glowing columns. Richly dressed merchant courtiers in embroidered dark frock coats and nobles in doorway-clearing pastel panniers milled together with equally agitated palace staff in silver livery. The light had faded from the warding runes around every door and window, but it was clear from the frustrated anger building in the crowd that the wards were still up.

"I've got to get home!" one voice lifted above the others. "My children are waiting for me."

"This is an outrage," an old woman with a splendid vermilion-plumed hat and a strong set of lungs cried. "We're free citizens of Loreice! The queen has no right to hold us against our will."

Lord Elford shook his head in disgust. "Locked and sealed like everything else. I thought there might be someone here to explain, but apparently not."

"It doesn't seem as if it'd be, ah, diplomatic to detain the Serene Envoy without consulting with you," I ventured.

"It's not only undiplomatic, it's illegal," Elford said flatly. "Neither the queen nor the Curia has the authority."

We stood gathered near the grand doorway that led from the

imperial wing into the entrance hall; a pair of palace guards flanked it, and I recognized the freckled face of the woman who'd met us on arrival. I approached her, smoothing frustration from my expression as best I could; whatever game the queen was playing, it wasn't the fault of some poor guard just doing her job.

"Hello," I said, "do you know what's going on here?"

She stared straight ahead as if she hadn't heard me. All the liveliness I'd seen at our arrival had fled her face, as if something had shocked her expression to blankness.

I dredged up her name from my memory. "Elia," I tried again. "Do you have any idea why the wards went up?"

She blinked at the sound of her name. A faint frown creased her brow, as if she were trying to remember where she'd heard it before. Slowly, she turned to look at me.

A silvery sheen fogged her eyes.

I stepped back. "Blood of the Eldest, what happened to you?"

Elia didn't react to my outburst. Her expression remained completely neutral—not guarded, but empty.

"I was told to stand guard in the entrance hall," she said, her voice flat and dull.

"No, your... your eyes!"

Elia blinked. I half expected silver tears to leak from between her lashes. "I have been honored to receive the queen's favor." Her lips curved in a smile, but it was as if someone else had shaped them with their fingers. There was no joy in it, no irony, no anything.

Silene must have done something to those guards she took into the mirror maze. Maybe it was a mind-influencing potion; maybe the reason she wouldn't let the Serene Envoy near the queen was because she'd given it to her, too, and she didn't want him to see those telltale silver eyes.

Or maybe something even more profoundly disturbing was going on.

A voice rang out behind me, cutting across the crowd. "I come with an announcement from Her Majesty, Queen Mirthaine. She has raised the palace wards, as you can see, but there is no cause for alarm."

I recognized that voice. I whirled to see Moreni standing before the closed palace doors, his arms spread benevolently, patrician confidence in his gaze. Ashe reached for her sword, but Kessa caught her arm. Moreni didn't have a good line of sight on the Rookery through the crowd; it was possible he hadn't seen them.

"Take it from a spy," Kessa murmured to Ashe. "When your enemy is talking, listen and learn."

The elderly woman with the vermilion plume squared herself in front of Moreni, gold embroidery flashing on her extravagant coat, fury in every line of her stance. "Explain this! The Curia was not informed that the wards would be raised. Why were we not consulted?"

"The queen has activated the wards for all of our protection, as there is a potential threat from across the border in Morgrain, Councilor Altaine," Moreni announced, his tone both grave and reassuring. "They will remain up temporarily, until the threat has passed."

My stomach flipped. Was this a real threat, or were they just using my domain as a convenient scapegoat, invoking its name to instill fear? Or worse yet, to prepare the people here to accept that a strike at Morgrain was necessary before they used the artifact. Hells, I might do something like that in their place, if I utterly lacked scruples.

Lord Elford drew an indignant breath.

"Your Excellency!" I hissed, before he could speak.

He stopped, surprised. Good—I had his attention, and the Rookery's as well.

"Don't draw any notice," I whispered. "You may be in danger. I think that silver haze in the guards' eyes is a mind control potion. Has anyone checked the queen's eyes lately? This could be a coup."

His mouth snapped shut. Difficult thoughts passed through his eyes.

Severin put a hand to his forehead. "The last thing you and I need is to get stuck in the middle of an imperial coup. Raverra will find a way to blame the whole thing on Vaskandar, just you wait."

Kessa let out a low whistle. "We can't let that happen. Bastian, if we're dealing with a mind potion, do you think you can cure it?"

Bastian hesitated. "Possibly. If nothing else, nearly all potions wear off within a few days at most, so we can cure it with time."

"All right, then!" Ashe said. "We stab Moreni and his friends, cure the queen, problem solved."

"This could still be the result of bad advice rather than alchemical influence," Foxglove warned.

Elford drew himself up. "Let's find out. I'm going to try one last time to have a private talk with the queen."

"I'd bring guards," I suggested. The last thing we needed was for the Serene Envoy to meet with the queen and come out with *his* eyes silver.

"Oh, I will." The envoy's tone went grim. "I'll give them this one chance. If they still block me from seeing the queen, or if Her Majesty refuses to open the wards, I'm going straight to the courier lamps to call in the Falcons."

My stomach dropped. Calling the imperial military on the seat of Loreician government could easily mean civil war—and with Severin and me in the middle of it, Vaskandar could get pulled in as well. But Lord Elford knew that.

I swallowed my instinctive protest. He was right; if this was a coup, we were out of other options. "If the Zenith Society has drugged the queen, Lady Silene probably *will* try to stop you from seeing her. What will you do if that happens? Walk away?"

Elford frowned. "We could likely force our way past her, *if* they let us through the wards on the royal wing—but I'd hate to cut down royal guards and functionaries who may not be involved in this treason."

If this were Gloamingard, I'd know some secret back way into the queen's quarters—some concealed passageway or forgotten space between the walls. This place was no Gloamingard, built with an imperial sense of order rather than the whimsical sprawling chaos of a series of Witch Lords. Still, surely a building of this size that showed the world such an extravagant face must have a reverse side to the mask, hidden from sight.

I drew in a breath. "There may be another way."

"I didn't realize the Serene Envoy kept a small army in the Summer Palace," I said.

Lord Elford chuckled, but there wasn't much humor in it. "Of course I don't. That would be far too undiplomatic. I have a handful of personal guards, no more."

"Did you pull these from your pockets, then?" I glanced at the well-armed, hard-eyed escort surrounding us as we marched through the spectacular Jewel Rooms on our way to the royal wing. There had to be more than fifty of them, and they moved like soldiers, their blue-and-gold Raverran uniforms just as bright as the long chain of dazzling gem-themed rooms we marched through, from emerald to sapphire to ruby.

"Every single member of my staff, from my second in command to my dishwasher, is also a highly trained soldier in the Raverran military—just in case." Lord Elford didn't look too pleased about it. "I never thought we'd have to use their other skills. Graces preserve us all."

The courtiers and palace staff we passed drew away from us, startled, and craned their necks wide-eyed after this open display of force. Whatever happened, the Serene Envoy would have diplomatic consequences to clean up.

"This is extremely uncomfortable," Severin murmured, walking beside me.

"Being smack in the middle of an internal conflict in the Serene Empire as a Vaskandran atheling? Why, yes," I agreed quietly. I had to thank the seasons no one in the palace would recognize me and realize a scion of Morgrain was at the heart of this pack of soldiers. "We've got to deal with this brash power play if we want to get what we need from the Zenith Society and get out, though." I didn't dare mention the artifact by name with so many people around us. "Hopefully my plan will let us stay away from any actual conflict—diplomatic or, seasons forbid, military."

Severin's fingers flicked out from his chest. "Avert."

We reached the Diamond Room, last and most dazzling of the Jewel Rooms, pale and shivering with reflected light. An arch of leaping golden dolphins framed the entrance to the royal wing; warding symbols surrounded it, ensuring that no one could enter by force or stealth without permission. A dozen guards flanked it, the same silvery haze in their eyes, turning away a steady stream of angry courtiers with blank, impassive insistence. The courtiers melted away before the Serene Envoy's retinue, alarm widening their eyes as they scurried to distance themselves from whatever confrontation was about to happen.

A functionary in a tailed coat of extravagant gold brocade bowed to Lord Elford in the doorway. "Your Excellency. I take it you're here to see Her Majesty about the wards?" A certain strain in the old man's voice suggested that he'd been expecting this, and was no more pleased about it than we were. I was relieved to find his eyes a clear blue.

"Of course, Bramant. Let us in." Lord Elford's tone left no room for refusal.

Bramant's wispy gray brows rose. "And your, ah, retinue?"

Elford made a dismissive gesture. "For my safety, since the queen's man at the main entrance said there's a threat from Morgrain. They can of course remain in the antechamber while I speak privately with Her Majesty." It came out smooth and casual; Elford was a good liar.

"Very well, Your Excellency." Relief colored Bramant's tone. He touched an artifice amulet at his neck and swept into a deep bow; the runes around the entrance flickered briefly with a pale light. "Please, come in."

We were through the wards. Good; that was half the battle.

The antechamber to the royal wing, a spacious hall completely in gold, resembled the inside of a giant's treasure box. Pale gold marble, delicately veined with caramel, sheathed the walls; gilded statues posed dramatically beside each window, and flights of gilded birds raced up the corners to spread their wings in clever patterns across the exultantly high ceiling. The frescoes peeking between the gaps depicted the Graces, clad in trailing swaths of wispy golden fabric, against a sky gone amber with sunset. The room was large enough to host a party with hundreds of guests; according to the Serene Envoy, it was often half full of people milling around, ecstatic at having made it this far into the queen's inner circles, hoping to be called in for an audience with the queen herself. Most of them would receive no such invitation. The glorious room existed as a sort of consolation prize, a lesser but still coveted honor.

Now it stood nearly empty. Aside from guards and palace staff, only a handful of courtiers waited here, a few in a tight cluster in the corner and another couple on a cushioned bench— covered in gold brocade, of course—that ran along the wall.

The elusive sense of ambient power returned, pressing at my senses, like a scent I couldn't quite pin down. The shadows in the room seemed darker, the sunlight dimmer. I had to repress a shiver.

"Something's not right," I murmured to Foxglove.

He gave me a sharp glance. "How so?"

I couldn't put words to it, but if I had hackles, they would be stiff and bristling. "This feels like a trap." I gestured around the room, nearly empty aside from our group. "There's a lot of magic in the air. I suppose it could be the wards." I'd just crossed through another set of them, after all. Still, I turned to Lord Elford. "Please be careful, Your Excellency."

He nodded, jaw set. "Believe me, I will. Should it come to violent treachery, I'm confident my people can handle any force currently in the palace, magical or physical. Still, if it's a trap, I admit I'll be glad to have you outside of it and free to respond, just in case."

More court functionaries in showy gold coats had been scurrying in and out through the door that led deeper into the royal wing, and servants in silver livery occasionally bustled past as well. I watched the latter carefully and spotted one of them easing open an entire wall panel a crack and slipping through this previously invisible door. I caught Foxglove's gaze to make sure he'd noticed; he gave a tiny nod. That was our way into the hidden servants' passages, which a bit of probing had revealed ran through half the palace.

Before we could detach from the Serene Envoy's group and begin casually ambling in that direction, Lady Silene entered the room.

She had presence; I'd grant her that. Every gaze turned to her at once, without her speaking a word. I only vaguely registered her extravagantly draped skirts or her tall imposing frame; it was her eyes that caught and held every soul in the room. Deep-set, intense, and full of a hard, piercing light, they swept the well-armed crowd before her and dismissed the lot of us before settling on Elford.

She was not remotely concerned that he'd brought so many soldiers. That wasn't good.

"Back again, I see," she said.

Beside me, Bastian drew in a sharp breath at her rudeness.

Unease prickled my neck. Even the queen shouldn't talk to the Serene Envoy like that, let alone a mere adviser.

Lord Elford didn't waver. "I'm here to speak to the queen of Loreice, not some inconsequential petty noble who isn't even in the Curia."

That should have irked Lady Silene; the functionaries around her winced, but she didn't so much as blink. No annoyance or shame flickered across her face—only a slow smile, spreading like the molten sliver of a rising sun.

"Of course." Her rich, resonant voice feigned mildness. "Naturally you must see the queen. Come with me."

Elford, taken aback, said, "I'm bringing an escort."

Silene waved a lazy hand, without glancing back. "Certainly. However many you wish."

Elford flashed us a worried look. That had been far too easy. "There's not room for all of you," he said, for Silene's ears. "Some of you should wait here."

I couldn't keep my unease bottled up anymore. I stepped as close to Elford as I could make myself. "Your Excellency," I said quietly, "this has got to be a trap. Don't go."

He hesitated, pulling out his fan and running its folded silk through his fingers. But then he shook his head. "If it's a trap, we're already in it. Go. You do your part of the plan, and I'll handle mine."

He gathered his guard about him and followed Lady Silene across the antechamber.

The couple dozen of us that remained drifted with as much seeming randomness as we could muster to gather along the wall that held the hidden door; some of our soldiers sat on the cushioned benches along the walls, and others stood talking to them, casually forming a barrier of bodies in conversational clumps around the door. Imperials were cursed good at this—my family would have been uselessly direct in this situation, good for nothing but a distraction.

"All right," Foxglove whispered, as the Rookery drew close about him at the heart of the group. "If she really does let the Serene Envoy talk to the queen, we're not needed; we stay hidden and do nothing. If she blocks him from seeing the queen, we find Her Majesty, figure out what's going on, and rescue her if necessary."

"And if it's a trap?" I asked. "Do we rescue the Serene Envoy, or the queen?"

"How about ourselves?" Severin suggested dryly.

Foxglove closed his eyes a moment, thinking, then opened them again. "If all the Serene Envoy's guards can't protect him, loaded with artifice devices and alchemy as they are, something has gone badly wrong. We try to save both, but we don't take foolish risks. We still have our mission to complete, and thousands of lives may depend on it. Getting out alive with information is our top priority."

"No one's looking," Kessa said abruptly, her voice clipped and low. "Let's go."

She eased the hidden door open. One after another, we slipped into the servants' passageway.

It wasn't quite like the dusty forgotten spaces between walls that I traveled in Gloamingard, but still, I immediately felt more at home. No one had bothered to adorn the plain, wood-paneled walls beyond a perfunctory coating of light blue paint. The hallway was close, a bit musty, and poorly lit. The Serene Envoy's intelligence officer had told us these corridors existed so that servants could remain unseen as they moved about—and also to facilitate the spying that seemed to be an imperial pastime. The royal family could spy on their guests and on each other, and naturally Raverra had its own agents placed among the servants to watch the queen.

The servants' corridors saw enough use that there was no guarantee we wouldn't run into anyone, and it was far too obvious that we didn't belong here, with all of us still wearing the courtier clothes we'd put on to blend in this morning. We hurried along as quickly as we could without making too much noise, pausing only for Kessa or Foxglove to take a quick peek through a hidden viewing hole or press an ear to the wall every time the corridor took us past a new room.

"Not this one, either," Kessa murmured, after the third time. "She must have let him in past the formal audience chambers to one of the private meeting rooms, which I suppose is a good sign."

Bastian let out a nervous laugh. "We're going to feel silly if he has a good conversation with the queen and sorts all of this out in a straightforward manner."

"I'll take feeling silly over the alternative," Foxglove said grimly.

A soft gasp cut the air.

A young woman in a servant's silver livery stood a dozen yards away, a basket of laundry in her arms. Her eyes stretched wide at the sight of us. *Curse it.*

Before anyone could do anything—before Kessa could step forward to defuse the situation, or the laundry maid could cry out and announce our presence—the servant suddenly swayed on her feet, her eyes rolling upward.

She collapsed in a graceless heap, spilling linens on the floor.

"Blood of the Eldest," Ashe blurted, hand on Answer's hilt. "Did one of you do that?"

Severin shook his head, wide-eyed. Foxglove said curtly, "I did not."

The shadows at the corners of my vision moved. I spun, but there was no one there.

Pox, pox, pox. Something was here, a power live and dangerous in the air. Gooseflesh stood out on my arms beyond the cascading lace of my sleeves.

"You feel that?" Severin gripped the hilt of his bone knife, glancing around the corridor. I nodded, jaw clenched too tight to speak.

Bastian ran to the fallen woman's side, already unclasping his satchel to get at any potions he might need. He laid two fingers on the side of her neck, peered at her eyelids, and made a startled noise. "She's only asleep. How odd."

Kessa let out a strained, nervous laugh. "Odd is an understatement. What— *Oh!*" She gasped and lurched backward into me, recoiling.

Something dark seeped down the walls, with a dull wet gleam in the flickering light of the luminaries. A sickening smell of blood filled the hallway.

I swore, reeling backward; immediately it was gone. But Kessa's gaze stayed fixed on the walls, her hands over her mouth.

"Oh, no. I know whose that is," she whispered, through muffling fingers. A shiver traced my spine.

Foxglove stood stiff and frozen, staring at the walls. "Is anyone else seeing this?"

Ashe's gaze darted around, looking for enemies. "What do you see?" she demanded. "Am I about to get my face ripped off by some invisible monster?"

"Just blood," I said, my nerves still buzzing. "I saw it when I touched Kessa, but it's gone now. It's not real."

It had *looked* real. It had smelled real. I'd never heard of anything like this—and given our current options for a source of unusual new magic, I'd have felt safer if the blood *had* been real and it were a simple matter of a few dozen dead bodies stashed in the ceiling.

A growing dread spread through me like cold fire sweeping along every branch of my nerves. The power I'd sensed earlier hung heavy around us now, humming in my teeth.

I'd felt something like that aching resonance before, only deeper and stronger, coming from the Black Tower.

"The Serene Envoy," I said sharply, fear coppery in the back of my throat. "We have to find him. He's in danger."

Foxglove nodded grimly. "Let's go."

We hurried along the corridor to the next set of spy holes. My mouth had gone dry as parchment. I had to be wrong, prayed to be wrong.

Kessa reeled back from her spy hole the moment she put her eye to it, choking off some sound of shock or anguish. I leaped to take her place beside Foxglove, my world narrowing down to one tiny circle that looked through into a sumptuous sitting room splashed with the scarlet light of sunset.

Bodies in the blue and gold of Raverra sprawled everywhere: across the gilt-and-brocade furniture, on the intricate designs of the Ostan rugs, in the cold ashy embrace of the hearth. Lord Elford lay among them, surrounded by the guards who had failed to save him. None of them bore any obvious marks of violence, but that almost made it worse.

Above this human wreckage loomed Lady Silene, indifferent to the fallen strewn underfoot. Her eyes locked on someone sobbing uncontrollably beyond the peephole's limited view; she advanced toward them with cruel exultation lighting her face.

"Now," she purred, "you must choose the next one to die."

Every muscle in my body tensed. We had to do something, had to stop this—but there was no door into this room from our corridor, and we had no power to match that which made the air around Lady Silene shimmer like a hot roof in summer.

From the floor, Lord Elford surged up in his plum brocade jacket, fashionable rapier in hand, eyes narrowed with grief and rage. An amulet at his throat glowed with a dull and fading spark—whatever magic had taken out his guards, he'd been shielded or revived. He thrust the slender gleaming length of his blade at Lady Silene's back, a clean and deadly strike that should have finished her.

Silene was half out of my narrow circle of view; all I saw was a flash of purple light, and the Serene Envoy stumbled back, gasping. Blood spread rapidly across his waistcoat, over his heart.

Silene drifted to stand over him, unscathed, shaking her head in disgust. "Humans. You never do know when to give up."

I reared back from the viewing hole as if she'd hit me in the face. My stomach contracted with horror. Everything in me rebelled, wanting to deny the clear evidence of my senses.

She was a demon.

"We have to get the queen out of here," I breathed. "We have to get *everyone* out."

She was

We have to

they'd caught up.

SEVEN

We found Queen Mirthaine on a wide terrace attached
to the royal dining room, gazing out over the long spill
of hillside down to the harbor. The sun had gone behind the
palace, casting the east side into shadow, and the young queen
gazing out at the sea looked pale and small against a sky fading
toward sunset.

She turned as we burst out onto the terrace, her blue eyes
widening with a sort of dreamy innocence rather than the alarm
that should have been there. No silver haze blurred them, thank
the Graces. She was bird-boned and wispy, almost buried in the
vast jewel-dripping expanse of her silver gown, and she couldn't
be much more than sixteen.

We had to get her out of here. Focusing on that was much
better than panicking over what it meant that there was a demon
in Lady Silene.

Foxglove swept into a flawless bow. "Your Majesty," he said,
urgency in every word. "You need to leave with us, quickly.
You're in danger."

Queen Mirthaine gave him a sweet smile. "How lovely to
meet you! But oh—you're hurt."

Startled, I glanced at Foxglove, but he didn't seem injured.

He shook his head impatiently. "I'm well, Your Majesty. But we have to—"

"No, no," she murmured, and lifted two pale fingers toward his chest. "Here. You carry it here. And in your hands. It's an old wound. I shouldn't look at it."

My shoulders prickled. She must be drugged, or perhaps the demon had done something to her mind. Foxglove's face went tense and unreadable.

"Your Majesty," Kessa said, her voice soft but infused with an actress's commanding presence. "Your adviser, Lady Silene, is a traitor. She's just killed the Serene Envoy. You need to drop the wards so we can get you and everyone else to safety."

The queen met Kessa's eyes and reached toward her face. "Sometimes," she said, with surpassing gentleness, "you can't save everyone."

Kessa jerked her head back, breath hissing inward.

"He was so happy to come with you," the queen murmured, still gazing at Kessa. "Surely it was good that you brought him." That made no sense—I must have misheard her. But Kessa stared at her as if she'd turned into a ghost.

"We don't have time for this," Ashe snapped, watching the door that Lady Silene or a dozen silver-eyed guards might walk through any moment. "Just grab her and let's go. We can apologize later."

I stepped forward, desperate to make the queen feel the same urgency the rest of us did. "Your Majesty, Lady Silene is a *demon*."

The queen gave the barest nod, her eyes drinking in my face.

Horrible realization sank into me like cold water through warm clothes. "You knew. You already knew she was a demon, and you were on her side all along."

"Yes, of course," Queen Mirthaine said, in her soft, breathy voice. "After all, we came here together."

My lungs froze. Whatever word I'd been about to speak turned to ice there, shattering.

She lifted a slim hand toward me, as she had with Foxglove and Kessa; her eyes suddenly widened. "Oh," she breathed. "Oh, could it be?"

Fear lurched in my chest, and I scrambled backward.

Ashe paced closer, her face hard, hand on Answer's hilt. "Right, you heard her. She's working with the demon. We can take her down or we can get out of here, but let's not waste any more time on a traitor to her own people."

"They're not her people," I croaked, staring into the queen's smooth young face. "She's a demon, too."

The Rookery all stepped back; Kessa uttered startled profanities.

The queen gave me a shy smile that softened those wide innocent eyes—eyes that had belonged to a living human girl, before the demon snuffed out her life and took her body to wear as if it were a new coat. My gut twisted with revulsion.

"I'm so glad you came," she said, with seeming earnestness. Raising her voice, she called into the palace, "Nightmare! This is wonderful. We have visitors!"

Pox. We'd started to drift toward the doors back into the dining room, ready to duck into the servants' passages and escape—but now approaching footsteps sounded from within. We bunched up and backed toward the stone balustrade, with nowhere else to go. The terrace overlooked the walled-in palace grounds, but the hill dropped off steeply enough below it that jumping would probably mean a couple of broken legs at best.

It would still be better than leaving ourselves at the mercy of a pair of demons.

Two of them. The back of my mind wouldn't stop screaming. Nightmare, she'd said. Not Hunger, not Discord. I'd let through more demons into the world than I'd realized.

Lady Silene appeared in the doorway, backlit by the luminaries in the dining room. A wave of power came with her that sucked the light from the sky and made the air humid with malice.

"How lovely," she said, her voice rich and deep and deadly. "We'll have to welcome them properly."

My heart beating with reckless ferocity, I opened my mouth to yell for Kessa to release my jess. It was the only way I could think to try to fight them, no matter how much I feared the consequences.

Behind me, Severin called, "Over the edge! *Now!*"

I spun to find him leaning on the balustrade, teeth gritted, both fists wrapped around the ivy that clung to it. His mage mark shone faintly with silver light.

Kessa was already sliding down the escape pole he'd woven from ivy and magic; I barely glimpsed her hair whipping out of sight. Foxglove came a heartbeat behind her. Bastian shot a glance at Ashe to make sure she wasn't looking and vaulted the balustrade with inhuman grace, trusting his chimera body to take the impact of his landing.

"Oh, don't go!" The queen sounded genuinely disappointed.

Ashe hesitated for a sliver of an instant, locking eyes with me—someone had to be last out, and Severin was still working on the ivy.

"Mage stuff," I barked. We couldn't lose a second over this, and I was mortally sure that if Ashe stayed behind to hold them off, she'd die. She nodded and went over the rail without another word, flinging herself nimbly at the pole.

"I didn't say you could leave," Lady Silene growled.

She lifted her hand. A pulse of power rolled over us, thick and smothering.

I swayed on my feet as my mind blurred and cleared, like the passing of a cloud—but whatever she'd done caught Severin straight on. The light dimmed in his eyes and he began to collapse, just as the servant with the laundry had. A cold needle of fear pierced my heart.

Without a second's hesitation, I tackled him over the balustrade. We fell, limbs tangling. I left my heart above me, a scream stuck in my throat, braced for the breaking force of the ground to hit me.

Something woody caught us, twisting an awkward leafy spiral around our fall, slowing and redirecting the force of it into a rustling tumble until we crashed into a heap on the grassy ground. Kessa stood over us, panting, a tendril of Severin's ivy vine clutched in her hand.

I didn't pause to check whether I was all right; I sprang to my feet, limbs surging with panicked energy that probably would have had me running on a broken leg. "Severin!"

"Asleep," Bastian said, scooping him up to sling across his shoulders. He added a slightly belated performative grunt and stooped more than he probably had to, with a furtive glance toward Ashe.

She didn't seem to notice. Her face was pale and bleak as the surface of the moon. "Let's run."

EIGHT

Bizarre shapes loomed around us as we fled through the dusky garden: topiary stacked cubes and pyramids, deer and leaping dolphins, their shadows stretching long across the grass beneath the sunset-bloodied sky. We followed the paths of crushed shell past the great tree where the queen held court and the strange glittering mirror maze, all the way down to the lowest terrace. We ran beneath manicured trees, through vine-clad tunnels and over fussy decorative bridges, as far as we could go from the palace. Finally its constellation of luminaries twinkled tiny in the distance above us, and we ran up against the rune-bound stone wall at the end of the grounds.

In the cover of a carefully groomed copse of trees, we caught our breath; Severin woke and surged up from the ground, staring around wide-eyed until his gaze fell on me and his shoulders relaxed.

"Two demons," Kessa burst out, slumping against a tree trunk. "*Two* of them! I knew we'd landed in trouble, but this is beyond anything I could have imagined."

"It's worse than that," I said, striving to keep my voice steady and failing. "Two *new* demons. Neither of them was Hunger."

Foxglove went very still. "You're sure?"

"I am." It hurt to admit it, the words molten lead in my throat. "You heard what she called Lady Silene, and the one in the queen didn't act anything like Hunger."

"Thank the seasons. I *hate* him." Kessa wrapped her arms around herself, as if for reassurance that she was still in sole possession of her body.

Severin shook his head, a fierce motion that traveled down into his shoulders. "No, no thanks. I don't care how much you hate him. I'll take the demon we know, no matter what a poxweasel he is, when the alternative is twice as many demons loose in the world. Two we could maybe deal with, but *four*? We're talking about the fall of civilization."

"Stop." Foxglove lifted a hand, holding it before him like a bared blade. "If we start thinking about how bad this is, we won't be able to focus on anything else." He swept his dark gaze across us all. "If the queen isn't Hunger, who is she? Bastian, any ideas?"

"I...I don't know." Bastian groped in his satchel for his notebook with trembling hands. "Most of what lore we have about the Nine Demons is old stories. The clever baker who exposes her possessed neighbor by throwing salt on him, the prince who bests the Demon of Discord in a riddle game, the kind shepherdess who sings a lullaby to the storm to put the Demon of Disaster to sleep. There's no field guide for identifying them."

Ashe tipped her head back to stare up into the tangled tree boughs and muttered, "*Nine I name the darkest powers...*"

Foxglove whipped to face her, startled. "What are you doing?"

"It's a counting rhyme. For skipping rope and such." Ashe shrugged. "It's how I remember all the demons. Everyone in Vaskandar knows it." Kessa nodded agreement.

"My brother would give me till the end to hide," Severin muttered, a muscle jumping in his temple. "It wasn't a game."

I didn't know it; I hadn't grown up playing with other children. A strange, bitter loss joined the unpleasant tangle of feelings in my stomach.

"Vaskandrans." Foxglove shook his head. "Even your children's rhymes are sinister. All right, say it."

Ashe dropped her voice to a low, ominous tone, as if she couldn't help herself.

"Nine I name the darkest powers:

"One for Hunger, who devours.

"Two for Discord, sowing strife.

"Three's Corruption, twisting life.

"Four's Disaster, fire and flood.

"Five for Carnage, steeped in blood.

"Six is Madness, minds laid bare.

"Seven's cold and bleak Despair.

"Eight for Nightmare, dreaming dread;

"Nine is Death, and now you're dead."

As she counted, it sank into my soul that now four of the demons she named had been unleashed into the world by my own hand. Everything humanity had built since the Dark Days—all our burgeoning lives, everything we'd become—hung fragile as soap bubbles before their power, ready to be blown away on the wind. Foxglove was right: it made it hard to focus on anything else.

"We know we've got Hunger, Discord, and Nightmare," I said, forcing myself to think practically. "Given what we've seen in the palace, I'd guess the queen is most likely Corruption, Madness, or Despair."

"Maybe Despair, given that we keep seeing awfully depressing things?" Kessa suggested, frowning.

"I'd lay down money Nightmare's the one doing that," Severin said, with an edge that left me no doubt he was thinking of his dream.

"We'd really need more information to make a guess that's better than wild speculation," Bastian said, with a sort of grimace I'd learned was his *inadequate sourcing* face. "Whichever she is, she's an immortal being with nearly limitless power who we know alarmingly little about."

One thing was certain: with so many demons loose, we'd tipped past a point of no return. Before this, I could believe that we'd catch Hunger and banish him, that my grandmother would somehow master her demon half—that my life could go back to what it had been, only with a jess and some new friends. Now I had to admit things were *never* going back to the way they were. Whatever new world we stood on the brink of, it wouldn't be the one I knew.

Kessa let out a hollow laugh. "And we're trapped inside the palace wards with two of them."

"So we're buggered," Ashe said flatly.

A gloomy silence fell. But Kessa's words set wheels turning in my mind.

I might be able to help with the wards. My power disrupted complex energy structures, like life—or magic. With my jess loosed, a simple touch might be enough to bring down the wards entirely.

But the last time I'd loosed my broken magic, it had stirred in me like some vast creature unfurling ragged wings. At the Shrike Lord's castle, it had almost slipped my control, and the glimpse I'd gotten of what might happen if it did was profoundly disturbing. Between that and my grandmother's attempts to push me to unleash my power, I was reluctant to use it.

These, however, were desperate circumstances.

"We might not be trapped." I drew myself up, resolve hardening. "Kessa, you should release me. I can try to disrupt the wards." There was no way I was leaving without the artifact, but we could have that argument after everyone in the palace was safe.

Bastian shook his head, his expression grim. "Unfortunately, I'm afraid that won't work." He pointed to the rune-marked wall, at a particular swirl in the design. "These are newer wards, and they've got a fail-safe cutoff loop. Most modern imperial fortress wards do. It's to keep the whole ward from going down if an enemy damages the wall in one spot. If you attack the wards in one place, the magic cuts that section off and the power flows around it, keeping the enchantment intact."

"Couldn't I just…touch it multiple places, then?" It seemed unfair that after the hard decision to use my power, it wouldn't even work.

Bastian grimaced. "Not unless your arms are twenty feet long. I'm sorry, Ryx."

"So, I reiterate, we're buggered," Ashe said, with a sort of triumphant gloom.

Frustration churned in my gut. I hated being away from my people and my resources, dealing with unfamiliar magic, in a land dead to my senses. This mission had gone so wrong so quickly, and I felt like a fish on dry land, struggling to adapt to a place where nothing worked the way I expected before it killed me.

One thing at a time.

We'd find a way to deal with the demons and the wards, somehow. But there was something we had to do first.

I took a deep steadying breath. "All right. We may not be able to get out, but we can at least warn the rest of Eruvia."

Foxglove nodded, jaw set. "The courier lamps." He turned to Bastian. "Scout the palace. See what the situation is, and whether they've got a guard on the lamp chamber."

Bastian stared at him urgently, his eyes flicking in warning to Ashe. Foxglove had slipped; it made no sense to send the gentle scholar to scout alone if you didn't know he was a chimera modified for stealth.

Foxglove turned smoothly to Severin. "Can you go find some birds or something to spy on the demons? I want to make sure they're not coming after us. Ashe, go with him; I don't want any of us to be alone right now."

Severin frowned, his annoyance at being given orders clearly warring with the sense of them. But he jerked his head in a nod. "Fine."

"Right! Come on, mage, time to earn your board." Ashe slapped him on the shoulder, which he accepted with resigned disdain, and they moved off.

"Sorry," Foxglove murmured to Bastian once they were gone. "I keep forgetting she doesn't know."

Bastian dropped his satchel, then stripped off his burgundy velvet jacket and the attached false shirt front in one fluid movement. "I don't."

For a brief instant his lean chest showed bare in the warm glow of sunset, his brown eyes reproachful. Then patterns swarmed across his skin, the color shifting until he perfectly matched the mottled green shadows of the trees. My eyes slid off him, even knowing he was there.

"You could tell her, you know," Kessa said softly. "She's not going to hurt you just because she used to be a chimera hunter."

Bastian's voice came from the blur of colors where he'd stood: "The only thing I control about what I am is whether I keep it secret. Perhaps it's foolish, but I prefer to continue exercising that power."

His breeches came off next, which I tried not to think too hard about; then his footsteps receded, and he was gone.

"Fair," Foxglove muttered to the empty air where he'd stood, "but it's cursed inconvenient having to dance around one of the Rookery's most powerful capabilities in front of our own members like this."

Kessa sighed. "Oh, we'll manage. Besides, you were the one who taught me that sometimes, you have to leave other people's secrets alone."

Foxglove went still. "Yes, I did."

Of course. He had secrets of his own. An odd relief flooded me; if the Rookery kept secrets from each other, I felt a bit better about holding back the truth of Whisper's nature, so long as it didn't hurt them to hide it.

A short time of tense silence later, Ashe and Severin returned;

not long after, Bastian reported back that there was a crowd at the entrance to the administrative wing on the second floor, angrily demanding access to the courier lamps, but the guards were turning them away. He'd mapped an alternate route to the lamp chamber using a back stairwell and some empty clerk's offices. Meanwhile, Severin's birds and mice determined that the demons had not left the royal wing.

"That makes a certain horrible sense," Kessa said, her voice subdued. "They've got a lot to keep them busy there right now."

All the Serene Envoy's people, left behind in the demons' clutches. That didn't sit well in my stomach. "Is there some way we can rescue them?"

Foxglove rubbed his hand as if it ached. "No," he said, with quiet regret. "They're behind the royal wing wards, inaccessible, with the demons present and active. We don't know if any of them are even still alive."

The brutal truth of it tore at me like war chimera teeth. "I know, but—"

"We're the best chance these people have." Foxglove waved an arm toward the palace. "We're the *only* chance Eruvia has to learn there are two more demons in the world right now. You said it yourself; that has to come first."

I closed my eyes. "I know. I just don't like it." But hard decisions to abandon lost causes were something I'd had to face before, as Warden. I steeled myself and opened my eyes. "All right. Let's go send that message."

The courier lamp room, it turned out, was deserted. We found the door locked and sealed with a hastily added artifice ward, with no one outside or inside.

"This isn't right." Bastian stared at the sealed door as if it were just as disturbing as everything else we'd seen tonight. "Imperial regulations require at least one clerk to be on duty at all times at an important courier lamp chamber like this."

"I think we're well past the point where anyone is following imperial regulations," Kessa said.

"At least it means that Raverra will notice something is wrong." I ran the end of my braid through my fingers; it had fallen free of its coil when we leaped off the queen's terrace. Somehow, knowing that hundreds of miles away dozens of courier lamp clerks were frowning and reporting to their superiors that they couldn't raise a response from the Summer Palace made it hit home exactly how much trouble we were in. Even now, the doge or the Council of Nine might be hearing those reports, knowing it meant that something dire had happened but without any idea what.

They'd probably assume it was something my grandmother had done. That the palace was destroyed, and the demonic invasion of the Serene Empire had begun.

"We'd better hurry," I muttered beneath my breath.

The Rookery was already on it; Foxglove was drawing intricate runes over the artifice seal with obsidian-dusted paint, while Kessa worked on the locks. Severin and Ashe stood guard down the corridor, watching for any sign of guards or lamp clerks returning. I wished I could seize time in my hands and make it run faster, to get us inside the lamp chamber as quickly as possible and send our message to head off impending disaster.

"You know I've been studying the demons rather intensively," Bastian murmured from my side, rocking onto his toes with the same pent-up nervous energy I felt. "There's one thing I keep coming back to—one thing I don't like at all."

I seized gratefully on the distraction. "What, only one?"

Bastian didn't seem to notice my irony. "Well, lots of things, of course. But when you come down to it, there's only one that matters."

"And what's that?"

He met my gaze, and the hopelessness in his eyes took my breath like a blow to the stomach.

"The math," he said bleakly.

I must have misheard him. "The... *math*?"

"Energy is always an equation." He waved his hand as if he could sketch one in the air. "Magic is all about transforming one type of energy into another. But the demons... they're dividing by zero." When I stared at him blankly, he clarified: "Approaching infinity—it shouldn't be possible. Their power appears to be functionally limitless."

"Because they're drawing it from the Hells." The cold implications trickled down through me.

"I keep thinking of an ancient stone pillar that stands outside an Ostan city legend says was devastated first by the Demon of Disaster, and then by the Demon of Despair. It's lain in ruins since the Dark Days." He closed his eyes, calling up the memory. "*This is a city of bones, of dust, kingdom only of the cursed and the dead. Forget the name this place once bore, and call it Desolation.*"

"Cheerful," I said hoarsely. This distraction wasn't helping after all.

"But here's the strange part." Enthusiasm caught in Bastian's voice, somehow. He could get fired up about the grimmest things if there was a scholarly conundrum involved. "The math says humans lose against even a single demon. All that energy should have turned Eruvia to a wasteland."

"You sound far too excited about this," I observed.

"But it didn't!" Bastian almost hopped on his toes. "Somehow, after a hundred years, humanity *won*. We got rid of them. How is that possible? What advantage did humans gain that let them surmount infinity?"

"The Graces?" I guessed dubiously. "That's what my mother taught me."

"That only begs the question. What advantage did the Graces have, then?" He sighed. "I wish I could interview your grandmother about the Dark Days, but that's not really practical."

"For a variety of reasons," I agreed, turning over everything Bastian had said in my mind. Something about it resonated strangely, as if I were on the cusp of some connection I couldn't quite make.

"Got it!" Kessa crowed, her triumph jarring me out of contemplation.

Foxglove appeared to be finished as well; he put his paint away, and Kessa pushed open the door on the empty, silent chamber.

Hundreds of lamps sat in niches on the walls, most of them off; several flickered intermittently with insistent lights, pulsing signals to clerks who should never have abandoned their posts. It was the only light. The fitful gleam picked out a great inlaid artifice circle on the floor, and hundreds of slim copper wires ran up from the lamp niches to weave into great drooping cables that wound up at last through a rune-ringed circle in the ceiling, finding their way to the sending spire on the roof. The place felt like a shrine, the lamps candles lit for prayers gone unanswered.

Foxglove scanned the lamps, spotted the one he wanted, and went to it at once, pulling up one of the stools scattered around the circular room for use by the clerks. Without another word he laid two fingers on the lamp crystal before him, and it flared to life; swift and sure, his fingers tapped, and the light flickered on and off beneath his touch. Hundreds of miles away, another crystal flickered simultaneously.

"What will the Empire do when they learn the queen and her adviser are demons?" I whispered to Bastian, nervous. This was not the kind of situation where I trusted Raverra to have a measured and thoughtful response.

Severin snorted. "Send in the warlocks, of course. I can't even blame them."

"I should like very much to think they'll try other methods

first." Bastian didn't sound convinced. "There are hundreds of innocent people in this palace."

A few moments passed in silence, save for Foxglove muttering bits of words to himself as he sent and received in the courier-lamp code. Bastian watched him avidly; he must know it as well.

Kessa wrapped her arms around herself. "I wish I knew what the demons wanted," she said softly. "If they were humans, we could negotiate with them, reason with them, flatter them, trick them. But what Lady Silene did to the Serene Envoy and his staff..." She shook her head. "She could have used them. The Zenith Society would have found a hundred uses for them." Bastian turned a bit green at that, and Kessa flashed him an apologetic grimace. "Sorry. But they would have. Nightmare just... cast them aside."

"Well, she's a *demon*," Ashe said, with an air of relentless logic. "Creature of pure evil, remember? Doing terrible things to people is probably how she gets her fun."

A pang pinched my heart at that. Becoming a demon had twisted my grandmother, made her impulses darker, perhaps—but I couldn't bear to think of her as a being of inherent evil.

Bastian, to my surprise, leaned against Kessa like a child seeking comfort. She put a protective arm around him. I couldn't help a twinge of... something, some mix of envy and a sad, aching loss.

"I must confess," he said in a small voice, "I'm more than a little alarmed to find ourselves at their mercy."

Severin gave him an odd look. "Don't put yourself at the mercy of someone who has none."

Bastian blinked. "I wasn't aware I had a choice."

"There's always a choice." Severin shrugged. "You have to be clever. I lived in my father's shadow, and then my brother's, and they might as well have been demons. I know this dance."

Ashe let out a harsh bark of a laugh. "True, in Vaskandar we're used to arrogant all-powerful beings lording it over us. We'll barely notice the difference."

It wasn't like that in Morgrain, I wanted to protest. But if it were, I'd never know.

"Severin's right," I said instead, with quiet assurance. "We may not be able to fight the demons straight up, but there's plenty we can do against them. We can hold out as long as we need to, like mice in the castle walls."

Foxglove pushed back his stool with an air of finality. The courier lamp before him had gone dark.

"That won't be necessary," he said. "The Serene Empire is sending Falcons up from the harbor fortress to take down the wards under cover of darkness."

Kessa let out an enormous sigh of relief, but the tension in my shoulders only knotted tighter. We still had to find the artifact and get everyone to safety—and if the wards went down, the demons were bound to respond. The Empire's move set the clock ticking.

"How long?" I asked.

"Two hours," Foxglove replied. We exchanged a grim look; he understood. "Let's get moving, and may the Grace of Luck go with us."

"Any sign of the weapon?" Foxglove asked Bastian, his voice low enough that I barely heard him over the sighing murmur of the wind. The air had gone damp with coming rain. I planted my feet with care on the sloping roof tiles, regretting the copious skirts swishing around my feet, hems torn and dragging after our rough escape. I was prepared to fling myself flat and grab for one of the innumerable dragon-headed chimneys that loomed around us if I slipped; it was a long way down to the gardens below.

Bastian, whose magic-viewing Verdi's Glasses turned his eyes to great round mirrors in the moonlight, shook his head. "There are so many enchantments on the palace that I'd only see the artifact if it were outside, or in the stables or some such."

"At least that narrows it down. These grounds are huge; if we know the artifact's not in them, that makes our search easier." Foxglove turned to Severin, who crouched a short distance away at the nexus of a chittering and chirping crowd of birds, bats, and mice. He had a whole sack of seeds ready, eyes closed to gleaming slits as he communed with them; they came and went in a constant flutter and scuttle of motion.

"What's the status, Atheling?" Somehow, Foxglove made it sound like a nickname rather than a royal title.

Severin grabbed two fresh handfuls of seed and held them out to his little hirelings; birds vied for position on his wrists. He stayed silent for a few extra seconds—just long enough to remind us all that he wasn't under Foxglove's command, I suspected.

"Moreni and his friends are all gathered together with food, talking," he said at last. "They don't seem agitated—at least, so far as a mouse can tell. No one's jumping up and yelling, anyway."

"They probably don't know about the poor Serene Envoy, then," Bastian murmured. "Moreni's not going to like that."

"Easier for the soldiers coming with the Falcons to arrest them if they're all in one place," Foxglove said. "How about the artifact?"

Severin shook his head. "I've got my spies searching Moreni's rooms and everything adjacent. No one's found it yet. Looks like they were smart enough to guess we might try something like this, and they've stashed it somewhere."

That wasn't good. We were running out of time. Kessa had asked around the cleaning staff to see if anyone had seen the weapon, and I'd used my deep knowledge of the sort of nooks and hidden places a castle could possess to scour as much of the palace as I could, but we'd had no leads whatsoever.

"What are the demons doing now?" Kessa asked Severin, nerves stretching her voice thin.

His face twisted. "They've been busy doing something to the survivors among the Serene Envoy's guard. I don't know what, but I can't imagine it's pleasant."

My stomach seemed to slip down off the roof. So there were survivors. It should have been good news, but it didn't feel that way.

"Hey." Ashe, who crouched on a gable scanning the palace like an owl searching for prey, suddenly straightened. "She's coming outside."

Sure enough, on the royal apartment terrace, Lady Silene swept out into the golden rectangle of light cast by the open dining room doors. She gazed out into the darkness, corset-straight and unnaturally still, something about the lines of her menacing even from here.

"What's she looking at?" Foxglove asked sharply.

I peered into the darkness beyond the garden wall, where the hill sloped down in green rolling folds toward the sea. I cupped my hands around my eyes to shield out the palace lights and the moon, so I could see into the deepest shadows better.

My heart jumped. Sure enough, something moved there: figures, many of them, climbing up the hill.

"It's them," I confirmed. "The Falcons and their escort. She's looking right at them. We have to warn them!"

Bastian tore a page from his notebook and began scribbling furiously. "We can send them a bird—hang on—"

"We can do better than that." Foxglove pulled a luminary crystal from one of the pouches at his hips and shook it vigorously to activate it. Brilliance kindled within it, white and clear; he cupped it in his hands at once to muffle it, then began lifting his top hand in a rapid irregular pulse, showing flashes of light. *The courier-lamp code.*

The figures kept scrambling up the hill. There must be dozens of them, close to a hundred; clearly they'd sent enough to arrest the Zenith Society and facilitate the evacuation as well as to protect the Falcons while they took down the wards. But we'd been counting on surprise. Today had already proved that against a demon, numbers weren't enough.

"Come on," I murmured. "See it. Turn around and get out of here."

The night air seemed to grow suddenly colder. The hair on my arms lifted; in the gardens, birds let out strange cries of fear. All of Severin's animals scattered at once.

Oh, holy Hells. Here it comes.

I couldn't quite *see* the torrent of magic that flowed from the Demon of Nightmares, but I sensed its passage. It swept down the hillside and engulfed the approaching soldiers like a swiftly descending fog.

At once, distant shouts arose, a clamor rising up from the darkness. Even from this far away, the panic in them was clear.

"What's happening?" I strained my eyes desperately, but all I could make out was a chaos of movement. Occasional quick flashes punctuated the night—magic and flintlock sparks.

Foxglove whipped his rune-engraved spyglass monocle out of one of his pouches. He lifted it to his eye and immediately let out a blistering curse.

"What is it?" Kessa demanded.

Foxglove lowered the monocle, his expression bleak.

"They're killing each other," he said.

NINE

I felt like I'd swallowed the dirty slush from the roadside at the ragged end of winter.

"What?!" Kessa snatched the monocle from Foxglove, let out a distressed noise, and lowered it again. "Oh, sweet Hells. It's chaos."

"How bad is it?" Bastian asked, dread in his voice.

She lifted the monocle to her eye again for a quick glimpse, then winced and looked away. "Most of them are attacking each other in a panic. Some of them are trying to get the others to stop, but it's no good. It's an absolute bloodbath."

"She's making them see each other as monsters," I guessed, with numb horror. "Like in the story of the seven unlucky brothers."

Ashe made a hissing noise through her teeth. "Curse it, you're right. But we don't have a magic mirror to show them the truth."

"We have to help them." The wild, urgent energy flooding my veins demanded an outlet. "We couldn't save Lord Elford, but there's got to be some way we can—"

"No," Ashe said curtly. "It's already too late. Listen."

The distant yelling was already shifting from the hot urgent shouting of combat to cries and wails of anguish. The savage flurry of movement had died down.

I knew the pain in those screams, rising up raw and wild over the lower groans of the wounded and the dying. The heart-tearing horror of seeing someone dead by your hand, impossibly and incontrovertibly dead, and straining with everything in you to turn back time and undo this terrible, final mistake that no amount of willpower or penance could fix. It twisted my heart to hear it.

"It's over," Kessa said heavily, looking through the monocle again. All the usual liveliness was stripped from her voice. "About two-thirds of them are down. I can't tell how many of those are dead. The ones still up seem to have snapped out of it and are running around tending to the fallen."

A surge of anger rose coppery red in me, and I glared at the figure on the royal terrace. Lady Silene spread her arms wide, head tilted back, as if bathing in the sound of the distant screams like rain.

She'd stopped when she did on purpose, to leave plenty alive and hurting. If this was what a demon was, Ashe was right: they were monsters, creatures of pure evil, unredeemable. A deep, bleeding ache opened up inside me again, if it had ever really closed: this was what I'd made my grandmother.

But no. They couldn't all be like this. Whisper wasn't this cruel. Was he?

Kessa handed the monocle back to Foxglove, her chin trembling. Ashe put an arm around her.

Foxglove took one last look and shoved the monocle back into its pouch. "Those wards aren't going anywhere tonight," he said curtly. "Everyone in a Falcon's uniform is down."

We sat among the dragon-mouthed chimneys in stunned silence, listening to the clamor on the hillside sort itself out into cries for aid, calls for specific names, the frantic flurry of hastily applied field medicine. Nightmare stood poised on the terrace, eyes closed as if enthralled by a transcendent symphony. She didn't raise her magic against them again; the soldiers slowly picked up their wounded, leaving the dead on the hillside for now, and began the long, awful trek back down to the harbor fortress.

"What do we do now?" Kessa asked, sounding lost.

I dragged my braid between my fingers, thinking furiously. "Our priorities haven't changed. We've got to get the artifact, take the wards down, and get everyone to safety before the demons can do whatever it is they're planning. It just got harder, that's all."

"I would say I'd feel better if I knew what they wanted with a palace full of people," Severin muttered, "except that I'm fairly certain I'd actually feel worse."

Foxglove rose to his feet, the motion stiff and weary as if his whole body hurt. "Come on. We've seen enough here, and we have work to do."

The commotion in the entry hall was so loud we heard it from halfway across the palace, the moment we descended from the roof. We headed straight to the soaring white hall with its delicate stonework and softly glowing columns and found it packed with hundreds of people. They milled and shouted, some banging on the closed doors or fruitlessly trying to break the warded windows. One group in plumed hats had faced off with another group in pastel finery, pointing fingers and shouting blame at each other. Silver-eyed guards ringed the room, impassive.

Right. They didn't know. The worst this frustrated crowd had to worry about was the possibility of a coup or a supposed attack from Morgrain. Which, in all fairness, would be more than enough by any normal standard.

"Should we warn them?" Kessa asked worriedly, from our vantage point in the clearer area by the imperial wing entrance, away from the press at the doors. "Make some kind of announcement?"

"No," I said immediately.

Everyone stared at me; Foxglove raised his brows. "Elaborate, please."

"Right now, they're a crowd." I'd had to give unpleasant news to the population of Gloamingard before, and I spoke with the certainty of experience. "They'll react to bad news like a crowd, which would make things worse. We want them thinking and reacting as individuals." At home, I'd tell Odan and Gaven and have them spread the word quietly down the chain of command, one calm conversation at a time. "We need to identify competent leaders in the palace—not necessarily political leaders, but senior palace staff; people who get things done."

Ashe lifted her head. "Good thing you didn't want to make an announcement, because it looks like someone beat us to it."

An old man in a gold coat had entered the hall from the direction of the royal wing: Bramant, the functionary who'd met the Serene Envoy at the door. A page boy set down a chair and steadied it for him, and Bramant stepped up onto it with a determined expression, clutching an artifice wire–wrapped amplification loop. A wave ran through the crowd as people started to notice him; he didn't wait for their attention before raising the golden loop to his lips.

"Thank you for your patience in this difficult time." His amplified voice boomed out, echoing from the walls and silencing the crowd. "Her Majesty recognizes that you are all understandably concerned about the wards being raised. She graciously invites you to the grand throne hall in one hour for an announcement that should help set your minds at ease."

"I doubt it," Severin sang under his breath.

Voices in the crowd lifted, shouting questions at him; Councilor Altaine stood front and center with her vermilion plume, fists on her hips. Bramant lifted his hands.

"I'm sure your questions and concerns will be addressed in one hour. If not, I will personally do my best to answer them afterward." The crowd surged toward him, and the page boy holding his chair flinched, but Bramant stood unwavering. "In the meantime—good people!—in the meantime, we have plenty of rooms available for those who were only visiting the palace for the day, in case you can't go home tonight. The housekeeping staff is waiting for you in the Sapphire Room to assign you lodging. Otherwise, I suggest you prepare for the announcement, as it will be a formal court occasion."

My respect for Bramant rose. That was clever, to give the crowd reasons to disperse and actions they could immediately pursue. Some people were already leaving. By his honest, harried look, he either had no idea who he was truly serving, or he was an exceptionally good actor.

"I wonder what he'd say if I asked him about the Serene Envoy," I murmured to the Rookery.

Foxglove eyed Bramant and the crowd that pressed in around him, shouting questions as he attempted to wave them off. "I'd say you should go ask, but we're not getting near him. Come on; we've got to get ready for this announcement."

Ashe gave him a skeptical look. "Really? You know they're just going to lie."

"But which lies they use should tell us something about what they're planning." Foxglove tipped his head toward me. "Besides, it'll be our best chance to identify and talk to key leaders, as Ryx said, and spread our warning. We need to tell everyone to keep their heads down, but be ready to move as soon as we can figure out a way to unlock the wards."

"I'll put on my fanciest dress," Kessa said, her voice dripping irony. "I do hope they'll serve wine."

"I wouldn't count on it," I said.

"You shouldn't be here."

I swallowed a yelp, but couldn't stifle the startled jump that dropped half my armload of skirts on the floor. I left them where they lay and turned, heart racing, to face Whisper.

Finally. He sat with his tail curled neatly around his paws on the rich burgundy-and-gold brocade bedspread in my guest room, surrounded by the borrowed clothes I'd laid out to replace my torn gown for the throne hall announcement. Half-lifted hackles roughened the smooth line of his shoulders. That was far from reassuring; not much rattled Whisper.

"Took you long enough to show up," I said gruffly, around a sudden knot in my throat. "I missed you."

"I was busy." He prowled a restless figure eight on the bed, his claws digging at the covers. "I had no idea there were demons here, or I wouldn't have delayed. That was a mistake; I won't make it again."

"As for being here, believe me, we'd love to fix that. None of us want to be stuck inside locked wards with a pair of demons." He gave me an inscrutable look, and I corrected myself quietly: "Three demons."

He looked away. "Suffice to say there are two who are extremely dangerous to you."

This was my opportunity to try to get answers from him— information that might save the lives of everyone in the palace. But I had to struggle to think of anything but how relieved I was that he'd returned, which made no cursed sense at all.

"Do you . . ." I swallowed. "Nightmare and the other demon. Do you *know* them?"

"Of course I know them." His muzzle wrinkled. "It's unfortunate that they're together. Nightmare and Madness are easier to deal with separately."

So the one possessing the queen was Madness. *Lovely.* Not that there had been any good options.

"They're your . . . sisters?" It was an impossible truth. No matter how I tried, I couldn't reconcile the soft-furred chimera who let me scratch behind his ears with the Nine Demons my mother cursed by or the horror-rich legends of the Dark Days.

"I suppose you could look at it that way, if you chose. Human families are different." His tail flicked human nonsense aside. "We are kin, certainly."

I sank down on the bed beside him, a strange cold ache settling into my bones. Discord, Hunger, Madness, and Nightmare were accounted for now. That left few options for Whisper—the only demon in this world I hadn't loosed myself.

"Who let you through the gate?" I asked. "It must have been a long time ago."

His yellow eyes narrowed. "Do you truly think me so easily vanquished?"

I blinked in confusion. "What?"

"Four of us the humans banished by force," he said. "Four went back through the rift through trickery or persuasion. But your legends like to leave out that there is one demon you humans never conquered."

The cold within me intensified, until it seemed as if surely my breath should frost the air.

"Death," I whispered.

"Naturally." Whisper licked a paw. "No one let me through. I've been here since the Dark Days."

TEN

An odd jumble of feelings cascaded through me, like a box of attic trinkets tipped over to disgorge a flood of old forgotten things.

"That must have been lonely," I said at last.

Whisper turned his head to stare out the window. "Of course not."

When I stroked his sleek head, however, he didn't object.

"Why don't you want me to be here?" I asked, prodding relentlessly for an undefended spot in his maddening reticence. "Not that I'm happy about it myself, but you won't convince me it's concern for my safety. You've let me go into far more dangerous situations without protest."

For a long moment, he was silent. At last he sighed. "It's not your life that you should fear losing."

There were a lot of things worse to lose than my life: my friends, my family, my home. Given the demons in question, however, he might mean something else. "Because it's Madness and Nightmare? Do they attack the mind rather than the body, then?"

"They attack whatever they please." He examined a paw, flexing his claws. "They cannot give you an illness of the mind, if that's your concern; those are natural. Their magic can *affect* your mind, yes—much like alchemical potions can—which is why humans gave them those names."

"Affecting the mind—like those guards with the silver eyes?" I guessed, my stomach performing a queasy flip. "Or Bastian thinking he heard singing, or Nightmare putting people to sleep, or the soldiers seeing each other as enemies."

"Yes, yes. Such things are the least of your worries."

"I don't know, they seem pretty worrisome." My voice came out too high. I ground the heels of my hands into my eyes, taking a moment to steady myself. I'd seen too many people die today, and there was a raw aching mess down inside me that tasted of tears, but I couldn't let it out now. I had to focus.

I sorted through the many questions crowding my brain and picked one I thought Whisper might actually answer. "Do they know you're here? Madness and Nightmare?"

"Not yet." His ears swiveled back with distaste. "I'll eventually have to pay my respects. You should leave this place well before then."

"I can't. There are wards." I narrowed my eyes. "For that matter, how did you get in?"

His tail swished dismissively. "Humans set such store by wards and walls."

That wasn't an answer. I pressed ahead anyway. "Could other people get out by whatever means you got in?"

"No. Not even other demons." He met my eyes. "I gather Madness controls the wards. I could likely persuade her to let you out, as a favor. You alone—no others."

"Thank you for the offer, but I won't leave everyone else behind while I save myself." The idea was repugnant.

He sat on his haunches and stared at me a long time, his tail lashing across the bedspread. It was unnerving. Had I offended him somehow?

"Why are you looking at me like that?" I asked at last.

"I'm thinking," he said, "about whether it would cause more problems than it solves to forcibly remove you from this place."

The hairs on the back of my neck rose. I didn't want to find out how the Demon of Death would *forcibly remove* someone. "How about if we try to convince each other with words instead?"

"Ryx." His voice went soft as an old sorrow. "I can't tell you my reasons. Trust that I'm telling the truth when I say that if you stay, it will destroy you."

"I believe you." I swallowed a knot building in my throat. "That's a risk I'm willing to take. I can't run away from this. If we don't destroy this artifact, I'll probably die anyway, along with the rest of Morgrain—and regardless, I won't leave my friends to the mercy of the demons I released. I'm sorry."

"If you stay," he said, his voice unexpectedly intense, "if you remain here even one moment more, you need to keep away from Madness and Nightmare. Do everything in your power to avoid attracting their notice, *at all costs*. Do you understand me?"

"I—" I couldn't agree to that. Not when my touch was the only thing we'd found that had proven remotely effective against demons. But Whisper so rarely asked me anything, and never without reason. I remembered the strange look Madness had given me—*Oh, could it be?*—and wondered uneasily what, exactly, Whisper was worried would happen if I captured the demons' attention.

His burning gaze didn't waver. Knowing it was the Demon of Death himself glaring at me made it even more impossible to say no.

"Yes. I understand." That much wasn't a lie.

Whisper gave me a long, skeptical look. He knew me too well, curse it.

"I don't think you do." He rose, placing his paws with delicate care, and turned half away from me in disgust. "You were always a terrible listener. But if you ignore me this time, Ryx, there will be consequences."

His words were enough to set a foreboding upon me by themselves. But the sadness in them made it unbearably worse.

"Look, you know I can't make any promises. But I'm taking your warning seriously." I attempted a smile, but it came out wrong. "I'll try to be good this time."

"You always do." His fur seemed to blur into the gathering shadows as he slinked away, and his weary voice resonated in my mind. "And it's never enough."

The king who'd designed much of the Summer Palace was, Kessa had informed me, obsessed with illusions. The topiary in the gardens, the glowing columns of the entry hall, the mirror maze, the Jewel Rooms, even the twinkling luminaries in the facade—he loved to make things look like something other than what they were. So I expected the throne hall to be the greatest illusion of all, but it still surprised me.

The arching ceiling stretched impossibly high and had been painted a deep, velvety midnight blue and scattered with tiny, twinkling luminaries that exactly mapped the constellations. To make up for the ornamental restraint necessary to create this surprisingly convincing illusion of a night sky, the bottom story of the walls swarmed with a riot of marble carvings and gold accents, a whole pageant of leaping dolphins and dancing Graces and inexplicably scantily clad heroes, all converging toward a raised dais lit up with the glory of the dawn. An extravagant backlit stained glass window in the shape of the sun hung over the golden throne; flanking it, above rows of less ostentatious seats for the leaders of the Curia, a later artist had added more glowing windows depicting the phases of the moon, in a pointed artistic revision to show the monarchy sharing power in the firmament of the Loreician political sky.

It was a space that should have lifted the spirits, whether

in wonder or in laughter at the sheer excess of it all. But even though Madness and Nightmare hadn't arrived yet, a thick pall of dread already lay over the vast throne room and the glittering crowd within it. Oppressive demonic power hung like a sick miasma in the air, crushing down on all the extravagantly gowned and jacketed people packing the hall. Tense murmuring rose and fell, with occasional laughter spiking above it, fever bright.

Everyone was afraid. They didn't know what had happened, but there was no possible *good* reason for the wards to be up. They could feel their lives teetering over an unknown abyss, about to plunge into a disaster that no one had yet named. Questions ran like hissing fires through the crowd: Who was really behind the decision to raise the wards? Why wouldn't they let anyone use the courier lamps? What was the Curia going to do about this? And where was the Serene Envoy?

Where, indeed. I closed my eyes, trying not to imagine his ashes in the queen's fireplace, or his body stuffed with dozens of others in some deep wine cellar to molder.

"Lovely people, Loreicians," Severin muttered. "A compulsion to make everything artificial so ambitious it literally reaches to the sky, a ruler so remote no one's noticed she's a demon, and a court so welcoming no one will talk to us."

"You have a point." I frowned at the crowd around us; whether nobles in bejeweled coiffures, commoners in fancy hats, or palace staff in silver livery, everyone seemed to melt away as Severin and I approached. I'd been instinctively relieved to find a space clearing for us; the crowd had me on edge, and every muscle in my body tensed if anyone came close to within arm's reach—but it made it impossible to talk to anyone.

We'd broken up into pairs to better spread our warning and gather information, and none of the others seemed to have this problem. I spied Foxglove and Bastian talking to Councilor Altaine—who I'd learned was one of the original leaders of the

Festival Uprising—and Kessa and Ashe deep in conversation with a man in a splendid uniform coat and matching filigreed artifice amplification cuffs on his ears. He must be the palace majordomo; both of them were among the Rookery's picks for key leaders to coordinate with. But the moment anyone met my eyes or Severin's they immediately averted their own and drifted off, as if suddenly aware of business elsewhere.

"Ah," I said.

Severin raised his brows. "Ah?"

"I know why they're avoiding us. For the same reason they would at home." I gestured toward my face, frustrated. "We both have the mage mark."

He frowned. "This is a high court, not a remote farm village. Surely they're used to seeing mages with the mark."

"But you're clearly Vaskandran." I gestured to his vestcoat with its striking asymmetric trail of gold brambles embroidered across the front, from shoulder to hem. It made a stark contrast to my borrowed Loreician gown, with its nipped-in waist and extravagant puff of blue and silver skirts. "I might pass for Raverran, but not you—and you don't have a jess."

"Ah." The confusion on his face cleared and settled into wry resignation. "I'm the villain of their stories, come to drink their blood and curse their children. Fair enough."

"They're afraid of the wrong story villain." I glanced at the empty throne.

"This is annoying," Severin muttered. "I'd hoped we could ask our own questions to hunt down the artifact, since we apparently can't trust the Rookery to remember why we're here."

"They remember," I objected. "They've just been busy dealing with the sudden unexpected demon crisis."

"Distracted by their personal grievances, you mean." Severin shook his head. "Suffice to say that if I made a habit of relying on others, I wouldn't be alive. But we'll find it, if I have to conscript every animal in this palace to help us look."

My mouth quirked. "Maybe not *every* animal. It might draw too much attention if the horses from the royal stables go trotting through the halls."

"You forget I'm an atheling; I hate being inconspicuous." He grimaced. "That's another frustrating thing—in the past I've always had at least *some* cards in my hand when visiting a hostile foreign court. Here, I don't even know how I'd bluff convincingly."

"Much as I normally love a diplomatic solution, it's generally considered a bad idea to make deals with demons." I tried a teasing smile. "Besides, wouldn't acting the arrogant visiting atheling be dangerous? I thought you claimed you weren't the type to put yourself at risk for strangers."

"I'm not," he said, without hesitation. "Despite what you seem to enjoy imagining about me, I assure you, I'm a murderer and a traitor. All I know how to do is survive."

"If that's all you know, you're not very good at it." The smile faded from my face. "You saved us tonight, with those vines and your quick thinking. You held on until the end to make sure everyone got out, even though you could have been killed. That wasn't the act of someone who only cares about himself."

For a long moment, he was silent, a struggle playing out across his face.

"I was waiting for you," he said at last, as if this truth gave him no solace—as if I were a curse he couldn't shake. "Only you."

A little thrill went through the core of me; I did my best to keep it from showing on my face. "Severin..."

The faint scars on his throat jumped as he swallowed. "I mean, you're the only ally I have, so you're valuable," he said quickly, pulling on a thin veneer of self-scorn like a hastily donned bathing robe. "Everyone else wants something from me, even the Rookery. You're just...the only one foolish enough to..."

"Shh." I reached out, my hand trembling at the terrifying newness of initiating touch, and laid two fingers on his lips. *Soft.*

I wouldn't have thought anything about him could be soft. His eyes went wide.

"Take it from an expert," I murmured wryly, "you don't actually *have* to ruin everything for yourself."

"Ryxander," he whispered, my name moving against my fingers, wreathed in his breath. And then, his lips twisting into a lopsided smile: "I'll ruin whatever I like."

A trumpet blared. I jumped at the sound, snatching my hand back from Severin's mouth. We turned with everyone else to face the raised dais at the far end of the hall as the light shining through the stained glass windows went from soft to intensely brilliant, flooding us with radiance. All around us, the great crowd dipped in deep bows and profound curtsies as Queen Mirthaine of Loreice entered the room.

Or rather, the demon wearing her body did.

She smiled shyly at the assembled throng, resplendent and pale as a ghost in her lace-dripping silver gown; Nightmare walked at her side, and a trail of guards and officials followed behind. In the wake of the blazing presence of the demons, they seemed faded and lost, like shadows in shifting light.

After them came Moreni and the Zenith Society, strutting boldly onto the dais to stand in the places that should have belonged to the Curia, challenge and triumph in their eyes. That set off a whisper of outrage among the commoners, running through the crowd like a gust of wind, but it quickly fell silent. Everyone's attention stayed riveted on the queen in dreadful anticipation.

"I'm sure this will go well," Severin breathed.

Madness fluffed her skirts and settled onto her throne; Nightmare stood by her side, surveying the crowd with eyes narrowed in apparent pleasure. I barely noticed the others, even the Zenith Society; I couldn't tear my gaze away from the two demons standing there bold as sunshine, power hanging palpably around them. The rest of the room seemed to grow darker, as if they burned from within with an unholy light.

"Welcome." Nightmare spread her arms wide, and her deep, rich voice filled the hall. "You've come in search of answers, and we are here to give you all the answers you need." The crowd stirred and settled at that; I spied hope on some faces, wary skepticism on others. "You stand in a time of crisis, when darkness gathers at your borders, when fear beats in your hearts." She took too much relish in the words, her burning gaze raking the crowd as if drinking in the strain and alarm in their faces.

"And whose fault is that, I wonder," Severn muttered.

"Even a demon is making Morgrain out to be the villain," I said through my teeth. "I'm growing weary of it."

"In the face of such a threat, you need unity and power," Nightmare continued. Her voice resonated in the walls, in my bones. "We have raised the wards to give you the chance to embrace both." She swept an arm dramatically at Madness. "The queen offers you her protection. I call upon you now to come forward and receive her blessing and her favor. Who will be first?"

Her piercing eyes swept the crowd. Madness sat with her hands folded in her lap, leaning ever so slightly forward, as if she were eager to meet her subjects.

An uneasy stir ran through the hall, a murmuring and a drawing back. I picked out Councilor Altaine's sharp voice from the general commotion: "That's not an answer!"

For a long, agonizing moment, no one stepped up.

"No one's that foolish," I breathed, but not with relief. I doubted very much the demons would simply shrug and move on if no one volunteered.

"Oh, just you wait," Severin said cynically.

At last, a middle-aged man with jeweled rings and a powder-blue silk jacket stepped forward to the foot of the dais, bowing subserviently to the queen. "You know my loyalty, Your Majesty, but I will gladly swear it again here to provide an example for my colleagues in the Curia."

Moreni stepped forward to extend a hand toward the man in warm greeting. "Ah, Lord Calvert. Please, approach Her Majesty the Queen and claim the favor you deserve."

A dizzying smile broke across Madness's face as the bejeweled lord mounted the dais.

"You have relinquished fear," she told him, her voice unnervingly gentle. "I hope you haven't lost too much of yourself with it."

Well, that's not reassuring. But he knelt before her anyway, eagerness shining in his face.

They seemed to exchange greetings, their voices pitched conversationally now and inaudible over the agitated murmurs running through the throne room. The crowd turned from riveted attention to quiet side conversations, but the tension wasn't gone; it had simply diffused into the general miasma in the air.

"Like a herd of deer after the wolves have made their kill," Severin muttered.

He'd put his finger on it. "I don't like this. She's just talking to him, but I can't shake the feeling that something horrible is about to happen."

I clearly wasn't the only one who felt that way. The unease in the crowd was palpable. People bunched up in clusters by affiliation, little knots of plumed hats or coiffed heads bent together to whisper, clumps of staff in uniform hanging together for reassurance. The commoners were less than pleased to receive a call for pledges of fealty in place of an explanation, and a hard note of anger sharpened the general susurrus of conversation.

Nonetheless, a short line had begun to form at the base of the dais as more people—mostly nobles—volunteered to receive the queen's favor. Moreni made conversation with the waiting courtiers, flashing a charming smile.

"Might as well line up to drink poison."

It was Ashe, arriving at our sides along with the rest of the Rookery. They all looked fabulous in their court clothing; Kessa took my breath away in a rakishly cut embroidered scarlet jacket to match her plumed hat, over a coordinated red-and-gold gown with a daring Loreician neckline. If you could even call them necklines, given how far below the neck they scooped.

I flashed them all an approximation of a smile. "I'm glad you're here. Looks like things are starting to happen."

Foxglove gave a slow nod, eyes fixed on the dais. "That's why I want us together and ready."

Severin's breath hissed between his teeth. "Look. What's she doing to him?"

Madness bent over the kneeling lord before her, some silvery object in her hand—a small bottle, perhaps. She straightened as if she'd just applied something to his brow, a dreamy smile on her face.

"There." Her quiet voice carried through a sudden lull in the conversation, as half the room stopped to stare. "Now I can see you better."

"Let it be known that Her Majesty has anointed Lord Calvert with her favor," called out an official standing by, in pompous tones.

Bastian peered at the stage, squinting. "It looked as if she dripped beads of quicksilver above his eyes."

A cold finger of foreboding dragged a line between my shoulder blades. "Is that what she did to the guards?"

"Part of it, perhaps." Bastian gave us a troubled look. "Quicksilver wouldn't dissolve in tears; that haze we're seeing in their eyes has to be a magical side effect. In alchemy, quicksilver is a powerful conduit for affecting the mind; it's good for *any* kind of mind magic. Memory potions, truth elixirs, you name it. So she could be doing whatever she did to the guards, or she could be doing something completely—"

"Oh dear," said the queen, with a soft sadness that somehow pierced the unsettled noise of the crowd.

Lord Calvert stiffened, his jeweled fingers forming claws. He let out a strangled whimper, swaying where he knelt. Nightmare closed her eyes and drew in a deep breath, like someone inhaling the steam from a particularly delicious cup of tea.

Moreni snapped his fingers. Just as Calvert seemed about to collapse, a pair of guards with shining silvery eyes stepped forward and seized him by the elbows. They hauled him to his feet and dragged him, moaning and struggling weakly, through a door beside the dais.

The room went still. The courtiers standing in line recoiled a step; a frightened murmur ran around the crowd like wind through the grass.

Nightmare lifted two fingers in a lazy gesture, eyes half-lidded. "Next," she called.

"Oh, Hells, no," I whispered, horrified.

"I would really, really like to stab my way out of this place now," Ashe announced, clutching Answer's hilt.

Moreni beckoned encouragingly to the woman at the front of the line, a young noble with her hair swept up in an elaborate tower of flowers and jewels. She hesitated, glanced between the queen and Moreni, and began slowly mounting the dais.

"Someone's got to stop her." I was half ready to be that someone myself.

"Anyone who volunteered is *choosing* this," Severin said. "You can't save them."

"Do you think they're going to stop when they get to the end of the line?" I demanded. Silver-eyed guards had moved to block every door leading from the hall, cutting off all possible escape.

"No," Foxglove said quietly, "I don't think they will."

Up on the dais, the lady knelt before the queen, face tipped up to receive whatever was in that silver bottle.

I felt a rash urge to dash up there and knock it from her hand. To cry out, *No, stop!* It was inconceivable that we were all going to stand around and let this happen again and again. Not least because I was beginning to suspect this was why they'd raised the wards—to trap hundreds of people here and force their silvery dominion on all of us.

But Whisper's warning resonated in my bones: *Avoid attracting their notice, at all costs.*

A single silver bead dripped onto the lady's forehead. She gasped, a terrified sound, and began clawing at her own face. Her nails dug red furrows into her skin, and her voice rose in a breathless scream that set every hair on the back of my neck to standing.

Madness patted the lady soothingly on the head. "It's all right. It'll be over soon."

The same pair of guards moved in at Moreni's signal to haul her off after Lord Calvert. What little line had remained for the queen's favor rapidly dispersed.

"Next," Nightmare called, in a voice rich and dark as drinking chocolate.

"We need to distract the demons," I said urgently. "Divert their attention to something else and get everyone out of here."

"I could start a fire?" Ashe suggested helpfully.

"I'm not sure they care about fire," Foxglove said.

The room *shifted*, a change in pressure or light or available air that everyone felt at once. The whole crowd turned to face the dais; my heart stumbled as the queen and Nightmare stood side by side, gazing out at all of us with the intent curiosity of predators whose hunger is not yet sated.

"I said, *next*." Nightmare's voice carried through the whole throne hall.

A disturbance ran through the crowd, a reflexive shiver as if it were a cat stroked the wrong way. Some tried to slip out the exits, but silver-eyed guards stopped them with crossed pikes.

"Hells," I whispered. "We're out of time."

Nightmare spoke again; the room seemed to darken with every word. "This will not do. Very well; if none of you will stand forth to receive the queen's blessing, she will choose someone herself."

On the dais, Moreni suddenly stepped forward and whispered in Nightmare's ear; she nodded, listening.

"That bastard," Ashe muttered.

"Guards!" A smile like a knife cut spread across Nightmare's face. "Bring them to me."

She extended one lace-dripping arm to point directly at us.

ELEVEN

The crowd flowed away from us like water from oil, leaving a clear line of sight to the dais. Lady Silene stared directly at us, dark eyes glittering with malice, Moreni smug at her side. The queen tipped her head inquisitively, pale tendrils of hair dangling from her diamond-crowned coiffure, her gaze falling on us with a disquieting intensity.

So much for not attracting their attention.

"Should we run?" Bastian whispered, his eyes wide.

"We wouldn't make it five steps." Foxglove's hands moved over his belt, checking pouches with deft little touches. "You saw what they did to those soldiers. We've got to talk our way out." He didn't sound happy about it.

"I'm not sure I can talk our way out of this," Kessa said, her voice strained.

"Think of something fast," Foxglove suggested.

Half a dozen palace guards marched up to us through the avenue the crowd had cleared for them, hands ready by their rapiers and pistols. I stepped in closer to the others instinctively, mind racing, trying to think of some way to turn this situation around when it was the demons who held all the power. The secret to negotiating when you were this outmatched was to find some lever to use, of need or avarice or vulnerability, but we had nothing on the demons at all.

The officer at the front of the guards faced us, her eyes sheened with silver. "You are the one known as Foxglove?"

Foxglove nodded warily. "I am."

"Come with us," the guard said. "Her Majesty the Queen commands that you and your companions present yourselves to receive her favor."

My stomach flipped over. That little silver bottle frightened me far more than all the guards' pikes and pistols. By the gray tinge that spread across Foxglove's face, he felt the same.

"Not a chance in the Nine Hells," Ashe growled, her hand falling to Answer's hilt.

"Stand down, Ashe," Foxglove barked. "We can't fight them."

"Oh, I'm fairly certain we can."

"Rule Five." Foxglove thrust out a hand between her and the soldiers, without looking back at her. "We'll talk to the queen. It'll be fine."

It wasn't going to be fine. We all knew it, but we went with the guards anyway, through the silent gauntlet of the staring crowd. The dais approached too quickly; I was almost out of time to think of something clever.

Queen Mirthaine drew the eye like a bright hole in reality, a drowning, shining void that pulled everything into her slight silver-wreathed form. Lady Silene's decadent butter-colored gown with its wide flouncing panniers and pinched waist did no more to reshape her than the borrowed flesh she wore; she should have been a flame, a cloud, a sickening light that scalded the senses. Her gaze struck me like an arrow, bottomless and brooding. I forced myself to meet her eyes, trying not to think about how they had seen the rise and fall of centuries and presided over the collapse of human civilization. I couldn't tell whether either of them recognized us from earlier.

Hells take it, I'd already lost my chance to avoid their notice. I could think of only one reason why the demons might find me dangerously interesting; time to see if I could turn it to my advantage.

I drew myself up as we neared the bottom of the dais, trying to radiate the kind of confidence and power my atheling kin possessed. Before the guards could present us to the queen, before Moreni could open his gloating mouth, before Nightmare could issue an order to make us kneel before her, I called out in a bold, ringing voice:

"I bring greetings to Your Majesty from my grandmother, the Lady of Owls."

The crowd, already giving us the distance accorded to the condemned, recoiled further. A few scattered gasps rose up, as if I were the most frightening thing in the room. *These people need some perspective.*

Kessa flashed me a startled glance, then fell into position behind me as naturally as if she'd practiced it, supporting my play. Moreni scowled at this unexpected twist. But it was the demons' reactions that mattered, and I kept my eyes on them, not daring to breathe.

The queen's blue eyes widened in her pale face, as if she could drink me in with her gaze. "At last," she breathed.

Oh, that couldn't possibly be good.

Lady Silene's eyes narrowed. "I see." She rolled the words thoughtfully on her tongue. "The ... Lady of Owls sent you."

Moreni glared at Foxglove as if this were his doing, offering the demons a quick bow. "Your Majesty," he murmured, "I know these people. This is some deception."

Severin stepped up beside me. He'd pulled on his arrogant atheling persona like a familiar cloak worn with long use; I wasn't entirely certain how I felt about that.

"Ah, a little flea, tickling the ear of your betters," he drawled to Moreni. "Best stop annoying them, or you'll get scratched."

I had to actually say something of substance now, something that would prove Moreni wrong and pull the demons' attention away from ideas of forcing quicksilver on us all.

"Indeed," I replied to Nightmare, ignoring Moreni. "Since there seemed to be some commotion involving the wards shortly after my arrival, I'm taking this opportunity to present myself to Your Majesty. My most exalted grandmother has concerns about what you're doing here on her southern border." It was probably true. I flicked my eyes significantly toward Moreni, hoping the demons would understand the reference to the artifact. "I'm here on her behalf to ensure that no threat to Morgrain will arise from your current...activities."

It seemed the marble should melt beneath my feet from the sheer force of the demons' attention as they considered me. Sweat prickled at my temples.

Moreni bowed to the demons, a muscle flexing in his jaw. "Shall we carry on with the silvering, Your Majesty?"

The queen laid a slender hand on Silene's arm. "I want to talk to them," she breathed, a yearning in her voice that sent chills crawling down my back.

A slow, delicious smile spread across Nightmare's face. "Well, well. I see no reason we can't indulge ourselves. By all means, let's discuss these matters further—in private."

Ice crystallized in my belly; her tone left me no doubt that this wasn't going to be a simple friendly conversation.

"The others don't need to come," I tried desperately. "I wish to speak of matters best kept between us."

Amusement danced in Nightmare's wicked eyes. "Oh, little one, it's too late for that." She turned to the guards, as Moreni's expression transformed from frustration to triumph. "Escort our *honored guests* to the Velvet Room."

True to its name, the Velvet Room was swathed in the stuff. Smothering green and gold drapes cloaked the windows and even the walls, save where paintings hung in massive gold frames. Perhaps the intent had been to muffle sound and give a sense of privacy to those granted a personal audience, but it would also serve to keep the rest of the palace from hearing if we screamed. *How thoughtful.*

The one small mercy was that the queen had dismissed Moreni and his crew at the door, much to his frustration. More silver-eyed guards flanked us instead; they laid no hands on us, but stood ready and alert as we came before the queen and her supposed adviser, both of whom waited in front of a modest, velvet-cushioned throne. Approaching the demons was like reaching toward an open oven, the sense of raw power increasing until I was surprised the air didn't blur and smoke around them.

The queen's blue eyes latched on to mine, a question in them that I didn't understand. A shiver crawled up my back. Lady Silene's gaze traveled over each of us with unabashed anticipation, her tongue running over her teeth.

"Such a delightful company," she said as we bowed and curtsied. "So much potential. I must thank Moreni for pointing you out."

I didn't like the look in her eye. Best to establish civil terms for this conversation right away. "Your Majesty. Lady Silene." I paused. "Or would you prefer I use your real names, now that no one can overhear us?"

Nightmare shrugged with easy disdain. "Call us what you will. We lived without names for an eternity before humans gave them to us."

My skin felt like it was trying to crawl off and flee. This was a being who had existed for thousands of years, who had no physical form of her own, who had nothing in common with humankind and no reason to spare us. Everything I knew about diplomacy came from dealing with humans; this was uncharted territory, the realm of monsters.

"What are you doing here?" I asked bluntly, in the thin hope that I could put them on the defensive. "You can understand my grandmother's concern, with you clearly up to something on her border."

Nightmare seemed unimpressed. "If Discord is concerned what I do outside her borders, she should have let me take a host within them. It's foolish for her to be so concerned about her little human pets." She tilted her head too far, eyeing me with the bright-eyed consideration of a hungry bird. "I suppose she'd raise a fuss if I destroyed you."

"Most likely," I agreed, my throat dry.

"But why would I do that? It would be a waste of a gift." Her lips curved in a satisfied smile. "She wouldn't have sent you to me if she needed you back unbroken. She knows what I do."

Oh, holy Hells.

"Now, that's a risky assumption," Severin said, dropping the words between us with a show of languid carelessness. "Witch Lords are possessive; they take care of their own."

Nightmare's gaze landed on him, and she sucked in a breath as if he were some particularly spectacular piece of scenery. Even though I had a great appreciation for his shining black hair, fine cheekbones, and wiry grace, something about the predatory sharpness of her stare repulsed me.

"Aren't you a lovely mess," she breathed.

Severin had plenty of practice not reacting when someone tried to unnerve him. He inclined his head politely. "I do try."

Madness was staring at me again. She took a step forward, her extravagant skirts swishing against the floor. "I need to see you better, to be sure." She extended a slim hand toward me, seemingly oblivious that she might be interrupting anything. "Will you accept my favor?"

A servant stepped from beside the throne, holding a silver bottle on a tasseled velvet pillow. My stomach flipped in horror.

"I...I'm honored, Your Majesty, but I'm afraid I must decline."

"I fear we are all exhausted from our long journey," Foxglove put in smoothly, "and the Lady Ryxander needs her rest. So with your permission, Your Majesty, perhaps we can continue this conversation another time."

Madness unleashed a slow, wondrous smile in reply and extended both hands toward Foxglove, like a benediction.

"You're so afraid." Her voice was soft, compassionate. "Afraid of what you've been, afraid of what they'd think of you. You don't need to be. It's all right. Take my hands."

The power in the air grew so thick it was hard to breathe. Nightmare stood behind Madness, one pace back, her eyes alight with unholy anticipation. A deep sound beyond hearing seemed to thrum in my bones. *Don't take them*, I urged him silently. *Don't do it.*

Foxglove was no fool. His eyes stayed locked on hers, but his hands didn't stir from his belt.

"You're right," he said slowly. "I do fear you. But as the Graces watch over me, I will not take your hand."

Incredibly, the queen's shoulders drooped, as if he'd hurt her feelings. The Demon of Madness, looking like I'd felt as a child when my grandmother told me I couldn't play with my cousins.

"It's not like that," she said softly. "I don't want to hurt anyone. You're all just so fragile, and so beautiful."

"Delightful though this digression may be," Severin cut in, "we should focus on business. You still haven't given Exalted Ryxander an answer to take back to her grandmother about what you're doing here." His half-lidded eyes and almost insolently casual posture might have fooled me if I didn't know him, but I could read the tightness in his face and shoulders: he was terrified. But then, Severin had gone most of his life breathing terror like a fish breathed water. It was his natural habitat.

Nightmare advanced toward Severin with a curious smile curving her lips. She reached out one long fingernail and dragged it down his cheek as he stood rigid, struggling not to react.

"Be patient," she told him. "You'll get your turn. Right now, we're playing with the other one." She glanced over her shoulder at Madness. "What are you waiting for? Open him up, and let's see what's inside."

"Oh! Of course." Madness returned her gaze to Foxglove. In the space of an eyeblink, her shadow stirred and grew; it reared up in a surge of terrifying darkness, vast and dangerous and jagged-edged.

"Wait!" I started forward instinctively, but couldn't move quickly enough. It crashed down over him in a great wave.

Foxglove stiffened, a knife-thin gasp sliding between his lips. Ashe dropped her hand to Answer's hilt, feet shifting, ready to draw.

"Foxglove!" Kessa called desperately. "Are you all right?"

"I'm fine," he snapped, even as he swayed on his feet. "Just disoriented. Stand *down*, Ashe."

"Let's see what you've got," Nightmare purred, drawing closer to him.

All at once blood cloaked Foxglove's hands to the elbows, like scarlet gloves, dripping onto the floor. For a brief moment, I was afraid it was his own.

He clenched his crimson fists. "This isn't real. It's an illusion."

"It's not real," Madness agreed, her voice soft, "but it's truth."

"Listen to your heart quicken," Nightmare breathed. "So afraid of what else we'll find, buried deep and hidden away. Shall I show them, little one?"

Nightmare's smile spread wide and sharp as the crescent moon. She twisted her hand in the air, as if she broke a branch off a tree; Foxglove fell to his knees, pressing blood-drenched fists to his temples.

Kessa started toward him, alarm on her face, but he waved her away. "No. Get back!"

On the floor beside him, a shadow began to form. A somewhat human-shaped shadow, lying in a pool of darkness. A sense of overwhelming dread gathered with it, sucking the air out of my lungs.

Foxglove reached toward the shadow. "*No*," he whispered, his voice hoarse with terror.

"Enough!" I threw myself between Foxglove and the demons, heart pounding. The shadow scattered as their attention snapped to me; Kessa ran to Foxglove's side.

I had to drag this back to being a conversation, somehow. Was this what it had been like for Lord Elford and his people, in their last moments? "We're not your playthings," I said. "We're here as envoys to your court. If you mistreat us, my grandmother will be greatly displeased."

Nightmare's eyes fixed on me, widening as if I were some incredible new present.

"Oh, this one is even better," she exclaimed.

That sure as Hells wasn't what I wanted to hear. "Are you listening to me?" I demanded. "I would honestly love to have a conversation with you, but that can only happen if we actually listen to each other."

Madness broke into a smile so sweet, so pure, that it took my breath away. For a brief, flickering moment, even as something screamed a warning in the back of my mind, I thought everything might somehow be all right.

"I'll listen," she said, almost reverently.

I froze in her gaze, dimly aware that I was in terrible danger, but it all faded before the brilliance of that smile like fog before the noon sun. She drifted closer. *No, run away, run away...*

Madness lifted dainty fingers and laid them alongside my temples, her touch gentle as butterfly wings but piercingly cold. I couldn't so much as flinch—could only stare at her, mesmerized, straining to understand the inexplicable tears gathering in her wide blue eyes.

"It's time," she whispered, "to show me your truth."

TWELVE

Panic gripped me, far later than it should have. "Wait—"

The queen's eyes seemed to widen and rush at me, as if I plummeted toward twin pools of pristine water. A wave of immense power flowed over me with drowning force, making the air between us shimmer.

Pox, pox, pox. Whisper had warned me, and I'd failed to avoid her notice, and now I was done for. I braced for something awful, the unraveling of my very soul.

But if her power was water, my mind was oil. The giddy rush of magic passed around and through me, tingling briefly along my nerves, and was gone.

I blinked. Madness blinked. We stared into each other's eyes, and I couldn't tell which of us was more surprised.

Nightmare's wide grin faded. "What happened?" she snapped.

Madness shook her head, frowning faintly. "She won't let me in."

Hope stirred in my heart, small and fierce. For once, my broken, destroying magic might be helping me.

"Try again," Nightmare demanded, her hand falling on Madness's shoulder. "We'll do it together, this time."

I stepped back, panic rising; the guards flanking us seized my arms to keep me in place, faces impassive, hands hard as steel.

"Let her go," Severin growled at them, hand dropping to the bone knife at his belt.

"Stay out of this, Severin," I said curtly. The last thing we needed was to kick things over the edge into violence ourselves.

The demons' combined power crawled over me, plucking with shivering fingers, pawing at my mind. I flinched, queasy from the pressure of it. Again their touch slid off, like rain down window glass.

Sounds of muffled distress rose from my friends and the servant who still stood by with the velvet pillow, as if they felt the edges of the demons' mental assault; the soldiers who held my arms swayed and let out low moans. But I stood unbowed, staring defiantly back at the two of them.

"We're not your playthings," I repeated firmly. I hoped to the Graces they didn't notice how my knees trembled.

"How strange." Nightmare's eyes narrowed. "Try the mercury."

Oh, Hells, no.

The waiting servant stepped forward and offered the queen a small, shining bottle and a narrow glass tube on his velvet pillow, staring expressionlessly from silver-filmed eyes.

A hot thread of fear snaked up my middle. I tried to step back, but the guards tightened their grip on my arms.

Ashe lunged in a blur of motion, unwilling to wait any longer; light crackled on Answer's hilt as it leaped into her hand.

"*No!*" Foxglove, Kessa, and I shouted at once—but it was too late. Nightmare flicked no more than a glance in her direction, and Ashe collapsed in mid-lunge, sprawling boneless on the floor. My heart seemed to freeze between beats.

"What did you do to her?" Kessa cried, running to Ashe's side.

"Relax, she's just asleep." Nightmare chuckled. "Though she may not enjoy the dreams she's having. I believe you're dying in them, again and again."

Seething with rage, I struggled to twist free of the guards' grip, but their hands only tightened with bruising force.

"That's enough," Foxglove growled, hands dipping into his artifice pouches. Severin lunged toward Madness, ripping his knife from its sheath.

"Shh." Madness lifted a finger to her lips.

They all tumbled at once to their knees.

I craned my neck around as far as I could in the guards' iron grip, my pulse pounding with fear for them. "Are you all right?"

"Ugh." Severin slipped, barely catching himself on an elbow; Bastian had turned a sickening shade of yellow-green. "My balance is gone, and everything is a spinning mess of random colors. It's...we're fine, but we can't move. Worry about yourself, Ryx."

"If you're quite done," Nightmare said acidly, "let's get on with this. Are you ready, Madness?"

Madness dipped the slim glass tube into the silver bottle, capturing a metallic silvery bead at its tip. "It's all right," she crooned. "It's all right. It'll be all right."

Unreasoning panic burst through me—sheer terror as if that gleaming silver drop approaching in the queen's hand meant something infinitely worse than death. Whisper was right; I didn't know how, but he was right. This would destroy me. Every animal instinct in me screamed to fight and flee.

Kessa called out, "Ryx! Should I release you?"

Sweet Hell of Death. Madness leaned closer, all encouraging smile and wide blue eyes, the drop of quicksilver hovering close to my forehead. All it would take was one word, and the guards who held me would be dead, and no one could seize me again.

But the last time I'd unleashed my power in fear and desperation, in the Shrike Lord's castle, it had surged out of my control. I might take the Rookery with them—not to mention half the government of Loreice if I couldn't stop it in time.

No. I'd rather die in torment.

"That will not be necessary," said a voice soft as distant thunder, deep as the drowning ocean, final as the fall of winter.

Madness's head jerked up, eyes widening. Nightmare let out a startled hiss. The drop of quicksilver fell to the floor, missing my face by an inch.

Whisper prowled across the room toward us, sleek and poised, his yellow eyes hard. I should have felt a surge of joy at being rescued, but all that welled up inside me was a profound dread.

He avoided intervening directly above all else. This couldn't be good.

The hands on my arms went slack. The guards fell, one half a second after the other, to land in boneless piles.

Dead, just like that. I stared at Whisper in horror.

The other guards in the room raised their pikes or drew their pistols, alarmed—and as each did, they fell, sudden as a cut string.

"No!" I cried. But Whisper paced closer, not so much as glancing their way or mine, his attention fixed on the demons.

Madness and Nightmare faced him; Madness tried a shy wave, while Nightmare's face went closed and wary.

"Why hello, brother," she said, all the rich resonance flattened out of her voice. "It's been a long time."

"That it has. Why don't you dismiss the humans?" Whisper's tail flicked with apparent contempt. "We have a lot to talk about."

Nightmare's eyes slid sideways to me, narrowing, then back to him. "Yes," she said slowly. "Yes, we do."

Whisper didn't look at me. But I heard his voice, clear as if he spoke in my ear: *Ryx, take your friends and get out of here. Now.*

His tone was a warning, a doom hovering over my head. It made one thing clear: this was not a victory.

I shut my mouth and hurried to comply.

Whatever Madness did to scramble my friends' senses, it mostly faded when her attention shifted to Whisper. Bastian, Severin, and Foxglove stumbled out of the room on their own, while

Kessa supported a semiconscious Ashe until she came fully awake, cursing, in the now-deserted throne hall. That was one small blessing of the Graces; with the demons absent and distracted, it seemed the guards had let everyone leave.

We staggered together out into the gardens, sharing an unspoken need for fresh air. The mad shadows of topiary loomed over us as we stumbled across the damp grass, following the glowing white shell paths down to the third terrace with its great looming tree. Moisture hung in the air, making it raw and cold, promising rain.

"I'm going to kill her," Ashe snarled, the lines of her face taut and stricken. "I don't know how, but I'm going to kill her. Some things cross a line." She held Kessa's hand so tightly it couldn't have been comfortable; Kessa wrapped an arm around her in return.

"Is everyone all right?" I asked, concerned. We'd veered into the first conversation garden, which held a circle of fancifully carved benches shaped like cavorting fish around a mirror-smooth pool that glowed from beneath with an eerie blue light. Foxglove dropped heavily onto a bench as if he couldn't support himself anymore, and the others followed his example. "What did they do to you?"

"Stirred up a mess of bad memories," Foxglove said, his voice rough and low. "It was hard to tell what was real for a while. Everything's steadying now."

"For me it was a jumble of senses and feelings," Kessa said, still holding on to Ashe protectively. "Odd smells, shocking images, random intense emotions, and everything was spinning." She grimaced. "The spinning was my least favorite part. Strange bursts of emotion and random unpleasant imaginings I've dealt with before."

Bastian, half reclined on his bench, looked as if he might like to dig through his satchel for his notebook, but gave it up as too difficult. "I suppose the good news is that we've learned more about the demons' powers." Enthusiasm began to creep into his voice, forcing its way through his exhaustion. "They do seem to have different capabilities—Nightmare is the one conjuring the visions, while I got the impression Madness was the only one who could look inside people's minds."

"She couldn't look in Ryx's mind, though," Kessa said. "Good trick, that. Any idea why?"

I shrugged, my nerves still jangling like shards of broken glass in a sack. "My magic must have unwoven theirs. I don't know how my power worked through the jess, though. Maybe because if they're in my mind, they're already inside the binding?"

"Maybe." Bastian's voice sounded almost distant, as if he were thinking of something else. "Or..." He trailed off, staring into space.

"I want to know why they're trying to put quicksilver on everyone," I said, frowning. "They clearly don't need it to use their power on people." Well, except me, apparently.

"It might be an anchor," Bastian said absently. "So they don't have to maintain concentration. You'll notice we were all fine as soon as they got distracted, but the guards remain in their suppressed state even when the demons aren't paying attention to them."

Foxglove straightened, seeming to drag himself up from some dark pit. "We can speculate later," he said. "The question now isn't what they did. It's what *we* are going to do."

"What I'd *like* to do is run away," Kessa said. "I'm all for getting the mission done in the face of seemingly insurmountable obstacles—very dramatic, makes a good story later, and I have the perfect hat for it now—but there comes a time to pull up stakes and get out."

"No," I said quietly, but without any hesitation.

Everyone looked at me. I became suddenly conscious of the straggling remnants of my braid, half fallen from its once-elegant coil on my head, and began stripping it out with brutally efficient fingers.

"One thing I've learned from being Warden of a castle is that when things go to the Nine Hells, you have to go on the offensive," I said briskly. "We've been reeling from one thing to the next all day—and that's fine, but now it's time to turn to the attack." I shook my hair free; it fell wild and dark about my face, but I didn't care how I looked. We were all a mess.

"I love your spirit, but how?" Kessa asked, sounding genuinely bewildered. "Forgive me, but we don't seem to have a lot of options right now."

To my surprise, it was Severin who answered. "We need to get that cursed artifact from the Zenith Society, like we came here to do." He crossed his arms. "I'm sure whatever the demons are doing with the quicksilver is impressively terrible, but it can't possibly be as bad as slaughtering an entire domain."

"Good point, and it's something we can act on," Foxglove agreed, straightening. "This palace is too big to search every possible hiding place; we need to spy on the Zenith Society, or get an inside informant."

Ashe ran her fingers over the swirls of artifice wire wrapping Answer's swept hilt. "Sure, but we can't just *ignore* the demons. That's like trying to play cards while a war chimera eats your face."

"About that," Bastian began slowly, frowning as if he struggled to catch an escaping thought. "I've been trying to figure out how humanity stopped the demons in the Dark Days. And after what happened tonight, I was wondering..." He laughed, then shook his head. "I had the strangest idea. I'm sorry, it's probably nonsense."

Foxglove leaned forward, intent. "No, tell us."

"Well..." Bastian gave me an odd look. "Maybe the Graces were a bit like you, Ryx. Maybe they had malformed magic that made them resistant to demonic power."

A harsh burst of laughter escaped my throat. "That *is* nonsense. I'm no Grace."

Bastian ducked his head. "Obviously not as we understand them, but I've been wondering a lot recently whether they were just people with unusual magical capabilities. If demonic power has no limits, you couldn't stand up to them with *more* power; you'd have to have some other unique advantage—like immunity. And here you are, able to unravel their magic and neutralize it. Infinity becomes zero." He shrugged self-consciously. "I told you—it's just a fancy, not a real theory. Not worth mentioning."

"But what if it's true?" Kessa seized my hand, her eyes alight. "Imagine it, Ryx! You could be the Grace of...of..."

"Murder?" I shook my head. "Kitchen accidents?"

Kessa laughed. "No, seriously, it would make sense! No disrespect to your Graces, but *miracle* is basically a word for *magic we don't understand* anyway, right?"

Foxglove's dark amber eyes fixed on me. "It would explain how you exorcised Hunger from Kessa."

"We already know how I did that," I protested. "Not to mention that it only worked because I was right there when it happened. In another minute I'd have been too late. And I almost killed you, Kessa! You probably wouldn't have survived if you weren't a vivomancer. Don't count on me to do that again."

"Yes, well, we certainly shouldn't get overexcited," Bastian admitted. "It's just wild speculation. We don't have any real evidence."

"I think we have a lot of evidence that I'm not anything of the sort," I said gruffly. Blood and ashes, what a terrible idea. It hurt too much to contemplate the notion that maybe the bitter accident that had twisted my entire life might have a meaning, a purpose; that would be worse than a random trick of fate.

Severin slumped against a statue as if the weight of the past hour had finally hit him. "It doesn't matter why you're resistant to their power—whether because of your flawed magic, or because you're a Grace, or because your grandmother shielded you somehow through your connection, or for however many reasons a thousand magical theorists could come up with." He stared at me with inexplicable pain in his dark eyes. "What matters is that now they know. And they're not going to just let it go and forget about you. When the powerful realize something can actually threaten their power, they never just *ignore* it."

I stared at him, the truth of his words sinking in. This must be why Whisper had given me his warning; he must have known their power wouldn't work on me, and foreseen the danger.

Kessa, however, waved at Severin as if he were an annoying bug. "Oh, let Ryx have her moment of glory. She's a dashing hero now! She faced two demons down and made them let her go, after all."

My face heated. "I—that wasn't me."

"Oh, don't be modest!" She grinned. "Wish I could have seen it, but my senses were too scrambled at the time, and I was mostly trying not to throw up. How did you get them to back off?"

"It really wasn't me," I mumbled.

"No, it wasn't," Ashe agreed, her voice as serious as I'd ever heard it. She turned to me. "Ryx, I think it's time you told us what in the Hells is going on with your chimera."

A surge of guilt rose up in me. "Ah. Whisper."

"Yes. *Whisper.*" Ashe folded her arms. "I started to wake up when he came in. I couldn't move yet, but my senses weren't scrambled; I saw what happened. He strolled in there and guards dropped like stones. And the demons *know* him, like they're old drinking buddies—except they're *scared* of him."

I'd known this moment was coming, but this wasn't how I'd wanted them to find out. I'd always vaguely assumed that someday the Rookery would clearly need to know that Whisper was a demon, and I'd simply tell them, having kept his secret as long as I reasonably could.

I fumbled for words that would set Ashe's concerns at ease, that would assure people it wasn't what it looked like—except that it was exactly what it looked like.

Ashe kept going. "He's always known way too much. And he's not afraid of *anything*—you can't fake the attitude of someone who knows they're untouchable. I've only seen it in Witch Lords before, and now demons." She jabbed a finger at me. "That's no chimera, and you know it."

I let out a long sigh. "No," I admitted. "He's the Demon of Death."

"Hells on a stick," Ashe blurted. "What, no, you were supposed to tell me I'm wrong."

Kessa's fingers flicked in the warding sign. Foxglove grabbed his anti-demon charm. "Holy Graces preserve us."

Bastian pressed his long fingers into his temples as if he had to contain his brain. "Well, *that* explains some things. Oh my."

"I thought he was some ancient and powerful chimera, not a *demon*," Severin objected.

"He's not a threat," I reassured them. Then I thought that over. "Or at least, he's been in this world since the Dark Days and he hasn't caused any problems that I know of. He seems to have strict rules about staying neutral."

Severin stared at me. "Ryx, are you seriously trying to claim that the *Demon of Death* is not a threat?"

"A demon," Foxglove said, with piercing intensity, "is a demon. By definition, they're creatures of pure evil."

"He's my *friend*." Anger warmed my face in a sudden surge. "He's been my friend a lot longer than any of you have."

"He's a *demon*," Foxglove insisted. "He's not anyone's friend. You've been taken for a fool, Ryx."

Kessa sank down on the bench Foxglove had vacated. "The Demon of Death. Blood of the Eldest, I wanted to pet him. The Demon of *Death*."

"We're going to have to deal with him along with the rest," Foxglove said, his face grim.

My hands clenched at my sides. "If you try to hurt him when he's done nothing to deserve it—"

"He's a *demon*, Ryx," Foxglove protested. "Of *course* he deserves it."

"—I'll stop you," I finished, unable to keep the heat from my tone any longer. "He just *saved* us back there. He's helped us more than once. He could have brought the other demons through anytime, living in Gloamingard all those centuries, and he didn't. I'm not saying we should trust him—"

"Good thing, because he's the most suspicious-looking little furry bastard I've ever seen," Ashe muttered.

"—but he is *not* our enemy, and we're fools if we treat him as such." I took a deep, steadying breath. "And, I tell you again, he's my friend. Which means I'll stand up for him."

"For the Demon of Death," Foxglove said, his face taut, barely controlled.

"Yes."

There was a moment of tense silence. My own breath sounded too loud, too fast, but I couldn't slow it down. Foxglove was right to look at me like that—what I was doing made no sense, and I knew it. These were my friends, my *human* friends; Whisper had never asked for my protection and certainly didn't need it.

Finally, Ashe grunted. "I can't believe these words are coming out of my mouth, but if he doesn't want to start a fight with us, maybe we shouldn't start a fight with him. He's the *Demon of Death*."

Severin let out a strained laugh. "She's got a point."

Foxglove closed his eyes. His lips moved a moment in something I suspected was a prayer. When he opened them again, they were no softer; whatever his prayer had brought him, it wasn't forgiveness for a demon.

"All right," he said. "I can agree he's not the imminent threat the others are, for now."

I had a sinking suspicion that this meant *I have made a note not to include Ryx in any anti-Whisper plans.* Curse it, they'd better not try anything foolish. The last thing I wanted was to have to choose between my oldest friend and my new ones.

Even if my oldest friend had just murdered several innocent people who were controlled against their will. I couldn't shake the image of those guards dropping one after another.

Kessa glanced between me and Foxglove, frowning anxiously. "I wonder if he could be an asset," she suggested with the cautious air of someone hoping to smooth things over. "Clearly he got in through the wards somehow; could he get us out?"

"No, he said that not even other demons could…" I trailed off, the full implications of that tidbit Whisper had let slip—or dropped on purpose?—lighting up like a series of chained fireworks in my mind. Excited, I turned to Bastian. "He said that the other demons couldn't pass through the wards. Could we trap them here somehow?"

Foxglove's head lifted, like a dog scenting its quarry. "Interesting. Bastian?"

Bastian blinked. "The palace wards are certainly formidable— meant to stand up to invading Witch Lords, with redundant power sources and fail-safes. They *might* hold a demon, but we'd need to alter them." His hand twitched as if it yearned to sketch out designs. "Right now they let defensive magic pass outward, like Nightmare attacking those Falcons, so we'd have to change that. And of course, we'd also want to add some of the demon-specific enhancements the Black Tower wards used…" He started rummaging in his satchel. "I do have all the notes I took on them. I'm not saying it would definitely work, but I *am* saying it would be an interesting challenge."

"You're not thinking of warding us in with the demons, I trust," Severin said, his sharp tone suggesting that he trusted no such thing. "Call me selfish, but I have no interest in sacrificing myself to bait a trap."

"No, we'd need to get everyone out," Foxglove agreed, frowning. "That means gaining control of the wards. Most imperial wards either have a physical key or a password; I'd guess a physical key in this case, since if it were a password the Serene Envoy would probably have known it."

"Another thing to steal," Kessa said, sounding almost cheerful. "That's not so bad."

"All right, then." Foxglove pushed up from his bench with the slow care of a man testing whether moving hurt. He dusted off his coat, tugged his cuffs straight, and lifted eyes once again full of their usual fire. "Let's get on the courier lamps. Time to report to our superiors that we've got a plan."

The Summer Palace had changed while we were out in the gardens.

The scintillating lights in the entry hall seemed dimmer, their colors more lurid and eerie: bloody reds, sickly greens, and the ghostly blue of foxfire. A bitter taste stung the back of my throat, and the scents of blood and rot and animal musk teased the air one after another, there and gone. The grand galleries that led toward the Curia had a haunted look, plunged into shadow for the night: the expressions of the statues seemed grim or leering, the figures in the paintings twisted in despair or agony. What few people we saw at this midnight hour scurried on their way with wide-eyed, furtive looks, jumping at things that weren't there. In a gallery celebrating the Festival Uprising, one servant curled miserably against a statue of Councilor Altaine, his face buried in his hands.

"I wish there wasn't so much blood on the walls," Kessa said, the cheer in her voice threadbare. "It's making it rather difficult to admire the art."

Severin kept his eyes on the floor. "Every portrait and statue has my father's face," he muttered. "Blood sounds charming by comparison."

"Nightmare's miasma has definitely gotten worse." Bastian rubbed his arms as if he were cold. "Maybe she was holding back before and doesn't care about being found out now."

"It's like Alrassa," Ashe muttered. "The City of Fear."

"Charming name," Severin said, "but I've never heard of it."

"Then you didn't have enough friends to tell you creepy stories as a kid, mage boy." Ashe gave him a sidelong look. "Story goes the Demon of Nightmares settled in there, pretending to be a rich traveler. It starts out with a few kids having bad dreams and gets worse and worse until by the end, people's fears are made flesh to hunt and devour them in the streets." She sighed. "Nice, gory story to tell around the fire."

"Not so good to live through, though," I said. "We're going to have trouble keeping people from hurting each other at this rate. It gets bad enough during the long winters in Gloamingard, when all that's bothering everyone is short days and cold."

I didn't mention that I wasn't seeing any visions like the ones that made my friends curse or flinch from random objects. Occasionally I heard a distant whispering, barely on the edge of hearing, or shadows moved in the corners of my eyes—but that was all. I refused to give Bastian's theory any credence, but for whatever reason, my flawed magic seemed to make me resistant to the demons' mind games.

It made absolutely no sense that I should feel left out, but here we were.

We paused on the stairs to the second floor, which housed the administrative wing as well as residential and guest quarters. Foxglove split the group to scout different possible approaches to the courier lamp chamber, mostly as an excuse to send Bastian ahead again. When we reconvened in a few minutes, worry creased Bastian's brow.

"They must be serious about not letting messages get out after what happened in the throne hall," he reported. "They've got five guards on the door to the lamp chamber now, and they've replaced the temporary artifice seal with a better one. At least they didn't destroy the lamps—the Zenith Society must be planning to use them."

Foxglove rubbed his hands. "I'm not worried about the seal."

Ashe grinned. "I'm not worried about the guards."

My stomach lurched, thinking of what Whisper had done in the Velvet Room. "We should try not to hurt them."

"Of course." Kessa turned to Bastian. "What do you think? Sleepy birds?"

He nodded and began rummaging in his satchel. "Sleepy birds."

Sleepy birds turned out to mean the vivomancers coaxing in a few birds from a garden-facing window and charming them to drop several glass vials of Bastian's sleep potion among the guards. While they put it into effect, we waited around the corner, holding our breaths. I did a quick and messy job of rebraiding my hair to keep it out of my face if this turned into a fight, my fingers clumsy with nerves.

There came the shattering of glass and a few heavy thumps—then cries of confusion and alarm.

The sleep potion hadn't taken care of all of them. My heart tried to climb into my throat.

Ashe's eyes lit up as if it were a festival day.

"Finally," she breathed, and launched herself around the corner, Answer ringing free from its sheath.

"Rule Three!" Kessa cried, and the rest of us sprinted after her.

THIRTEEN

Two out of five guards already lay on the floor, knocked out by the potion; a third looked woozy, as if he'd breathed in some of the fumes. The remaining two fixed their silver-hazed eyes on Ashe as she charged up the corridor. One drew a pistol, and the other a sword.

I'd never run at someone holding a weapon before; my instincts screamed against it, and I faltered.

Ashe had no such hesitation.

Before the guard with the pistol could fire, Ashe lunged in and flicked a shallow cut on her hand. Green crystals on Answer's pommel sparked with light, and the guard seemed to go boneless at once, collapsing with a slurred curse. Relief washed through me—she was stunning them, not killing them.

The second guard seized the opening created by Ashe's extension, slashing down at her sword arm, but Ashe was too fast. Answer swept up, knocking her attacker's blade aside, and continued the circling motion to slide in and prick the guard's shoulder. The green crystals flashed again, and the second guard tumbled down to join her comrades.

The rest of us fell in at Ashe's back as she leveled her sword at the third guard, who swayed on his feet from the potion fumes, his pistol just now clearing its holster.

She slow-poked his chest with a disappointed expression. Answer's hilt flared green a third time, and the guard dropped with the rest.

Ashe wiped the traces of blood off her sword on a fallen guard's uniform, glancing over her shoulder at Kessa. "See? Rule Three. I was as gentle as if I were their own damned mother."

Kessa raised an eyebrow. "You have interesting notions about parenting."

Foxglove pulled a handful of slim twists of artifice wire from one of his pouches and tossed them to Kessa. "Bind their wrists with this. The potion and the stunning charge won't last more than ten minutes each; these will keep them paralyzed for a little longer." He turned to Bastian. "Come on, let's break that seal and get to the lamps. The rest of you stand guard."

At my side, Severin stiffened at the command, his eyes narrowing. But then his shoulders relaxed, and he sighed.

"I need to get used to that," he murmured, softly enough for no one but me to hear. "It's hard to take orders from anyone who's not my brother." He seemed to turn that over and added, "Actually, I was never good at taking orders from my brother, either."

"Just as well, in his case," I replied.

He sighed. "I'm realizing more and more that I actually have no idea how to interact with people in a normal way."

I let out a soft little laugh. "Me too, Severin. Me too."

Bastian handed Foxglove a brush and a bottle of artifice ink, and he began carefully editing the runes that sealed the door. Kessa and Ashe moved between the unconscious guards, tying their wrists. I strained my ears for any sound of approaching footsteps or voices, staring off down the corridor. My limbs trembled even though I hadn't gotten involved in the fight. I'd still been about to attack people who were essentially minding their own business; it was somehow more upsetting than the times I'd been on the other side of that equation.

Kessa froze over the last guard, her breath catching in her throat as if something had hurt her.

Ashe spun immediately, Answer in her hand, eyes wide. "Kessa! Are you—"

"Loren," she gasped. Her younger brother, who she'd found murdered.

She spun away, eyes squeezed shut, and stumbled immediately over another fallen guard.

Ashe caught and righted her, smoothly as if she'd seen it coming. "Easy. It's not real, remember?"

"I know." She took a shuddery breath. "But it's still upsetting, because he's dead, and *that's* real."

Foxglove swore, and sparks and smoke rose from the seal he was working on.

"My apologies," he muttered. "My hand slipped on the final rune. It's open."

Ashe folded Kessa in her arms, awkwardly patting her back, as Foxglove and Bastian slipped into the courier lamp chamber.

I exchanged a meaningful glance with Severin. We were all exhausted to the point of making mistakes. It had been such a long and terrible day, full of death and horror; my own legs felt weak under me, and weariness dragged at my friends' faces. I tried to think when any of us had last eaten. Breakfast with Lord Elford, before we went out to the gardens to identify Moreni. Hells, had that only been this morning? It seemed like a hundred years ago.

One of the fallen guards began to stir. Ashe pricked him with her sword tip, then made a full round of all of them.

"That's about it for my stunning orb," she muttered, frowning at Answer's pommel after the last flash of green proved a mere flicker. "Not much power left in the obsidian."

Kessa wiped her eyes and straightened her hat. "I'm sure

Foxglove can make a new one for you," she said, adopting a pale imitation of her usual jaunty stance. "We're all in favor of you having nonlethal ways to take out opponents."

Ashe eyed Kessa sideways. There was a certain gentle calculation in her glance, adding up cues to determine exactly how much teasing Kessa needed right now.

"I could switch to the fire one or the bone-cleaving one in the meantime," she suggested at last. "Those aren't always lethal."

Kessa crossed her arms, voice strengthening. "I'm not even going to dignify that with a response."

"You can be on fire or missing limbs and not dead," Ashe pressed. Her grin was pure mischief, but her eyes stayed soft.

"Rule Six, Ashe." Kessa wagged a finger at her. "No avoidable maiming."

Ashe let out a theatrical sigh.

"I've been meaning to ask," I said, glad of the diversion. "What's Rule Five?"

"Stop when Foxglove says stop. It's a catchall." Ashe started counting on her fingers. "Rules One and Two I made up myself: no hurting friends, no hurting kids. Rule Three was Kessa's idea—no killing unless absolutely necessary—though sometimes we disagree on the definition of necessary."

Kessa lifted an eyebrow. "Which is why we have Rule Five."

"Rule Four is talking before stabbing." Ashe rolled her eyes as if this were a ridiculous imposition. "You just heard Rules Five and Six, and Rule Seven is no torture."

"You needed a rule against torture?" I asked, incredulous. I'd believed Ashe capable of murder, but she was pragmatic, not cruel.

Kessa glanced at Ashe, whose eyes had gone clouded and her jaw set. "Well, the Furies unfortunately had a certain type of training that didn't sit any better with Ashe than it did with us," she said carefully. "She didn't *need* Rule Seven, but she wanted to add it when we were talking about the differences between how the Furies did things and how the Rookery does things."

"There's a reason I left them," Ashe said, in a tone that shut the door on any questions. "But I don't have the rules because I'd *do* all this stuff if I didn't. I have them so I don't have to make poxy moral choices in the middle of a fight. People make bad decisions when their blood is up."

From what I'd heard about the ruthlessness of the Furies, I had no doubt Ashe had seen plenty of those bad decisions, and maybe made a few herself. I nodded slowly. "Sounds like a good system."

Bastian and Foxglove emerged from the courier lamp room, their faces grim. Foxglove moved as if his body were stiff and aching; Bastian clutched his notebook to his chest.

"More good news?" Severin asked ironically. "Should we sit down?"

Foxglove didn't smile. "It's going to be a while before we have time to sit down again." He bent to retrieve his wire from the wrists of the guards, his movements sharp as if he were repressing anger.

Bastian licked his lips. "Well, there *is* some good news. The doge and the Council support our plan to alter the wards and trap the demons here, and they're willing to let us try it."

"But?" I prompted, my heart sinking at his phrasing. *Willing to let us try* implied that the Serene Empire had an alternative plan in mind.

"If we fail..." Bastian glanced at Foxglove, swallowing.

"They'll destroy this place and everyone in it." Foxglove straightened, binding wires dangling from his hand, face set. "They've got a fleet moving into position off the coast, loaded down with enough artifice cannons to turn the Summer Palace to a smear of glass."

I yanked at my braid as if I could pull it off and whip the doge with it. "What in the Nine Hells do they think that'll accomplish? It won't kill the demons, just the humans trapped here!"

"Apparently there was a fierce argument in the Council, but the winning side felt we can't assume that overwhelming magical force won't hurt a demon until we try it." Foxglove shook his head with bitter disgust. "They're afraid. And when power reacts to fear with violence, people die."

Severin threw his hands up. "Why are you even talking to them? You report to Vaskandar as well as the Empire. While the Witch Lords have their flaws, at least they don't jump to *burn everything to the ground* as their first recourse!"

"Because we can get courier lamp signals out through the wards, but not birds." Foxglove rubbed his temple. "I may be Raverran, but I have to agree with you in this case that my government isn't handling this well."

"Well, the Empire *does* think our plan is better," Bastian said in a small voice. "That's why they're giving us three days."

"*Three days!*" That was far longer than I wanted to be stuck here, but a terrifyingly short amount of time left for everyone in the palace to live if we couldn't pull this off.

"We don't have time to waste," Foxglove concluded wearily. "Let's go."

"How long is it going to take us to modify the wards?" Foxglove asked Bastian as we entered a spacious hall full of clerks' copying desks on our way back to the imperial wing.

Each desk held a single luminary lamp flickering out the last of its charge from the day's sunlight as the deserted room descended into shadow. This room impressed me more than all the extravagant showpieces glittering with imperial glory. In its precise organization lay the true strength of the Serene Empire: paper and pens and ink all laid out and awaiting an army of clerks the next morning, their task fitting into a hundred others like the perfectly aligned gears of a clock.

"Oh, you're the artificer, you'd know better than I would," Bastian said, surprised.

"Bastian. When it comes to artifice, I'm a carpenter and you're an architect." Foxglove rubbed his forehead. "You've got the plan for modifying them. All I can do is hold the stylus and carve runes as fast as I can until my fingers get too stiff." There was a certain ruefulness in his voice, as if it pained him to admit it.

"I think you're exaggerating, but all right. Three days will be a little tight, but if I help you scribe the symbols, I think we can—" He broke off, stopping where he stood.

"Oh my love lay down in silence, with a cold unbeating heart . . ."

The familiar voice echoed eerily from somewhere ahead of us, singing its unsettling song. Bastian's face went pale as cheese. I stepped closer to him, ready to offer support if he needed it.

"But I knelt by him and swore that we would never be apart . . ."

Kessa scowled. "That demon doesn't know when to leave it alone. Bastian . . ."

Bastian took a deep, shuddering breath. "It's all right. I know it's not real."

"Oh my love lay down in silence, in his flowers and his gold . . ."

A sliver of ice slipped between my ribs, piercing deep into my chest. "Wait. We can hear it, and we're not touching you."

Everyone stared at me. Foxglove let out a soft curse, his hand dropping to his pistol.

"But I took his skin and made a coat to keep me from the cold."

Footsteps echoed on marble, and a dozen people sauntered into the room with unmistakable menace. Shadow half masked their faces, but it was easy enough to recognize them across the sea of desks between us, even in the poor light.

The Zenith Society. Moreni stood front and center, an ironic smile pulling at his lips.

"Ah, the Rookery." His voice filled the room, from wall to wall. "How fortunate that we should meet you here. I believe we have unfinished business."

This was not what we needed right now. My pulse hummed like a bee's wings, anticipating violence. The Zenith Society outnumbered us, and by the way they moved, they weren't here for a friendly conversation.

"Moreni." Foxglove's hand slipped down to hook a thumb in his belt, equally close to his pouches full of artifice devices and his pistol. "I should have known that when you dared show your face again at last, it'd be to lick crumbs from a demon's boots."

"Boots that will grind your bones into the dust," Moreni replied, his lip curling. "You can bluster all you want, my dear Foxglove, but you're a rat in a trap, and you know it."

Bastian drew himself up, radiating a scorn I'd never known he was capable of. "I'm disappointed in you, Moreni. I used to admire you so much—to think you were intelligent. But only an utter fool would make a deal with a demon."

Moreni chuckled. "I beg to differ, my dear pupil. Only a fool would stand against a man with a demon on his side." He pressed a hand to his heart. "But I'm touched to hear that you remember me so fondly. Won't you come back? I've missed you."

"I'm sure you're just mocking me," Bastian said, with quiet strength. "But in case you're not—there's nothing you could offer, nothing you could do, to draw me back into the Zenith Society again."

Moreni shook his head with mock sadness. "That's two out of two wrong. I expect better from my students, Bastian. Clearly we'll have to resort to remedial training to bring you back up to my standards."

In response to his words, the Zenith Society began to spread out in a casually menacing arc. Bastian took an instinctive step back; I moved in front of him, anger simmering in my belly like an alchemist's cauldron.

"Ignore him," I murmured. "We'll handle this."

Foxglove removed his dove-gray coat with graceful precision and tossed it over a desk.

"I told you earlier, Moreni," he said with deadly calm, "you've lost the right to speak to Bastian."

Moreni spread his hands, wirework rings gleaming on his fingers. "Now, now. The bonds between student and teacher aren't so easily broken. After all, we made him what he is today. Wouldn't you say so ... Cortissa?"

Bastian sucked in a sharp, ragged gasp.

Cortissa. Oh, Hells. *The Skinwitch.*

A Raverran woman with a tumble of mahogany-colored hair twisted her face in anger. "Damn you, Moreni, I've kept this cover for five years—I reshaped my *own face*—and you blow it to the Rookery for dramatic effect!"

Bastian slid to his knees, shaking as if his whole body might fall apart, his eyes wide with terror.

"Bastian!" I whispered, alarmed.

"She's supposed to be dead," he choked. "They executed her. That *can't* be her. It's not her face. But it's her voice, holy Graces, it's her voice."

"Oh, don't worry," Moreni said to Cortissa, relishing the distress on the Rookery's faces. "The knowledge won't leave this room."

"Hey, that's a threat," Ashe exclaimed.

Answer flashed free of its sheath, bright as lightning and just as deadly.

That one motion set off an instant flurry in response, pistols and blades whipping out on both sides. I drew my own rapier, mouth dry, hoping I could use it well enough to survive a real fight.

"*Wait!*" Moreni threw up a hand. "I wouldn't do that if I were you, little rook."

"*Little.* Oh, very clever, no one's called me that before." Ashe sounded bored. She edged forward half a step, the movement so smooth it was easy to miss that she was advancing.

"Show them what I mean, Cortissa."

Cortissa tossed her hair. "I'm not your underling, Moreni. But very well." She lifted her voice. "Bastian, kill your friends."

What—I started to turn, apprehension lurching in my gut.

With a despairing cry, Bastian tackled me to the ground.

FOURTEEN

The marble floor hit hard, jolting my senses; I glimpsed a flash of metal above me and barely managed to grab Bastian's arm before he plunged a dagger into my throat. I could only stare at him in shock, straining with both hands to hold his knife back from falling on me, as he sobbed and shook.

Gunshots shattered the air, one after another, stabbing at my eardrums; someone cried in pain, and the sharp scents of smoke and powder filled the room. Desks skidded across the floor, crashing into each other and toppling over.

I'm Bastian's friend. He's trying to kill me because I'm his friend. I'd be touched if a swirl of horrible violence hadn't erupted at the edges of my vision, with shouting and Ashe leaping from desktop to desktop toward the Zenith Society and now another gunshot. Or if Bastian weren't inhumanly strong, forcing the knife inexorably closer to my throat despite the trembling of his arm against both of mine and the wild helpless despair in his eyes.

Severin hauled him off me, struggling to hold him as Bastian squirmed and writhed, his joints bending in ways a human's shouldn't. I scrambled to my feet and knocked the knife out of Bastian's hand; it skittered across the floor, the sound almost lost in the general racket.

I whirled, heart exploding with terror that someone had gotten killed already, to quickly count my friends. There was Ashe, pulling her red-dripping sword from someone's chest, and Kessa, who'd drawn aside one of our opponents and was talking to him urgently, keeping him out of the fight. Foxglove crouched on one knee behind an overturned desk, coolly reloading his pistol, blood staining his leg. Several of the Zenith Society lay on the floor or sprawled across desks and chairs, some moaning, some still. Moreni and Cortissa stood unscathed in a knot of armed comrades, the former readying a small, glowing object to throw at Ashe while the latter stood with her hands open, waiting for some fool to come within her reach.

A Skinwitch, with death or worse in her touch. The one who'd turned Bastian into a chimera.

"Ashe!" I called, fear making my voice ragged. "Look out!"

Ashe whirled, blood flying from her sword. The bright spark of one of Moreni's artifice rings flew from his hand, arcing toward her, leaving a sizzling trail of runes burned into the air behind it. Foxglove cocked back the hammer on his pistol, took quick aim at Moreni over the top of his desk, and pulled the trigger.

In the same instant, a figure appeared in the doorway.

The luminaries guttered and nearly went out.

The hammer of Foxglove's pistol snapped harmlessly down— a misfire. Moreni's ring went dull and dark, its light winking out, before it pinged harmlessly off Ashe's raised blade and skittered across the floor.

What in the Nine Hells?

A sudden wave of weakness passed over me briefly, and I swayed on my feet. Severin staggered, losing his grip on Bastian, who dropped to his knees with a strangled gasp. One of the wounded curled on the floor let out a fading wail.

My heart dropped from its place in my chest, but anger caught it mid-plunge with a squeezing hand of fire.

A familiar figure stood in the doorway, one finger casually lifted, a smirk twisting his lips.

Aurelio. Once my friend, before he'd betrayed me. Host to the Demon of Hunger.

"Now, now. What's all this? Why are you fighting?" A terrible grin stretched his mouth, showing gleaming teeth. "We're all friends here. Aren't we?"

"Like Hells we are," I growled.

Ashe paused, quivering on the verge of launching herself at Cortissa, sword bare in her hand, impulses warring on her face.

The Skinwitch grinned and beckoned her. "Oh, come here, little brat. I'd love to tie your bones in knots."

"Ah, ah, ah!" Hunger shook a finger at her, strolling forward. "What did I just say? My sisters don't want you breaking their toys." He surveyed the wounded and dying on the floor and sighed. "Though I suppose these are past repair."

Cortissa shrugged. "I can knit them back together."

"No, no, don't bother." He held a hand over a man who sprawled on the floor clutching his middle in a spreading pool of blood. The air around his fingers shimmered. "I'll take care of them."

"No, please," the man gasped, flinching away in terror.

It was too late. His face went gray and sunken; the blood leaking between his fingers turned black. He let out a horrifying, rattling gasp as if Hunger drew even the breath from his lungs, and then went still.

Hunger let out a delighted sigh, as if he'd just sipped a fine wine.

My stomach turned over. It was what he'd done to Severin when we'd fought him in the Black Tower, only much worse. Severin averted his eyes, paling.

"That's enough." I stepped forward, fury overcoming fear. If Aurelio was still in there, I hoped he felt shame down to the bottom of whatever he called a soul for harboring a monster that would do that to his own people.

Hunger lifted Aurelio's auburn brows. "They're your enemies."

"Some things aren't acceptable to do even to your enemies." I lifted my chin. "Though I wouldn't expect *you* to know that. Either of you."

That hit home. His face twisted into a new expression: hopeless, haunted, disgusted.

Aurelio's expression. Good—just as I'd hoped. I'd rather deal with a treacherous human than a demon; at least I could try to manipulate the former.

Aurelio dropped his hand and crossed half the room toward me, stepping neatly around desks and over bodies, his footsteps echoing from the high ceiling. Everyone watched with the tension of deer eyeing a wolf.

"Give me some credit, Ryx," he said, his voice light and smooth, belying the pain in his face. "I wouldn't let him do that if the man weren't already dying."

With the Zenith Society all behind him, he stopped in the next row of desks, met my eyes with drowning desperation, and mouthed clearly, *Help me.*

My heart jumped and staggered. I'd expected him to mock me, or maybe offer me vile slippery bargains—not this.

"Wouldn't *let* him?" The words came hot out of my mouth, unchecked by Aurelio's plea. "You didn't seem to have any hesitation about killing *me*. And do you expect me to believe you can *control* this demon?"

Aurelio threw back his head in sudden laughter, viciously amused. "Of course he can't. Arrogant boy! It's convenient for me to allow him to share this body for now, but if he actually got in my way I'd consume him and possess this vessel fully. And he knows it. Don't you, boy?"

A flicker of fear passed across Aurelio's face. "Yes," he muttered, but once again he mouthed, *Help.*

Pity and disgust twisted in my belly. *Good Graces, Aurelio, what did you think would happen when you invited a demon in?*

This was my old friend, one of the few I'd ever had, asking for help.

This was also the man who'd shot me with poisoned arrows and nearly killed me, having the sheer nerve to ask for my help. Staring into his desperate eyes, it seemed impossible to reconcile the two.

Before I could untangle that mess enough to form a reply, Hunger pivoted on his heel and strode back toward the Zenith Society.

"Come!" he called to them. "We're not here to play."

"My lord," Moreni said smoothly, "we should finish this first. You could kill them with a snap of your—"

Hunger didn't so much as glance at him. "No, no killing them. It's not worth hearing my sisters complain that I stole their fun. Besides, we have plans to make; it's time for you to fulfill your promises."

Oh, I didn't like the sound of that at all.

Moreni swept a mocking bow at Foxglove. "Another time."

He and Cortissa followed Hunger from the hall, barely glancing back, their focus now riveted on the demon. I couldn't tell if the light in the eyes they locked on him was worship, fear, or simply ambition. Foxglove and Ashe stared murder after them.

Whatever showed on my face as the ragged, wild energy of fighting for my life still surged along my nerves, I doubted it was any kinder.

The rest of the Zenith Society group went with their leaders, some of them cradling injuries—except for the man Kessa had been talking to. He hesitated, staring after his companions and the demon, then bent to help one of his fallen comrades instead. Kessa handed him a jar of something with a soft word, to which he uttered curt thanks. Trust Kessa to have spotted the one who wasn't as much of a complete waste as the rest of them.

She returned to us with a pale face and haunted eyes. "So Hunger's here, too." She sounded utterly weary, as if his arrival had defeated her. "*Three* demons."

"Four," Ashe corrected, with a *your fault* glance my way.

Severin shook his head. "It's good to confirm that things can, in fact, always get worse."

His irony couldn't lighten the dismal weight of truth: we were, as Ashe would say, buggered. Even assuming Whisper truly was only here because he'd followed me, the idea of several demons combining their powers in one place was chilling.

"Let's get out of here," Foxglove said at last. He winced. "Someone give me a hand up."

Bastian offered him a shaking hand. He'd gone a greenish shade, and tears left raw tracks down his cheeks, but at least he wasn't trying to kill me anymore.

"How bad is your leg?" I asked Foxglove, my insides still seething with energy and throttled emotion.

He groaned as Bastian heaved him to his feet. "I've had worse," he said through his teeth. "It'll need patching."

"I can..." Bastian's voice shook. He swallowed. "I can do that. Let's go."

We made our limping way out of the room. Bastian supported Foxglove; Ashe seemed to walk with a bit of a hitch as well, though I couldn't tell whether any of the blood splashed on her clothes was hers.

"Are you hurt?" I asked her, worried.

Ashe snorted. "Fine. Pulled a muscle in my ass doing that long lunge to poke the soldier's gun hand before she could shoot me earlier."

Kessa clapped her hands over her mouth. Tears stood in the corners of her eyes, and her muffled laugh sounded half like a sob.

Ashe's brows swooped down into a frown. "I'm just sorry I didn't get to skewer that rancid bitch for you, Bastian. Stupid demon, showing up ten seconds too early."

Bastian made a sort of strangled noise in his throat.

Severin stopped, whirling on Bastian, his vestcoat flaring. "Right. Now that we're clear of that place, what in the Nine Hells was that about? Why are we all acting like it's fine that you tried to murder Ryx?"

Bastian covered his face with both hands, shoulders hunching. "I'm sorry. I'm so, so sorry."

Foxglove, deprived of his support, grabbed a nearby pillar to keep upright, his teeth bared with pain.

"Severin, leave it," I hissed. "Now's not the time."

"No, I suppose it's not." Barely checked anger drew Severin's face taut. "The time to tell us the Zenith Society has some kind of control over you would have been *before* we got into a fight with them."

"I didn't know." Bastian shivered. "I thought Cortissa was dead. We were *so sure* she was dead."

Kessa threw a protective arm around him, glaring at Severin. "Leave him alone. He feels awful about it already, can't you see? None of this is his fault."

"I don't care whose fault it was." Severin shook his head. "If it's anyone's, it's mine, for starting to consider trusting all of you." My heart twisted at that; he said it so dismissively, as if it were a trivial and foolish error he wouldn't repeat. "No, what I care about is whether the people I'm standing next to are going to stab me in the back. Secrets are well and good—wrap yourself in them for comfort on a cold day, by all means—but not when I'm going to get killed for not knowing them. Why can she control you? Can she do that to anyone else?"

"It's because..." Bastian's eyes widened with panic. He shot terrified glances at Ashe, swallowed, and tried to force himself to continue. "She can do it because I'm..."

"A chimera," Ashe finished for him.

Severin stepped back in shock. "Blood of the Eldest."

Bastian's face cycled through a variety of interesting colors. For a moment, I was worried that he'd faint.

"You knew?" he managed finally, his voice thin and high as a squeaky door.

Ashe gave him a skeptical look. "Sure. I'm a former chimera hunter. Did you really think I wouldn't notice? We had months of training in how to recognize human chimeras."

"That's why I didn't want to tell you," Bastian rasped, the fear still in his eyes.

"I figured." She shrugged. "I pretended not to know so you wouldn't feel weird about it. I've known since the first week I met you."

Severin shuddered. "*I* didn't know. What she did to you is an abomination."

Bastian looked ready to pass out. "I...yes. Cortissa was the Skinwitch who...who changed me." He swallowed. "It appears that since she created me, she can control me."

"She didn't *create* you," I snapped, still furious at her cruelty. "Any more than I'd be creating you if I gave you a bad haircut."

That elicited a hollow laugh from him. "If you gave me a haircut, you couldn't use that to make me attack my friends. I'm so sorry, Ryx."

I caught his eyes. "I'm honored you cared enough to attack me."

"This is touching," Foxglove said through gritted teeth, "but can we keep moving? Some of us are bleeding."

"Means you're alive," Ashe said. She offered Foxglove an arm for support, and we all started walking again. Bastian moved as if he were in a daze; Severin kept sneaking covert glances at him, no doubt looking for traces of what made him inhuman.

"How is Cortissa not dead?" Fury simmered in Foxglove's voice. "I saw them burn her body and scatter the ashes in the lagoon. Even a Skinwitch can't come back from that."

"She said something about reshaping her face," I said, queasy at the thought. "She must have done a swap—made someone else look like her, taken their appearance in return, and escaped that way." Molding some poor woman's flesh and bone like clay, stealing first her face and then her life as her victim was executed in her place. It was as bad as anything the demons had done.

"Bastian doesn't go anywhere alone," Foxglove commanded. "Let's get everyone some sleep potion, or some other way to neutralize you if she tries to command you again, Bastian."

"We won't let her touch you," Kessa said fiercely, squeezing his shoulders tighter.

"I . . . right. Thank you." Bastian blinked and shook his head, as if he were coming awake, his color slowly returning to normal. "Let's treat your leg first, Foxglove."

"Speaking of which." Foxglove swiveled toward Kessa, the sweat of pain and effort beading on his temples. "You'd better have learned something good from that scoundrel I saw you give some of our best alchemical healing salve. I try not to kill when I don't have to these days, but spending limited resources on our enemies strains my charity."

"Even our enemies have families who'd miss them," Kessa murmured. But then she lifted her chin, putting her hands on her hips. "Besides, I made a useful connection. You have to play the long game, Foxglove. I've already learned some things from my new friend Girard."

"Distract me," he suggested.

"He's less than pleased with how the Zenith Society changed when Aurelio came back from Vaskandar—catering to this demon, binding their fate up with him, making him central to their plans. He thinks it's folly, and is upset with Moreni. I think I can flip him."

"The Graces reward the good," Foxglove approved. "Nicely done."

Pleasure at the compliment lit Kessa's strained and exhausted face. "Just doing what I do best. I'll follow up tomorrow and see if I can get him to leak the location of the artifact."

"That would be the best thing to happen since we came here," I said. "I don't like Hunger's talk about making plans." If those plans involved activating the weapon, we had to use any lead we could to get it first.

Any lead . . . There had been genuine desperation in Aurelio's face as he mouthed pleas for help at me. Much as I loathed the thought of helping my aunt's murderer, finding the artifact was more important than any vengeful impulse I might have toward letting him boil in his own pot.

Which would require me talking to yet more demons. Whisper wasn't going to like that.

I'd be less worried if he hadn't been so very right the first time.

We stumbled back to the imperial wing to find it depressingly empty. We passed a tea tray someone had hastily set on an urn when the call came for all hands to throw on uniforms and accompany the Serene Envoy to face the queen; the cups on it stood cold. No one would ever drink them. Hastily discarded jackets lay cast over furniture where functionaries had tossed them when throwing on military uniforms, and papers still scattered a table along with a half-eaten plate of biscotti where some of the envoy's staff had abandoned a meeting. We were the last people left in the entire wing; no one else had returned alive.

Kessa searched the Serene Envoy's quarters and found an artifice key that raised our hopes for a moment, but it activated wards on the golden door that closed off the private section of the imperial wing, not the greater wards on the palace. Still, Foxglove not only raised those wards but sketched out an additional trap seal from a carefully positioned chair while Bastian worked on his injured leg.

"Moreni and Cortissa won't leave us alone just because Hunger told them to," he said when he'd finished, packing his artifice tools away with shaking hands. "This should deliver them a nasty surprise if they try to tamper with the wards."

"Good," Kessa said, with some asperity. "Now we can get some sleep."

"There's no time for sleep. Bastian and I need to design the modifications to turn the palace wards into a demon trap." He fumbled his brush; Kessa caught it before it hit the ground and gently returned it to him.

"Bed," she said firmly. "Any enchantments you design in this state will blow up in our faces."

She wasn't wrong. We were all a mess; my mind felt numb with shock and my whole body ached with exhaustion, and most of the others had been through worse than I had. It didn't take much chiding for Kessa to usher us all off to sleep.

I was the only one who didn't have nightmares.

When we dragged ourselves from our beds into a dreary gray morning, we found chisel marks at the edges of the warding symbols on the golden door, and a ring of scorch marks surrounding Foxglove's seal. It had saved us all from being murdered in the night.

FIFTEEN

A surprising number of people congregated in the palace gardens for the queen's morning court, but a dull pervasive horror had choked the social swirl of lively activity. Power hummed in the air like a note just below hearing; sometimes the water that streamed endlessly from the fountains turned dark as blood in the corner of my eye. The great tree spreading over the heart of the gardens had a sinister aspect to it, like a raptor mantling over its kill.

Gone were the throngs of courtiers strolling grandly along to make a spectacle of themselves. Commoners huddled in whispering knots, their plumes drooping dispiritedly, while nobles hovered around the queen in various orbits, like moths gathering the courage to fling themselves into the flame. Instead of flirting, couples comforted each other in nooks and corners, glancing around with hollowed eyes. One fine lady in panniers stifled a shriek and leaped back from some threat not everyone could see; a lord ripped off his resplendent brocade coat, crying out in horror at whatever he saw on it—Flames? Spiders?—and flung it into a fountain.

I lifted Foxglove's borrowed monocle to my eye and trained it on the crowd of courtiers—almost exclusively nobles in their shiny pale silks—clustered around the queen beneath the great tree. The demons had been selecting them in little handfuls to speak privately in the mirror maze, and every single courtier had gone willingly. They stumbled out later weeping and shaking, or were half dragged out, limp and sagging, by palace guards.

"I don't understand people," I muttered, blinking to adjust my surprised eye to how close everyone suddenly seemed. I trailed my gaze across glittering jewels and brocade, searching for the queen.

"Some of them refuse to see what's happening," Severin said, with the cynicism of someone well familiar with this particular power dynamic. "Some of them see it just fine, but think it won't happen to them."

We'd gulped down coffee and some day-old pastries Kessa had found in the imperial wing kitchen, then immediately split up: Bastian and Foxglove to work out the design for the ward trap, Kessa to get her new friend Girard alone to weasel information out of him, and Ashe to see whether any of the palace guard might have escaped silvering and be recruitable. Severin and I had the job of attempting to discover where the queen kept the ward key, but since everyone in the palace was cringing away from me as if I were a ravening war chimera after my rather public introduction as an atheling of Morgrain last night, we'd come equipped with Foxglove's listening and viewing devices so we could do our spying from outside conversational range.

"Also," Severin concluded with disgust, "from what I've overheard this morning, a fair number of those nobles are signing on with demons with their eyes open because Silene promised to kick the commoners out of the Curia. They'd rather give power over their country to demons than to merchants and tradespeople. Charming, really."

"Oh, there are plenty in Vaskandar who'd do the same thing if they were forced to share power with non-mages," I said darkly, focusing the monocle on the queen's silver-swathed figure. "It's—ah!"

I'd caught a gleam of artifice wire. Yes—a cluster of dainty artifice amulets adorned her pale chest, and front and center hung an elaborate jeweled key.

"She's got the cursed thing hanging right over her bosom," I muttered.

Severin flashed me a wicked grin. "That explains how you spotted it so quickly."

My face heated as I lowered the monocle. "I swear I'm not ogling demons, the gown styles in Loreice just..." I trailed off helplessly, snatching my hands back down before I could make regrettable gestures near my chest.

"Sounds like you're ogling demons to me," Severin observed.

"Look, the *point* is that it'd be hard to steal."

He let out a laugh that quickly faded to a bemused look. "It's still so strange," he said quietly. "I can't believe I'm plotting to steal something from a demon in some harebrained scheme to save the Loreician court."

"I have to admit I thought we'd have destroyed the artifact and be heading back to Castle Ilseine by now," I agreed ruefully. "This mission went up in flames rather quickly."

"No—or yes, but that's not what I meant." Severin gave me a sidelong sort of look. "You enjoy this, don't you? Not all the horrible things that have happened on this mission, but what the Rookery does in general. You *like* fixing other people's problems."

I blinked. "I suppose I do." Fixing other people's problems was most of what I'd done as Warden, come to think of it—that, and preventing them from occurring in the first place.

"You see, I find it profoundly irritating. My own problems give me enough trouble, and these people aren't even part of my domain." He shook his head. "It's why you fit in so well with the Rookery and I don't—why I'm not particularly interested in trying, to be honest. I don't know what I'm going to do with myself as an atheling in exile, but I know it won't be this."

He said it idly, staring off northward across the gardens, but the words hit me like a blow to the stomach. Granted, I planned to go back to being Warden of Gloamingard as soon as I could possibly manage it, but in the meantime, it felt so good to have found another home, perhaps even another family—and Severin, for all his prickly edges, was part of that.

Except that apparently he wasn't, and didn't want to be.

I spotted Kessa approaching across the lawn, her worried frown in stark contrast to her jaunty plumed hat. I seized on her arrival with relief; I was in no mood to poke around under the rock Severin had tipped up to find out what feelings crawled there.

"That was quick," I greeted her. "You look like you've learned yet another disturbing thing."

"Well, the good news is that I found Girard, and we had a nice chat." She sighed. "The bad news is that while he confirmed they do have the artifact somewhere in the palace, he doesn't know where it is."

"He sounds remarkably forthcoming," Severin said skeptically.

"Oh, he didn't say it in so many words. Give me some credit for subtlety." Kessa wagged a finger at him. "Now, the *worst* news is that I get the impression he was glad for the chance to leak a warning because he only learned what the artifact does last night and was appalled... Which likely means they were discussing plans to use it."

Severin went still. "We can't have much time, then."

"We can still find it." I said it as much to ease the tightening in my own chest as to reassure Severin. "I'll try talking to Aurelio."

"That's a novel approach." Severin's brows lifted. "Sure, talk to Aurelio. Maybe we should ask Moreni, too, while we're at it."

"He's the only lead I have." Never mind the sick dread accumulating in my gut at the thought of talking to Aurelio at all, let alone Hunger, who would perforce be part of the conversation.

"What about Whisper?" Kessa put in. "Do you think he might help? Seems like there's a decent chance the Zenith Society would want to use this thing on Morgrain, and that's his home, too."

"Oh, yes, let's ask *all* the demons." Severin shook his head.

"I . . . I'm not sure. He's so adamant about staying neutral." My instinct was to say no, flat-out, but Kessa had a point: with Morgrain potentially on the line, his priorities might change. "I don't know if I can find him quickly, though."

"That's another point that concerns me." Severin's face hardened. "We don't know what he talked about with the other demons last night. We don't know where he is this morning. I'm willing to grant that overall he's been helpful, but frankly the idea that the Demon of Death is now here as well, being chatty with Nightmare, Madness, and Hunger, is more than a little alarming."

Fierce words in Whisper's defense leaped to my tongue, but I let them go. Whisper, of all the beings of terrible power I'd met, didn't need defending.

"You're right," I said quietly instead. "Half the Hells are here, putting their heads together. I'm scared, too."

Kessa elbowed me, tipping her head toward a page boy in silver livery who approached us at a trot, a creamy square of paper in his hand. He looked like the same thatch-headed boy who'd held Bramant's chair; his eyes seemed mercifully free of silver, alight with nothing more sinister than determination to perform his duty. He bowed to me and extended the paper in his hand.

"Lady Ryxander of Morgrain," he said, his voice trembling just a bit on the dread name of my home. "An invitation from the queen."

I stared at him, my heart sinking through increasingly murky layers as if I'd dropped it to the bottom of a pond.

"There must be some mistake." I didn't think for a second there was a mistake, but I could hope.

He shook the paper at me, ever so slightly, as if I might not have seen it. "No, my lady, it's for you. Tea with Her Majesty, this evening."

I reached out and took the letter with as much wariness as if I were plucking it from a war chimera's maw. "Ah. Thank you."

The boy bowed again, crisp and buoyant, and trotted off.

"Bloody pox," I said.

"Don't go," Severin urged the moment the boy was gone. "I can push you off a balcony and break your leg if you need an excuse."

"Tempting." My stomach had clenched up until it felt hard and small as a walnut.

"I'm serious." Severin frowned. "I'm normally all for chatting with your enemy and seeing whether you can tease any information from them. But not in a situation like this, where they've already shown us what they're willing to do in private conversations and you'd have no way to make a quick exit."

"I assure you, I've got no intention of walking into this trap, no matter how politely they ask." I crumpled the card, hiding it in my fist.

"Good," Severin said, with clear relief.

I wished I could feel any myself. I harbored no illusions that this was an invitation I could so easily decline.

"Speaking of the queen, have you found the key?" Kessa asked. By the way her glance flicked to the paper peeking between my fingers before landing on the group of courtiers beneath the tree, I suspected she had her own thoughts on the tea party but was waiting until Severin wasn't around to share them. A spy might have a very different perspective on what we stood to gain from such an invitation.

"As it happens, Ryx was so riveted by..." Severin broke off before my ears had a chance to start burning. "Ah. Sorry for the bad timing, but I have to go receive a report."

I followed his gaze. A gray tabby cat sat under a bench, staring at him. When I met its eyes, it looked away, pretending not to be interested.

"One of your scouts?"

"Yes. I've been waiting for this one; I had him searching for the artifact." Severin sighed. "Though I suppose there's an equal chance he just wants more fish. I've been feeding the palace cats."

I blinked at him, distracted. "You're feeding the palace cats in the middle of a demon crisis?"

"Look, someone has to do it. Since that guard who said she was feeding them turned up with silver eyes yesterday morning, I didn't want them to..." A trace of the smile I was trying to suppress must have shown on my face, because he drew himself up haughtily. "I'm gaining their loyalty so I can use them in scouting and stealth missions."

"Of course," I said, as seriously as I could manage. "I'm certain that's the only reason."

"It could be a very important report, if he's found the weapon. Oh, stop looking at me like that!" He threw up his hands and stalked off toward the cat.

I exchanged amused glances with Kessa. It was almost enough to make me feel better. But the mangled square of stiff paper remained in my hand, its edges digging into my skin, more dangerous than any knife.

Once Severin was gone, Kessa cast a final glance after him and angled between me and the great tree, worry creasing her brow. "Ryx," she murmured, "be careful. The queen—Madness—she's staring at you. She's been watching you this whole time."

I couldn't help it; I looked. Sure enough, the queen's distant pale face turned in my direction, her wide eyes seeming to suck in all the space between us and devour it, pulling me toward her as surely as a child yanking on a tablecloth might drag a glass to the edge.

I quickly turned away, my mouth dry. "That's alarming."

"A bit, yes." Kessa grimaced. "Let's go for a walk and interrupt her line of sight. Severin can catch up."

"Right," I agreed, my nerves tingling.

Kessa and I followed the white shell paths away from the tree, deeper into the conversation gardens where subdued knots of courtiers gathered to speak in low tones. I still hadn't gotten used to the rustling cloud of skirts I moved in, or the sword, which had an annoying tendency to slowly drift too far forward on its fashionably slender belt and need correction so it wouldn't foul my stride. I drew a lot of glances; fans snapped open to hide whispers, reminding me of the flicking fingers of the warding sign that followed in my wake back home.

Well, at least I was used to it. Unlike my other, more disturbing source of unwanted attention.

Ashe found us before we'd gone far, striding up to us in a hedge circle centered on a false fountain with an extravagantly joyful pod of leaping bronze dolphins and blue-tinted glass frozen in intricately rendered motion instead of real water. Hells, *she'd* better not have some disturbing revelation, too.

"I couldn't find a single damned guard left without silver eyes," she reported, without preamble. "Tried talking to some of them anyway, but it was pointless. I think they're not much more than puppets."

Kessa grimaced. "That's unfortunate, but not surprising."

"They don't go down easy, either," Ashe added, rubbing her knuckles.

Kessa and I stared at her, aghast.

"What! I had to find out," Ashe protested. "It was science."

"Please tell me you didn't kill anyone," I said, trying to sound calm and reasonable.

"No, no. Knocked him out and stashed him under a bush." Ashe grinned. "The best part is I'm pretty sure their brains are too addled for him to report me."

Kessa sighed. "So much for getting the guard on our side. They're going to be a problem when it comes time to evacuate."

"Maybe," Ashe said. "They seem pretty suggestible. I bet you could come up with something clever." She gave us a jaunty salute. "What next? I'm free for a new mission."

"Why don't you check to see whether Bastian and Foxglove are close to done with the ward alteration designs?" I suggested. "As soon as they're ready to start carving, we have to get moving. That's the single piece that's going to take the longest of this whole puzzle."

Ashe hesitated, the moment stretching on. At last, her grin fell into a scowl. "Bit hard to talk to Bastian when he's flinching from me like he expects me to rip his arms off any minute."

"He'll come around," Kessa reassured her. "He just needs time."

"I can't even blame him, given some of the stuff the Furies did to people like him." Ashe shook her head.

"But *you* didn't do any of that," Kessa reminded her. "You quit over it."

Ashe gave Kessa a long, level look. "I quit, sure. But that's not enough." She slumped into a sort of crouch on the base of the fountain. "I promised myself I'd protect him, to help make up for the chimeras I couldn't protect. That I'd always keep him safe."

"Seems like you're keeping him safe right now," I observed.

"He's so *soft*, though." Ashe made squishing motions with her hands. "Strong enough to break me in half, and probably faster than me if he really tried, and who knows what else—but a complete cream puff. And he's scared of me. What do I do with that?"

Kessa put her hands on Ashe's shoulders and planted a gentle kiss on her forehead. "What you're already doing. A fantastic job."

"Hmph," Ashe said. But her ears went pink. "Oh, fine. I'll go check on him."

I could feel the queen's eyes on me, even with trees between us. Her attention ran cobwebby fingers whispering across the edges of my mind.

"We should move on," I said quietly to Kessa, once Ashe was on her way. "Madness is still watching me."

Kessa nodded, with a lingering glance after Ashe. "How unrelentingly creepy of her. All right. They say demons balk at running water; let's put some fountains between you."

No matter what course we chose, the queen's attention still prickled at the edges of my senses. Even circling to the far side of the mirror maze building didn't seem enough, with its glittering bulk *and* the massive tree *and* a fair bit of distance between us and Madness. It was no good; I'd have to hope she got distracted by something else and get back to business. I turned to Kessa to ask whether she had any ideas for how to steal the ward key.

I'd caught her with her guard down. She stared off across the gardens with lines and hollows of exhaustion cutting into her lovely face, the sparkle dulled in her kind brown eyes. I swallowed my question and asked a different one.

"How are you doing?" I was unpracticed at being gentle, but I tried to sound sympathetic.

Her face transformed immediately; she flashed me a bright smile. "Oh, I'm fine! I'm just worried about everyone else."

We'd reached a towering stone fountain, a moss-slicked bulk of a coiling sea monster with water trickling down over its sides from its roaring mouth into a great pool. Its eyes bulged with rage, a bronze ship trapped in its coils with tiny bronze people tumbling to their doom. Incongruous lilies floated in the pool, and sparrows fluttered at the rim.

I stopped and gave Kessa my full attention. "No, really. You can tell me. I don't need to lean on you, like the others do; I won't be upset."

"I…" Her chin quivered, and suddenly her eyes were damp. She dragged a sleeve brutally across them. "Oh, this is ridiculous. I just… Nobody ever calls me on it, because they'd rather accept the lie." She gave me a shaky smile, this one much truer, with pain underneath it. "I'm a wreck, thank you for asking."

Kessa liked touching people. She probably needed a hug or something. I tried patting her shoulder. "I see you caring for the rest of them all the time, but you're going through the same things—the Zenith Society, the nightmares. That's got to be exhausting."

"A bit, yes." She gave a small, rueful laugh. "But I'm better at functioning through this kind of thing than the rest of the Rookery. After Loren died, I had a bad bout of melancholia, you see. Lost a month to it, like a long bad dream. Foxglove helped pull me out of it, giving me a purpose, helping me get elixirs and mental training so I'd be ready the next time it hit—and it turns out that training is remarkably useful for putting aside all Nightmare's nasty images and feelings as well." She lifted her hat and smoothed back her hair, letting out a breath that held no small amount of tension. "So it's like anything else. Since I'm the one with the relevant skills, I've got to do the job; in this case, that job is keeping everyone else from falling apart."

"Just because you're better at it than the others doesn't mean it's not hard," I said.

Her mouth twisted wryly. "It would be easier if I were still as thoughtless as I was five years ago, and didn't feel like I had to hold them all up with my own hands. My arms do get tired, emotionally speaking."

"You? Thoughtless?" I shook my head. The idea was impossible. "You're the kindest person I've ever known."

"That's very nice of you, but let me assure you, I used to be… well, very young, and very caught up in being a spy. Always the star role in my own show."

"I can't imagine that," I protested.

"People change, Ryx." Her gaze left mine, going soft and sad. It landed on the stone sea serpent looming above us, with far-away sympathy, as if she understood that sometimes everything became too much and you had to drown some sailors. "I lost Loren because I was so wrapped up in my own cleverness at discovering the Zenith Society's secrets that it didn't occur to me that I'd put him in danger. Now...well, now all I want is to play a supporting role. There's a great satisfaction to it—keeping the others going, helping them stay whole when the world tries to break them."

"Still," I said, my heart aching, "you shouldn't have to carry them all by yourself."

"I know." Her mouth twisted wryly. "It'd be easier if they weren't all so..." She broke off, staring past my shoulder, her eyes going wide. "Blood of the Eldest. It's *him*."

An all too familiar figure was heading directly toward us, his Falconer's uniform exchanged for a scarlet coat in the Loreician style, so thick with decadent gold embroidery and pearl accents that the cloth barely showed through. A golden clip held back his short auburn ponytail, though his beard was less neat now, as if he'd neglected it.

Aurelio. My friend, my enemy, my would-be murderer.

"Why don't you go find Severin and see whether that cat was really reporting anything?" I stepped between them, my jaw tightening. "I'll talk to this traitor."

SIXTEEN

I met Aurelio beside the glittering jagged swirls of the mirror-chip mosaics on the back wall of the maze building, trying to swallow enough of my anger to appear civil. *Information*, I reminded myself. *You need information. He has it.*

"Hello, Ryx," he greeted me, exhaustion dragging at his voice. New hollows dug shadowy pits beneath his eyes. "I admit I was surprised to find you here last night. I'd have thought nothing could drag you away from Gloamingard right now."

That stung. I wasn't sure what was worse—the implication that I'd fallen short of what he expected from me as Warden, or the way he said it. Casual and rueful, with his usual Aurelio voice in his usual Aurelio way, as if he were still the person I'd thought he was and our friendship hadn't been a lie.

"My grandmother kicked me out," I snapped, rattled. "What about *you*? I thought all you wanted was to protect the Serene Empire. It seems odd to find you involved in overthrowing the government of an imperial client state."

He winced. "That was Madness and Nightmare. They'd already taken over by the time we arrived."

It was always someone else's fault, with Aurelio: he was acting on orders, it wasn't his idea, he was terribly sorry. Was that how it came to this? He'd seemed decent enough, when we sat on the terrace together and shared our dreams years ago. Perhaps he'd slipped a little more each day, contorting himself further and further to not look in the mirror and see what he was doing.

"*We*. Do you mean the Zenith Society? Or your new friend, the Demon of Hunger?" I couldn't quench the anger that burned in my chest, and I didn't want to. But seasons witness, what a waste. "You became a murderer because you wanted to protect the Empire, and now you're working to destroy it. And I thought *I* made a mess of things."

Aurelio stared at me in helpless anguish. He leaned against the wall of the building next to us, his fingers nervously tracing the patterns of the mosaics. "I'll admit I've made some mistakes."

That did it. So much for diplomacy; I cared too much. "A mistake is when you knock over a bottle of wine and break it. Carefully coating arrows with rare paralytic poison and firing them repeatedly into someone before cutting her throat is not a *mistake*."

"Look, I'd say I'm sorry, but we both know that's not enough." His fingers dug into the mosaic chips as if he might pry them off the building.

I spread my hands. "Then what do we do?"

He drew in a breath as if gathering strength. "I was hoping you could help me with something."

I struggled to master my anger. This was too important; I needed what Aurelio knew, and he apparently needed something from me. But I couldn't seem too easily mollified, either. "I hope you're aware of the audacity of you asking me that."

"Extremely. But it's a little thing, for you. Important to me." He grimaced. "Please, Ryx. I know this is going to sound foolish, given everything that's going on, but I don't know who else to turn to." He flicked his gaze toward the strange building, an odd tension entering his voice. "I can't ask anyone in the Zenith Society. It's a personal matter. I need to write to my father."

That blindsided me. "What?"

At last I realized: Aurelio's hand was still moving on the wall, still tracing the same patterns.

Letters.

"I want to try to explain to my father what's happened," he said, choosing his words with slow care, his eyes burning urgently into mine. "I don't know how to tell him that his own son has a demon in him—sharing my eyes and ears at all times, seeing and hearing everything I do."

I got the message: Hunger was listening to us. I worked my jaw, trying to look as if I'd just turned away from him in anger, not because I was staring at the movement of his finger. It wasn't hard; I was genuinely furious.

T...A...R...T... He'd better not be trying a bizarrely elaborate method to insult me. He kept tracing more letters on the wall—*I...F...A...C...*—and then started over again. *Tarty face?* Really?

Hells, it wasn't an insult. I'd been starting with the wrong letter. *ARTIFACT.*

I had to keep talking, to avoid rousing Hunger's suspicion. "Have you tried asking him to leave?" I asked, striving to still sound annoyed despite my pounding heart.

He let out a despairing sort of laugh, slapping the side of the building. "Oh, he could leave at any time, if he chose. But then he'd simply take a new host. No, I'm doing Eruvia a service by continuing our partnership."

His finger traced a new word, as his stare remained fixed urgently on me. *D...A...N...G...E...R.*

That was hardly news, but of course he couldn't be sure I knew about the doomsday artifact. I tried to think of a way to ask where it was without being too obvious.

Before I could frame one, Aurelio's eyes hardened, and he straightened away from the wall. "Which reminds me," he said, all the weary urgency gone from his voice, "I still haven't forgiven you for ripping me out of my vessel earlier. That was rude."

Kessa. He meant Kessa. This was Hunger again. The dread of realizing I was speaking to a demon mixed with frustration—I'd been so close to learning something from Aurelio.

Anger made me bold. "You were trying to *kill my friend*," I said through my teeth. "That's even more rude."

"*Friends*. Such a foolish human concept." He traced a finger idly up the wall beside him, unconsciously mimicking Aurelio's movements; in its wake, the bright reflections of the mirror chips faded, as if a cloud had passed over the sun. "Your little trick worked because I was startled. Now I know what you are, and what you can do. So let me warn you: we've learned from the Dark Days. Do you doubt for a moment that any one of us could destroy this palace and everyone in it as easily as a mortal draws breath?"

A chill settled on my heart. "No."

"Then why haven't we?"

By the avaricious gleam in his eye, I knew my answer. "Because that's not what you want. That was never what you wanted. You want to *possess* this world, not destroy it."

"Exactly." He laid a hand over Aurelio's heart, an affectation he must have learned from humans. "It's so unspeakably *boring* back home in the Hells. It didn't seem so bad before we knew there was more; but now that we've tasted all the glorious complexities of physical existence and sampled the exquisite palette of human life, we'll do anything to stay here. *Anything*, including destroying anyone who might try to stop us. Do you understand me?"

"I've been threatened before," I said stiffly. "I'm familiar with the procedure."

"Then you know that if you act against us, you risk those *friends* you value so highly." He curled his hand closed, and the air seemed to grow thin in my lungs, as if I were up on a high mountain. "Yes, we learned many things from the Dark Days. One was that human attachments are a great vulnerability."

"Why are you bothering to threaten me at all?" I crossed my

arms to cover the hollow of fear in my stomach. "You said it yourself—you could destroy us all with a thought. Shouldn't we be beneath your notice?"

Hunger laughed, as if what I'd said was genuinely surprising and delightful. Then he reached out before I realized what he was doing and laid Aurelio's hand on my cheek.

For one brief instant a sickening emptiness pulled at me, like the feeling of missing a step, or the dizzy swarming rush of trying to stand up when you've lost too much blood. I twitched my face away, and it stopped at once.

His power worked on me better than the more ephemeral mind magic of Madness and Nightmare did, it seemed. That made this game I was playing even more dangerous.

"Oh, we've noticed you." His tone was amused, almost caressing. "Believe me, Ryxander of Morgrain, we've noticed."

My face was icy cold where he'd touched me. Cold, too, was the certainty in my mind: he *knew* something—whatever it was Whisper hadn't wanted the demons to figure out.

I know what you are, he'd said. I stared into his wicked, mocking eyes in horror. If he thought I was a Grace, like Bastian did, I was in deep trouble.

His face twisted, and Aurelio let out a long, frustrated sigh. "I'm sorry, Ryx. He keeps interrupting."

I blinked at him. Aurelio again. "What...what were we talking about?"

"My letter. The one to my father." He held my gaze urgently. "Please, won't you help me?"

I gave a slow, cautious nod. "All right."

"I know how I want to start it, but I'm not sure where to go from there."

Aurelio's hands trembled as he laid out an inkwell, pen, and paper on a gleaming wooden table in a quiet corner of the royal library. The old king's fanciful aesthetics hadn't reached here; it was an older, truer part of the palace. Wooden shelves reared around us, wrapping us in privacy and the scent of dusty old books, their end panels carved with scenes of scholars studying, the Grace of Wisdom unrolling her scroll, even a whimsical detail of a cat balancing on top of a teetering pile of books. Afternoon light streamed golden through the tall narrow windows, dust dancing in the beams. It would have been a pleasant place to spend time with a friend, if the friend hadn't deeply betrayed you and wasn't hosting a demon.

"Show me what you've got," I suggested, every muscle locked tight. I'd have to lean closer to Aurelio to see what he wrote. Once I would have been thrilled to be able to safely do so; now the idea was repellent. I forced myself to bend, stiff and creaking as an old dry branch.

Aurelio caught my eye, dipped his pen, and began to write with a sort of utilitarian elegance.

Dear Father, he began.

I wished I knew what his gambit was with this letter. I prepared to look for clues—maybe the beginning letter of each word would spell something.

Pretend I'm writing to my father, Aurelio continued, his gaze flicking up from the paper to meet mine, an urgent plea in his eyes. *Hunger shares my senses, but not my thoughts, and he can only read ancient Ostan runes. The Raverran phonetic alphabet didn't exist yet in the Dark Days. This was the only way I could think of to talk to you without him hearing.*

I stared at the paper, then at Aurelio, a shock of hope coursing through my veins.

"Is that too formal?" Aurelio asked, his voice stretched a bit thin. "What do you think? He *is* my father."

"Given the depth and gravity of your mistakes, a little formality isn't misplaced," I said, my heart pounding.

Aurelio nodded as if this were great wisdom and kept writing. *I need help and I don't know who else to ask. I know you have good reason to hate me.*

I let out a short, bitter laugh. "That part's certainly true."

Aurelio's fingers tightened on the pen. He dipped it in the ink again, the nib clicking against the jar. *Fine. But we can still help each other. Hunger is TERRIBLE. I want him gone, too.*

His writing paused. He looked up at me, desperate. "This is the part where I'm hoping you can help me."

"Hmm." I made a pretense of thought, laying a finger beside my temple. So he wanted Hunger out—not just gone from him, but banished, if his earlier comment about doing a service to Eruvia by hosting him had any grain of truth. Much as the idea of working with Aurelio galled me, having Hunger's vessel as an ally against him could be a big advantage.

Except that the trap we currently had planned for the demons would seal Aurelio inside the palace with all three of them, which I doubted was the kind of help he was looking for.

I held out a hand. "Might I suggest some phrasing?"

Aurelio passed me the pen. I leaned over, my skin cringing away from his nearness, and wrote: *The Rookery is working on finding a way to banish the demons, and I assure you that if we do, we'd be thrilled to work with you to toss Hunger back through the gate like a chewed-up chicken bone. Do you have any idea how the Graces got rid of him in the Dark Days?*

Aurelio shook his head glumly. "I have no idea. What to write next, that is."

"Maybe try something like this, then." I dipped the pen again and pressed down too hard, the nib digging into the paper. *If you really want to help against Hunger, tell me what his plans are. Back there you were trying to warn me about the artifact.*

Aurelio started to reach for the pen, then hesitated. "If I tell my father about that, he could get in trouble. All my friends in the Zenith Society could."

"I think it's far too late to worry about that," I said, holding his eyes. "This isn't a situation *anyone* is getting out of without making sacrifices, Aurelio. Not your friends, not me, not you."

He chewed his lip. "You have to promise—"

"You're the one who asked me for help with this letter. I don't think I have to promise anything." I tried to sound disinterested, and hoped he couldn't tell how my heart was racing. This was the first lead we'd had on the artifact, and we were almost out of time to stop a massive catastrophe; I was ready to tackle Aurelio to the ground if he tried to leave without passing along what he knew.

"It's important," Aurelio protested.

I gestured to the paper. "If it's that important, I think you need to tell him."

Aurelio closed his eyes a moment, then began to write. *Do you know about the artifact the Zenith Society stole? And what it's designed to do?*

"Yes," I said, peering over his shoulder as if I approved of his words.

Do you know how Hunger wants to use it?

I braced my palms on the table. "I'm not so sure about that part."

Aurelio drew in a ragged breath. His hand hesitated as if he had to write the next words across razor blades. Finally, he continued. *The Zenith Society has an artificer with them here, Lutani. Skilled but without the mage mark. He's modifying the artifact for Hunger—removing the part that produces the killing pulse and reversing the polarity of the part that delivers energy to the network of life linking a Witch Lord to their domain.*

I frowned. "That part you just wrote is a bit strange. Are you sure it makes sense?"

"Think about it," Aurelio said, his voice rough with some suppressed emotion. The pen trembled in his hand. "It'll come to you."

I didn't know much about artifice. Reversing the polarity sounded like he meant changing the direction of the flow of power. So he wanted to use this artifact to somehow draw on the web of life magic in a domain to power something, instead of delivering a killing burst? That sounded relatively benign compared to wiping out all life in a domain. Unless...

I grabbed the pen from his hand. Beneath his words, I scrawled, *Hunger? Does Hunger want to use this to drain all the life out of a domain?*

Aurelio nodded, his face twisting bitterly. "Now you get the gist of what I'm trying to say."

But why? I was tearing the paper, too agitated to care. It was all I could do not to spill the ink as I dipped the pen again. *Can't Hunger drain the life out of everything around him anyway? Why does he need an artifact?*

"Not bad, but I want to add some details." Aurelio took the pen back. *His range is nowhere near great enough to get a whole domain at once. The demons consider the Witch Lords a potential threat, and Moreni offered up the artifact as a way to destroy them. Hunger is thrilled at the idea of getting to glut himself on so many lives.*

I stared queasily at the terrible words in Aurelio's swooping handwriting. This was worse. Somehow, they'd found a way to make it even worse than simply killing every living thing in a small country; Hunger was going to *consume* them.

"When?" I breathed. Aurelio shot me an alarmed glance, and I cleared my throat. "When are you going to send this letter? How long do we have to work on it?"

A variety of emotions chased each other across Aurelio's face, settling at last on cold disdain.

He threw the pen down. "How long, indeed. You're wasting my time, boy."

Hunger again. No, this was terrible—I had to get Aurelio back. He hadn't told me where the artifact was yet.

I swallowed. "It's important to him."

"It's not important to me." Hunger pushed back his chair, preparing to rise. "Sharing a body like this has its advantages—there's no risk of merging with your host, like poor Discord did, *ugh*. But I despise having to sit through boring human foolishness."

Suddenly, he gripped the table as if to hold himself in the chair, his knuckles going white. "Just a few minutes," Aurelio pleaded. "We're nearly done. I was planning to send this *tomorrow*, so there's not much time. Let me write just a few more lines."

My heart seemed to contract to half its usual size. *Tomorrow.* Holy Hells. "I think we can finish it in just a few minutes," I agreed, my mouth dry.

For a few agonizing seconds, Aurelio was still, gripping the table and braced as if for a blow. Then he let out a long, relieved breath and seized up the pen again.

"Let me finish this off quickly, and you can tell me if it looks good," he said, his voice quavering.

They mean to test it to see if Lutani's modifications work, he wrote. *They picked a Witch Lord they think no one likes, and a domain they think is short on allies, in the hopes that this won't unite the Witch Lords against them.*

My stomach knotted tighter and tighter. Morgrain—he must mean Morgrain. Everyone was turning against us because Grandmother was a demon.

But Aurelio wrote, *They're targeting the Shrike Lord of Alevar.*

Holy Hells. *Severin.*

I gripped the back of his chair. "Where is the ... your father located? If he's hard to find, this letter may not reach him promptly." My words came out hoarse and strained. If Hunger was any good at reading people, he must realize I was upset; I had to hope his utter lack of empathy would serve me well for a change.

"I'll write out the address." Aurelio's pen moved to the top of the page.

On the mantelpiece, queen's bedroom, royal wing.

Well, pox. "That's a hard address to deliver to," I managed, after a moment.

"I've done what I can by writing this," Aurelio said, his voice shaky. He lifted his eyes to mine, full of doubt and remorse and fear. "All I can do now is trust in the postal service to get it done."

The postal service indeed. It seemed the Rookery had been promoted.

"Thank you," I told him, then hastily added, "for reaching out like this. It means a lot to me." It was strange and uncomfortable, feeling gratitude to Aurelio. What he'd done was unforgivable—but if the risk he'd taken let us save Severin and all of Alevar, it might be difficult to hold on to even the most deadly of personal grievances. "I'll work on helping you with that thing you mentioned, too."

Now we had to find a way to get into the queen's bedchamber and steal the artifact tonight, or Severin—and every other living thing born in Alevar, down to the smallest blade of grass— would die.

SEVENTEEN

Severin stared at me, drowning darkness in his eyes. Everyone else stared at Severin. The clocks in the Serene Envoy's sitting room ticked, the sound measuring and filling the silence.

"We have until tomorrow," I concluded, desperate to put some hope back in his face. "We can still stop this."

Severin's teacup sagged in his numb hands. I reached to try to catch it, but he set it on the mantel beside him instead of letting it slip from his fingers. It took him two tries, the cup rattling against the marble.

"I see." His throat jumped.

Foxglove had gone very still. "You're certain they're going to do it? No chance this is a bluff."

"Yes."

Severin slumped against the wall. "I dislike my brother as much as anyone, but I hadn't realized he was so universally loathed that anyone would eradicate my entire domain to get to him and expect no one to care."

"They're wrong about that," I said grimly. "The act itself is too appalling—and too dangerous. Even the Shrike Lord's most virulent enemies would unite to destroy them."

"I'd have said nothing could bring together the whole Conclave, but that'd do it," Kessa agreed, her eyes wide. "We'd see the Eldest unleash their full power, and all nineteen Witch Lords."

Ashe coughed. "Eighteen, at that point. But yeah. The Eldest versus the demons—I'd watch that fight. From several countries away."

"Forgive me if it's not much consolation that we'd be avenged." Severin's face hardened from shock to anger. "Curse my brother. It should never have come to this." He gripped the mantel so hard his fingertips paled. "Hells, I'm the heir. I should have *kept* it from coming to this."

"It hasn't come to anything, yet," I said sharply. "And it won't. We're going to stop them. We know where the artifact is; we'll tear down the whole palace and pick it out of the wreckage if we have to."

"We might." Kessa took her hat off and turned it thoughtfully in her hands as if this were any other problem we could think through and fix. "Getting into the queen's bedroom is going to be difficult. It's as if they don't want spies and assassins in there."

"Inconsiderate of them." I sank into an empty chair. My legs were trembling from the sheer nervous energy of having had to tell Severin they were targeting his home. "But surely there's got to be a way."

"We'll find one," Foxglove said. "This takes priority over the key and the wards; we throw everything we've got at breaking in there." He looked as if he very much wanted to get up and pace. He started to heave his wounded leg down from the footstool on which it rested, experimentally; sweat bloomed on his temples, and he hissed and settled it back in place. "There are two main obstacles."

"Just two?" Kessa's brows lifted. "Let me guess: their names are Madness and Nightmare."

"The demons are one," Foxglove agreed. "The servants' corridor we used last time doesn't go back into the queen's private quarters, only as far as the royal audience chambers. We can't sneak past them if they're in the private apartments; we're going to need some kind of distraction to keep them out of there."

An idea began unfolding in my mind, slow and terrible as the petals of a poisonous flower. I didn't like it one bit, but it made an awful kind of sense.

"I'm assuming the second obstacle is the wards," Bastian said, without raising his eyes from his lap. He'd picked a chair as far away from Ashe as possible when I called the Rookery together, and seemed to be avoiding looking at anyone but Foxglove and Kessa.

"Yes." Foxglove grimaced. "They're too good. I can't crack them. We need someone to let us through."

My sense of foreboding deepening, I reached into my pocket. "I can get us in. I have an invitation."

I laid the crumpled ball of the tea party invitation on a drink table and smoothed it out for all to see.

"Perfect," Foxglove approved.

"Not perfect," Severin objected, straightening. "I'm obviously desperate to get this artifact, but that's a terrible idea."

"Listen to the man with his life on the line, Ryx." Kessa gave me an alarmed look. "Are you sure about this? I know you're jaded at the idea of being in a room with demons because you grew up with the *Demon of Death in your house*—which I still can't wrap my mind around, by the way—but this little tea party sounds incredibly dangerous."

"Believe me, I'm not excited for it," I said. "But I'm not going to sit back and let an entire domain become a lifeless wasteland because I didn't want to put myself at risk. This is our way in; let's use it. I don't want you to die, Severin."

He slashed the air with an angry hand. "And I don't want you to throw your life away for me!"

Silence fell over the sitting room. He stared at me as if I were the only one there, his breath coming fast and angry. The clocks ticked, counting out the seconds slipping away until Hunger unleashed devastation on Alevar and it was too late.

"I'm not throwing my life away." I tried to sound calm and reasonable, but I couldn't quite keep the quaver out of my voice. "And I'm not doing it for you."

Something flickered in Severin's eyes. Hurt? Relief? His expression closed, and I couldn't tell.

"Fair enough," he said softly.

"Listen," Foxglove cut in, his deep voice steady. "Whatever the demons want with Ryx, they could just walk up and do it. They don't *need* to invite her to a tea party. Whatever danger accepting this invitation might put her in, she's likely in more if she declines it."

I gestured to Foxglove. "As he says. I'm not happy that I've attracted their attention, but I may as well use it to save lives." I tried to force a smile, but I could tell it didn't come out right. "At least this way, I might get tea out of it."

Bastian cleared his throat, looking nervous at speaking up in the middle of our argument. "Do we know *why* the demons seem to be so interested in you, Ryx?"

A light kindled in Foxglove's deep amber eyes. "I'd lay odds they've got the same theory you do."

It was the very thought I'd been trying to put out of my head since talking to Hunger in the gardens.

"I'm no Grace," I protested, but it sounded weak even to me.

"Are you so sure?" Foxglove's eyes burned with intensity. "The demons would know better than anyone. They've seen it before." He straightened in his seat. "It fits together. You shrugged off the combined power of Madness and Nightmare; you banished Hunger from Kessa when he tried to possess her. There's no denying that for whatever reason, your magic is effective against them in ways that nothing else is."

"Because it's *broken*." My fingernails dug into my palms. "Look, I'm happy to use this resistance I've got to draw them away from the artifact. Just don't pin your hopes on me. I've made too many mistakes." All my life I'd wished someone would have faith in me, and now that they did, it was terrifying.

Whatever Bastian saw in my face, it made him grimace and rise suddenly to his feet. "Ryx, can I have a quick word in private?"

Foxglove and Severin gave him odd looks, but Bastian ignored them, keeping his gaze fixed on me with a sort of desperate sincerity.

"All right," I agreed.

We headed into the adjoining formal dining room, large enough to host a party of fifty; I could feel Severin's eyes on my back as we left, as sure as if he'd rested his hand there. After we'd moved out of earshot, Bastian stopped by a massive ornamental vase and met my gaze square on at last.

"I'm not sure how to say this, but... Well, I think Foxglove *is* pinning too many hopes on you."

My heart sank. I forced a laugh. "At least I'm used to disappointing people."

"No, no, I didn't mean that." Bastian waved his hands, eyes widening. "I'm not worried you'll fail to meet his expectations. I'm worried that he's pressuring you into a dangerous situation because he wants to find out whether you can deliver a miracle."

His words struck a jarring chord. My grandmother had done almost the same thing—seeking to put me in danger in the hopes that I'd unleash my power. I wished I'd never heard Bastian's cursed theory that I might be somehow like the Graces; now I was seeing confirmation of it everywhere, even though I *knew* it was just my brain seizing on a pattern and trying to make all the pieces fit.

"And what do *you* think?" I asked, not bothering to hide my skepticism. "It's your theory, after all. Do you agree with Foxglove that I'm some kind of... heir to the Graces?"

Bastian winced. "Foxglove is a man of faith."

"And you're not?" I held his gaze, waiting for him to tell me this whole idea was ridiculous.

Bastian hesitated, his dark eyes going clouded. "I used to be. My parents raised me to pray to the Graces. But when I...well. How shall I put this?" His mouth twisted in something that was not a smile. "When Cortissa gave me my new skin, first she... she took off the old one."

It took me a too-long second to realize it wasn't a metaphor. My hands flew up to cover my mouth, and I stared at him in horror. "Oh Hells, Bastian."

"Yes, it was, ah...it took a long time. The song I've been hearing—she sang that while she did it." He looked down at his hands, laced together over his stomach; his knuckles had gone white. "I prayed, Ryx. I begged the Graces to save me. And, well..." He sighed. "I suppose I'd prefer to believe the Graces were more or less human, and are passed away and gone now, rather than that they possess the divine power to help me but instead stood by and let her do that."

I couldn't move past the sheer horror of it. "And you had to face her yesterday. I'm so sorry."

He winced, his eyes dropping from mine. "I won't deny I'm a bit of a mess this morning. But that's not what I meant to talk about. The point is that normally I'd look to Foxglove for a completely rational assessment of risk, but he might be a bit, ah, compromised here. I agree with you that we may not have any other workable plan, but I don't think this one is safe."

"I know it's not." I was too aware, in fact, the knowledge twining in my stomach like I'd swallowed a live snake. "But it's what we've got to do to save Alevar." *And Severin.*

"Well, then." Bastian gave me an odd sort of smile. "So long as you know what you're getting into. We're the Rookery, after all; unsafe plans are our specialty."

We started back toward the sitting room together. But just as we reached the door, Severin came storming out of it, the gray rings of his mage mark smoking in his eyes.

"Severin!" I stopped, surprised; Bastian cast a glance at both of us and scurried into the sitting room. "Where are you going?" It seemed a better question than my first instinct of *are you all right*, since the answer to that was clearly *no*.

He paused, pent-up violence gathered in every line of his body. "To show the Zenith Society what happens when you threaten my domain."

"You're not going to *challenge* them," I protested, stepping in front of him in alarm.

"Do I look like a suicidal fool?" he snapped. "No, I'm not going to challenge them. I'm going to *ruin* them. They're going to learn what it means to face the wrath of a Furwitch."

I recognized the fury boiling off him; I'd be as incandescent with anger if it were Morgrain. But that only alarmed me more, because I knew all the rash things I'd be willing to do in his place. "What do you mean, ruin them?"

"Remember that cat in the gardens?" His smile was sharp as an unsheathed dagger. "He didn't find the artifact, but he *did* find a way for small animals to bypass the wards the Zenith Society put up on their guest quarters after our little altercation. Mice and rats will chew through the wire on their artifice devices while they sleep. I'm going to plague them with every stinging and biting insect I can find in this palace, targeting eyes and ears and mouths. It's not my domain, so I'll have to individually enchant each creature, but it's worth it." His hands clenched at his sides. "I've never made a chimera before, but I'm going to figure out how to make spiders more venomous just so I can murder them one by one with tiny assassins they can't see coming. And I'm going to send birds to shit in their coffee, because my rage is both vast and petty."

I stared at him. A good friend, part of my mind argued, would try to talk him down—would tell him that vengeance wasn't the answer, and that it would consume him.

But I was an atheling, too, and I understood. So I just said, "All right."

That seemed to take the edge off his fury. He focused on me as if he'd only now fully realized who was standing there. "This is what I get for thinking the situation here was someone else's problem," he said, more quietly. "I don't believe in cosmic justice, but I *do* believe in irony. Well, now I'm invested."

I reached out, fighting my instinct to keep my distance, and laid a hand against the sharp line of his cheek. His jaw muscles flexed against my palm.

"I won't let you die," I promised. "No matter what, I won't let that happen."

He closed his eyes for a moment. Then he took my hand from his face and returned it to me with exquisite gentleness, as if I might have lost it.

"You focus on keeping yourself alive," he said. "I have a feeling that's going to take all of your concentration."

Oil lamps flickered in elegant filigree cages on the walls of the Hall of Portraits. The bloodred marble hall conducted visitors who made it past the antechamber deeper into the royal wing, like a long throat swallowing the queen's guests whole.

I paced its length alone, the Rookery left behind in the golden antechamber with the scant staff who'd still reported to duty after the majordomo passed on our warning. I tried hard not to think of Lord Elford walking this way a few days ago, unaware that he was experiencing the last moments of his life.

Grand, stern-faced portraits of dead Loreician monarchs in massive showy frames took on a shifting life around me in the unsteady light. Reflections of the lamp flames danced in the highly polished marble floor, as if another corridor ran through an underworld sealed beneath my feet. The silence became achingly loud, a deafening hum of nothing in my ears, broken only by my own footsteps.

I forced myself to keep walking, knowing that every step likely plunged me deeper into a trap. Tea, the page had said. Did demons even drink? I'd better not find her serving up cups of blood.

This was just another diplomatic meeting. I'd had tea with hostile Witch Lords, who were equally capable of snuffing me out like a candle; I could do this.

The oil lamps all dimmed and brightened at once, as if the whole grand hall had taken a sudden breath.

A small black shadow stood in the center of the room ahead, poised and elegant, waiting. I blinked. He hadn't been there a second ago.

"And this, at last, is where I draw the line," Whisper said.

EIGHTEEN

I stopped, sure as if Whisper's words had encased my legs in solid ice. *Oh Hells.*

"I warned you that you should take my offer and leave." The silk of his voice had steel beneath it. "You ignored me. I can't allow you to do so any longer."

"My friends need my help." I forced the words through my dry throat. "An entire domain is at stake. This is too important, Whisper."

"They'll manage without you. Leave this place. Run as far as you can, to the ends of the earth, and don't look back." His voice left no room for argument. It wasn't a request. I'd pushed him as far as he was willing to be pushed.

It was axiomatically pointless to argue with Death. But I never did know when to give up.

"Be reasonable. If I walk away now, the Rookery will fail. Nightmare and Madness will catch them, terrible things will happen to them, Hunger will use this artifact, and Severin will die." Emotion roughened my voice. "This is our one chance to save tens of thousands of people from a cruel and pointless death. I can't run away from it just because it's dangerous."

"You and I," he said, tail lashing, "have different priorities."

He was willing to let Alevar die. The chill certainty of it settled in my chest. I'd never let myself ask who, exactly, he was protecting—but if I were being honest, it had never been humankind.

"Maybe so," I said quietly. "But you're still my friend. You know me. And you know I have to do this."

His blurred reflection in the marble floor shifted, swelling larger and darker, even as Whisper himself didn't move. A subtle pressure of power grew in the air, slow and inexorable as the fall of night.

"And that is why I came prepared to stop you."

My heart lurched. He could kill me where I stood without so much as twitching a whisker, if he chose.

"Why?" I demanded, all my frustration rising up in a furious wave. "Why is it so important that I don't go to this stupid tea party? Why is this so much worse than all the other risks I've taken, all the mistakes I've made, all the trouble I've caused?"

"Because once you step into that room, it's over." He spoke so softly I had to strain to hear it. "You'll have crossed a line, and you can never return. This is my last chance, my very last chance, to salvage my promise."

His promise. Something stirred deep in the back of my mind, like a great fish moving beneath dark water—some connection I was on the brink of making at last.

"What will you do," I asked him slowly, "if I try to walk past you?"

His gaze met mine, shining with sulphureous intensity. "If you try to pass me—if you don't leave this place with me now—I will sever your memory. I'll drop you in some remote and distant land, with no idea who you are, and you can start over."

He was serious. Dread and anger stirred a volatile cocktail in my stomach. "Hells take it, Whisper! That would be like killing me!"

He stared at me through gleaming yellow slits of eyes. "You know who I am."

Death. But that was never what had mattered to me. My eyes stung. "I thought you were my friend."

"I am," he said, soft as falling snow. "More than you know. That's why I'll do it."

Listen to him, something within me whispered. He knew more than I did of what perils might wait behind the queen's gilded door. I could find the Rookery and tell them it was no good, we had to call off the mission. They could come up with some safer scheme to sabotage the artifact, one that didn't involve me. If the Demon of Death himself was opposing us, this wasn't going to work.

But the Rookery was trusting me to do my part. If they failed tonight because I backed out, an entire domain would turn to an abattoir tomorrow. I'd be abandoning Severin to his death.

I had to find a way to convince Whisper to let me pass, and there was only one thing I was sure he cared about.

"You're trying to protect an outdated promise." It was a guess, a gamble. "Things have changed too much since you made it. You say this is your last chance, but it was already too late once I opened the gate and let Discord through."

His tail swished restlessly, cutting the air like a whip. "That may be true," he acknowledged. "And yet still it binds me."

"Is..." I licked my lips. "Is there anyone who can release you from it?"

"I don't want to be released."

"But is there?" I pressed. "I have no doubt it's important—but the last thing I want is for anything to set us against each other." Hells, now my throat was tightening, and dampness collected in my eyes. I should be afraid that he was going to obliterate my memory and take me away from everything I cared about forever; I should be angry that he'd consider doing so. Here I was getting all sentimental over an actual demon instead. "I couldn't bear that, Whisper. So please, if there's any way to set aside this promise, tell me."

He stared at me in silence a long time. Finally, he breathed something between a hiss and a sigh. It set the lamps to a mad, brightening dance.

"You can," he admitted grudgingly. "You could release me."

Ah. That confirmed what I'd long suspected; his promise had been made to my family. That would make this easier. I drew in a breath. "Then I—"

"Don't," he interrupted sharply. "I urge you not to do this. You *will* regret it."

I paused, uncertainty churning within me. "You've been right every time with your warnings," I said. "But you're also right that we have different priorities. I can live with regret if I have to."

For a moment, he was silent, as if considering his response. "This promise is the only thing that overrides my neutrality," he said at last, the words coming slow and reluctant, as though he hated to make the admission. "Without it, I'll have a hard time finding excuses to help you."

An odd warmth bloomed in my chest. "I'm honored that you'd want to."

"Hmph." He licked imaginary dust from the fur of his shoulder.

"But I can't put myself first." Before I could have second thoughts, before he could stop me, I rushed the words out: "Whisper, I release you from your promise."

A hot wind blasted down the hall from nowhere, stirring my hair and ruffling his fur. Power tingled across my skin. Panic spiked through my veins for one brief instant, a horror that I'd done something terrible and foolish that couldn't be undone. Then everything was still again.

"Fool," Whisper growled. His ears swiveled back. "I warned you."

"I'm sorry," I said, my chest aching. "There's too much at stake."

Whisper paced up to me, glaring. I dropped down to a crouch and reached out a hand, tentatively, hoping I hadn't destroyed everything that lay between us, hoping we were still somehow friends despite the promise shattered in pieces on the floor.

I'd expected him to perhaps give my fingers a grudging sniff, at best. But he shoved his furry head into my chest, rocking me back on my heels.

I scratched the soft fur behind his ears for a while. "I'm sorry," I murmured again.

"I tried," he said, more subdued than I'd ever heard him. "I tried, Ryx. But you made it harder for me at every turn."

"I do that," I said ruefully. "But I have to confess that I still have no idea what you're talking about."

"You will." A great weariness lay on the words. He lifted his head, and for one moment I could see all the millennia within his ancient eyes. "Soon enough. Remember that I did what I could to save you."

I must have blinked, because he was gone. I crouched alone in the shadowy marble corridor, the ancient rulers of Loreice staring down at me from oil-painted eyes.

Bramant opened the door I wanted desperately to stay closed, bowing me in to meet with the queen. He moved differently than I remembered from my previous glimpses of him—looser, less precise. He straightened from his bow, and I realized with a lurch that his eyes were silver.

I had no time to react. It was too late to change my mind; I was already in motion, stepping through into the Rose Room.

The first thing that hit me was a suffocating wave of power, so thick the air felt like blood. My next impression was eye-assaulting opulence. The ceiling burgeoned with artfully worked gold flowers studded with jeweled dewdrops and tiny twinkling luminaries. Heavy swaths of pink and gold silk brocade draped the windows, holding in a sickly sweet miasma of roses; graceful white marble sculptures of flower-draped dancers accented the pink marble walls.

It took me a moment to triage my overwhelmed senses enough to focus on the table set with an elaborate silver tea service—and the Demon of Madness on the far side of it, waiting for me with a shy smile in acres of lace and puffed silver silk.

She was not alone.

Hunger and Nightmare flanked her at the damask-covered table, teacups in hand. They raked me with eyes sharp as diamond shards, tension straining between them.

Too much tension. The silence held an edge; their stares pressed it to my throat.

The door swung shut behind me.

"And here she is," Nightmare said, with apparent relish. "Now we can finish this."

That wasn't what I wanted to hear at all. I dipped a stiff bow, nerves taut as violin strings. "Your Majesty. Thank you for receiving me."

"Don't pretend," Madness said gently. "We don't need to keep secrets anymore."

"Indeed." Hunger leaned forward, cradling his chin in his hand. "It's time to drop our masks and reveal the truth. Wouldn't you agree?"

No trace of Aurelio showed in the hazel eyes that stared at me across the table, drinking in my every movement. Whatever I'd walked into, that slippery traitor was smart enough to stay out of it.

Hunger expected something from me, sure and eager; I couldn't guess what it was, let alone whether it would be safe to pretend to deliver it. A mistake here could be deadly. I eased down into the chair left open for me, slowly as if it were made of needles. *Stall them. Keep their interest and stall them. That's all you have to do.*

"Forgive me if I'm reluctant to agree to something you make sound so much like a trap," I said carefully.

Nightmare made a hissing noise that could perhaps have been a laugh. "Oh, it is. Do you know why you're here, little one?"

"Of course she does," Hunger snapped, before I could say anything.

"Perhaps she doesn't?" Madness sounded dreamily astonished, as if this were a breathtakingly novel idea.

Brooding tension hung between the three of them like impending thunder. A horrible realization crawled up the back of my neck and into my mind: they were having an argument about me.

"You're curious why your power didn't work on me," I guessed. I could only hope said curiosity wouldn't have them taking me apart to examine the pieces.

"That's one way to put it," Hunger said, grinning.

"You have an unusual mind." Nightmare laced her fingers around her teacup. "You're not like other humans. We've been having a *debate* as to why."

Not like other humans stuck a sharp edge into an undefended place. It called up years of keeping everyone beyond arm's reach, of scuttling through the walls of my own castle, of my people making the warding sign against me as if I were a curse.

My fingertips whitened on my teacup. "Perhaps you simply aren't familiar with what humans are like now, after four thousand years."

Hunger let out a disbelieving hiss. "A normal human couldn't rip me out of a new host."

"My magic is flawed." It was the same explanation I'd given year after year, a hundred times, but I'd never uttered it with so much urgency. I could feel whatever small control of the situation I'd walked in with sliding away through my fingers. "I was ill as a child, and it formed improperly, unweaving instead of weaving. That's all there is to it."

Madness tilted her head. "Is that truly what you believe?"

I looked quickly away from those drowning blue eyes. "I ... Of course I do."

Nightmare struck her cup triumphantly with her sugar spoon. "See? I was right. You're imagining things, Hunger."

His eyes narrowed. "Prove it. Show me her fears."

Panic leaped in my chest. "Wait, I—"

"Fine." Nightmare's hand shot out, fast as a snake, and clamped onto my arm. I tried to wrench away, but her fingers dug in with uncanny strength.

Once again there came the feeling of something skittering against the edges of my mind, claws scrabbling against glass and sliding off. I froze, holding my breath, ready to try to push back if she found purchase.

"I can do it," Nightmare said through her teeth. "I just need a foothold. Madness, get the quicksilver."

Madness started to rise. "Yes, that should open the door," she agreed eagerly, her eyes still fixed on me. "I'll be able to see you clearly, and then you'll see, too."

"No!" I leaped to my feet, yanking my arm back, heart trying to kick its way out through my rib cage. The spots where Nightmare's fingers had dug in ached with blooming bruises. I struggled to regain a shred of poise. "With regret, I must decline."

Madness looked crestfallen. "All I want is to help you," she said wistfully.

Nightmare and Hunger watched me like cats who've let a mouse scuttle beyond reach of their paws, purely for the pleasure of catching it again. Words were my only armor against them; I had to think quickly.

"Quicksilver is unnecessary. Tell me your disagreement, and I can help you settle it without—"

"Oh, hush," Nightmare said. A fog pressed at my mind, and for a moment I swayed beneath it, but it passed.

Hunger gestured eloquently to me. "See? You can't put her to sleep, either."

The room darkened, the breath pressed from my lungs. Nightmare growled, "There's *plenty* I can do to this little worm."

"You can," I agreed. I had to stabilize this situation somehow, turn it back into a dialogue and reclaim some scrap of power, before it was too late to recover. "But once you do, this conversation is over. Given that you could have had your guards bring me in at any time, I'm assuming you invited me to tea because you wanted to *talk*."

"She's got a point," Hunger said, but there was something strained about his voice, not careless enough—Aurelio, struggling to the surface long enough to intervene. Once again, an unexpected wave of gratitude to a man I hated surged through me.

Annoyance flickered on his face, and Hunger was back. He shrugged, deciding not to disagree with his host.

Nightmare's eyes stayed locked on mine. No trace of humanity softened them, hard and glittering with ancient malice. After a long moment, she gestured to my chair.

"Very well." Her voice was deadly quiet. "Sit, and we'll talk."

I sank back into my seat as if I were easing into a pool I knew was full of sharks.

Madness gave me a dazzling smile. "That's better. See? We're not your enemies."

I was fairly certain they were, but it would hardly be diplomatic to say so. "The greater the differences between us, the more we can learn from discussion," I acknowledged instead.

"Now." Nightmare began dropping sugar into her tea, one spoonful after another. "You arrived here with a pack of other humans. You care for them, do you not?"

Apprehension settled in my stomach. "It's a characteristic of humans to care for the people around us," I said. "It gives us strength. You might try it sometime."

Hunger chuckled as if I'd made a joke. He started loading little cakes on his plate from a platter on the table that I hadn't touched, settling in as if he expected a show.

"Does it truly give you strength?" Nightmare's deep voice dripped skepticism. "Caring for others always seems to inevitably be a human's greatest weakness."

This was dangerous ground. Without thinking, I took a sip of tea to buy time. *Pox.* I'd have to hope it didn't have quicksilver in it; at least I only tasted roses.

"Caring for each other lets us work together and build societies," I said at last. Best to keep this general and philosophical, and try to move her thoughts away from my friends who even now were committing burglary a few rooms over. "We can accomplish a great deal more that way than we ever could alone."

Nightmare smiled as if what I'd said proved her point. "Is that so?" She took a long sip of tea, showing no reaction to the mountain of sugar she'd piled in it. "Look out the window and tell me what you see."

I glanced to the windows; they faced the sea, with a view of the lights twinkling in the harbor town below. "Luminaries shining in the night."

Her smile stretched wider, too wide. "Look closer."

I tore my eyes away from her face to give the window a longer look. From this distance, all I could see was that scattering of lights in the darkness. The steady, cold pinpoints of luminaries contrasted with the warm orange glow of . . . *Blood of the Eldest.*

Fire.

I rose without thinking and went to the window, breath caught in my throat, and stared down at the harbor town. Several hungry orange patches of fire bloomed in scattered spots; this close, I caught a faint scent of smoke under the miasma of roses, and I could make out the urgent peal of alarm bells.

The sickening pressure of power I'd felt in the room flowed over me in a strong current, pouring down the hill toward the town below.

I whirled back to face the demons, anger kindling an answering flame beneath my breastbone. "You're burning the town!"

Nightmare calmly stirred her tea with a silver spoon. "They're burning it themselves, I'm simply stoking their fears. It takes so little to make humans turn on each other."

If that was true, there must be a lot more terrible things happening in that town than just fires. My heart twisted. This was how the Dark Days must have begun; at the bottom of this hill, they'd already come again.

Nightmare watched me avidly, drinking in my reaction. I struggled to control my face. "Why are you doing this? They're no threat to you."

"Of course they aren't. I'm doing it for the beautiful colors their minds make in anguish." Her pupils grew, inky blackness swallowing up her irises. "Now, yours...ah! Your colors are so bright, so *intense*." She shivered with pleasure. "Extraordinary. Perhaps there's something to Hunger's idea after all."

Hunger paused mid-cake to level a glare at Nightmare. "Of course there is. Push her, and you'll find out."

It sounded almost like a warning. As if there was something I could do that Nightmare might regret. Seasons, what I'd give for that to be the case.

Madness tilted her head, as if she'd heard some distant noise. "No," she whispered, so softly I almost didn't hear it. "You mustn't."

I kept my attention fixed on Nightmare. "You're a coward," I told her through my teeth. "Sitting here in this warded palace and torturing people you know can't reach you."

Hunger laughed. "Cowardice is a ridiculous concept. Humans should listen to their fear; it carries important messages."

Nightmare's eyes stayed locked on me, black and ravenous. "Would you prefer that I torture the people *inside* this palace, then?"

I tried not to show my flare of alarm and revulsion at the thought, but Nightmare sucked in a breath as if she'd seen it anyway and it was the most beautiful thing she'd ever witnessed.

"Glorious," she breathed. "Oh, you don't like it when I hurt people, do you? This is *marvelous*."

This was going nowhere good. I mustered all my anger; if they believed I was a Grace, or that there was something I could do against them, perhaps I could at least use that to bluff.

"Don't test me," I growled. And within the safe confines of my jess, I uncurled the fist I kept clenched tight around my power, just a little. Enough to let it flare for a brief instant, for anyone who could sense it.

Their reaction was immediate and startling. Hunger hissed like a cornered cat, pushing back from the table. Madness rose, her eyes widening, straight and stiff. And Nightmare recoiled, gasping in shock as if I'd struck her.

They were afraid of me. Three of the Nine Demons, afraid.

For a fleeting moment, I held them in my hands. They stared at me, tense and riveted, waiting for what I'd do next. But there was nothing. The next breath I took, the next word I uttered, they'd realize it had been a bluff; that if I held some power against them, I had no idea what it was.

Something fluttered at the corner of my vision: a pale green moth, big as my spread hands, bumping against the window glass. Severin's all clear signal.

"I'm weary of being talked about, threatened, and prodded at," I said with cold courtesy, clenching my hands to keep them from trembling. "Good night. Perhaps we can speak again tomorrow, if you want to hold an actual conversation."

I stalked out of the Rose Room with as great a show of offense as I could muster and slammed the door behind me. No one moved to stop me, but I could still feel their eyes on my back through the wood.

What in the Nine Hells did they think I could do? They recognized something terrible in me, something I'd almost unleashed in the Shrike Lord's castle, whether it was the power of a Grace or just my own broken magic unfolded from the bottle I'd stuffed it in all these years. Maybe I could use it against them—maybe it could turn the tide—but the sick lump sitting in my stomach didn't feel like victory.

I had to get out of here before they rallied from their surprise. Bunching my skirts in my fists, I ran through audience halls and antechambers, past silver-eyed guards and hovering servants, breath coming hard and nerves on fire. I needed to get away from the miasma of roses, from their questions and suspicions, from their devouring looks and prying minds.

I wanted more than anything to run all the way home to Gloamingard, where I could be myself, with my castle wrapped around me, familiar as an old quilt. That, at last, might be far enough.

But the scent of roses lingered in my hair and on my skin, and I couldn't shake the dread that it was far too late.

I took a wrong turn fleeing the royal wing and found myself in the palace shrine. Marble columns lifted a high arched ceiling into shadow; night-dark windows riddled with complex stained glass loomed above. Countless candles flickered at the altars to each of the Nine Graces, and the offering tables overflowed with flowers, food, and other gifts left by a palace population desperate for divine aid. A pair of servants knelt praying before the altar of the Grace of Mercy; an elderly courtier lit a mourning candle in the alcove dedicated to the Grace of Love, to remember someone lost. It was a hushed, holy place, full of watching presence, waiting for something to happen.

My nerves jangled like a string of broken bells, too loud for a place this quiet. Somehow, I'd come out of that tea party alive and unsilvered. Whatever doom Whisper had predicted, it hadn't yet come to pass, but I wasn't fool enough to think I'd escaped it; I could feel its jaws closing around me.

The looming statues of the Graces gazed down on me, each from its niche: Bounty with her horn of plenty, Luck with her mask, Victory with her fiery sword. Figures of myth and story, power and virtue—they always lifted people up and helped them, never accidentally murdered them with a stray touch.

I had no place among them. Even if it turned out that something about my power was the same as theirs, there was more to being a Grace than the ability to frighten demons, and I wasn't qualified.

It was a strangely reassuring thought.

I whispered a brief prayer of thanks, gathering myself to go meet the Rookery at our prearranged spot in the gardens. Clearly it was becoming urgent that I figure out what the demons saw in me, but right now destroying the artifact took priority. My familiar solace came to my rescue once more: I had work to do.

Silk rustled behind me, and a prickling chill came over me.

"You don't like me right now," Madness said, with deep sorrow.

NINETEEN

I turned, dread a cold-pawed beast sitting on my heart. I thought I'd gotten away—but of course, I couldn't really get away. This palace was their domain now, and we were all in their power.

She stood alone in her fanciful silver puff of a gown, diamonds sparkling in her hair, her presence in the shrine pure blasphemy. For all I could tell, she seemed genuinely distressed.

"That's because you're hurting people," I said quietly.

"I don't want to hurt the humans," she said. "I like them."

It made no sense, but she seemed so sincere, so wistful, that I believed her. "Yet you keep hurting them."

"I'm like the light. All I want to do is look. But when I look…" She lifted a hand, delicate fingers reaching, as if she could see something beautiful hanging in the air just before her eyes. "I touch." She sighed, her hand dropping. "And when I touch, they scatter, like ripples in water. If I do it too much, the pattern is destroyed. I try so hard not to harm them, but time after time I fail."

Unexpected sympathy twisted my gut. "I'm sorry. I know what that's like."

"I know you do." She gazed at me again, seeking something, but I couldn't begin to guess what. "That's why I want to help you."

"I don't…" I swallowed. "I don't think you can help me."

She tilted her head and stared at me a long time in the dim, flickering light of the shrine candles. It was profoundly unnerving. I didn't dare leave, but couldn't find words, either.

"You don't know, do you," she breathed at last.

She was a demon, and my enemy. All that had gotten me out of the Rose Room was bluffing that I knew what they saw in me. The moment I admitted my ignorance, I lost whatever edge their suspicions had granted.

But I had a feeling Madness would know if I flat-out lied to her. And despite knowing how powerful and dangerous she was, it was insidiously difficult to see her as a threat when she stood before me like this, looking sad and lost.

"I don't," I agreed quietly. "Would you care to enlighten me?"

Her eyes lit up as if I'd promised her a present. *Oh pox.*

"Yes!" She clasped her hands, rising up on her toes in excitement. "Yes, of course!"

"Wait." I lifted a hand, alarmed. "What exactly are you—"

"I can help you." She unleashed a dazzling smile on me. "Oh, I'm so glad. I'll go get the quicksilver."

My stomach lurched. "No, that's all right! If it involves quicksilver, I'll pass, thank you."

Madness had already turned and was all but running out of the shrine, a rustling mass of silver silk trailing behind her.

"What have I done?" I whispered.

I had an unpleasant suspicion I'd find out sooner than I'd like. But there was no time to dwell on it now. I had to go meet the Rookery and find out whether Severin and all the thousands of people living in Alevar would get to see another sunset.

I stumbled out of the palace and into the gardens as if waking from a bad dream, the cool evening air hitting my face with the welcome relief of a splash of clear water. I drank in great gulps of it, trying to chase away the lingering scent of roses. Unsettling thoughts buzzed in my brain, released by the demons' reactions to me; I did my best to stuff them away into a box and shove it into a far corner of my mind. *Later.*

The Rookery waited for me beneath the great spreading tree at the heart of the gardens. Its reaching layers of tangled boughs and whispering leaves stretched above them in the darkness, complex and ancient as the rule of a Witch Lord. I couldn't tell in the silvery moonlight whether they were clustered around an object on the ground or simply huddled together talking.

Graces, please let them have it. I didn't think it would end well for anyone if I tried to distract the demons like that again.

Kessa broke away from the group to meet me as soon as she saw me coming, a broad smile of relief lighting up her face. "Ryx! You're all right!"

That was perhaps optimistic. I couldn't shake the feeling that something significant and terrible had happened, that I'd tipped past the edge of a cliff and was only beginning to plummet—but I was all in one piece, and that was something.

"Against all odds, it seems so," I agreed, peering past her shoulder through the gloom. *Yes*—a strange metal-bound box lay on the ground, covered in startlingly intricate wirework and marked with layers of overlapping diagrams and runes. Relief slumped my shoulders. "You got it."

"We did!" Kessa beamed. "Took a fair bit of work breaking some protections, and there was a chancy moment when we had to talk our way past a servant who showed up at a bad time, but we got it. Thanks to you."

"And now," Severin said sharply, "we destroy it."

Foxglove raised the hand not currently leaning on his cane. "Wait. We can't."

I rounded on him, still full of unspent nervous energy and not in the mood to dance with any more demons tonight. "That thing *has* to be destroyed, and you know it. It's an abomination."

Foxglove caught my eyes, a relentless spark in his. "Listen to me, Ryx. The Rookery can't destroy this artifact. We'll be disbanded if we do."

Severin bared his teeth in something no one could mistake for a smile. "Oh, disbanded, how terrible. In that case, I'll *certainly* sit back and trust the Serene Empire, my country's historical enemy, to safeguard this device they've already lost once and never use it to inflict unspeakable destruction upon my people."

Foxglove didn't so much as glance at him. "I haven't checked it yet to see if it's intact and operational," he said, still holding my gaze. "It clearly got roughed up in transport at some point, and the wirework is so complex that if it were physically damaged, I very much doubt anyone could ever restore it."

Severin blinked. He slid me a half-disbelieving glance, as if seeking confirmation that yes, for once in his life, someone who owed him nothing was doing right by him.

I nodded to Foxglove, careful to suppress my smile of gratitude. "I understand."

Foxglove turned to the others. "Ashe, Kessa, why don't you go find us a good place to hide it until we can get it out of the palace. Bastian, you and I should get to work on altering the wards."

Kessa grinned and saluted. "We'll make sure to take our time picking the best possible location. Wouldn't want it to get horrifically damaged, after all. Come on, Ashe."

Bastian frowned for a moment as if he might argue, and then realization visibly dawned on him. "Right! Yes, lots of work to do on the wards. Let's go—but after that, you should rest your leg."

"Of course." Foxglove started off, maneuvering his cane with the ease of someone who'd used one before. "Ryx, Severin, you can guard the artifact until Ashe and Kessa get back. I trust you to do what needs to be done."

Severin and I watched them until the damp night air swallowed them.

"Well," he said. "I feel foolish now."

I turned to the artifact and drew my belt knife. "Delicate and irreplaceable wirework, he said."

Severin drew his, grinning. "Indeed."

Several minutes later, we'd kicked hacked-up snarls of golden wirework under bushes, tossed it up in trees, buried it in flower beds, and thrown it in lily ponds. Only a few ragged stumps of wire remained on the box, and we'd bent them into new shapes to be sure.

"Not bad," Severin said, surveying our handiwork.

"That should do it," I agreed. I'd managed to cut my hand on a wire and lifted my finger toward my mouth.

Severin caught it, his hands gentle. "Don't do that; it's not sanitary. Let me see."

A thrill ran up my arm at his touch as he examined the little cut, angling it to catch the moonlight.

"It's tiny," I said. "I'm fine."

Severin didn't look up from my hand. His twin locks of hair dangled down on either side of his bowed head; one tickled my wrist. "I had a fairly stern talk with myself while you were at your tea party," he said huskily. "I was fully prepared to spend the rest of my life trying to atone if you got killed on my behalf in there. I'm glad I get to continue living out a selfish existence."

The tea party. Hells. For one brief moment, I'd forgotten. Everything that happened came crashing back, tied up in a heavy bundle by one single urgent concern.

"Severin, I…" I took a deep breath. "I'm sorry. I think I've put you all in danger."

Severin laughed, lifting his face in surprise. "What, *more* danger? How is that even possible?"

"Because I made a mistake." I took my hand back, plunging on. "I tried to use the demons' interest to draw attention away from the rest of you, to make you safer. But I'm afraid it's going to have the opposite effect."

"Oh, yes, very surprising that attracting a demon's attention would be the opposite of safe." He shook his head.

"Curse it, I'm serious!" I stepped closer, wishing I dared grab him to somehow shake into him how afraid I was. "I could get you all killed because I relied too heavily on being resistant to their power."

"Ryx." Severin's hands closed on my shoulders. "Stop trying to take responsibility for every horrible thing the demons do."

"But it *is* my—"

"Don't flatter yourself." The moonlight caught in the stormy rings of his mage mark. "Oh, I get the impulse. I used to think that about my brother all the time. That the terrible things he did were my fault because I didn't stop him, because I didn't kill him and become my father's heir instead, because I found a way to avoid his ire one day and it fell on someone else." He made a rueful grimace. "I've gone down that road. It doesn't end anywhere useful. It's arrogant to blame everything on ourselves; we're just not that important."

That got through like nothing else could have. *Useful.* I turned the word over in my mind, examining it from different angles.

"All right," I agreed, surprised at how calm I sounded. "Instead of worrying about whose fault it is you're in danger, I'll worry about how to protect you."

"Yes," he said approvingly; and then immediately and with suspicion, "No. Wait. I know you. You're going to do something reckless again."

"Only if I have to." I gave him a wry smile. "I'm too practical for needless heroics."

"Good." His throat jumped, shadows sliding down the clean lines of his neck like spectral fingers. "Maddening though you may be, you're all I've got left. I don't want to lose you."

The words sent a little shiver through me. To hide it, I let out a skeptical laugh. "Now you're just being dramatic."

"Me? Never." The faintest ghost of a smile moved his lips. "I spent my whole life focused just on surviving, until you came along. Now I have to go to all the tedious trouble of figuring out what more I can do. Since it's your fault, I want you to survive this *with* me, if that's not too much to ask."

"It might be," I said. "We're neck deep in trouble and sinking fast, Severin."

His eyes traveled over my face as if he could read words written there. At last he said hoarsely, "More than neck deep. I think I went under a while ago."

His thumb moved on my shoulder, the slightest gentle brush.

My world flipped inside out. *Oh.* We were having a different conversation than I'd thought. *Well then.*

Heat flushed my face. The distance between us narrowed, vanishing like the moonlight when a cloud passed overhead.

We kissed, a quick brush at first, warm and soft. The light touch sent a deep reverberation all through me, as if I were a great bell. *Sweet Hells.* I needed more.

Our arms went around each other, hard and urgent; our mouths met, melding together, the boundary blurring between us. I could feel his heart pounding against my chest, alive, *alive*, and seasons witness I'd never been this close to anyone before, ever in my life. He was all lean muscle, pressed warm against me; I ran my hands up into his silky hair at last, and it was just as soft as I'd imagined. I closed my eyes and melted into him.

He gasped, stiffening in my arms, and pulled suddenly away from me.

"What?" I asked, alarmed. "Did I do something wrong?"

He shook his head, eyes wide and desperate. All the heat that had crept through me vanished as surely as if someone had flung a bucket of ice water on us.

I gave him a gentle shake, afraid. "Hey! Are you—"

"*Help*," he whispered hoarsely.

And he collapsed like an empty garment.

I caught him, his weight staggering me. He struggled to stay upright, but all his strength seemed to have left him.

"Severin!" Hells, he was choking, or poisoned, or under magical attack—he could be dying. I'd never learned to treat emergencies; I had no idea what to do.

"I can't..." he gasped. "Both of them..."

Worry twisted a knife in my side. Fighting off panic, I eased him gently down, cradling him against me. "What's happening? How can I help?"

"They're *here*."

His eyes went dull as a silver sheen began to creep across them.

My heart froze. "*No!*" I grabbed him tighter, as if I could squeeze the demon's touch out of him somehow. "Fight them off! *Severin!*"

It was no good. The silver covered his eyes, and he went limp in my arms.

From the shadow of the looming tree came Madness and Nightmare, trailing lace and radiating power, hand in hand. The air shimmered around them, and a skittering sound scratched at the edges of my hearing.

I should have been afraid of them, but all my fear was bound up in Severin with cords strained to the breaking point. All I had left was fury.

"What did you do to him?"

Nightmare chuckled, deep in her throat. "Nothing compared to what we're about to do."

"It's to help you," Madness said soothingly, her misty eyes sad. "He would want to help you. He wants you to be happy."

Nightmare held out her free hand, imperious. "Now, give him to us."

I pulled Severin's unresponsive body closer, as if my arms were a warding circle that could protect him against all the power of the Hells. "I won't let you take him."

"Oh, my dear," Nightmare purred, "you don't have a choice."

They lifted their joined hands, faces taut with concentration. The air seemed to grow thick and heavy, pushing down on me like a smothering blanket. I struggled against the weight of their full combined power, but it was too much; I might as well try to hold back an avalanche with my bare hands.

I swayed and collapsed as my mind plunged down into suffocating darkness.

TWENTY

"Ryx! Ryx, wake up!"

Someone was shaking me, urgently. The ground pressed cold and hard beneath me. Severin's warmth was gone.

I lurched up to a crouch, gasping. Kessa bent over me, eyes wide with alarm, and Ashe stood by scanning the gardens with Answer in her hand, but there was no sign of Severin or the demons.

They were going to torture him just to get at me, and I didn't even know why. It was my worst nightmare made real.

Of course it was. The Hells could have that evil wretch back anytime. "Did you see anything?" I demanded. "Did you see where they took him?"

Kessa gave Ashe a wide-eyed glance; Ashe shook her head, still on the watch for enemies. "We just got here," Kessa said. "We figured you'd had enough time to, ah, deal with the artifact, and we came back to get whatever was left of it. But we found you lying on the ground instead. What happened?"

I opened my mouth to reply, but a giddy wave of disorientation swept over me, and a soft voice whispered in my ear:

Please don't be angry. Nightmare says this is for the best.

"Where is he?" I hissed aloud.

Don't worry, we're keeping him safe in the mirror maze. Come find him, and we'll give him back.

The voice faded at once, leaving me digging my fingers into the lawn all the way to the roots. All I could think of was the guards who'd gone into the mirror maze as lively individuals and come out as silver-eyed automatons.

"Ryx?" Kessa asked, sounding alarmed. "Are you all right?"

Grim resolve settled over me like a leaden cloak. "They've got him in the mirror maze."

"Fresh roasted Hells on a stick," Kessa swore.

I surged to my feet, brushing off my skirts, ignoring the hollow dread inside. "I suspect Nightmare and Madness are annoyed I left their tea party without permission, and they want me to finish our conversation before they'll give him back."

The tip of Ashe's sword dipped, and she gave me a skeptical look. "But you're not going, of course. Because it's an obvious trap."

"I assure you, going into any kind of labyrinth with a pair of demons is not on my list of clever things to do, but I'm not certain I have a choice," I said.

"The maze part isn't the problem," Kessa put in, rising hastily to her own feet. "Remember what Bastian said about quicksilver? All those mirrors are probably backed with mercury. The whole building will amplify and conduct their magic."

That must be why they wanted to lure me in there. To get past whatever resistance my flawed magic gave me. But why involve Severin? Their combined strength might not allow them to breach my mind, but it had been enough to put me to sleep. They could have dragged me in there instead of him.

I could only think of one reason: because they were afraid of me. They'd taken a hostage to make me cooperate.

I was not feeling *remotely* cooperative.

"Can you think of any way to rescue him without going in there?" I asked.

Kessa frowned. "Lure the demons out somehow?" she suggested dubiously. "We could create a distraction. Maybe burn down part of the palace? Though I don't know how we'd keep from burning down *all* the palace in that case."

"There was that one rescue we did where Bastian mixed up some explosive potions and we blew a hole in the building," Ashe reminisced.

Kessa shook her head, the plume on her hat bobbing. "Don't you remember how that ended? Sixteen people injured! We're lucky no one died."

"Oh, right." Ashe shrugged. "Set the mirror maze on fire, then. Smoke them out."

"Severin was unconscious last I saw him," I protested, only more anxious now. "He could die."

"I could send an animal in to scout," Kessa offered.

The world went giddy again. Madness's voice whispered in my ear once more, with childlike wonder. *I can see why you like him. His mind is so pretty, so complicated. Oh, and Nightmare says to hurry if you want him undamaged.*

"Pox take it." I started for the mirror maze, fear coppery in the back of my throat. "We don't have time. By the time we've got a clever plan ready, they'll have done something irreversible to him."

Kessa hurried to catch up, Ashe hovering at her side. "We're coming with you, of course."

"No." I stopped and faced them. "Normally I'd think that was a fantastic idea, but they took Severin as a hostage, and you said yourself that if we step in there we're in their power. We'd just be handing them two more hostages. It makes more sense for you to stay outside, go get Foxglove and Bastian, and come up with a plan to get us *both* out."

Kessa put her fists on her hips. "By that logic, you shouldn't go in there, either. Why would it be any different for you?"

I stared at her. The uneasy emptiness in my belly grew,

stretching into an abyss. I knew what I had to do, but Graces help me, I didn't want to do it.

"Because," I said, "you're going to release my power."

Kessa's face went still and wary. I couldn't tell if it was sadness or fear in her eyes. "I don't know, Ryx. It'll take at least a day for the jess to work again, and we don't even know whether your unsealed magic will protect you."

"It'll give them a reason to be wary of me, after what I did to Hunger," I said grimly. "Whether it provides me any additional defense or not, it'll give me offense. And I'm in the mood to fight back."

"This is a terrible idea," Kessa said, with absolute certainty. "I should know. I'm an expert in terrible ideas, having participated in countless of them."

Too much anger had gathered in me, like a rising storm. "I have to go in there, and I'm not doing it unarmed. This is the only weapon I have against them. Release me, Kessa."

I stepped back to give them both room and spread my arms, the end of the jess dangling from my wrist.

Kessa shook her head. "I won't keep your own power from you; I don't have the right. But I have to tell you that I can't support this, either." She took in a long breath. "*Exsolvo*."

The world went keen and dangerous. My fingertips tingled with possibilities, all of them terrible. The carefully mown lawn withered and died in twin ovals beneath my feet.

A rush of magic swarmed up my arm, and the jess lay cold and inert on my wrist. I stripped it off, chest aching, and tossed it to Kessa; she caught it gleaming in midair, her face solemn.

"I don't know what's going to happen," I told them. "Be ready for anything."

Kessa nodded, lips pressed tight, silent for once.

"Go show those bastards," Ashe said, lifting her sword in salute.

I nodded in acknowledgment and stalked across the grounds

toward the mirror maze, leaving dead brown footprints in my wake.

The silence in the mirror maze was oppressive, as if a deafening bass hum sounded just below my threshold of hearing. Power lay heavy in the air. Ghostly luminaries hung from the ceiling and occasionally between the mirrors, reflected back a hundred times in every direction.

Dim illusory halls stretched around me, some curving toward infinity, some turning corners or breaking up into a dozen unexpected angles. Darkness hovered behind everything, barely held back by the pale glow of the luminary crystals, dissolving the more distant images into nothingness.

And all around me, from every angle, stood the same pale woman in a bedraggled sapphire-and-silver gown, her dark braid half undone, mage mark standing out sharp as lightning from the harrowed pools of shadow in her eyes. I looked like a ghost, at home in the labyrinth of nonexistent space around me, already dead and gone.

"Severin?" I called. My voice fell flat as if I'd shouted into a smothering curtain, barely reaching my own ears.

I took a few steps, my hands lifted tentatively before me; my fingertips met glass. For a brief moment, my breath made a soft cloud in front of me.

You can still leave, a sensible voice in the back of my head reminded me. *A few more steps, and you won't be able to, but you could turn around and walk out of this trap right now.*

I ignored it. I had to find him. It was my fault he was in here in the first place.

I tried another angle, straining to listen; no calls for help or anguished cries met my ears, but there came a barely audible whispering, a skittering like claws across a polished marble floor.

A dozen copies of me receded and approached as I took one turn and then another, following walls I couldn't see. My fingers skimmed across glass.

It rippled in their wake, like water.

My stomach flipped. *Impossible.* But I supposed nothing was impossible when demon magic wormed its way into your senses.

I stopped. The reflection in front of me stopped. We stared at each other. Her head tilted at an ever so slightly different angle than mine.

My heart pounded so loud I half expected it to echo back a hundredfold from every mirror.

"Who are you?" my reflection asked, in a voice like mine, but with a strange shimmer to it.

Seeing my own face move, my own expression shift, when I wasn't the one doing it sent a chill down my back—and rekindled a steady candle flame of anger within my rib cage.

"I'm not talking to you," I told it.

I felt my way down another half-invisible corridor, leaving smudges on the glass that quickly faded into nothingness, surrounded by images of myself.

They turned their heads to watch me. One by one, as I passed them, they disappeared, winking out of existence. It was more unnerving than I wanted to admit.

Ahead, another reflection waited, head cocked to the side.

"How much do you remember?"

I stopped, breathing fast, and glared at the mirror Ryx confronting me. My own eyes stared back. My own brow creased faintly in a frown that was unquestionably mine.

"She never told you anything, did she? Your grandmother. She kept so many secrets from you. Aren't you angry?"

"No," I snapped, and turned back the way I came. But I ran into glass, face-first, where there hadn't been any before. I clutched my nose, cursing; my reflections stood and watched, solemn, waiting.

"Of course you're angry," one whispered.

"At least a little," another agreed.

"She should have told you *something*."

I turned in a slow circle, nerves jangling, looking for a way out. Half a dozen reflected Ryxanders surrounded me, each with a corridor stretching to infinity behind her, marked by lines of pale lights bending gradually into obscurity.

"Where's Severin?" I growled. "I'm not here to talk about my grandmother."

"Let's talk about *you*." A reflection on my left raised her hand to touch the glass of her mirror, then vanished, leaving her corridor empty.

A cool breeze seemed to blow from it. In the distance, I heard a small child crying, weak and sickly.

Something about that sound struck dread deep into the core of me, an unreasoning terror. I turned away from it, hurrying in the opposite direction, feeling my stumbling way along angles and corners of glass. My own eyes stared back at me from a dozen directions, wide with fear.

"What are you afraid of?" my reflected lips whispered, desperate, nearly pressed against the mirror by my ear.

I didn't know. But whatever it was, it touched a primal terror deeper than anything I'd felt since I first stepped inside the Black Tower.

I reached for another reflection, hoping to find a way onward—but that one popped like a soap bubble as my fingers met cold, hard glass.

"What about Whisper?" murmured my own voice, behind me. "He knows. He's always known."

"But ah," said another, reasonably, "there was the matter of his promise."

I turned slowly toward the speaker, drawn despite myself. *His promise.* The one I still felt a sick, nameless dread at having released him from, though I'd never learned what it was.

There was no one there to have uttered the words. All my reflections were gone. Only empty mirror corridors surrounded me, illusory and endless, and enough reflected lights to fill the starry sky.

The sound of crying returned, louder this time.

"Don't you want to know about his promise?" whispered a voice.

I did, Graces help me. But not like this. I tried to tell them that, but my mouth was too dry.

In the infinite distance, a light went out.

"I don't want this," I managed at last, my voice cracked and husky.

"*Too late,*" voices whispered all around me. "*Too late.*"

In every reflected corridor, the most distant light disappeared, cutting the illusory passageways short of infinity. Then the next light went out, and the next, and the next, darkness creeping toward me. My reflected world shrinking, devoured piece by piece.

I tried each direction in turn, panic rising in my throat, but no matter which way I went, my fingertips met only mirror. It was a trap, just like I'd known it would be. There was no way out.

"Enough!" I cried desperately. There had to be some trick, like in the story of the seven unlucky brothers—some way to shatter the illusion, to find Severin and escape. "Here I am, in your stupid maze. Let him go!"

The darkness advancing down the mirror corridors was my only reply.

Horror strained to bursting in my chest. If I couldn't escape before the last light went out, something terrible would happen; I was sure of it. Something I'd fled from all my life, something worse than death—

"I warned you," said Whisper's voice, tired and sad.

The last lights went out, plunging me into darkness.

TWENTY-ONE

The child's wailing filled all my senses, reverberating in my bones.

"Hush, little one. Not much longer now."

It was my grandmother's voice. She held me against her chest, small as a puppy, and I could feel the sound rumbling comfortably through me. Her power folded around me like a warm, familiar cloak. I stopped crying, too exhausted to keep it up any longer. All I'd known was struggle for so long, and now I couldn't even hold my head up anymore.

A memory. This must be a memory from when I was a child, long ago. My parents always told me I was very sick, but my grandmother's magic saved me.

The grinding of stone against stone scraped my ears. Red light flooded the inside of my lids. I opened my eyes.

All around me, lurid red runes and diagrams glowed against obsidian walls, rising impossibly high to meet in a complex seal on the distant ceiling. At the center of the round room, a flat black obelisk stood in a glowing scarlet circle, dark enough to be a hole in reality, a window to a starless night sky.

We were in the Black Tower.

Oh, holy Hells. Grandmother, what did you do?

Whisper sat a few paces away, ears pricked and alert. "You're sure about this?"

My grandmother's arms tightened around me. "It's the only way." I'd never heard her so sad, so exhausted, so desperate. "Yes, curse it. If you're certain it won't hurt her, I'm sure."

No, this is a terrible idea. Don't do it.

Reality rippled, as if a drop of water had fallen into the center of my perception.

White light blazed across my vision, energy crawling over me, through me, inside me. I knew this power—it was the limitless pale fire of the Hells, magic in its purest and most terrible form, which I'd unleashed three times by my own hand. It should have been agonizing, terrifying, overwhelming; but in this mirror vision, it flowed through me harmlessly, as if I were floating in water.

A gap opened, a vertical slit, the blazing white light parting like a curtain. On the far side stood my grandmother, her face grim as death, a small dark-haired child cradled sleeping in her arms.

"You can save her?" she asked me, through that slender gap between worlds.

A memory. This is a memory, too.

Oh, no.

"I can," I said, forming the words from pure intent as I drifted closer to the gap.

"And you swear you will not harm her." My grandmother's mage mark burned fierce in her eyes, twin wheels of orange fire. "You won't possess her or take control."

"I swear." All the power swirling around me trembled with how hard I willed it. This was my chance—my one chance to take a step toward atonement. She *had* to believe me.

My grandmother half turned toward Whisper, her teeth bared in an uncertain grimace. "And we can trust its word? You're certain?"

"*This* one, yes." A thrill leaped through me at the sound of Whisper's voice; it had been so long, so very long, since I'd seen my brother. "None of the others. But this one will keep her word."

"All right." My grandmother stepped back, squaring her shoulders. "Come through, then, and honor our agreement."

No, this can't be right. She wouldn't have. Grandmother, surely you didn't.

Reality rippled again. Colors swirled around me, red and black and a blaze of blinding white, mixing in a confusing swirl from two different perspectives. I cried out in fear. It was too much to take in, too alien and strange . . . .

But then the perspectives began to merge.

A great surge of *rightness* rose up in my chest; I drew in a breath, a real breath, with working lungs, sucking in power along with air, and let it out with a delighted laugh. *I know you. I* know *you*, I sang silently to the two halves of myself as they joined blazing together. Everything about you. All your fear of making a mistake again, of everything you do bringing only sorrow; all the wild chaos of energy within you, the uncontrolled joy and love and fear—*I know you.*

This wasn't right. It hit me in a moment of desperate, drowning terror—this wasn't what we'd wanted.

I was supposed to wait in the back of my mind, unseen but separate, a quiet passenger, sustaining my life—that was the plan. But now two scant years of sickly yearning tangled up in an eternity of power and light, merging inexorably into one, and I couldn't extricate myself, couldn't fix this, had ruined everything *again*.

"Whisper!" I cried, desperate, squirming in my grandmother's grasp. "Whisper, help me!"

His yellow eyes met mine. Thought to thought, intent to intent, we communed for an anguished instant.

I can't. Merging can't be undone. I'm sorry, my friend. What would you have me do?

"Promise me," I said aloud, my voice small and fierce. "Swear to me, Whisper. Promise you'll do everything in your power to make sure she—I—live a normal human life."

His tail lashed across the floor. "I don't make promises. You know that."

"And I've never asked you anything, in an eternity of friendship! Promise me this one thing." Hot tears streamed down my cheeks. I couldn't hold all this knowledge in my tiny human mind; it was too much to absorb at once, too terrifying, too strange. All I wanted was for my mother to come take me back and hold me. "Sever my memory, Whisper, and let me live a human life. My life, *her* life, as we agreed. Please, quickly, I can't take this much—"

"I promise," Whisper said, his voice resonating through the bones of the Black Tower itself.

And his power came across my mind like a knife.

I surfaced from the memory, gasping, a long, anguished cry torn wild from my throat. All around me, a dozen reflections threw back their heads and howled with me. I dropped to my knees, shaking as if I would fall apart, sure I'd throw up in a minute.

No, no, no. I'd never wanted this, never wanted any of it, should have listened to Whisper when he tried to warn me. I covered my eyes and dug my fingers into my face—reassuringly human flesh, reassuringly human pain.

It couldn't be true. Never mind the raw *realness* of the double memory—it was Madness and Nightmare playing with me, plunging me into delusion.

"But who *are* you?" my own voice asked, plaintive.

I lifted my head to find a reflection looking down at me, head tipped to one side. "I need to know for certain," it said, with a soft wistfulness. "Which of us are you?"

Another reflection put my hands on my hips. "Hmph. Whoever you are, you're a fool, taking a bargain like that and merging with a human. And leaving the rest of us behind in the Hells! I'm half inclined to break this pretty human toy of yours out of spite."

Madness and Nightmare. Anger flooded me, driving out the horror. No matter whether this was more hallucination or horrible truth, no matter who I was or what I was, I sure as all Nine Hells wasn't taking any more of this from them.

I rose to my feet, hands curling into fists.

"That's enough," I growled. "Give him back, now."

The reflection that spoke with Nightmare's words sneered and crossed her arms. "Not until you tell us who you—"

A pulse of fury white-hot as the Hells themselves rose in me in response to her words, and for one instant, my power slipped through the iron control my grandmother had worked so hard to drill into me all those years.

The mirror that Nightmare stood in cracked.

And the one beside it, and the one beside that. Cracks spiderwebbed across every mirror—all the ones surrounding and trapping me. The high *ping* of popping glass scattered around like applause.

All at once, every single mirror in the maze exploded into a shower of shining fragments.

A vast and terrible chiming crash cascaded around me, a cacophony of shattering glass rising to the stone ceiling and ricocheting off the walls. Broken shards of mirror tumbled down in a great rain of glass, all through the building. The floor and walls shuddered, rumbling like thunder, and then were still.

Teeth gritted, I wrestled my power back down under control. Severin was in here; I'd never forgive myself if I'd hurt him.

I stood in a great empty stone building on a field of shattered glass. It stretched like snow around me, interspersed with blasted fragments of wooden framework and the occasional stone support column. Luminary crystals glowed feebly, scattered through the wreckage, casting a pale light up toward the shadowy ceiling.

In the center of it all stood Madness and Nightmare, clinging together in apparent alarm, broken shards of mirror glittering on their elaborate gowns. They stared at me wide-eyed, struck silent at last by what I'd done.

Severin lay curled in a tight protective ball on the floor at their feet. Glass dust silvered the dark sprawl of his hair. *Alive.* Thank the Graces.

I marched toward them, silvered glass crunching under my feet, still overflowing with rage. I didn't dare think, didn't dare feel anything but the desire to make them pay for what they'd done to Severin——and to me.

Madness lifted a hesitant smile to me, her wide blue eyes shining. "I *knew* it was you," she breathed. "Oh, I missed you."

The vulnerable hope in her voice threatened to slide a knife through a gap in the armor of my fury. I couldn't look at her; I focused on Nightmare and kept advancing.

Nightmare took a step backward. Her face had gone closed and wary, but her eyes were alight. "I can't believe it. They were right—I can't believe it. I know who you are."

"Don't say it," I barked.

Nightmare met my eyes. A smile curled her lips, one of reckless abandon and gleeful anticipation, as if this moment were too delicious not to savor even if it might turn to poison in her mouth.

"Disaster," she greeted me, lifting her palms in exaltation.

TWENTY-TWO

Disaster. The word sent a shiver down my core. I stopped ten feet away from them, glass grinding under my heels.

"My name," I said through my teeth, "is Ryxander. Warden of Gloamingard and Exalted Atheling of Morgrain."

"Call yourself what you wish," Nightmare crowed. "I know you now. I've known you for thousands of years, sister."

No. I was not going to accept that word. Not from her.

"*Get out,*" I growled.

Thunder rumbled as punctuation to my words, shaking a high singing whisper in response from the drifts of broken glass.

Madness's face fell, as if I'd genuinely hurt her feelings. Nightmare seized her hand.

"Come on," she said. "We did what we came to do."

They left, broken glass chiming in their wake.

I dropped to my knees beside Severin, ignoring jabs from the few shards that made it through my layers of skirts to slice my legs.

He still lay curled up, eyes squeezed shut; blood ran down his temple and the back of his hand from cuts inflicted by the glass, and I didn't doubt there were more. Yet again, I'd hurt someone I cared for.

Maybe I finally knew why that kept happening. *No, don't think about that. Focus on Severin.*

"They're gone," I told him. "Are you all right?"

I yearned to reach out and brush glass particles off him, but I didn't dare touch him with my power unsealed unless I was sure he was ready for it. *Don't think about your power and where it comes from, either.*

Severin's head jerked up. The silver sheen drained from his eyes, sharpness and color coming back to them; my shoulders slumped with relief.

He lurched to his feet, staggering away from me, his fingers flicking out from his chest in the warding sign.

"Stay away!" His chest heaved as if he'd been running. "I don't know who you are."

I froze, stricken. Blood ran down from Severin's hairline, and the scars on his neck stood out livid against his golden skin. The horror of whatever he'd been experiencing in Nightmare's care still marked his face.

I dropped the hand I'd reached out toward him. "I won't hurt you." Despite my fierce struggle for control, my voice shook. "I'm not—I'm not like them, Severin." I swallowed. "We should get those cuts seen to, and... you should rest."

Thunder shook the building again, drawing a chiming protest from the sea of broken glass and setting the shadows to trembling.

Severin kept backing away, staring at me as if I were some dangerous stranger.

And maybe I was.

My chest hurt with the deep, sick ache of a mortal wound. I turned on my heel and made my way toward the door across the field of razor-sharp glass.

Rain pelted my face and ran cold fingers down through my hair as I blundered out into the gardens, paying no attention to where I was going. The chill went straight through my court clothes, setting me to shivering.

Good. *Good.* If I could feel it, maybe I was still human.

I left a trail of dead grass and cracked flagstones behind me, a clear swath of destruction as I staggered away from the glittering lights of the palace. No human did that. Hells, it should have been obvious—of *course* I was a demon.

Disaster. One of the worst of them all, among the most terrible and grandiose villains of the Dark Days. I had no memory of whether those stories were true—nothing beyond that one moment Madness and Nightmare had pried up from the secret sealed vault in my mind. I shied instinctively away from trying to remember more, as if the past were made of fire and knives.

I wanted so badly to believe this wasn't real—that it was a torment concocted by Nightmare, so she could lap up my suffering. That what I'd experienced in the mirror maze was hallucination, not memory. That my entire life hadn't been a lie I told to myself.

But now I remembered being fire and light. I remembered sensations I had no words for. And I knew, I *knew*, that what I'd seen was true.

A soggy bed of ornamental rosebushes blocked my path. I couldn't bring myself to plow through them and destroy the gardeners' careful labor with my ruinous touch. I fell to my knees on the slick lawn, grass dying beneath me as the muddy earth soaked through my stockings.

Lightning tore the sky in half, blue and wicked. Thunder rattled my bones.

"I tried, Ryx," said a soft voice behind me. "I did everything I could. But you made my promise impossibly hard to keep."

Whisper. I swiveled to find him sitting in the grass, ears drooping slightly. The rain poured down all around him, but only a light mist silvered his deep black fur.

Half of me wanted to scream at him. Half of me wanted to wrap my arms around him and sob into his fur. I couldn't do either, so I dug my fingers into my bedraggled hair, yanking it free of what remained of my braid.

"What do I do, Whisper?" The words tore out of my raw throat. "I can't go back and pretend nothing has changed, pretend that I'm human."

Whisper regarded me with unblinking calm. "Nothing *has* changed, and you *are* human. You're simply also a demon."

So he confirmed it. A surge of restless anguish drove me to my feet; my indoor shoes slipped on the wet grass, and I caught myself on a statue of a leaping dolphin. It fractured at my touch.

"It's not that easy." My voice rose, out of control like everything else. For so long I'd managed—bottled up all the terrible things happening and moved on. But the bottle had broken, the horrors inside overflowing in a sickening wave that set my whole body shaking. "Whatever I am, whoever I am, I'm *done*. I can't—this is too much."

The wind picked up, howling through the palace chimneys. Thunder boomed, ominously close, and lightning flickered in the sky.

Whisper's tail lashed. "You are Ryxander of Morgrain," he said, his voice a whipcrack. "You are also the Demon of Disaster. And that makes you twice over my friend." He rose, and shadows seemed to gather around him; his voice sharpened to hold an edge. "And you do not have the luxury of being done. As for what you should do, you need to get your power locked down right now, before the palace slides into the ocean or catches fire. You're leaking."

Pox. *The lightning.* That was me.

I'd known all my life I couldn't afford to lose control; now I knew the stakes for losing it were higher than I'd ever realized.

Anger and pain and confusion tangled up with the power that trickled out of me, wild and loose, stirring up the sky to chaos.

Wrestling it all back under control was like fighting a flock of razor-winged geese with my bare hands, but it was something I could *do*. I clenched my jaw and forced the fist of my power closed, struggling against all the furious surging energy that yearned to break free.

The rain lessened at once, and the rumble of thunder faded and gentled. That only made me feel worse.

"All the power of one of the Nine Demons, and I use it to get myself soaked." I collapsed down against the broken statue, wrapping my arms around myself to try to stop shivering. My many layers of skirts dragged at me, heavy and waterlogged.

"You can't *use* it for anything." Whisper's voice had gone gentle. He laid a paw on my leg. "You tried for thousands of years to control it, but you can't."

"*You* can," I protested.

"We are each a fundamental type of energy, expressed in a particular manner. Some of us are orderly, and some chaotic; some are precise, directed, and others…" He sighed. "You are a creature of pure generalized entropy, Ryx. Control isn't in your nature. The best you can do is contain it."

I scrubbed the salt-streaked mess of my face. "So I really *can* only wreck things."

"As a demon, yes," Whisper said calmly. "As a human, you can do more."

A shudder wracked my shoulders. Hells take it, all those years I'd been trying so hard not to destroy everything I touched, hoping I could do better, and of *course* I'd failed. I was lucky I hadn't burned Gloamingard to the ground and killed everyone who lived there.

What had my grandmother been *thinking*?

I closed my eyes, letting the moaning of the wind flow over me. "Do my parents know?"

"No. They begged your grandmother to save you, and she told them she'd do everything in her power to do so. I'm afraid she kept her promise better than I did."

I laughed shakily. "You kept it well enough. Graces know I had no idea."

It was blasphemy for me to invoke the Graces. My own religion literally existed to celebrate my defeat at their hands. I was the enemy—one of the greatest evils the world had ever known. What in the Nine Hells was I supposed to do with that?

"Maybe..." I cast around the dismal gardens as if the answer might lie before me. Yearning flooded me for my own safe bed at Gloamingard, for my grandmother's bony hand on my brow. "Maybe all I can do is find a place as far away from humans as possible, where I can do the least harm."

"You've...tried that before." Whisper gazed off into the murky night. "Strange you should mention it now, after all the fuss you made about not wanting to abandon your friends back when it could actually have helped."

I grabbed fistfuls of my own hair. "No, of course I can't abandon them. But I can't face them, either. Severin *knows*." It was an impossible situation.

"Then sit here in the rain until your human body dies of starvation and exposure, if you wish." He shook off the light mist he'd allowed to accumulate on his fur. "I've given up on advising you."

My human body. The dread certainty struck me that it wasn't the only one I'd ever had.

I buried my face in my knees and hugged my own freezing, trembling flesh and bone as tight as I could, forcing down the hysterical bubbles that threatened to break free as laughter, sobs, or worse. I had to keep control, no matter what. I had to find a way forward. We were still in the middle of a crisis; I needed to tie the pieces of myself together with twine and prepare to face it.

Whisper remained silent. I wasn't sure if he was still there. The roaring of the wind had softened to a moan that was almost lulling, as if maybe I could lie down here and forget who I was for a while, and let it soothe me to a watery sleep.

"Ryx...?"

It was Severin's voice, hoarse and uncertain.

My head snapped up. Severin stood well beyond arm's reach, bedraggled in the rain; his embroidered vestcoat was gone, his shirt plastered to his chest. Blood still ran down his face, barely missing his eye. There was no sign of Whisper.

"Severin!" I lurched to my feet. "What are you doing out here?"

"I was afraid you'd—" He checked himself, rearranging his face from its haunted, vulnerable lines into a more controlled expression, forcing his mouth to approximate the shape of his usual half smile. "I don't know what in the Nine Hells just happened. One moment I was trapped in a lengthy and rather unpleasant hallucination featuring my dear family, and the next I was covered in broken glass. I'm afraid my vestcoat was ruined."

That's right. On top of everything else, I'd left him bleeding and alone when he needed help. But—did that mean he didn't know after all?

"We should get your cuts seen to." I stepped toward him.

He flinched. Only barely—he'd almost suppressed the reaction—but it was there.

I froze, an empty gulf yawning in my chest.

"I heard what they called you." He didn't say the word *demon*, but it was in his eyes. "I was going to walk away. I got halfway to my room when I realized I have no reason to trust them, and came back. They're toying with you, of course. It can't be true."

"Can't it?" I could lie to him, I supposed, but I was done with lies.

He looked away, the rain tracing trails over his cheekbones and down his throat. "One of the things Nightmare, ah, reminded me about was that my brother almost killed you. If you were a demon, you would have never let that happen. You'd have leveled his castle and killed everyone in it."

My gut twisted. "I...Severin, I nearly did."

He stared at me. For a moment, it looked as if he might try a laugh. But his face fell and he whispered, "You're serious."

"I didn't know." I pushed my soaked hair back from my face, wishing I could as easily claw the realization from my mind. "I didn't understand what I was doing. But the only reason I didn't tear that castle down was because you were in it."

"Well." He was silent a long moment. Far behind him, the twinkling luminaries set into the palace facade began to wink out one by one, their gathered light expended. "Thanks for not killing me, I guess."

He sounded so tired, defeated, hollow. I wished I could wipe the blood from his face, brush the hair back from his eyes. Severin alone, of everyone in this palace, I could safely be close to, to claim some kind of human comfort; but he might as well have been on the far side of the mountains. Whatever right I had earned to touch him, it was gone.

I swallowed. "You should go inside. You're hurt."

"And what about you?" His voice took on an edge. "Where will you go?"

I could only stare at him, lost. Going back to my room seemed impossible, but I hadn't forgotten what Whisper had said about abandoning my friends. "I don't know."

"Don't leave." The words burst out of him uncontrolled, almost violent. His hands clenched, then uncurled again. "Please," he added grudgingly.

"I can't," I pointed out. "We're all stuck here."

"Don't vanish into some hidden corner of the palace to sulk, then." Every line in his body was rigid with tension. "Or turn to mist. Or move in with the other... with the queen. I'm already exiled and far from home; don't leave me to the conversational mercy of the Rookery."

"You're afraid of me." My heart ached at the truth of it. "How can I stay, if you're afraid of me?"

He let out a harsh laugh. "I've spent my whole life being

frightened of the people closest to me. I thought you were finally going to be the one exception, but apparently I was wrong."

My breath hitched. "Hells, Severin." Somehow, he'd found a way to make it worse.

"Look, you know I'm terrible with feelings." He made an impatient gesture, as if throwing that nonsense away. "Yes, I'm absolutely terrified. No, I don't want you to disappear off into the night forever. I don't know any more than that, and we're not going to figure it out standing in the rain. You should come inside."

"I can't," I protested.

For a long moment, we stared at each other hopelessly in the darkness, drenched and dripping. More than once, he seemed to hover on the verge of saying something, emotion driving some word to his lips before it died there.

At last, he crossed his arms. "Well, I'm not going without you. And you might not have to worry about things like cold and wet—"

"Oh, I do," I said, shivering.

"—but I'm a mere mortal human. An extremely stubborn one. So if you don't come with me, I'll get sick, and it'll be your fault."

I stared at him, incredulous. "You wouldn't."

"You know I would. I'll die of exposure right here if it means I win." The faintest hint of a smile lighted on the corner of his mouth for an instant.

"You rotten bastard." It was the most bullheaded, maddening, kind thing anyone had ever said to me, and I didn't know whether to throttle him or break down crying.

Voices cut through the wind, calling our names. I whirled in alarm to face the Rookery as they came running toward us through the darkened garden, Foxglove limping and leaning on his cane.

"Pox," I breathed. I wasn't ready for this.

"Don't tell them," Severin said, his voice low and urgent. "Ryx, for blood's sake, you can't tell anyone."

Before I could think of a reply, or much of anything besides the loud white noise of blank panic, they were upon us.

"Ryx! You rescued him!" Kessa cried, flinging her arms wide. "We came here ready to save you both, but you did it already!"

Ashe grabbed the back of Kessa's dress, jerking her to a halt. "You unleashed her power, remember?"

"Right!" Kessa stopped with the others in a cluster near Severin, grinning with broad relief. "We had a plan, but I'll be honest, it was pretty terrible, so I'm glad yours worked. Are you both all right?"

"Severin's hurt," I said, pushing the words out through a throat that wanted to lock up in pain at how *normally* Kessa was treating me, as if nothing had changed.

"I'm fine," Severin said, glaring at me as Bastian closed in to peer at the cuts on his face. "But we *both* need to get warm and dry."

"How did you get him out?" Foxglove asked, his piercing eyes scanning me as if he could see straight through to all my secrets.

The truth sat in my belly like a hot coal. I remembered what Foxglove had said about Whisper: *A demon is a demon. By definition, they're creatures of pure evil.*

"They just wanted to talk to Ryx," Severin cut in, before I could form an answer. "To try their power on her again. But she was having none of it."

To me, it sounded weak and hollow, too intentionally vague. But Foxglove nodded with a satisfaction that only made me feel worse.

"I'm sure you're fine," Bastian said to Severin in the patient tone of someone who'd been told that by a lot of seriously injured people, "but I do want to get some alchemical salve on those cuts, because you don't actually have an infinite supply of blood, you know."

"Let's go," Kessa agreed, with worried glances all around. "We've still got lots of work to do on the wards and a key to steal, and we only have two days left to do it before those imperial warships off the coast level the palace. If we don't sleep, we're going to botch this so spectacularly no one will ever find the pieces of us."

She wasn't wrong. I had to try to find a way to help that wretch Aurelio, too, on top of everything else. There was work to do; that hadn't changed, even though the entire world had rotated ninety degrees and settled again. Somehow, I had to keep going.

Everyone started without hesitation for the palace, an air of excitement putting more energy in their steps, their voices, the way they carried themselves. Excitement because they thought I'd achieved some victory, held some upper hand over the demons.

I couldn't make myself take a step from where I stood. I stared at their backs, knowing that if I said nothing and came with them, it would be a lie. If I didn't crush their fragile hope here and now and make it clear that I came not from the Graces, but straight from the Nine Hells themselves, I was committing a deep betrayal of the trust my friends placed in me.

Severin paused and gave me a meaningful glare over his shoulder. Kessa glanced back, too, and beckoned me on.

My chest aching as if shards from the shattered mirrors had lodged inside it, I followed.

TWENTY-THREE

It was a long, awful night of staring at that cursed ceiling mural as the moonlight crept across the wall and finally faded into the sinister gray of a sleepless dawn. I shouldn't even have tried to sleep, but my body ached with bone-deep weariness. Terrible thoughts chased each other around my head as I lay there in the dark, trying to somehow patch myself together enough that I could get out of bed in the morning and do what needed to be done.

Mostly my stunned mind kept presenting me with the central awful fact, over and over: I was the Demon of Disaster.

I didn't *feel* like a demon. I felt human.

But then, I supposed I didn't know what being human felt like.

This doesn't change anything wasn't a comforting thought. It recast my whole life in a darker light. All of the hopes I'd been building that my jess would let me live a normal life, that I could stop being a danger to the people around me at last, were shattered.

My secret weighed unspoken in my chest like blood pooling in my lungs. I was going to have to tell the Rookery sooner or later; this was the sort of information that might get people killed if I held it back too long. But every time I tried to imagine telling them, a wave of nausea gripped me, and cold sweat prickled my skin.

Bastian. I could tell Bastian. He'd understand; he wasn't entirely human himself, and he'd believed my grandmother wasn't irredeemable. Maybe telling him would be enough, for now.

Morning broke fully over me with all the pale unpleasantness of used dishwater. It was time to make my bones move, to face the world that I only half belonged to. Time to go forth into the awful newborn day and keep it from becoming worse.

Dragging against the weight of my own shattered world, I got up.

All too aware of how little time we had, the Rookery wasted none of it. We'd split up and gotten to work by the time the sun had finished clearing the hills. Foxglove and Bastian carved away at the wards, Severin continued his work of subverting every animal on the palace grounds to be his spies and saboteurs, and Kessa and I met first with the majordomo and then with Councilor Altaine and a handful of other Curia leaders to discuss procedures for swiftly evacuating the palace.

I was glad to get moving. It had been unbearable to face everyone acting so *normally*, gulping down the tea and coffee and increasingly stale pastries Kessa had brought from the kitchens, treating me like one of the company. Everyone except Severin— he'd stared at me as if I'd transformed into a mountain leopard and he wasn't sure whether to cautiously approach me or run away. Thank the seasons I had a good excuse to avoid everyone as much as I could, with my jess still inactive.

It felt good to dive into something as comfortable as castle logistics, and even the familiar dance of keeping my distance from important people during meetings. I didn't have to think about what I was, or what it meant, and could focus on simple tasks like setting up a chair barrier to keep Loreician officials unclear on the danger from wandering into my side of the meeting room, or organizing a communication chain to quickly spread the word when it was time to get everyone out.

But then Bastian needed someone to act as a lookout while he worked on the wards along the outer edge of the conversation gardens, where the wrong people might wander by and catch him in the act. Kessa had to go talk to the queen's maids to find out whether Madness ever took the ward key off, so that meant me—and then I had nothing to keep my hands and mind busy, and no excuse not to work up the courage to tell Bastian the truth.

He'd set up behind a tall row of hedges. I stood at the end, peering between the branches, watching for anyone who might approach. I was most concerned about the Zenith Society. By the Rookery's report, they weren't early risers, but at some point they were bound to notice that their stolen artifact was missing. So far there was no sign of them among the people who'd taken to the grounds as relief from being stuck inside the palace—some huddling in whispering clusters, others walking briskly alone or in pairs as if they could outpace the deadly trouble they were in. A determined crowd of sycophants remained around the queen under her great tree, and gardeners worked on clearing up the damage done to trees and bushes by last night's storm. I couldn't help a guilty twinge at that.

Unfortunately, everyone seemed distant enough that I didn't have to concentrate on being a lookout, and was free to worry about how to broach the topic of my secret.

Bastian, I'm a demon. It sounded both foolish and dramatic at the same time, somehow. *I discovered something about myself last night*...Ugh, that sounded like the lead-in to a love confession. *Do you remember that conversation we had back at Gloamingard about my grandmother being a demon?* Too roundabout.

His stylus scratched away at the stone wall, carving more symbols into the wards with an alchemical engraving potion. I had to get this over with. *Do it, Ryx.* My throat tightened up as if the air had turned to poison.

The scratching stopped. Bastian let out an explosive sigh. "I suppose I should just come out and say it."

I spun and blinked at him. "What?"

Bastian fidgeted with his stylus. "I understand if you don't want to be alone with me, after what happened. You don't have to do this."

"What are you talking about?" Now I was completely lost.

He stared at me in equal incomprehension. "I tried to kill you." When I didn't say anything right away, he added helpfully, "With a knife."

"Oh!" I had genuinely almost forgotten. Hells, I was an ass. "Don't worry about that. You were controlled."

"That's exactly the problem." His shoulders hunched. "If Cortissa walks up to me right now and tells me to try again, I'll have to do it. It's not even an unlikely chance; we know they want to take us out of the picture, and it's an easy and logical move. I'm faster than a normal human and would have the advantage of surprise. It's legitimately dangerous to be alone with me right now."

I shrugged. "It's been dangerous to be around me for my entire life. We'll manage."

"I hate this," he said quietly, his shoulders drooping. "There's so little in this life we *can* control; knowing I could lose command of my own body at any time is terrifying."

"I know." I wished I could reach out to him somehow, but I couldn't even take a step closer without killing off patches of garden. "My grandmother did that to me once, and it wasn't pleasant. I'm sure it's a thousand times worse when it's someone you hate."

"If I'd killed you . . ." He trailed off, shaking his head. "I could still kill you. Or Kessa, or Foxglove, or any of the others." He grimaced. "Maybe not Ashe. But the point is, if I hurt someone, even if I was controlled, their blood is still quite literally on my hands."

"No it isn't," I said immediately. "You're not a killer, Bastian. Whereas Cortissa—well, if she'd ever learned to give one whit about human life, she wouldn't be a Skinwitch. You'd never hurt anyone; she's the one with murderous intent."

Bastian still looked skeptical. Searching for words, I fell back on a very Vaskandran way of looking at it, hoping Bastian would understand. "If she forces you to do something terrible, that's a grievance we hold against her, not one anyone should hold against you."

"I suppose you're right." His smile held more pain than relief. "It doesn't feel that way, though. Not when it was my hands that tried to kill you."

"I understand." I held up my own hand, with its naked wrist. "I've killed... well, more than one person. I don't know exactly how many. None of them were on purpose."

He nodded, his dark eyes gone thoughtful. "You certainly shouldn't feel bad about that. So... maybe I should try not to, either."

"It's not easy," I admitted.

"Very little in life seems to be." He lifted his stylus again, with a rueful sigh. "Including rewriting the wards to an entire palace. I suppose I should get back to work."

I gave him an encouraging smile, and he turned his attention to the wall again, his shoulders a bit more relaxed.

I still hadn't told him. Pox take it.

A flurry of color and movement drifted toward us, coming from the great tree: a knot of nobles in pastel silks and silver-eyed guards, with Madness and Nightmare at the heart.

My stomach shriveled up around the bit of pastry I'd nibbled that morning. I wasn't ready to face them, or to think about last night. But I couldn't let them discover Bastian.

They probably couldn't see him, but I was standing at the end of the row of hedges behind which he worked, and Madness had clearly spotted me. She sailed relentlessly in my direction, trailing exquisite clouds of silver lace and her whole retinue of courtiers.

"The queen's headed this way," I murmured to Bastian, trying not to sound as queasy as I felt. "I'll see if I can draw her off."

I started wandering away from him through the conversation gardens, trying to look as if I were just pacing around and brooding, which seemed plausible enough after last night. Out of the corner of my eye, I saw Madness stop and exchange a few words with Nightmare; the other demon seemed to first resist, then give in as Madness shook her head. They split, Nightmare taking the train of courtiers, and Madness drifted my way alone.

My pulse quickened. I paused, made sure I couldn't see Bastian from here, and let her catch up to me.

Her young face—no, the stolen face she was wearing—broke into a hopeful smile. My belly twisted with revulsion and something else, something softer and hard to name.

"Disaster," she greeted me.

"Don't call me that," I snapped.

Her smile faltered. "Oh. Like Whisper, then—you have another name. I see."

I jerked my head in a stiff nod. I had no idea what to say to her. I should be trying to figure out a way to get the ward key—it was dangling right there on her chest, sparkling with jewels and wrapped in artifice wire—but strange gears shifted in my mind every time I met those wide blue eyes, rust falling off them as they threatened to turn into motion.

Her pale brows drew together. "You don't remember me at all."

"No." Graces help me, there was something about her voice. Something familiar in the back of those eyes, elusive as a scent I hadn't smelled since childhood. "I'm sorry. Or rather, I'm not sorry." I took a deep breath. "I don't *want* to remember. I just want to be who I've always been, living my human life."

Her head tilted. "You never lived a human life."

The words slid between my ribs like a stiletto. No, I supposed ghosting around in the walls and shunning living touch wasn't quite the normal human experience, in retrospect. "Nonetheless."

She reached for my face; I jerked back instinctively. "I miss you," she whispered. "You protected me."

My stomach lurched as if I'd missed a step. "What?"

That strange, tentative smile touched her lips again. "I was... quiet and small and strange. I made little patterns and I broke them, made them and broke them, by myself in odd pockets of the Hells." She swirled a finger in the air, watching its path as if she could track the invisible turbulence it caused. "The others were cruel, sometimes. But you didn't let them bully me." She touched my shoulder, gently; a tingling rush of power trickled into me. I flinched, but apparently demons overflowed with so much energy that she didn't even notice the amount I took from her. "You understood how sad it makes me, that I keep breaking the patterns without meaning to. Because you're the same."

"In this world, some of those patterns are human minds," I said, my voice tight. "And human lives, in my case. *People*."

Madness nodded, her face grave. "So beautiful. So fragile. Do you remember now?"

I shook my head. Something pressed on my chest, a deep inexplicable grief, making it hard to breathe.

"That's all right." The smile that lit her face could have melted snow. "I'll help you."

"I don't need help," I assured her, alarmed. "I'm fine."

"You always say that. But you never are." She patted my cheek with a cool, slim hand. "Don't worry. Now it's my turn to take care of you, sister."

Sister.

Her handprint remained cold on my cheek as the silvery train of her gown hissed away over the grass.

I was still staring after Madness, my mind in a loathsome gray space, when a flash of wine-colored brocade caught the corner of my eye. *Aurelio.*

Or Hunger, more like it, by the force in his stride as he advanced across the lawn toward a cluster of courtiers lingering in the sprawling shade beneath the great royal tree. A cluster that included some familiar figures I was pretty sure were Zenith Society, and—curse it, that was Moreni. The gardens were *full* of people I didn't want to deal with this morning. I scanned for any sign of Cortissa, thinking anxiously of Bastian carving away unprotected on his wall, but I didn't see her. That could be good or bad.

Just as I was about to hurry back to Bastian, Hunger reached the group and started shouting, terrible rage swelling his voice. I caught the words *stolen* and *promised* and *gone.*

Uh-oh. It seemed he'd found out about the missing artifact.

The courtiers recoiled before him; Moreni stood stiff, spreading his hands in a *What can I do* gesture. Hunger must not have liked that, because he seized a random young man in an apricot silk jacket by the throat.

Even from this distance, the boy visibly withered, clawing weakly at Hunger's wrist, his mouth a wide cave of horror. Within three racing beats of my heart, he went limp.

Hunger threw him down on the grass, an empty husk. By the way his body bounced and lay still, I knew with sick certainty he was dead. *Holy Hells.*

Some of the courtiers ran, screaming; others threw themselves down to cower before him. Moreni backed a step, hands up and explaining, his people grouped tight around him. He lifted a finger and pointed to the palace.

I made out one word: *Rookery.*

The wave of power Hunger unleashed didn't reach to where I stood, but everyone left standing beneath the tree swayed and dropped to their knees.

Without a word, Hunger stalked off toward the palace, murder in his stride.

He was going to kill them all.

TWENTY-FOUR

I ran after Hunger, thinking furiously. Foxglove and Kessa were in the Rookery quarters; she'd made him take a break from carving runes to rest his leg and eat. They didn't stand a chance against an enraged demon. I had to pacify or divert him somehow.

I brushed past a topiary bush, leaving a yellowed streak, and reeled away from a silver-eyed palace guard I'd almost bumped into. Voices rose beyond a hedge, warning me before I risked colliding with a pair of plume-wearing Curia members muttering something derogatory about nobles cozying up to Lady Silene. This was too dangerous—I had to slow down, pox take it.

Hunger disappeared into the palace through a grand door framed by leaping bronze dolphins; I chased him through galleries populated enough to set my heart pounding, walking as quickly as I dared and swerving to give the hollow-eyed clumps of people as wide a berth as possible. At last I caught up to him in the imperial wing, before the warded golden door with its crest bearing the winged horse of Raverra.

"Aurelio!" I called, hoping to startle him into taking back control of his body.

But it was Hunger who whirled on me, fury in his face. A wave of power hit me like a wall, rocking me on my feet.

"You," he snarled. "These are *your* humans, Disaster. They took something that was mine!"

It wasn't yours, I wanted to retort, but that would only feed his anger. If I'd learned one thing in my years of mediating diplomatic relations between Morgrain and the Serene Empire, it was the importance of understanding what mattered to the party you were negotiating with.

"Actually," I said, trying to sound as casual as I could given that I'd just chased him all the way here, "they saved you from making an ass of yourself."

He checked himself, narrowing Aurelio's eyes. "What do you mean?"

"Isn't it obvious?" I shrugged, clasping my hands behind my back to hide how they were trembling. "That artifice toy was bait. A cheap bribe, so they could use you. How do you even know it was really stolen? They could be hiding it from you themselves, to string you along and keep their leverage over you."

Hunger's frown deepened. "They'd better not be. Boy! What do you have to say to this?"

Aurelio winced, human uncertainty softening his hazel eyes. "I . . . I don't think the Zenith Society knows where it is, either," he said, with an alarmed glance at me that I read as *Please don't get my friends killed*. "I suppose it's true that Moreni hates the Rookery and would point the blame at them no matter what actually happened."

Fine, if he didn't want me to aim Hunger's wrath at the Zenith Society, I could try another angle. "The point is, you never needed this thing. They were trying to entice you to do what *they* wanted with it, but it wasn't really what *you* wanted. You can't possess something if you've destroyed it."

I'd hit home; something flickered in his eyes. "It's true that I haven't had my own country in ages. Not since that place by the water, back in the Dark Days—what did the humans call it?"

A distant, nostalgic look came over his face. "It doesn't matter. They worshipped me, brought me sacrifices. It was glorious."

The thought turned my stomach, but at least his focus was shifting away from retribution. "Yes," I agreed. "Like that."

Cruel amusement pulled at his mouth. "You didn't seem so approving four thousand years ago."

That was news to me. I had no memories of him, no feelings bubbling up from some buried past. For all I knew he might bring thousands of years of grudges or friendship to this conversation, or all the complex layers of beloved familial spite, but I had no idea if we'd even liked each other.

Good. It didn't matter. I was Ryx now, and I hated him.

Hunger inspected me more closely. "You didn't know, did you? You genuinely thought you were a human." He shook Aurelio's head in disgust. "Look at what's happened to you. First Discord, now you—completely debased. It's revolting."

He was trying to upset me, but I had plenty of practice bottling up distress to conclude a delicate negotiation. If he truly abhorred the idea of merging with a human, maybe I could somehow use that to help free Aurelio.

"It wasn't my idea," I said. "Perhaps you could get the Zenith Society to make you some kind of artificial host, if you hate humans so much."

"Like Whisper's chimera body?" He snorted his contempt. "No need for such contrivances. All it takes to avoid a merge is a willing host who hates the idea as much as you do." He smacked Aurelio's chest with his palm, proud as if he were showing off a fine horse. "Right, boy?"

Had I been a willing or unwilling host? In my scrap of memory from the mirror maze, I'd been mostly very small and very tired, with no real understanding of what was happening. Maybe some part of me had *wanted* this—the sickly child to be eternal and strong, and the demon to be human and loved.

Aurelio's expression had gone resigned and haunted. "Of

course I'm willing. No one else will invite you in voluntarily, and you'll just possess me by force if I try to evict you. And I'd sooner shred my own eyeballs with a cheese grater than merge with you."

Hunger laughed. "Exactly. This vessel is mine." He stretched luxuriantly, enjoying Aurelio's body like a fine wine. "Very well, then; you've given me some ideas. I'll have to talk them over with Nightmare before the council."

"Council?" I asked.

Aurelio's brows lifted, his expression sliding across Hunger's in apparent alarm. "Do you mean the Zenith Society meeting in the library? We—that is, I thought you weren't coming."

So Aurelio was conspiring with his friends in the Zenith Society behind Hunger's back as well. I supposed I shouldn't be surprised; if he was adept at one thing, it was treachery.

His face twisted into Hunger's sneer of contempt. "Why would I want to sit in a boring human meeting? Ugh. No, this is a family council. Nightmare wanted to have one." An idea seemed to come to him, and his lips spread in a cruel smile. "In fact, *sister*, you should come. After all, you're one of us."

I had no doubt the invitation was a taunt, meant to rub salt in a bleeding wound. My first urge was to repudiate him, to tell him that we were absolutely *not* on the same side and that he could take his council and stuff it. But I'd sat down at a negotiating table with enemies before, and I'd be a fool to turn down a chance at this kind of information.

"I'll think about it," I said.

He put a hand to his chest and inclined slightly in a mocking bow. "It wouldn't be complete without you. Until then, sister."

At last, he stepped away from the door to the imperial wing, moving off with all the jaunty confidence of someone with no concept of consequences for his actions.

My shoulders slumped with relief. He might decide he was still annoyed about the artifact later—and we had Moreni's displeasure to reckon with—but for now, at least, he'd let it go.

And whether on purpose or not, Aurelio had dropped another gem for me. So the Zenith Society was having a meeting in the library, were they? The destruction of their weapon was bound to change their plans, and I doubted very much their response would be to concede defeat and sit quietly while we subverted the wards.

It was time to go get the Rookery and do some eavesdropping.

Once you got past the initial grand, impressive chamber that existed to show off to visiting dignitaries, the royal library turned into a warren of tall stacks, narrow aisles, and little nooks and side rooms set up for reading, study, or academic discussion. It was a fine place for a private conversation if no one knew to look for you there, but the sightlines for spotting anyone who might overhear you were terrible. And if the people sneaking up on you included a powerful vivomancer who'd already used mice to scout out your exact location and the best spots for listening, well, you'd better have brought an anti-eavesdropping artifice device.

Moreni, unfortunately, had brought one.

I peered at the doorway to the study room where they were meeting through the slim gap between a pair of old leather-bound books, breathing in the scent of aging paper. They'd hung a slim chain woven with copper artifice wire and glittering crystals across the door. A faint humming sound rose from it; the enchantment muffled and garbled all noise escaping the room. Past the chain, I could glimpse a smallish book-lined room and one end of a table with several people clustered around it.

Kessa gave me an encouraging nod from her spot a safe distance away down my aisle. My turn.

We'd all taken our shoes off for this; my stockinged feet padded quietly on the elaborate mosaics of the Grace of Wisdom that covered the library floor. It was easy enough to edge around to a position by the doorway to the study room, pressed against the wall and out of sight. Seasons, it felt good to be doing something as reassuringly human and normal as tiptoeing around a library, even if the situation remained dire. Foxglove had worked his way to the far side of the doorway; he eyed the artifice device analytically and gave me a sharp nod.

I slid my hand along the door frame and carefully touched one finger to the end of the chain.

A swarming rush of magic flowed up my arm. The humming stopped, and voices rose up in the room beyond.

"...Pox-rotted Rookery, that's who stole it, Hell of Corruption take them," Cortissa growled.

Foxglove flashed me a brief, fierce grin.

"It's got to still be in the palace." That was Moreni, his voice gloved in calm. "We'll find it. As for the Rookery, while it's a shame Hunger didn't finish them for us, we'll deal with them—or our allies will."

"Will they, though?" This was a new voice, dripping cynicism. "We've already seen that we can't count on them to stay focused on our goals. They'd rather muck around in people's heads. And they have no sense of loyalty; it's only sheer luck that Hunger grabbed some hanger-on and not one of us this morning. I don't like how all our plans rely on support they could take away at any moment."

Cortissa let out a wicked little chuckle. "Oh, they won't, Lutani. I know how to hold their interest. I'm going to make them presents."

"Presents?" Lutani sounded wary, and I couldn't blame him; my own skin prickled at the way she savored the word.

"Human chimeras to be their lieutenants." I could hear the smile in Cortissa's voice. "With all the people in the palace at our disposal, I've got plenty of materials to work with. Our sponsors hardly want the trouble of actually running a country, after all—they only want the foothold that controlling the symbols of power gives them. If I gift them a set of powerful and absolutely loyal servants, they'll be delighted to use them."

"Absolutely loyal to *us*, of course," Moreni added smoothly. "And then we control Loreice and all its weapons and resources. The demons can entertain themselves however they please; we won't be reliant on them anymore."

Hells. I glanced toward where Bastian hid, deeper in the stacks, but couldn't see him; I hoped Kessa was in range to give him some comfort. It was turning *my* stomach to hear this, so I could only imagine how he felt.

"I'm concerned." I could see the speaker this time: Girard, the man Kessa had given the healing salve to. He sat with his chair pushed back a bit from the table, arms crossed. "With all respect, my lord, what are the demons going to *do* with Loreice? We're supposed to be protecting the Serene Empire, not handing pieces of it to them."

"To us," Moreni corrected him. "The important thing right now is that we need an unassailable base of power here, to operate from until we can take control in the Serene City. The current leadership doesn't have the stomach for doing what needs to be done to keep the Empire forever safe from Vaskandar; we do. If that means the demons have their fun in Loreice while we consolidate our control, then that's the price we have to pay."

"This sounds less like it's about protecting the Empire and more about attempting another coup," Girard objected. "I've got plenty of reservations about what we've already done, but what we're helping them do tonight... Well, it's beyond the bounds. If this is just a power play, count me out."

"We have to seize power *in order* to preserve the Empire," Moreni explained, as if Girard were being obtuse. "And to protect ourselves." Footsteps sounded, and the light in the room changed, as if he'd drawn back a curtain. "Look out the window. See that fort overlooking the harbor? A fine imperial fortress, full of the most advanced artifice weapons to help protect our border. Right now, all aimed at us." Another rustle, as if he'd opened another curtain. "See those ships off in the distance, on the horizon? Full of more weapons and Falcons, likely including a storm warlock. All pointed straight at the Summer Palace."

Uncomfortable stirring and exclamations came from some of the Zenith Society members. I exchanged glances with Foxglove. I should have realized they'd notice; they had spyglasses and working brains and a knowledge of how the Serene Empire tended to respond to threats.

"Of course we don't want to fight the Empire," Moreni continued. "The only way to avoid that, given that they've outlawed us and are coming for us, is to show this government that violence is not a strategy that will serve them. The doge and the Council aren't fools; if they see that military force can't prevail, they'll try something else—hopefully negotiation, but if not, no matter. It'll buy us time to seize control in Raverra either way."

"And how do you intend to show them that military force can't prevail?" Girard asked dubiously.

"Our patrons will handle that," Moreni said, with satisfaction. "Shortly after their council today, I believe. I'd make certain you're behind the wards on our quarters within the next hour, as I gather there may be . . . side effects in the palace."

That didn't sound good. Foxglove stiffened, his eyes narrowing.

"Ah yes, their little council." Cortissa's nails drummed on the table with a rolling patter. "We need to get one of us into that meeting."

"I've tried. We're not invited." Disgust infused Moreni's tone. "More's the pity."

"Anything else?" Cortissa asked, with the voice of someone easily made restless by meetings. Her chair scraped the floor. "I want to talk to Nightmare before this council of theirs. We were having the most lovely discussion about possibly letting her watch while I make my chimeras."

"And I've got to repair half my artifice devices," Lutani complained. "Something's been chewing on the wire."

We should get out of here. They were about to leave, and when they did, they'd walk right into us. I glanced at Foxglove, who seemed to agree; he jerked his head toward the exit.

Slowly and silently, we started creeping back along the library walls, barely daring to breathe, the conversation fading with distance but holding the unmistakable tone of a discussion in the process of wrapping up. As we neared the door, one final comment from Cortissa drifted over our heads:

"And the Rookery?"

"Given what I know," Moreni said, "after tonight they won't be a problem."

Foxglove pulled us aside as soon as we were out of sight of the library entrance. "All right. I'm worried about what they're planning for tonight—"

"I can talk to Girard," Kessa offered. "He didn't seem too happy about it, and I bet I could coax a warning out of him."

"Good." Foxglove nodded. "But first we've got to get on the courier lamps right away and warn the Serene Empire to prepare for an imminent attack on that fortress and those ships."

Kessa gave a low whistle. "That's going to be tricky. The majordomo said the queen has really upped the protections on the lamp chamber in response to these inexplicable repeated break-ins. We're going to have to be clever."

"Then we'll be clever," Foxglove said, with grim resolve. "Teodor used to be stationed in that fortress; it's bigger than Castle Ilseine, with thousands of people. And it's a hub for training mage-marked children to control their power. There are families there."

Kessa gave her hat a decisive tug to a rakish angle. "Well, we can hardly let those baby mages get hurt, can we? Come on."

Everyone started to move. I gathered my courage and cleared my throat. "You go. I'm going to spy on the demon council. We need to know what they're doing."

Kessa frowned. "An admirable goal, but you shouldn't try to sneak up on a bunch of demons by yourself. Do you want me to come with you? We'd need listening devices and—"

"No, I..." I took a deep breath. "I've been invited."

Everyone stared at me with puzzled expressions—except Severin, whose eyes had gone wide with alarm. He shook his head minutely.

Bastian frowned. "Why would they invite you to a council of demons?"

Severin answered before I could, with a nonchalant shrug. "To represent the Lady of Owls, of course."

The words I was marshaling dried up in my mouth. *Curse it, Severin, this is hard enough.*

"Oh, well done," Kessa approved. "I know you've been working that angle. Still, claiming to be her emissary didn't protect you before. Are you sure you'll be safe?"

"Safe is a relative term. But I think I'll be all right." After all, they knew who I was now; they'd gotten what they wanted.

Foxglove gave me an odd look. "Does this have to do with your... *friend*? Because I'm not sanguine about relying on the protection of the Demon of Death."

"He... he's not protecting me anymore." A knot tried to form in my throat; I swallowed it ruthlessly. I could tell Foxglove the truth—*I don't think they'll attack me because they've promoted me from human victim to peer*—but we needed to hurry, and this wasn't the time for shocking revelations. I settled for a piece of it. "After how things ended in the mirror maze, I think they'll be a bit more cautious around me."

His eyebrows flew up. "Sometime you have to tell me what happened in there."

"Excuse me, but we should go," Bastian said, shifting from

foot to foot with frustrated urgency. "If we want to warn the Empire in time for them to actually do anything, that is."

"And then get behind our own wards before those side effects they were talking about happen," Kessa added. "Not to mention getting a warning to our contacts in the palace."

"Fine." Foxglove angled toward the courier lamp chamber, ready to start down the hall. "Your judgment so far has been on the mark, Ryx. I trust you to know whether you can do this. Just be careful."

My judgment had been questionable, and I kept getting in so far over my head I'd forgotten what sunlight looked like. But the moment when I could have told them the truth without holding up the mission was gone.

I gave him a sharp nod. "I'll be as careful as I ever am."

Ashe snorted and gave me an *I heard what you did there* look as she followed Foxglove.

"I'll catch up," Severin called after the Rookery. "I need a quick word with Ryx."

Oh, I bet he did. I certainly needed a word with him.

We glared at each other as the Rookery's footsteps receded. Severin's gray mage mark smoldered like the smoke from a sullen fire.

The moment they were out of hearing range, he burst out, "What in the Nine Hells was *that*?"

Heat built in my face. "I could ask you the same thing! Why did you lie to them?"

"To keep you from making a colossal mistake!" He threw his hands up. "What were you *thinking*? You can't tell them!"

"I don't want to lie to them," I protested. "They're my friends."

"You *have* to lie!" Severin stepped closer to me, his voice going softer, but no less intense. "You have to lie for the rest of your life. Otherwise, it's over."

I crossed my arms. "I can't accept that. How can I ask them to trust me if I won't trust them?"

"Stop thinking of the Rookery as your friends and start thinking of them as what they are: an international government agency." Severin flung an arm in the general direction they'd gone. "What happens if you tell them? *Think* about it. What will they do?"

"They'll..." I struggled to say, *They'll understand, because they're my friends.* But it was too much to ask them to simply understand; frankly, it would be strange if they did.

"They'll make a report to their superiors." Severin pronounced every word with ruthless precision. "They *have* to; it's their job. Don't you see? The question isn't whether you trust your friends with your secret. The question is whether you trust the Serene Empire and Vaskandar with it."

My stomach dropped as if Severin had kicked it down a well. "I hadn't thought of that."

"And what do you think they'll do, when they know?" Severin reached out as if to grip my shoulder, but hesitated. "The Council of Nine and the Witch Lords aren't your friends; they have no reason to hold back. They'll want to kill you—or study you, or use you as a weapon. I'm not sure which is worse."

He wasn't wrong. Seasons witness I hated it, but he wasn't wrong. "I have to put the good of Eruvia first," I insisted. "And Eruvia—"

"Doesn't need to know." Severin let out an explosive breath. "Look, *I'm* struggling to accept your exciting news, and I'm *used* to strange and terrible things being part of my daily life. Anyone you tell is going to panic, whether it's your best friend or a head of state. And right now, if heads of state panic, we get a demon war."

"Maybe." I frowned at him. "Or maybe you're saying that because you know that's what will convince me."

"At least take a few days to think the full implications through before you take a rash, irreversible step that will get you killed."

His eyes were so desperate, pulling at me from shadowy hollows dug by lack of sleep. Something fluttered in my rib cage, a beating of trapped wings.

"I..." My voice came out thick and strange. I swallowed and tried again. "I assure you, I've been thinking of little else besides the full implications. But you've got a point. Thank you for still caring, given...everything."

Severin seized my hand; I stifled a flash of instinctive panic. He lifted it in both of his, trembling, and laid it against his heart. I could feel it beating against the backs of my knuckles, warm and alive and frightened. My breath caught in my throat.

"Thank *you*," he whispered. "For last night. No one ever cared enough to save me before."

Slowly, tenderly, he let my hand go. I left it hanging in the air, frozen, unsure what had just happened. It felt far too much like a good-bye.

"I'd better catch up with the others." His voice had gone husky, and he didn't meet my eyes.

Words deserted me utterly. I stared after the graceful sway of his ponytail as he strode away.

My skin crawled as if it wanted to run away right off my body, and I couldn't blame it. The power in the air nearly crushed the breath from my lungs. But I belonged here, at this table full of demons—and that made it even worse.

"Last time, the humans beat us because they were organized. They worked together, while we all pursued our own fancies without any kind of coordination." Nightmare steepled her fingers and leaned forward over the oval table she'd had set up on the airy terrace outside the royal wing. Past the ivy-clad marble balustrade we'd escaped over two impossibly long days ago, the green hillside swept down to the distant, restless blue eternity of the sea. "We can't repeat our mistakes. So I've copied a custom the humans have and called this council of all of us."

I couldn't help but notice she'd seated herself at the head of the table. I doubted that Madness, at her left hand, knew what that meant; she was gazing wistfully out at the ocean and might not be listening at all. Hunger, at her right, certainly knew; dissatisfaction marred Aurelio's features as he rolled the stem of his wineglass between his fingers.

I'd sat at the foot of the table, as far away from Nightmare as I could get. It felt deeply wrong to be here. The only thing remotely reassuring about this situation was Whisper, perched on an elevated cushion between me and Madness. His tail tip swished back and forth, his yellow eyes narrowed in disdain or disapproval.

What it meant that the Demon of Death was a comfort to me, I didn't really want to examine.

"It's not all of us, though, is it," Hunger said, eyeing the empty seat between the two of us.

Nightmare shrugged. "I invited her. But do you really expect that *Discord* would attend a meeting about working together?"

Hunger laughed. "No, I suppose not."

"You forget," called a heart-stoppingly familiar voice, "that I also like surprising people and ruining your careful plans."

My grandmother vaulted over the balustrade from nowhere, her orange-ringed eyes burning with mischief.

<u>TWENTY-FIVE</u>

My grandmother's winglike mantle settled around her as she landed on the terrace. I had to stop myself from lunging to my feet.

Nightmare's eye twitched. "Hello, Discord. Glad you could make it."

"No, you're not." My grandmother grinned, too wide, showing her teeth. "But I'm glad to be here."

She didn't take her seat, leaning against the railing instead, arms crossed. I gripped my chair to keep from running to her. For a moment I thought she wouldn't even greet me; but her eyes slid sideways to mine, and she winked.

A wink. *Holy Hells, Grandmother.* Everything I had to say to her, everything unspoken between us, all I'd learned about what she'd done to me and for me boiled in my chest, splattering scalding feelings around my rib cage. But this wasn't the time for that. I clamped my jaw shut and stayed in my seat.

"How did you get in through the wards?" Nightmare asked through smiling teeth.

"Oh, didn't I tell you? I let her in." Madness turned her shy, brilliant smile on my grandmother. "Welcome, Discord. The merge suits you."

My grandmother offered her a mocking half bow. "I certainly think so."

"So we're all here, then." Nightmare's voice held a slight edge of annoyance, but she spread her arms as if to welcome everyone. "All six of us who've come through the gate, back in the material world with its many pleasures at last. Some of us have already begun pursuing our goals. I ask you now: What will we do?"

My stomach tightened. At least no one contradicted her claim that this was all the demons who'd come through; part of my brain had been worried that there might be more, and we could be facing the full nine as we had in the Dark Days. We didn't have to deal with Carnage, Corruption, or Despair, who by all accounts were some of the worst. But six was still more than enough to cause incalculable human suffering.

And I'd just counted myself in that number. I felt like throwing up.

Hunger jabbed the table with Aurelio's finger as if it were a knife. "I want the Serene Empire."

"That's half the continent," Nightmare objected. "I've looked at a map. Also, it wasn't our arrangement."

Hunger shrugged. "You can keep Loreice as your little playground. There should be plenty of humans here to occupy you. I'll take the rest."

My fists curled in my lap. No matter how outraged I was at what they said, my priority had to be getting information. "And what would you *do* with it?" I asked, trying to keep my voice even.

Hunger stared at me as if I were talking nonsense. "Do? I *want* it." He crossed his arms. "You're the one who pointed that out to me, remember? Since apparently I'm not going to get to drain Alevar today after all, I need *something*."

It seemed inconceivable that Aurelio would sit silent while Hunger talked that way about the Empire he'd been willing to murder me to save. Pain flickered across his face, his hazel eyes meeting mine with a sort of miserable understanding, but he didn't speak. I wondered if Hunger had threatened him with retribution if he reminded the other demons of his demeaning presence.

"You're so short-sighted, Hunger." Nightmare shook her head. "The entire point of possessing a country is to savor the anguish of the humans within it."

"Let me make one thing clear," my grandmother said, her voice cutting through the conversation like a knife. "Whatever games you play with the rest of the world, stay out of Morgrain."

Nightmare shrugged. "No one cares about your little toy box, Discord. It's yours."

"I care," I protested, through my teeth.

Whisper's tail whipped as if he could flick away the whole table and everyone around it. "You know I always remain neutral," he said, his voice soft and ominous. "But I ask that you bear in mind one thing."

Everyone fell silent and listened, attentive and wary.

"We're all here because we *like* the material world." He swept his sulfurous gaze across us like a beam of fire. "But if I have learned one thing from living in it for millennia, it's that this world is fragile. We are power, and it cannot easily withstand us. Unless you move through it with profound restraint, you will destroy it."

Hunger frowned. "Oh, come now. Maybe Disaster or Carnage could, if they weren't careful." My spine prickled at that. "But most of us aren't disruptive on that level."

"I assure you, you are," Whisper said. "The effects may be subtler, but they can be just as devastating."

"My amusements don't destroy anything," Nightmare protested. "The humans are no use to me dead, after all." But Madness cast her eyes down at the table, as if she knew better.

I kept my mouth clamped shut. The deaths of the Serene Envoy, of all his retainers, of the Falcons and their escort who'd come to take the wards down—all of them called her a liar. But I could tell by her face that she didn't even remember them. They were inconsequential to her; I suffered more of a pang of conscience from killing grass when I stepped on it.

"Believe me if you wish, or find out the hard way." Whisper licked a paw, as if he couldn't care in the slightest.

Hunger shrugged. "If it looks like we're doing more damage than the world can sustain, we can always adjust our behavior then."

That did it. I'd been struggling not to say much; my goal was to listen and learn their plans, and it was uncomfortable enough being here at all without actively claiming my place at the table. But I couldn't sit silent and let them talk so carelessly about their potential to destroy everything I cared for.

I braced my hands on the table. "This world is not yours to break," I said. "You can't divvy it up between you and run roughshod over it, without any care for who or what you're hurting so long as it doesn't cease to exist completely."

Nightmare's eyes glittered. "I assure you we can. We've done it before."

Hunger's grin spread broadly across Aurelio's face. "The Graces are gone. Who's going to stop us?"

I stood up. "I will."

I expected them to laugh. To dismiss me, without the veneer of respect with which they'd disregarded Whisper's advice. But they all stared at me with varying degrees of wariness or calculation.

"Is that a threat?" Nightmare asked flatly.

The thought of me threatening a table full of demons was ridiculous. But I couldn't back down. "If it has to be."

Madness's eyes had grown so wide they threatened to drink in the sky. "Don't," she whispered. "Don't fight them, Disaster— Ryxander. You were so sad last time."

A chill colder than the bottom of an icy lake in winter settled in my stomach. *Last time.*

"She's right," Whisper said, meeting my gaze with the inscrutable depths of his slit-pupiled eyes. "You don't remember the reason I remain neutral. No matter what else unfolds, we must not fight each other, at all costs. The damage to this world when we do is catastrophic."

Oh pox. I sank back into my chair, stunned. What had I done in the Dark Days that was so terrible that even other demons urged me not to risk repeating it?

There were plenty of stories about the Demon of Disaster. Earthquakes, floods, fires, hurricanes; cities destroyed, civilizations ruined. I couldn't conceive of having done anything like that, no matter how different I might have been before the two halves of my current whole merged on that fateful day in the Black Tower. But by the looks the others were giving me, I had to consider the possibility that those stories could be literal truth.

I shivered, as if the day had gone suddenly icy cold. *No.* Whatever had happened four thousand years ago, it didn't help anyone for me to dwell on it now. I had to stay sharp and do what I could to keep the callous beings at this table from wrecking the world haphazardly with their power.

The others had moved on; Nightmare turned to Hunger. "Now, you have your little plan with the humans to take control of the Empire. I won't get in your way so long as you let me do whatever I like to the people in it."

Hunger shrugged. "That's fine."

My grandmother snorted. "Don't be a fool, Nightmare. He's saying that now, but you know Hunger. Once he has what he wants, he'll want what *you* have, too."

Nightmare's eyes narrowed. "She's not wrong."

"She's trying to turn us against each other!" Hunger protested. "She's *Discord*!"

"She's still not wrong," Nightmare said stubbornly.

My grandmother turned to Hunger. "And once she gets her hooks into your humans, she'll make everything in your empire all about *her*." She jerked her head contemptuously at Nightmare. "You'll be an afterthought at best."

Hunger frowned. "I see what you're doing."

"But I'm right."

"Yes," Hunger agreed through his teeth, "but I still see what you're doing, even if you're right."

My grandmother laughed, hopping up to perch on her railing like one of her own owls. "That's the sheer beauty of it."

The embers of my anger had flared up again. "Have you ever considered simply living in this world, rather than trying to twist it for your own amusement?" My jaw felt stiff, and the words came out clipped. "If you followed Whisper's advice and walked lightly here, then maybe you could stay for thousands of years, too, because no one would feel compelled to drive you out."

Madness tilted her head in consideration as if this had genuinely never occurred to her before, but Hunger gave me a condescending look, and Nightmare laughed.

"Oh, I do hope they try!" She licked her lips. "Some of my favorite memories are the times humans sent armies against me. So many fears to work with! The suffering was *exquisite*, the colors breathtaking." Her eyes shone at the memory, as if she could almost see it unfolding before her. "Thousands of humans, living out their worst nightmares... Oh, it took days and days for all of them to die, and it was *beautiful*."

I was kin to this. The thought was so deeply repugnant that I wanted to dig my nails into my skin and pull out my own soul, if that would somehow repudiate her. I gritted my teeth.

"Yet it was humans who banished you to the Nine Hells in the Dark Days." Banished *us*, I realized as I said it. "Don't underestimate what they can do."

"Last time was a fluke, because we weren't ready for them." Hunger waved a dismissive hand. "Whisper's point about being careful not to destroy the world by accident is far more valid than any concerns about what the humans might try to do to us. Especially with the gate in our hands this time!"

"My hands," my grandmother corrected, grinning.

"Yes, the gate." Nightmare leaned forward. "What are your opinions about the others? Do we bring them through to join us, or leave them in the Hells and keep this world for ourselves?"

I clamped my mouth shut. If I wanted to learn from this—to be humanity's spy at this meeting—I had to let the others talk.

Madness almost seemed to crumple in on herself. "Not Carnage," she whispered.

Nightmare grimaced. "Ugh, no. She's certainly not one to, ah, *walk lightly*."

"Not Corruption, either," Hunger said with distaste. "He ruins everything."

"We're not letting any of them through," my grandmother said firmly. "It's not your decision; I hold the gate."

Hunger straightened. "You can't just claim the gate as your own. It's vital to all of us."

"I already have," my grandmother countered, showing her teeth.

"Hah! You can't even get close to it because of the humans' wards." Hunger crossed his arms. "If you want to do anything with it, you'll need help from someone who can drain their magic, like me."

I filed that away, scanning everyone's faces for a sign of who else might be able to circumvent artifice wards. Nightmare was frowning, which probably meant she couldn't; good. Madness was harder to read—she was staring at a butterfly—but I'd guess her power probably worked similarly to Nightmare's. We should still be able to trap them either way, given that Bastian hadn't thought *I* could drain the wards due to that little cutoff swirl, but we'd have to keep a close eye on Hunger.

"Oh, I doubt you could bring down the Black Tower wards," my grandmother said, still grinning at Hunger. "But I don't want to open the gate, so it hardly matters—unless any of you would like to go back through it."

"It sounds as if none of us want to bring the others through anyway," Nightmare said, cutting off Hunger before he could rise to the bait. "I wouldn't mind Despair, but if they weren't quick enough to make it through when the rest of us did, that's their loss."

My grandmother made a face. "Despair is tedious. We don't need them."

Nightmare spread her hands, a certain cunning light in her eyes. "Can we at least promise not to interfere with each other, then?"

"No," I said bluntly. No one seemed surprised.

Whisper's ears swiveled back. "My neutral stance remains unchanged. I will not bind myself with a promise."

Hunger leaned his chin on his hand, gazing at Nightmare. "Would you swear not to interfere with *me*, sister dear?"

She hesitated visibly.

My grandmother laughed. "No one's *that* naive, Hunger. Not when it could mean standing back and watching as you swallow up all of our own interests." Every time she spoke, it tugged at me in strange ways; her voice was so familiar, but there was a mocking edge to her that was new. The almost–but–not–quiteness of her burned at me like salt in my eyes. "As for me, I hope you didn't seriously imagine I'd promise not to interfere in anything. It's against my nature."

Madness let out a long, wistful sigh. "I never *mean* to ruin things."

Nightmare's expression seethed in frustration, pulling in directions a human's face wouldn't. "Then what is the purpose of this council?" she hissed. "Have we learned nothing? Think of all we could accomplish if we unite our strength together!"

"You can't," I realized, the words falling out of my mouth in sudden triumph.

They all looked at me. Hunger scowled. "Why not?"

"Because you're not human." I was sure of it. "You're too driven by your own natures to bend to meet someone halfway." Relief swamped me; the world was still in horrifying peril, and we might not be able to avert a new era of darkness—but we had a chance. If the demons had truly been able to join forces, there'd be little hope for humanity. "That's why you need the Zenith Society. You can't even make a decent scheme without human help."

Hunger scowled at me. "You've lost not only your dignity, but your sense as well, merging with that human. I don't need their help. They're beneath me."

"Then prove it," I challenged him. "Cast off the Zenith Society and do it on your own." I doubted he'd fall for it, but anything I could do to drive a wedge between them was worth a try.

Before he could respond, Whisper rose, stretching. "I've delivered my warning. I have no interest in staying here to listen to the rest of you argue."

Nightmare wrestled her annoyance under control, bowing her head in a respectful nod instead. "Of course you must do as you see fit."

Madness stood, too; Nightmare's eyes widened with shock at that. "You tried," she said, laying a gentle hand on Nightmare's shoulder. "Our colors are too strong and sharp. We can't blend them."

Nightmare shook her hand off, getting up as well. "Very well, then," she said. "Perhaps our goals are too different to work together. But I hope we'll at least have the sense this time to talk to each other. To stay out of each other's way as much as we can, and to warn each other of threats we see coming."

"The threats you don't see coming are more fun," my grandmother murmured.

Nightmare ignored her, turning to Hunger. "Come. You and I can finish the more fruitful discussion we were having earlier somewhere else."

"Indeed." Hunger rose, too, and they linked arms. They strolled off together, Madness trailing behind them.

For one brief moment Aurelio shot me a desperate, pleading, terrified look over his shoulder. I couldn't tell if it meant *Stop them* or *Help me.*

That look pulled at me to follow them, a hook sunk into the mass of worry in my gut. Moreni had said they were going to launch some kind of attack after the meeting—I should eavesdrop, try to figure out how to counter them. And no matter how deep and righteous my grievance against Aurelio might be, he'd been helping me; if I could think of a way to help him in return, I would.

But another need, far deeper and more profound, kept me here as surely as roots winding down through the earth.

As soon as they were gone, I turned to face my grandmother.

TWENTY-SIX

The light of mischief left my grandmother's eyes, leaving them dark and troubled as she stared at me. The wind teased the white shock of her hair.

"So now you know," she said quietly.

"What were you thinking?" The words burst out of me, uncontrolled, pent up since last night. "You defied the Gloaming Lore! *Nothing must unseal the Door.*"

"I did it for you." She stepped toward me, an odd smile crossing her face.

"It was our family's duty! Our purpose!" I spread my hands. "And look at what's happened now. You should have left it closed."

"Should I have?" She cocked her head. "I'm rather fond of you, Ryx. I have no regrets."

"I do." I swallowed a burning knot in my throat. "Not about what you did, but about what came after. I may not have opened the gate deliberately like you, but I've done a great deal more harm. Harm that can never be undone."

She knew what I meant. The wild, gleeful fires burning in her eyes tempered and softened.

"I wouldn't have chosen this," she admitted. "As a human or

as a demon, I wouldn't have wanted to be both. But it's only fair. I did the same to you."

"Would you ever have told me?" I tried not to make it sound like an accusation. As if I were merely curious, not wondering why in the Nine Hells she hadn't warned me about what I was ages ago.

My grandmother snorted. "After I merged, I wanted you to know right away, but Whisper made it clear that he'd stop me if I tried to tell you. So I had to resort to other means to get my message across."

"Like leaving me to be tortured to death by the Shrike Lord." All right, that *was* an accusation. That abandonment still hurt, a raw and open wound.

"Oh, you wouldn't have died." She paused, considering. "Or I suppose your body might have, if you didn't unleash your power to protect it—which I expected you to do far earlier than you apparently did, to be honest."

An icy vise clamped down on my belly. "Wait, what do you mean? Are you telling me . . . What happens if I die now?"

"You can't." Her mantle fluffed in an uncomfortable shrug. "Not really. If your body dies, you'll claim another—whether you like it or not. You can hold out a little while, searching for one you prefer—but you can only resist the pull for so long before you get sucked into whoever's around. It's like holding your breath."

A yawning void seemed to open beneath my feet. I would far, far rather simply die than possess some poor soul. "That's awful," I croaked.

"I'm not thrilled about it myself. Possessing a new host is always chancy, but now that I'm human with a human perspective, well—" She grimaced. "I'm rather vehemently opposed to the idea."

I clutched my braid in both hands as if it were a lifeline, still working through all the horrifying implications. "That means that if I die, I murder someone. And *wear them like a shirt*."

"Probably, unless someone invites you in," my grandmother agreed. "So I recommend you try very hard not to die."

My eyes stung, and an awful feeling surged up in my chest—guilt? Shame? It made no sense, an instinctive reaction without an underlying cause.

Except that I'd done this before. I must have; long ago, in the Dark Days, my own body hadn't been born yet. "Thank the Graces I can't remember," I breathed, sickened.

The fierce orange rings of my grandmother's mage mark fixed on me. "I can."

"Oh, Hells." I hadn't thought that through. My hands flew to my mouth. "I'm sorry."

Her shoulders twitched as if she were shaking off an annoying insect. "I'll admit I envy you. If I couldn't remember—if this existence were all I knew—it would be easy."

"Not entirely easy," I said, my voice rough.

"Oh, I don't mean my *life* would be easy." She brushed the idea off. "I mean the merge. The settling of the dust. The swirling of the milk into the tea."

I didn't feel like milk and tea. I felt like myself, the same as I always had.

And that was a debt I owed to my grandmother and Whisper.

"Thank you." The words caught inside me on feelings pointing seventeen different ways, but I forced them out.

My grandmother lifted a brow. "For what? For lying to you all your life? For leaving you to die? For exiling you from your home? I'm forced to admit I've been a terrible grandparent."

"For giving me a chance to be myself. Whoever that turned out to be." I shrugged uncomfortably.

"Oh, Ryx." She reached out and laid her strong, warm hand on my shoulder, as she always had when encouraging me. "You're a monster."

My heart lurched.

"We both are," she added, with a sad half smile. "This is what we've made each other, and now we have to live with it."

It was too dangerous to stand alone on the terrace after my grandmother left. When I was alone, and standing still, everything threatened to catch up to me; I had to keep moving to stay ahead of the heavy tight feeling that kept trying to close like a claw around my middle, squeezing the breath from me.

So I ground the heels of my hands into my eyes, drew myself up, and followed Nightmare and Hunger, without any clear plan besides trying to stop them from whatever they were about to do.

They'd ascended a set of steps to a smaller and higher terrace, sized to entertain no more than a handful of guests rather than an entire large party. Nightmare stood there alone now, gazing out over the sparkling ocean; there was no sign of Hunger or Madness. If I hadn't known better, I might have guessed she was simply enjoying the view.

"Ah, there you are, Disaster," Nightmare said, without turning. Pleasure infused her deep, rich voice. "I'm so glad you came to join me. Your reaction to this will be *delightful*. Come, stand with me."

I forced myself to advance to the railing, with about as much eagerness as if someone had asked me to pet a lethally venomous chimera known to be a biter.

Standing at her side felt wrong and dangerous. Still, I was here, and that meant I had a chance to do something that mattered.

"The Zenith Society were talking about how they'd arranged for you to attack the imperial forces nearby." I tried to sound casual, as if thousands of lives didn't hang in the balance. "They seemed rather smug about using you for their own purposes."

I'd hoped Nightmare would take offense at that, but she shrugged it off. "Hunger's pets have been useful. If they hadn't explained how your Witch Lords use magical connections to extend the range of their power, I wouldn't have thought to try what I'm about to do."

I asked the obvious question, trying not to show how much I dreaded her answer. "What are you about to do?"

She gazed down at the harbor town, where sullen black smoke still rose to the sky in places. The few slips of sandy road I could glimpse through folds in the hills showed thick with wagons and coaches—people leaving, fleeing for their lives. "I couldn't normally reach that far, you see. Power dissipates so quickly when it's only anchored at one end. Do you know how I did it?"

I shook my head, gripped with the increasing surety that something dreadful was about to happen.

Nightmare gazed fondly down at the ravaged town. "Getting your hooks into a human's mind is easier if you have a foothold. Quicksilver works wonders; knowing a bit about them helps, or the human thinking about you—there are so many back doors and shortcuts. In what you call the Dark Days, I noticed that once a human had steeped in my power long enough, I could get into their mind easier, reach them from farther away—as if I'd established a pathway. So after I heard about your Witch Lords, I tried something with some of the humans we let leave before Madness raised the wards. I put a speck of my own power in them." She gestured to the town, with great satisfaction. "And they brought it home."

I remembered what Moreni had said about the demons wanting the foothold the symbols of power gave them, and a chill settled over me. "That's why you're taking over the Loreician court. To spread your power over the entire country."

"Eventually." An anticipatory smile curled her lips. "All the leaders here are our little seeds, to be soaked in our magic and blown on the wind. It takes quicksilver to anchor our power in a human for more than a few days, though—my experiment with the town showed that—so we have to go through the tedious process of silvering them all first. But that should be over soon."

The way she said it sent chills crawling between my shoulders. Hells, this must be what Moreni had been hinting at; they were planning to do it tonight.

"Right now, however," Nightmare said with slow relish, "I've got other seeds ready to sprout and die."

Her gaze fell on the fortress that stood beside the town, its thick rune-scribed bastions strong against magical and physical assault—and no use at all against a power that could pry open people's minds like walnuts.

"They sent me a gift, you know, after we raised the wards." Her voice became a purr. "They didn't realize that I sent a gift back with them in return."

Blood of the Eldest. The survivors of the Falcon group who'd already lost so much—killed their comrades and had to carry their wounded home off that dark hillside. She'd left hooks in their minds.

"They can't hurt you." I clenched the marble railing before me, ivy rustling under my fingertips. "You don't have to do this."

Nightmare's smile was a knife-edge black with heart's blood. "I know."

The bright daylight seemed to darken, as if heavy clouds descended. Power thick as molasses flowed over me; I staggered under it, distant wailing and scraping dragging at the edges of my mind before sliding off. On the slope below the terrace, a bird let out a mournful cry.

"What are you *doing*?" I demanded.

"Unfurling." She closed her eyes, bliss transforming her face. More cries of birds and animals sounded from the gardens and the hill, following a broad swath toward the distant fortress.

From the palace rose up human screams.

Pox. Were they killing each other? I tensed, ready to tackle Nightmare and try to rip her out of her host like I had Hunger.

She opened one eye, giving me a sidelong smile. "I don't need to read your mind like Madness to know what you're thinking. Kill this host, and I'll take one of your friends for my next one. And then I'll get right back to what I was doing."

My nails broke on the balustrade with thwarted fury.

More cries rose from the palace; below in the gardens, someone ran screaming through the carefully cultivated flower beds as if war chimeras slavered at their heels. My friends were in there, and they didn't share my resistance to Nightmare's power.

I couldn't stop her, but I could try to protect them.

Cursing, I spun away from Nightmare and ran back into the palace.

I didn't need to be susceptible to demonic power—with my jess off, a building full of people staggering and running around unpredictably, unable to see me and in the grip of panic, was already my worst nightmare.

I dodged a pair of elderly gentlemen falling out of a door with their hands around each other's throats, swallowing a scream at how close they came to touching me. A young boy in a servant's uniform sprinted toward me, wailing; I could only flatten myself against the wall and pray to the Graces that he wouldn't suddenly swerve. The people huddling in corners and crying were easier to avoid, but wrenched at my heart.

Somehow, I made it to the imperial wing, its empty halls for once a blessing rather than a haunting. My footsteps echoed in its grand chambers; the suffocating press of power around me started to lessen, as if the wave Nightmare had sent forth had peaked and was barely beginning to pass. *Thank the Graces.* I'd been afraid there'd be no end to it—that she'd sustain her nightmare aura at this level until everyone in the palace was incapacitated or dead.

Several rooms away, something gave a heavy crash, and Bastian screamed.

I swore and broke into a run.

TWENTY-SEVEN

I burst into the Serene Envoy's sitting room to find Bastian pressed into a corner, staring in horror at something only he could see, shaking his head with the cords standing out in his neck and wild colors chasing each other across his skin. But it was the source of the crash that grabbed my immediate and urgent attention.

Severin and Ashe rolled on the ground, half in the fireplace, spattered with scarlet; Severin's bone knife and Answer lay on the floor, both bloodied. Severin had bound up Ashe's right arm with a twist of woody vine and struggled to hold her other arm with both of his, in which a bare knife gleamed. Shadows loomed and writhed around them, faint echoes of whatever they saw instead of each other.

My eyes fell on a large open wine bottle on a side table; I grabbed it and started flinging streams of wine at them, desperate to make them stop and unable to come any closer.

"Wake up!" I shouted, my voice raw with panic. "It isn't real! You're hurting each other!"

Ashe growled and whirled on me, purple wine and crimson blood staining her pale hair. Severin lurched to his feet, clutching a wounded forearm, and snarled at me like an animal. At least they didn't seem too badly hurt—but if they jumped at me, they could both die.

"It's me, Ryx!" I cried, waving my arms at them. "Stop fighting!"

Recognition flickered in Ashe's eyes. The knife sagged in her hand. Severin swayed, blinking at me as if he were coming awake. Whether I'd gotten through to them or Nightmare's power was simply continuing to ebb, they were coming back to reality.

"Whoops," Ashe said, lifting a hand to her bloody temple. "Turns out you're not a chimera."

Severin waved an exhausted hand, and the vine around Ashe's arm unraveled and fell off. "Sorry I attacked you like that. I thought you were...someone else."

"Good thing I saw you as about six times your actual size and was stabbing nothing." Ashe retrieved Answer from the floor, grimacing at the blood on its edge. "Mostly."

Bastian had curled into a ball on the floor, whimpering; his own nightmare hadn't yet faded. I hesitated, wanting to help him but not daring to get any closer. "We need to get your wounds treated," I told Ashe and Severin, worry still keeping its anxious grip on my heart.

"Aw, they're just scratches," Ashe began, and then froze. "Kessa. Where's Kessa?"

As if summoned, Kessa burst into the room, eyes haunted, hat feather straggling. "Here," she said, short of breath. "I woke up halfway to the—Ashe, why are you covered in blood?"

"This is hardly *covered*," Ashe scoffed.

"Let's wake Bastian up and—"

I didn't get to finish. From the hallway leading to the guest quarters came a strangled cry and a muffled thud.

Foxglove.

The sound had come from his room. Severin stayed with Bastian, calling his name, while Kessa and Ashe ran in through Foxglove's open door; I peered anxiously through it from a safe distance behind them.

Foxglove knelt on the floor, his hands lifted trembling in a posture that left me no doubt that to his eyes, they were covered in blood. I could almost see it if I tried: a shadow dripping down his wrists and from his fingers, sheathing his arms to the elbow.

Another shadow darkened the elaborate Ostan carpet before him, roughly the size of a man, spreading in a widening pool.

Kessa let out a strangled shriek, her hands going to her mouth. "*Loren*. Not again. I can't look."

Loren. Her brother. Hells—they were seeing the same thing. They shared the same nightmare.

Foxglove gave the slow blink of a man emerging from sleep, but the horror didn't leave his face—it settled deeper, sinking into his eyes like a beast slithering back into the hole it had always dwelled in. Ashe stared at Kessa, then Foxglove, her eyes widening. She must have had the same realization I did, because she silently mouthed a curse.

And then it hit Kessa. She turned, slowly, toward Foxglove, a movement as powerful and inevitable as that of a glacier.

"Why are *you* seeing my brother?" she asked him, all the color bleached from her voice.

Foxglove returned her gaze with haunted eyes, his shadow-dripping hands still held before him.

"Curse it," Ashe whispered, looking desperate and grim with blood trickling down from her temple.

Kessa drew in a long breath, white and ragged, that stretched the moment to the point of tearing. I wanted desperately to intervene somehow, to stop her, to make things right, but there was nothing I could do to fix a past that was already broken.

"It was *you*!" Rage twisted Kessa's face, all the kindness and humor I knew gone, all softness replaced by thorns and fire. "Hells take you, Foxglove, it was you all this time! You're the one who killed him."

"Yes," Foxglove said softly, a deep and stricken darkness in his eyes. "I did."

Kessa let out something between a roar and a wail, a terrible sound that seemed larger than she was, as if her grief itself uttered it. She unleashed a vicious kick that caught Foxglove square in the chin and knocked him sprawling. I flinched in sympathy.

He'd closed his eyes in the instant before it landed. He could have dodged, but he took it.

Kessa hurled herself at Foxglove where he lay on the floor, but Ashe caught her, alarmed. "Whoa! What are you doing? Rule One!"

"He's not my friend," Kessa spat, her eyes narrowed in fury. "He killed my brother. Let me go, Ashe!"

"I can't just let you attack him," Ashe protested, snaking her arms into a better hold even as Kessa struggled to free herself. "He's not even defending himself!"

Foxglove had rolled onto his elbows, watching Kessa with a sort of resigned sorrow that broke my heart, as if he'd known this was coming. As if he'd always known.

I stepped away to open up more space, my chest sick and aching. "He was an assassin, Kessa," I said. "He was following orders. He didn't know."

"I don't care! *Look* at him! Loren's blood is on his hands!"

Foxglove rose slowly to his feet, rubbing his jaw. "The imperial contact who gave my assignments was compromised by the Zenith Society," he said, his tone controlled and even, as if he had practiced this speech dozens of times. Maybe he had, trying to get the courage up to tell her. "He told me you and your brother were Vaskandran agents sent to kill the doge. But when I completed the first part of the mission—"

"When you *murdered my brother*, you mean," Kessa snarled.

"Yes. When I murdered your brother." Foxglove bowed his head. "He was clearly no assassin."

"He was a *musician*! He couldn't even fight!" Tears roughened Kessa's already raw voice.

Foxglove winced more than he had when she'd kicked him, but his voice stayed level. "As you say. So instead of going after my second target—you—I reported the situation straight to the Council of Nine. That discovery—that they'd infiltrated and were abusing the chain of command—made it possible to bring down the Zenith Society, to stop the coup they were planning, to free Bastian from Cortissa's laboratory."

"I don't want to hear it!" Kessa cried, loud enough to reverberate through my body like a thunderclap. "I don't care what you realized after you did it, or how well it turned out for the Empire. He was my little brother, and I was supposed to keep him safe, and *you killed him*."

Foxglove bowed his head. "I did. I'm—"

"Don't you *dare* say you're sorry," Kessa hissed. "I can never forgive you for this. Never."

Ashe's brow creased. "Don't say never," she objected. "He's not an assassin anymore. You have to give him a chance."

"I most certainly do not." Kessa twisted, struggling to turn to face Ashe; Ashe released her, and Kessa jabbed a finger into her chest. "You should stay the Hells out of it, Ashe. Nothing can wash out the blood on a killer's hands. *Nothing*."

Ashe stared as if Kessa had slapped her. "People can change," she insisted, a desperation in her voice that echoed in my own heart. "He's like me. Used to follow orders, used to be just a killer, but now he knows better. Right? It's why we're in the Rookery."

"Don't you defend him, Asheva!" Angry tears poured down Kessa's face; her normally fluid actor's voice had lost all control, coming apart in raw pieces. "Anyone who'd do what he did is a monster. I *hate* him."

Ashe stepped back, her face even paler than usual, words struck from her lips.

This had spiraled out of control. "I know everyone is strained right now, because of the effect of the demons," I began, trying to sound reasonable, calm.

Foxglove shook his head. "No. Kessa, you're right about me. But leave Ashe out of it."

She whirled on him, eyes flashing. "You do not tell me what to do anymore."

He stood very still. I didn't breathe. After a long moment, he nodded. "All right. That's fair. As of this moment, I step down as leader of the Rookery."

"Don't," Ashe objected, an edge of panic in her voice. "Kessa, tell him he doesn't have to do that."

It was the wrong thing to say. Kessa peeled her lips back from her teeth, snatched her beloved hat from her head, and threw it on the ground.

"Get out," she barked. "Not another word. Out, now."

Foxglove headed for the door; I quickly stepped out of his way. He moved with his usual grace and poise, but his eyes brimmed with utter desolation.

Kessa pointed at Ashe. "You too. I won't listen to you defend him. Out!"

Ashe's lips tightened as if she were struggling not to cry. She jerked her head in a quick nod and started after Foxglove.

Curse it, this kept getting worse. The Rookery was falling apart like waterlogged paper, and my clumsy hands couldn't salvage the weeping shreds.

"Do you want me to..." I began, my heart straining in multiple directions.

Kessa turned her back on me. "You too! I can't stand to look at a single one of your faces. *Out!*"

I followed the others from the room. Kessa's broken, messy sobs rose up behind us.

The hard, sick feeling in my stomach wouldn't leave. Ashe and Foxglove were gone by the time I caught up with Severin and Bastian; the latter had recovered enough to treat Severin's arm with trembling hands, but he looked as if he needed to be tucked in bed with a cup of his choice of reassuring beverage.

I wanted to stay with them and make sure they were all right. My heart ached to run after Ashe and Foxglove and Kessa, and find soothing words somewhere within that would magically mend everything between them. But there was something that needed to be done, and right now I was the only one not too much of a wreck to go do it.

I headed out to find a vantage point from which I could figure out the state of the fortress and whether there was any way we could save it.

The roof was a logical choice; it had a clear view, and there should be no one up there for me to run into. But when I stepped out of a dormer window in the servants' attic and scrambled up the slanting tiles to the rooftop with its dragon-mouthed chimneys, I discovered that I wasn't alone up here after all.

Hunger stood perhaps a hundred feet away, the wind ruffling Aurelio's hair, gazing out over the sea.

I froze. He didn't act like he'd seen me; his focus remained riveted on the fortress and the ocean beyond. I could climb back down and avoid his notice.

But that wasn't what I'd come up here to do. I took a deep, steadying breath and forced myself to make my way across the roof toward him, walking into the power radiating from him as if it were a contrary wind.

His presence was normally subtler than Nightmare's, for whatever reason, but now he'd uncloaked the sheer magical force that made up his very being. Instead of pressing or scraping at my senses, it plucked at them, dragging at me with greedy invisible fingers, stealing bits of warmth from my skin or shine from my hair.

Would I give off such an aura, if I stopped suppressing my power? What would Disaster feel like? A sense of overwhelming doom, perhaps. My insides twisted unpleasantly at the thought.

Hunger's end of the roof had a much better view of the

fortress. I was relieved beyond measure to find no smoke rising from it, no corpses strewn around it, at least so far as I could see from this distance. Perhaps Nightmare's attempt to shroud the place in her miasma had failed, whether due to distance or lack of numbers among those she'd touched with her power.

Or maybe she'd been trying to do something else entirely.

As I approached Hunger, he murmured with great satisfaction, "Here it comes."

A light flared on the fortress battlements, and another. Twin golden streaks launched from the great cannons there: enchanted cannonballs, blazing with fire and light, leaving trails behind them like shooting stars as they arced out over the water toward...

Hells have mercy. Toward the three imperial warships waiting off the coast.

The cannonballs struck their target with a great flash of light; one of the three warships went up in flames.

Hunger laughed with delight. "I have to hand it to those human friends of yours, Aurelio," he said. "They do have some entertaining ideas."

His face twisted in apparent pain. "This isn't right," Aurelio said. "This isn't what we wanted. We were supposed to *protect* the Empire."

I couldn't hold back my frustration. "If you'd remembered those scruples earlier, maybe we wouldn't be here."

"Do you think I don't know that?" Aurelio turned eyes sharp with bitter anguish toward me, but something seemed to catch his head and force it back around. Hunger stared intently out at the ships again.

"Shh, boy," he said. "If your friends are right about what happens next, it's my turn."

More flashes of light erupted in the distance—two from the fortress, and one from one of the warships. The golden streak from the ship angled too high to hit the fort.

It was heading straight for us.

"Oh pox," I breathed, fear lurching in my chest.

Hunger made a gathering gesture, as if he were scooping something from the air before him. A golden light to match the glow of the cannonball flared briefly in his eyes.

The cannonball dropped, its fiery trail angling suddenly and sharply downward as if someone had swatted it from the sky. As if Hunger had stolen the force that hurled it toward us.

It struck the hillside below in a flash of light, but no flames billowed up from it, as they had from the others. Instead a faint glow streamed to Hunger's outstretched hand, and the light in his eyes grew brighter.

A sound rumbled like distant thunder. With a flash, the second ship burst into flames.

Hunger shook his head. "I wanted to drop it on the fortress, but I missed. Oh well, one more try. And no, boy, you can't have the body back, I'm using it right now."

Thousands of people lived in that fortress, including families with children. There was no way in the Nine Hells I was letting him drop a cannonball on them. I contemplated one quick well-timed shove—but no, that wouldn't even kill Aurelio, let alone Hunger, given the sort of damage I'd seen him heal before.

A physical or magical attack might distract him, but that wasn't where my skills lay. I was the Warden of Gloamingard, and I fought my battles with subtler weapons.

One thing I'd noticed about demons: they loved to talk.

"Why would you want to kill them?" I demanded, playing up my distress. "What would you possibly gain from it?"

Hunger raised Aurelio's brows at me. "This was that human Moreni's plan, to keep them from shooting at us. It would be tedious to stand up here catching cannonballs all day, so better to destroy them."

I let out a sharp laugh. "I see he didn't tell you how much magic there is in an imperial border fortress like that. He probably knew you'd want it for yourself."

Something flickered in the hazel eyes that Hunger gazed from with so much more cruel intensity than Aurelio ever did. "What magic?"

"Weapons. Mages. Wondrous devices. Power sources. You name it." I kept my eyes locked on his, trying to keep his attention. "Aurelio would know better than I would; he was a Falconer. You could ask him."

"It's true," Aurelio chimed in, his eyes flashing gratitude at me. "The Serene Empire concentrates a lot of its most powerful magic in border fortresses, to keep Vaskandar at bay. That place would be a treasure box for you."

Beyond his shoulder, lights flashed again, and fire arced through the sky.

Hunger licked his lips. "That's...interesting."

The incoming cannonball sailed toward us, high over the fortress. Hunger whirled, hissing, and lifted his hand just in time; it dropped straight from the sky and plummeted to the hillside with a dull thud, not far beyond the palace walls. This time, there was no flash, and Hunger's eyes glowed even brighter with all the energy he'd absorbed.

"You distracted me on purpose," he accused, whirling back to me. His eyes glowed golden; power roiled around him, pulling at me with a low sound like wind blowing across the mouth of an empty cave.

"You were making a mistake," I tried to sound hard and certain. "Moreni tricked you. He's *using* you—again. Nightmare might not care about that, but surely you do."

Hunger stepped toward me. My legs began to feel weak, as if I'd climbed up a tall mountain without drinking enough water; my heart beat with dull labor in my chest. By the sheer force of power assaulting me, I had no doubt that if I were fully human, I'd be dead.

"No," he snarled. "I'm using *him*. He's *mine*. All his little band are mine, my tools, my pets, to use as I see fit. I can see what you're doing, trying to take them from me—just as you're trying to take this host from me. But you won't. They belong to me."

His face shifted suddenly, screwing up in an agony of struggle.

"Go," Aurelio gasped. "He's angry, Ryx. Get out of here."

"But the fortress—"

"*Go.*"

The power around us kept building; a hollow wind sucked the breath half from my lungs. If I stayed here, I only had two options: fall before Hunger's power, or unleash my own.

I might survive the former. With a palace full of people beneath me, I couldn't live with the consequences of the latter.

I scrambled off across the roof while I still could.

TWENTY-EIGHT

I found the Serene Envoy's sitting room empty save for Severin and the ticking of the clocks when I returned, nerves still on fire and pulse racing, from the roof. He, by contrast, draped across a sofa with the forcibly relaxed, slightly glazed look of a man on pain potions, his bandaged arm across his chest. He lifted his head when I entered, managing half a smile.

"I gather the Rookery isn't quite the perfect happy family they seemed," he greeted me. "And I thought my history with my brother was complicated."

I yanked on my own braid, in no mood for banter. "This is the worst possible time for all this to come to a head."

"It's a mess." Severin tipped his head back over the armrest, baring the scars on his throat. "Normally I'd follow the old adage about staying out of other people's grievances, and I wouldn't touch this with protective gloves and a long pole. But I didn't live to adulthood by being a slow learner, and recent experience would suggest that in a massive global crisis, I can't afford to stay out of *anything*."

"They need to move past this," I agreed—too roughly, even though my heart ached for all of them, especially Kessa. She hadn't done anything to deserve this. "The demons have struck at the Empire; things are going to keep escalating quickly."

"I've been lying here coming to the conclusion that they're going to need help, and the subsequent conclusion that much as I recognize I can no longer maintain an aloof stance, I am notoriously bad at feelings." Severin spoke with precise elegance, but too slowly, and without lifting his head. He reminded me of my mother when she'd had Raverran friends over and drunk too much wine.

"You're not going anywhere," I realized.

"Bastian said the same thing when he gave me these potions, yes." Severin gestured toward a row of empty cups beside him. "So I'm afraid the somber task of ministering to wounded rooks falls to you."

I found Ashe in the garden, hacking the corners off a topiary cube. She'd left her vestcoat inside, and the wiry muscles in her shoulders were clearly visible through her thin white shirt as she mutilated the inoffensive bush with precise, vicious flourishes. A fair number of people had come out to the gardens to gawk at the lights in the sky and wonder what horrible thing was happening now, but they gave her an extremely wide berth.

I tried to forcibly calm my jangling nerves, with mixed success. Eruvia needed a functioning Rookery right now. Which meant that no matter how shaken I was by everything that had just happened, I needed to be calm enough to pull the others back from the edge.

"Kessa needs you," I said at last, once I was ready.

"Then maybe she shouldn't have kicked me out." Ashe sliced the entire top section off the topiary; it slid to the ground and landed with a rustling crash in a pile of severed branches.

I winced. "She's upset. She didn't—"

"She meant it." Ashe slammed her sword home in its sheath. "She's not wrong. I know I'm a monster. I just thought she cared about me anyway."

"Hells, Ashe, you know she does." Ashe's words cut too close to the bone to be comfortable, and she didn't even know it. I sank down on a nearby bench, too weary to stand anymore. "Of course she's lashing out, after learning Foxglove killed her brother. Even Kessa isn't kind enough to not be angry about *that*. And I'm sure it doesn't help that Nightmare is rubbing our minds raw."

Ashe scowled. "Maybe so, but she was saying what she thought. Killers are monsters—you heard her. That means you and me."

"I'm all too aware of that." I passed a hand across my face. "We don't have time for this kind of drama. Listen to me, Ashe. The demons are planning to quicksilver everyone in the palace tonight. They just crippled all the nearby imperial forces, so no one is coming to help us. If we don't stop them, steal that ward key, and get everyone out of here, we're all done for. You, me, Kessa, the entire country." Her eyes flickered at that, sharpening from the dull haze of misery that had come over them. "You need to pull it together. Everyone's a wreck; there's no one who can take your place if you go off and sulk."

She stiffened. But then her shoulders slumped, and she sighed. "You're right. We've got to stay sharp. Ugh, this thing with Foxglove stepping down—that's a disaster."

I winced at the word. Ashe didn't seem to notice.

"We can't lose him now," she went on. "Mind you, I'm mad at him, too—I trusted him with Rule Five, for blood's sake; he was supposed to be my moral compass, and turns out he's no better than I am. But he's our leader, and we've got to get the group back together somehow, to finish the mission."

"As quickly as possible," I agreed. "That's why I came to get you."

"Right. But I'm no good at plans—I just follow orders. So it's got to be you."

"Me?" I lifted my hands to ward off the idea, alarmed. "I'm new to the Rookery."

"That's why they'll listen to you. You're not tangled up in all these old secret dramas."

No, I had a *new* secret drama.

It seemed impossible that she could be right—that I could be better positioned to help hold the Rookery together right now than Foxglove or Kessa or Bastian or even Ashe herself—but she was right about one thing: it had to be done. And I hadn't spent years as the Warden of Gloamingard to sit by knowing something needed doing and wait for someone else to handle it.

"All right." I took a deep breath. "We'll fix this."

Ashe nodded, her expression more than a bit relieved. "Good. Because I hate it."

"Step one…" I pointed to her. "Go to Kessa and tell her you're sorry."

"Sorry?" Ashe stared at me. "For what? I'm not the one who called *her* a monster! And I'm sure as Hells not sorry I didn't let her jump on Foxglove. She might've stuck a knife in him."

"It doesn't matter," I said. "It just tells her you want to be friends again."

"Well, if it'll work, I guess." Ashe rubbed the back of her head, mussing up her pale shock of hair. "Let's give this a try."

Ashe didn't even get a chance to apologize. Kessa, who we found sitting alone on the floor of her room, rushed at us and threw her arms around Ashe's neck. Ashe stiffened, then hugged her back, stunned.

"I'm sorry," Kessa whispered.

Ashe burst out laughing.

Kessa drew back, confusion creasing her brow. "What?"

"Nothing." Ashe wiped her eyes. "Ryx gives either terrible advice or good advice, and I'm not sure which."

My mouth felt strange, twisted. It took me a moment to realize this odd sensation was a smile. "Probably terrible."

Ashe touched Kessa's cheek, gently, as if it were made of

smoke and might dissipate. "Listen," she said, her voice subdued. "I don't blame you for being mad at Foxglove. It'd be weird if you weren't. But—"

Kessa caught her hand, keeping it pressed against her tear-streaked cheek. "Don't defend him."

Ashe let out a frustrated breath. "He's my friend, too, Kessa."

"Maybe he shouldn't be." Kessa's voice had gone tight again. "My life stopped on the day Loren died, Ashe. I built a new one—but Foxglove helped me build it. If he lied to me so deeply, does that mean this whole life is a lie, too?"

"Buggered if I know," Ashe said roughly, "but I can tell you I'm here in your life, and I'm not a lie. And Foxglove, well—"

Kessa slashed the air with her hand. "I don't want to hear his name."

I couldn't stand by and let what was barely mended between them tear again. "By name or otherwise," I said, too tired to attempt gentleness, "the reality is that we need him. He's our artificer. We can't do this without him."

Kessa turned anguished eyes on me. "How am I supposed to work with him? I hated Loren's killer for *years*! And Foxglove—he was my mentor. He gave me purpose, he took me in; he was the one I could talk to when my melancholia hit, because he didn't panic if I mentioned having dark thoughts. I trusted him, I *loved* him, and all along..." She shook her head. "I can't. I'm sorry, but I just can't. He *killed my brother.*"

"Yes," Ashe said, an edge in her voice, "and he's sorry. He's spent every day of his life since trying to atone. Can't you see that?"

Seasons have mercy, I'd thought I was no good with feelings, but Ashe was worse. *Give her time*, I wanted to snap at her, but I couldn't.

"Look," I put in before Kessa could let loose a heated reply, "I'm not saying you have to hold hands and sing songs with him. The rest of us can act as intermediaries, so you won't have to work directly with him more than is necessary. But getting everyone out of here alive has to come first, and running from one crisis to the next today has set us back far enough without losing any more time."

Kessa gave the barest nod, but the pain only deepened in her eyes. "I understand we have to finish the mission. But I can never trust him again."

"Sometimes..." My insides twisted into a knot. "Sometimes it's hard to tell the truth when you're afraid it'll end a friendship."

"That's no excuse." Kessa shook her head. "I can't stand the thought of so much as looking at him. Once this is over, either he leaves the Rookery, or I will."

Kessa's words stuck with me like the poisoned burrs my grandmother grew to guard forbidden places in Morgrain. She'd caught me in a trap with no exit: I needed to tell her the truth, or risk losing her friendship. But if I told her now, when she already felt so betrayed by Foxglove and I was somehow one of the last pillars of stability, I'd only hurt her and split the Rookery further.

I'd just learned my true nature myself, but already my silence had become a lie.

No time for that. Save the world first, existential crisis later.

Now I had to remind someone else of that rule.

I'd left Foxglove for last because I wasn't entirely sure what to make of him anymore. I'd known he'd been one of the legendary imperial assassins, and that he had some deep regret in his past that had led him to quit; but somehow there was a visceral difference between vaguely understanding that he'd killed and being friends with one of the people whose lives he'd destroyed. Maybe there shouldn't have been.

I'd always thought he was the most like me, of everyone in

the Rookery. After all, I'd killed, too, and I had plenty of my own regrets. Now... Hells, he was still probably the most like me, but that wasn't any consolation.

I couldn't find him anywhere in the imperial wing. I ventured out into the long sequence of spectacular galleries that formed the main spine of the palace and found sobering signs of the wreckage, material and human, caused by Nightmare's unfurling. Someone had toppled a statue of an urchin throwing a stone, a symbol of the Festival Uprising; pistol balls had left holes in a portrait of a dead king, and blood smeared the floor in one room. Items discarded or dropped in hallucinatory frenzy lay everywhere: a broken sword with a ruby-bedecked hilt, a single well-worn boot, a scattering of jeweled hairpins with half a fistful of blond hair still wound through them. Dazed and shaken people wandered the halls, too—enough that I had to creep warily along the walls to avoid them—calling anxiously for missing friends, helping the injured to safety, hugging each other in corners and weeping.

Everything I saw twisted at my heart. And all this was just a side effect of what Nightmare had done to the fortress.

I racked my brain for where Foxglove might have gone. With his wounded leg he wasn't in any shape to climb to some out-of-the-way spot on the roof to brood, and I hadn't seen him in the gardens when I went looking for Ashe. My best guess was that he'd plunge himself into duty to avoid facing his feelings—it was what I'd do in his place. Which meant working on the wards, either somewhere along the wall that encircled the grounds or on the stretch that ran inside the front wall of the palace.

Sure enough, I finally found him working on the warding runes that circled a window in a back corner of the library, shielded from the world by rows of shelves full of leatherbound books and a heavy, dusty silence. The library must have been fairly empty during Nightmare's attack, and seemed to have survived the chaos reasonably intact; I spotted a single librarian moving through it now, picking up books from the floor and restoring them to shelves with gentle hands and soothing noises, as if they were wounded birds.

I waited while Foxglove finished the rune he was working on, his teeth bared in concentration, the tip of his stylus smoking as alchemical etching fluid burned a fine line into the window frame. I took the time to slow myself down: my thundering heart, my frantically racing thoughts. This conversation was going to be like a delicate diplomatic negotiation. Going in with my nerves still buzzing wouldn't help anyone.

At last he slipped the stylus back into its pouch, his face a door not only closed, but locked and sealed.

"If you've come here offering pity, I don't want it," he said.

There were so many things I could say to him. Hard words, railing at him for having brought the Rookery to this, or for running away. Soft words, soothing little lies, telling him that it wasn't his fault, that it would be all right. True words: that I understood too well, that he was still my friend.

The wrong words, for this man in this moment.

Instead, I let out a huff. "No. People like us don't deserve pity."

His shoulders relaxed at that, and his face creased into lines of honest pain. "Damned right we don't."

I was so cursed tired. I hadn't slept in a thousand years. The bookshelves bracketing us seemed strong enough, solid wood embellished with whimsical carvings of scholarly forest animals and polished to a dark shine; I leaned against one, elbows braced on a shelf, book spines pushed into an arc to embrace my back.

"Are you sure that was wise, what you did?" I asked quietly. "Stepping down as leader of the Rookery *now*? This mission was hard enough already."

Foxglove let out a long breath. "I had to. Kessa was going to quit otherwise. It bought us time to deal with this after we're out of here, away from the demons and their miasma, where we can think straight again."

"That's the most sensible thing I've heard anyone say all day," I approved. Now wasn't the time for hard truths and bitter reckonings—his or mine. "Everyone's bound to react in the worst possible way when Madness and Nightmare are twisting their emotions."

"I should have told her years ago." He rubbed his forehead. "I don't know what I was thinking. No—I know exactly. I thought I could kill that man. The assassin. I thought I'd buried him, and he was dead."

A strange prickle walked up my spine as I realized he was talking about himself. "Do you really think that's possible?" My voice didn't come out quite steady. "Cutting off the person you used to be, and becoming an entirely new one?" If, for example, the Demon of Death had severed your memories of the being you once were.

"No," he said quietly, looking at his hands. "I told myself I could do it. I believed it. But I was wrong. I'm still the same man, no matter how much I like to think I've changed, and I have to face the consequences of what I did back then."

That wasn't an answer I wanted to hear, given what I'd been and what I was. But this moment was about Foxglove, not about me, so I didn't try to argue.

Foxglove's hand had stolen to his cravat pin. I did some quick emotional math. "Do Lia and Teodor know? That you killed him?"

He let out a bitter little laugh. "They don't even know I was an assassin."

I blinked at him. "What? How come *I* know, and your partners don't?"

"Because you're on the Rookery side of the divide." He absently brushed stone dust from the freshly carved runes. "I split myself into one dead assassin and two living people. I have to be hard, as the leader of the Rookery, and sometimes violent. I never want that to touch my family. But this place is muddling up all the pieces of me. I've been thinking too much like the assassin lately—plotting out ways to kill Moreni and Cortissa in my head, reliving all those old memories, considering the political implications to be someone else's problem. He may not be dead after all."

"Maybe." I suppressed a shiver at the idea that my own past might not be dead, either. "Most importantly, we have to find a way to mend things between you and Kessa. We've got to move fast; the demons are pushing ahead with some exciting new plans I need to fill you in on. There's too much going on for healing, and I'm sorry for that, but we need some way to slap a bandage on the wound and keep going." It was the only wisdom I had, and I was aware that it was garbage. But it was garbage that worked for me.

"You can't mend a taken life." Foxglove began carefully cleaning his stylus with a silk pocket handkerchief. "After the mission I'll do whatever she wants, up to turning myself in for murder."

"How would Lia and Teodor feel about that?" I challenged him.

The handkerchief went still in his hand. He closed his eyes. "Ryx," he said, "I have enough nightmares right now. I would appreciate you not giving me new ones. Now, tell me about these exciting new plans, and let's get this done."

"Hundreds dead in the fortress, and most of the crew of the three warships." Bastian clutched his notebook; his cheeks looked hollow, as if he hadn't been eating. "That was the report I got from the fortress; we've been flashing lights back and forth through the windows, since the courier lamps are too well defended now for casual trips."

Kessa looked up from where she'd been staring into the fire.

Her eyes showed red; her usually glossy black hair hung dull and unbrushed. Ashe, perched behind her on the sofa back with all the protective ferocity of a mantling hawk, began gently finger-combing it.

My heart hurt looking at all three of them. And for Foxglove, off working relentlessly on the wards; and Severin with his bandaged arm, who leaned wearily next to an open window, coordinating an intermittent stream of birds and mice scuttling up to exchange a report for a handful of seeds. This was what the Dark Days must have been like: everyone ground down, exhausted, trying to function with their emotions in bloody ribbons and the crushing weight of the demons' power pressing on them like a cairn of stones.

"What happened?" Kessa asked, voice vague as if she were forcing herself to shake off a bad dream.

Bastian consulted his notebook, but I suspected it was more to gather himself than because he needed to refer to his transcription of the courier-lamp code. "All the survivors of the attempt to bring down the palace wards suddenly saw the imperial warships and everyone *not* under Nightmare's influence as some kind of enemy. Exactly what they saw seems to have varied."

Ashe shook her head. "Wouldn't take many people to seize the cannons with a surprise advantage like *that*."

"Do we know if the children survived?" I asked Bastian quietly.

"Our warning let them evacuate the civilians in time—and they're smart enough to keep the school for mage children far away from the artifice cannons. But honestly, I didn't ask too many questions about casualties. I was afraid."

"This was Moreni's plan." I rose to my feet, too full of nervous energy to sit despite the aching exhaustion of my limbs. "One thing I learned at the council is that demons are terrible at planning. That's what they get from the Zenith Society, or any human partners—not just knowledge of how this world works, but the ability to come up with a complex scheme like this at all."

Bastian tipped his head. "You realize this makes Discord much more dangerous than the others. Since she's also human, she doesn't have that weakness."

The perpetual knot in my chest tightened. "Being human doesn't make her more of a threat. It could make her our greatest ally."

"She hasn't acted like an ally," Ashe said bluntly.

"She hasn't acted like an enemy, either," I insisted. "She just wants to protect her people."

Severin gave me an odd look. "Believe me, I understand about feeling familial loyalty to horrible monsters, but you can't pretend she's not dangerous."

You're a monster. We both are. I swallowed an aching lump in my throat. "She's always been dangerous. I...Look, it doesn't matter. Right now, she's not the problem. We've got to take out these demons before they can do any more harm. Kessa, we need that key. Were you able to learn anything from the maids?"

Kessa roused herself. "Actually, I've learned quite a few things today." She let out a laugh that teetered on the edge of plunging into something darker. "Eldest, that was a terrible choice of words. Better to say I kept myself busy before everything went to the Nine Hells." Ashe squeezed her shoulder, and she put on her usual smile like a battle-worn shield and continued. "First of all, the maids tell me that it's not so much that the queen doesn't take off the ward key to sleep—it's that she doesn't sleep at all. So we're going to have to steal it right off her neck."

My heart sank. "That sounds difficult."

"Yes, but not impossible." Kessa lifted a finger. "Back to that in a moment. The second thing I learned—from my friend Girard—is that your theory is right, Ryx. They're planning to get quicksilver into the whole population of the palace at once tonight. Moreni apparently seized the palace apothecary's entire stock of soothing elixirs, which contain mercury and—unlike the pure stuff—dissolve in water or wine."

Ashe grunted. "I can tell you flat-out we're not evacuating this palace if they turn everyone into silver-eyed stiffs like the guards. Going to be hard enough as is."

Bastian frowned. "Counterintuitive though it may seem, I don't think the quicksilver is what makes the guards like that—or at least, not directly. I think the mercury is an anchor, and it's Madness's controlling presence that causes the change in their eyes, as well as the suppression of their personality."

I shivered, remembering Severin's eyes turning silver as the demons forced their will upon him. They hadn't needed quicksilver then. "That makes sense."

"The nobles they gave quicksilver to at that lovely gathering in the throne hall don't have silver eyes, either," Kessa noted. "They're acting fairly normally, by all accounts. From what you said, Ryx, I think they just want to get their hooks into everyone for later."

I caught myself about to turn toward the mantel, waiting for Foxglove to pull us back to the plan. But of course he wasn't there. I realized with a twinge that it would have to be me.

"Right." I took a deep breath. "So we need to figure out how they plan to distribute this soothing elixir to everyone tonight."

"Aha!" Kessa's eyes twinkled; it was good to see her enthusiasm back again. "Now we come to my third and final tidbit of the day. I suspect I know how they're going to do it, or at least where and when." With a flourish, she produced a square of creamy paper from some hidden pocket in her gown. "A page gave me this appalling little announcement on the way back from talking to Girard. Her Majesty the Queen is holding a ball tonight, and attendance is mandatory."

"What fun," Severin said, his voice thick with irony. "We've got so much to celebrate."

"The mandatory attendance part does sound rather suspicious," I said.

"Transparently so," Kessa agreed. "Though, to be fair, can anyone think of a reason a demon would throw a ball that *isn't* deeply sinister?"

Silence. My heart contracted. *Maybe if she just liked people*, I wanted to say. *Maybe some demons like dressing up with their friends.*

"So here's how I pull this all together," Kessa concluded, with the air of a stage conjurer directing attention to her next trick. "We go to the ball, stop the poisoning, and steal the key. One fancy party and we're done except for the wards, and we get to look fabulous while we're doing it."

"Or," Severin suggested acidly, "we could stay away from the obvious trap, warn everyone not to eat or drink anything at the party, and use the distraction to set up an ambush for the Zenith Society."

Ashe straightened. "Ooh, I like it."

I shook my head. "Tempting as it sounds, I don't think it'll work. I'm sure they'll sweep the palace to make sure everyone shows up to this party—and both the Zenith Society *and* the demons will notice if we're not there. Besides, forgive my cynicism, but I've run a castle and I know how bad people are at following instructions. We can't just count on people not to eat or drink anything; we have to be there to deal with heedless fools and unforeseen circumstances." Severin didn't look convinced; I turned to Kessa before he could argue. "Do you have a plan for how to steal the key?"

Kessa bit her lip, thinking. "Maybe if you distracted Madness, Ryx. I've seen how she latches on to you—she gets completely focused. She probably wouldn't notice if I climbed up on her shoulders and started restyling her hair."

An uneasy shiver brushed my spine. Talking to Madness frightened me much more than talking to Nightmare or Hunger, even though she seemed least likely of the three to do anything terrible to me. With Nightmare and Hunger, anger sustained me, and I felt resolutely human. Madness kept teasing at buried things, severed memories, lost pieces I didn't want returned. Kessa was right, though. It was our best chance.

There was one other problem. I held up my bare wrist. "Excellent idea, but I can't go to any balls until my jess is working again."

Bastian tipped his head. "Well, jesses absorb energy from around them, and Foxglove put it on a chunk of obsidian in a windowsill in direct sunlight, so it should be recharging about as quickly as possible. It might be ready by tonight."

I nodded, steeling myself. "If it's ready, then I'm up for it."

"So we're doing this," Ashe said, with weary resignation. "We're going to the terrible-idea ball being thrown by a set of demons."

"We have to," I said. "Besides, if it goes well—if we get the key tonight and finish the wards in the morning—we can be out of here by this time tomorrow."

Ashe waved a hand. "Oh, you don't have to convince me. Certain doom, nine o'clock, wear a nice dress. I'll be there."

TWENTY-NINE

My jess recovered its power just in time for the ball. Bastian examined it with his Verdi's Glasses—magic-detecting spectacles—and confirmed that it should be working again.

I'd never been so eager to slip my hand through its shining golden loop, the beads gleaming like blood as Kessa held it wide for me. The world went muffled with it on, less raw, less sharp-edged. I touched the leaf of a potted plant to be safe, and it remained green and unwithered; an old, familiar tension fled my shoulders.

"There." Kessa patted my arm once we were sure it was safe, her smile more real than I'd seen from her since Foxglove's revelation. "I'm so glad. Honestly, I'd be terrified to face the demons without you—you've been so effective at dealing with them. I don't want to think what would happen if you weren't there."

"I'll do everything I can to protect you," I promised, ignoring the unease fluttering in my belly at her misplaced trust. The Rookery only saw the tea party, the mirror maze, and the demon council as victories because they hadn't been there.

"I'm looking forward to my first time working with you as my partner in guile. Normally it would be..." She trailed off, pain creasing her brow.

Hells, everything was going to be complicated for a while. I swallowed. "Those are hard shoes to step into, but I'll do my best."

Kessa let out an explosive sigh. "I wish I could stop caring about him. Snuff it out like a candle. But I keep wondering what he would think, worrying about whether he's eating and taking his joint elixir." She raised a shaking hand to her face. "Hells, I promised Lia I'd take care of him. What am I going to say to her? How am I going to explain to her and Teodor why I can't come over for dinner anymore? This is rotten and I hate it. But I don't want to forgive him, either."

I understood. Foxglove was her family. Some ties you couldn't cut, even when they made you bleed.

I didn't know what to say. I couldn't tell her it would be all right, I wasn't willing to tell her she was well rid of him, and it was too early to try to reconcile her to Foxglove. Tentatively, I lifted my arms, with all the awkwardness of a wet bird spreading its wings to dry.

Kessa dropped her face on my shoulder, all but falling against me. I patted her back as she trembled, grimly fixing my focus on trying to make her feel better and not on how warm and soft she was. I hoped holding her was enough; I'd never comforted anyone before in my life.

After a long moment, she straightened, wiping her eyes. "We'd best get ready for the ball. We'll stand out if we're not dressed to excess."

My heart ached for Kessa, but as I headed to my room to change, I couldn't help but feel more optimistic with the jess on my wrist. And as I turned the golden wirework thoughtfully beneath my fingers, it gave me an idea exciting enough to quicken my pulse.

When I opened my door, yellow eyes waited for me, gleaming down from a patch of shadow atop my wardrobe.

I caught my breath. "Whisper. You can't just walk up to someone and say hello, can you? You have to wait in ambush, or sneak up by surprise."

"Naturally." He leaped down onto my bed in a long, graceful arc, finishing with a flip of his bushy tail.

I closed the door behind me. I had some questions for him, and I'd rather keep them private. "Listen," I began. "I was wondering—"

"It won't work," he said.

I blinked at him, nonplussed. "How did you know what I was going to ask?"

"Because I know you. And it's natural for you to wonder whether you could use a jess to seal a demon's power and render them harmless. You're not completely ignorant; it was only a matter of time until you asked."

"Well, thanks." I sank onto the edge of my bed beside him, trying to hide my disappointment. "Why won't it work?"

He tipped his head, as if searching for an angle that might allow my too-human brain to understand. "Jesses are meant for humans, who have...attachment points, you might say, which they use to manipulate magic. The jess locks them together with each other instead."

"Bastian told me that. But...the jess works on me." I spread my hands. "Why wouldn't it work on other demons?" *Other* demons. That had rolled right off my tongue. I was getting used to this, Graces help me.

"Don't rely on the jess to keep your power contained." His voice dropped to a low hum of warning, almost a growl, sending a chill down the back of my neck. "Those human attachment points are an easy escape for your power; they focus and concentrate it, too, which is why your touch is so devastating to living things. But demons *are* power. We don't need to rely on such fine manipulation." His tail swished. "I suppose you could think of it as the spout of a teapot. If your power overflows the pot entirely, however, the spout is irrelevant."

"And if I overflow..." I swallowed. "A lot of people die."

"Most likely," Whisper agreed. "Though your power works differently when you fully unleash it than when it escapes through those human attachment points. Without the concentrating and focusing effect, you won't kill people and unravel magic with a touch. You'll disrupt things on a much larger, more diffuse scale."

I shuddered. "Like storms."

"Among other things, yes."

There was something I needed to know—a question that had gnawed at me since last night, lurking in the corners of my mind, keeping me from sleep. But the sick apprehension in my gut whenever I thought of it made me afraid of the answer.

Still, I had to ask. "The legends of the Dark Days speak about the Demon of Disaster."

Whisper glanced away. "I have no doubt that they do."

"They, uh." I licked my dry lips. "I know these are stories, not histories, and they're thousands of years old. But they say the Demon of Disaster did some terrible things." My stomach hurt, and cold sweat broke out on my palms. "Hurricanes and earthquakes and volcanic eruptions that..." My throat closed, sure as if someone squeezed my windpipe shut. But I forced it out. "That killed thousands of people. Wiped out whole cities. There are...lots of stories like that."

For a long moment, Whisper was silent, and the only sound was my heart beating fiercely in the dim shadows of my room. Finally, he sighed.

"You must understand," he said, his voice so quiet I strained to listen, "that when we first came through, we had no comprehension of what life even was. We were beings of pure energy, from a realm of pure energy; matter itself was strange to us. We didn't know we'd stolen human bodies, didn't understand the information our human senses were giving us. It was all completely new."

I held my breath. Somewhere beyond the severed ends of

memory, his words resonated, like a trembling deep within the earth. Every syllable had the terrible weight of pure truth.

"It took a long time to learn," he continued, soft as the fall of twilight. "We absorbed some knowledge from the humans we took as vessels—but by inheriting bits and pieces of their understanding of the world, their understanding of *us* shaped what we became. I was a severing energy, precise and unanswerable; the hosts I took knew in their fear that they were dying, and named me Death. Nightmare was a reflecting energy, complex and subtle; it was their terror that resonated with her, and their fear gave her a name, too."

"And I was Disaster," I whispered, my eyes stinging.

"Yes." He briefly touched his nose to me, cold and regal, in a sort of formal greeting. "You were a disruptive and chaotic energy, vast and unbridled and destructive, and that was how their terror defined you."

"Curse it, Whisper." I scrubbed my face, fiercely; there was no clear reason for this surge of grief that welled up within me like some underground spring to flood my eyes with tears. "I don't *want* to destroy anything."

"You never did." He laid a paw on my leg, his pads rough and warm. "Some of the others didn't care what effect they had on the world even after they came to understand it, as you saw at that mockery of a council today." Contempt passed through his voice like a cold wind, there and gone again. "You spent a hundred years learning to contain your power. It's why you don't have a harmful aura like Nightmare and Madness do. Why you didn't destroy your home and everyone around you when you were a tiny pup with no memories and no common sense. You've clamped your power tight beneath your skin for so long that you do it instinctively, even in your sleep." He removed his paw, leveling his yellow gaze at me. "But every time you relax that grip, it will come easier, like a loosened knot. You must be very, very careful, Ryx."

The last thing I wanted to do was risk deserving the name my ancestors had cursed by for four thousand years. "I will."

"Hmph. You'd better."

"What…" I didn't know how to ask this question; it was strange in my mind, and stranger on my tongue. "What was I like? I mean, I was two different people—two different beings. And now I'm me. I must have changed."

His tail swished across the bedspread. "You're the same, but different. The same friend I've always had, but…" He made a strange sound, a quiet huff, as if he'd surprised himself. "You've matured."

"Matured?" That wasn't what I'd expected.

"Yes. The sense of duty is mostly new; that came from the human side. And you're much better at approaching things logically and thinking them through now. I like the new you better."

"Good," I said. "I think." Seasons, this was an odd conversation. It was hard to wrap my feelings around it.

"But you always cared for your friends," Whisper added, almost to himself. "That's not new."

That made me feel better, somehow. If I'd loved my friends even as a pure demon, I couldn't have been a creature of absolute evil. "I do care for them, and I'll always protect them."

Whisper gave me a clouded look, long and secret and somehow sad. It set a shiver of foreboding in my bones.

"Yes," he said, with a great heaviness. "Yes, I don't doubt you will."

Palpable fear smothered the grand ball. Absolutely no one wanted to be there.

The musicians played terribly, with some of their number clearly missing or injured from the chaos Nightmare had unleashed earlier in the day. It didn't matter, because nobody danced, except for a handful of people with silver-sheened eyes who swayed and stumbled through their steps as if they were half asleep.

There was food, but no one ate. We'd put out the word for no one to drink, either, but I still saw a few people sneaking glasses of wine, and I almost couldn't blame them.

"I've been to livelier executions," Severin murmured, scanning the room.

"But have you been to a prison this fancy?" Kessa countered.

The ballroom itself staggered the senses. Intricate chandeliers of dripping crystal sparkled in glacial splendor above a cavernous space wrought in writhing shades of intricately veined marble. Vast, dark oil paintings celebrating the glories of the Loreician monarchy brooded in gilded frames; dramatic statues of the common merchants and tradespeople who'd led the Festival Uprising posed defiantly beneath them. Flickering oil lamps in ornate wall brackets supplemented the luminaries, which would dim by midnight, but they seemed to add unsteady shadows more than light. There was no peaceful spot for the eyes to rest.

Most of the people clumped in tight clusters in bedraggled finery, whispering, casting glances over their shoulders. Some sported bandages, or new spreading bruises, or the telltale shiny patches of alchemical healing salves. A few slumped against the wall, heads down in apparent despair. Many hadn't bothered to put on jewelry or makeup, or even to brush their hair.

Everyone knew, now, how much trouble they were in. Some of the nobles had donned plumed hats and stood apart from both the commoners and their fellows who still cleaved desperately to the queen, clinging to power to the very last. The Loreician court seemed shaken by the exchange of fire between the fortress and the warships in a way that the mere presence of demons among them couldn't match; demons were a legend, after all, but the serenity of the Empire was the foundation on which their world rested.

We were certainly no exception to the crowd's ragged, haunted appearance. Foxglove, talking to Councilor Altaine halfway across the ballroom, had a brooding and unshaven look at odds with his crisp gray frock coat. Close at his side, Bastian cast hunted glances around as he bent over a wineglass, testing it for traces of quicksilver; we'd glimpsed Cortissa in attendance, and were doing everything we could to keep him away from her. Even Ashe, standing wary guard beside him, looked leaner and more brittle, like a sword at risk of breaking.

"Right," I said, trying to pull together my overwhelmed senses to focus on business. I still wasn't used to crowds like this; I wasn't sure I ever would be. "Do you see Madness anywhere?"

Kessa snorted. "Spot the demon is an easy game. Just look for empty space."

She was right. At the center of a wide berth of deserted floor, a tight knot of people surrounded the three demons—Zenith Society, courtiers who'd made dubious choices, and a few silver-eyed attendants. Hunger laughed with the Zenith Society, drinking up their attention. Nightmare stood smiling by his side, satisfied as a cat in the cream. Madness—

Madness was already looking at me. Her stare tugged at me, like a hand plucking on my sleeve from all the way across the ballroom.

"Well, looks like it'll be easy for you to get her attention, anyway," Kessa murmured. "The tricky part will be getting her away from the others, so they don't notice. Stealing something's not much good if you can't get away clean with it."

"We might be able to get Aurelio's help in diverting Hunger," I suggested, a bit dubiously.

Severin's face tightened. "I don't want to rely on that wretch. Frankly, I don't know how you can trust him, either, given the grievances you have against him."

"He's helped us more than once. He's not... It's not that simple." My stomach churned at the words coming out of my own mouth. "Look, don't make me defend the man who murdered my aunt. But Hells, Severin, you wouldn't be alive right now if he hadn't told us where the artifact was."

"And I wouldn't have been in danger from it in the first place if he hadn't brought Hunger to the Zenith Society," Severin snapped. "I don't owe him anything, and neither do you. Don't let him convince you otherwise."

"I *know* we don't owe him anything. I *despise* him. But our interests align; we want to get rid of Hunger, too."

Kessa's brows flew up. "Does he know that our current strategy for getting rid of Hunger involves trapping him in this palace?"

"I'm not so foolish as to tell someone like Aurelio our plans." But she was right—if we went through with our plan, Aurelio would be trapped in here with the demons, possibly forever.

Hells. Did I hate him that much? He used to be my friend; lately, he'd been my ally.

He killed my aunt. Even more than trying to murder me, that I could never forgive.

"I suppose the best possible outcome would be if we give him just enough warning to evict Hunger and slide out the door before we seal the wards, then arrest him on the doorstep," I muttered. Severin was looking at me skeptically, and I couldn't blame him; the precise timing required for that stunt would be daunting. "Anyway, point taken. We can't rely on him, and it wouldn't be right to deliberately use him if we know we might have to leave him to rot like that."

"It'd serve him right," Severin said. "You're more forgiving than I am."

A swirl of movement detached from the cluster around the demons, heading our way: the Zenith Society, Moreni and Cortissa at the forefront. Hells, their timing was as horrible as everything else about them.

"Here comes trouble," I said.

Kessa followed my gaze and sucked in a breath through her teeth. "They haven't seen Bastian, have they?"

I glanced toward the corner where the others were working on tracking down the quicksilver, but found my line of sight blocked. An escort of silver-uniformed guards was marching more guests into the middle of the ballroom, no doubt having rounded up those who thought they might escape the mandatory event. I spotted Elia among them, and felt a pang at how indifferent she seemed to the fear of the people she was herding.

"I don't think so, with all those guards in the way," I said. "Moreni looks like he means business, though, and there's a lot more of them than us."

The party crowd stirred uneasily as the tight knot of the Zenith Society group moved through them, almost in formation. Hostility radiated from them like a demonic aura.

Kessa's eyes hardened as she watched their approach. "*They're* the ones who killed him," she muttered. "I can't forget that."

"No matter what happens, I'm not letting them get out of here alive," Severin said through his teeth. "It's lovely that you all want to save Loreice, but my priority is destroying those wretches before they come up with some other plan to annihilate my domain."

"Not now, though," I said, alarmed.

"Oh, don't worry, not here. I won't let them see it coming." A small smile tugged at Severin's mouth as they got close enough for us to see the rashy patches of insect bites on the faces and necks of several of their number.

Pure animosity glittered in Moreni's dark eyes. "I'm surprised you have the gall to show your faces," he said, turning one of his wirework artifice rings on his finger. "After what you did, why do you think we'll let you walk out of here alive?"

Kessa gave him a contemptuous glance, up and down, dismissing every part of him. "It seems to me that you couldn't stop us."

Severin flashed a murderous grin, but my shoulders tensed. Much as a brawl with the Zenith Society might be cathartic, they had a Skinwitch, and Moreni was dripping with artifice devices. Whoever won, we wouldn't emerge from any serious fight unscathed—and with half of our number out of sight across the ballroom and Bastian needing to stay the Hells away from Cortissa regardless, we were woefully outnumbered.

None of this escaped Moreni. His gaze traveled over the three of us, noting Severin's and my mage marks.

"And where is your dear leader?" Moreni asked mockingly. "And my beloved protégé? Not to mention your little attack dog. I do hope no misfortune has befallen them."

Kessa winced at his mention of Foxglove. She did a good job of hiding it, but by the flicker in Moreni's eyes, he noticed.

"Wouldn't you love to know," I said to cover for her, trying my best mysterious smile.

"You seem rather...vulnerable without them." Moreni exchanged an amused glance with Cortissa, as if our reduced numbers were an inside joke. This close, I could see the rings of the mage mark around her pupils, a deep red like dried blood.

Severin lifted his brows in mock surprise. "Is that a threat? I do hope so. Because as a visiting atheling of a foreign domain, it would be inappropriate for me to start a fight, but I'd be delighted to end one."

Cortissa let out an impatient snort. "Enough of this posing. We're not going to murder you here—not when it would be so much more effective to murder you while you sleep. Or you could tell us where you've hidden the artifact, and we could let you live." She snapped her fingers. "It's an easy choice."

Something wasn't right. They were going through the forms and motions of antagonizing us, like actors rehearsing their blocking without putting their hearts in their lines. I frowned at them.

"You've got to know you won't gain anything from this

conversation. Why did you come to talk to us?" I glanced around, suspicious. "Is this a distraction?"

She burst out into raucous laughter. "Oh, you'll *wish* you were distracted."

Moreni lifted a lazy hand. "Now, now. No hints, Cortissa." He gave me a polite nod, halfway to a mocking bow. "We just wanted to see your faces before we left. Please give my regards to Foxglove and Bastian, and enjoy the ball."

He flicked two fingers toward the main exit to the ballroom. Cortissa gave us a parting smirk, and the whole group of them headed toward the doors.

I was sure they'd swerve at the last minute to mingle back into the crowd—perhaps to go after Bastian or Foxglove or return to their demon patrons. But they sauntered out, with nods to the silver-eyed guards flanking the door, and were gone.

"That can't be good," Kessa muttered.

Severin frowned. "The question is, are they leaving to go do something sinister somewhere else, or to avoid something nasty that's about to happen here?"

I bit my lip. The more I thought about it, the more the implications of their departure disturbed me. "If it were just a matter of quicksilver in the wine, they wouldn't need to leave. One way or another, there's more to their plan."

Severin gazed in the direction they'd gone, eyes narrowing. "That's it. I'm going after them."

He started to move; I put myself in front of him, alarmed. "To do what?"

"Oh, relax. I'm not going to murder them." He paused. "Yet. I'm going to round up some of my furry friends to follow them."

"That's not a bad idea," Kessa approved.

My heart jumped unaccountably. "I don't like the idea of you going off alone right now."

He gave me a strange look.

Embarrassed, I admitted, "It could just be nerves. But you

heard them; something big is about to happen, and I think we should stick together."

An odd disappointment flickered in his eyes. Had he wanted me to come out and admit I was worried about him because I cared for him? I'd been trying not to make him feel uncomfortable, given what he knew about me. To step back, make it businesslike, and give him safe distance.

"Much as it pains me to say it, my safety isn't what matters right now." Severin gave an uncomfortable sort of shrug, as if selflessness were an ill-fitting vestcoat he planned to return to the tailor. "I'm the heir to Alevar, and my brother is apparently doing such a poor job that the consequences almost destroyed us. I've got no choice but to step up." He sighed. "I'm probably going to have to spend years doing diplomatic cleanup, but in the meantime, I need to latch on to this threat like a whip-hound and prevent them from ever trying to harm my domain again."

A surge of pride welled up in me for Severin, to see him assuming responsibility when he usually avoided it like an unwelcome guest. "Still, please be careful. If they catch you skulking around after them, when you're alone and unprotected—"

He lifted an eyebrow. "You're mistaking me for someone brave, I see. A common error." A strange mix of amusement and pain edged his voice. "I assure you, I'm not going anywhere near them. I'm not like you; I can't stand up to monsters with impunity, human or demonic. I've got too much to lose."

"You're plenty brave," I objected. "You just use indirect methods. You're highly effective."

That same disappointment hooded his eyes again. "Highly effective. Such a warm compliment." He shook his head. "I'd better go after them, or they'll be too hard to track down. Good luck, Ryx. Don't do anything rash without me."

He walked away, the shining tail of his hair swaying behind him. Curse it, I'd fumbled this and hurt him again.

Kessa sighed and put a sympathetic hand on my shoulder. "And I thought *I* was bad at romance."

"Look, I couldn't come closer than rock-throwing range to anyone until a month ago," I protested, my ears burning. "Also, we're not... I mean, I'm not..."

"Mm-hmm."

"Anyway, we'd better get that key." There was no way to explain to Kessa that getting involved with someone would have been a bad enough idea when I thought I just had a killing touch; now it was a terrible plan on a cataclysmic level.

A stir ran through the room. Not just a murmuring reaction in the throng of people—though there was that, too—but a ripple in the heavy layers of power smothering the place, like a fresh stream pouring into murky seawater. An achingly familiar scent of pine and musky feathers teased my nose.

I didn't have to see the source of the disturbance to know who had just entered the ballroom. I could feel her approach in my soul, the missing piece of me that was Morgrain drawing nearer.

"My grandmother's here," I breathed.

Kessa sucked in a sharp breath. "Another demon. This might be a controversial opinion, but I'm going to say that's *not* what this party needed."

"I should talk to her." I could feel her pulling at me—not a command, but a request. "I'm sorry, I know we need to go after the key now—"

"Oh, I have to get a closer look at it first," Kessa assured me. "The clasp, her hair, other jewelry around her neck, and so on. And the last thing I'd do is step between you and your grandmother, not least because she'd probably turn me inside out if I tried. Besides, maybe you can learn something from her."

Oh, I was sure she could teach me plenty. I swallowed. "I'll try. Good luck."

"You too. I suspect you'll need it more." Kessa gave me a sympathetic grimace and headed off through the crowd.

I moved toward the parting wave of alarmed courtiers to meet my grandmother.

No matter how many times I told myself she wasn't the grandmother I knew anymore, no matter what she'd done to me, seeing her face was like coming home. Her crest of white hair, the laugh lines beside her eyes, the lean angles of her face—they were all as familiar as the view from my bedroom window back at Gloamingard. The wave of power that surrounded her enfolded me like comforting wings.

But the smile that showed her teeth had too much of an edge to it, her eyes too much of a cruel glitter.

"Hello, Ryx. Enjoying the party?"

"Hello, Grandmother. To be completely honest, I don't think anyone is enjoying this party."

She laughed. "Oh, I am. I've already started a fight between Hunger and Nightmare."

I glanced toward the tight cluster of three demons, incredulous, and found only two; sure enough, the crowd swirled around Hunger as he stormed off, scowling.

"You didn't even go near them." I shook my head. "I shouldn't be surprised, but I have to admit I'm impressed. Did you do that for fun, or do you have some clever plan?"

She raised an eyebrow. "Have you ever known me not to have a plan, even when I'm doing something for fun?"

"No," I admitted. "Not that I don't approve, but why?" Hells, it was so easy to fall into old conversational patterns with her, talking as if nothing had changed. But a current of wrongness flowed down those familiar channels, setting my nerves on edge.

"You and I are in a difficult position, Ryx." She laid a hand on my shoulder—warm, supportive, sympathetic. I went rigid under it, wanting to trust her, not at all sure that I could. "We want to protect this world from the unchecked ravages of our less responsible demonic kin." She cast an exasperated glance toward Nightmare.

"That's one way to put it," I agreed.

"At the same time, if humanity gains too much of an upper hand over demons, things will go poorly for us."

My brows climbed my forehead. "Is that even possible? I'll be honest, we—humanity, that is—don't seem to have many advantages right now."

My grandmother chuckled. "The others certainly don't think so, but they're fools. I remember the Dark Days, and I remember how the Graces beat us—each in a different way, learning and adapting, matching strengths to our particular weaknesses. And I know what we're capable of now, with all the advances humans have made in the four thousand years since then. I won't deny that right now the demons are very much the surer bet, but humanity has an enormous talent for coming back from the brink of doom and managing to scrape out a win."

That was strangely reassuring. "I hope we do."

"*We?*" My grandmother gave me a cynical look. "If humanity finds a way to banish the demons, I assure you they won't make an exception for us. They'll send us back to the Nine Hells with the others. Is that what you want?"

Horror gripped me with prickling claws. "I..." *I don't belong in the Nine Hells.* But that wasn't true. We were discussing an eternity of exile in a place I'd been taught was one of infinite torment—and it was also apparently my home, just as much as Gloamingard was. "No, I don't."

She nodded. "So we have to make sure neither side wins. We have to keep them in balance. We stand on the fulcrum, you and I; if both sides need us, neither will dispose of us."

It was similar to the strategy I'd often used when building Morgrain's relationships with our neighbors in Vaskandar and the Serene Empire. I could understand it; I could appreciate it. At the same time, if it meant undercutting humanity's efforts to neutralize the demons, I could never support it.

"So you're causing division among the demons, because their side is stronger now."

"Yes. We can't let them unite." She cocked her head. "Just like we can't let the Serene Empire and Vaskandar truly join forces, but right now there's scant chance of that."

"I couldn't work against humanity," I objected.

"Couldn't you?" The orange rings of her mage mark pierced me, seeing all the way through my soul like they always had. "There will come a time when you have to choose whether to let them attack us. Not demons as some nebulous concept of evil, but you and me and Whisper. You'll have to either stand by and let them cast us into oblivion, destroying the bodies you and I were born in and robbing us of the domain we are bound to by blood and sworn to protect—ripping away from us the very world that is as much ours as theirs. Or you'll have to fight back."

The idea of making such a choice was nauseating. I stiffened, rejecting it. "I've been a diplomat of sorts for my entire adult life. I refuse to believe we can't find some kind of peaceful solution."

My grandmother grunted. "Tell it to Nightmare and Hunger. Tell it to the Council of Nine and the Conclave." Her hand dropped from my shoulder. "I wish you luck, but I've been around long enough to spot a conflict that can't be solved by words alone. We have to play a harder game."

"Not until I absolutely need to," I insisted. "I haven't given up yet."

"I look forward to seeing how long you last." She lifted her head abruptly, as if she'd caught a scent in the air. "Hmm. There's something I have to look into. Enjoy the rest of the party, Ryx. I'll see you soon."

I stared after the ruffled feathers of her shoulder mantle and the pale shock of her hair as she moved off through the crowd. The air around her seemed clearer, sharper; the people near her took deep breaths even as they moved instinctively away in fear, and their eyes lingered on her as if they could take some bitter strength from her passage.

Then she was gone. And the smothering presence of Madness and Nightmare fell upon the room as if only her power had been holding it back.

Shadows writhed at the corners of my vision. Some of the people around me staggered, or recoiled from things I couldn't see; scattered cries of alarm rose from the crowd, and the music faltered. One woman not far from me sank in a puff of skirts and put her face in her hands.

I could almost see shapes in those swarming shadows that disappeared when I looked at them straight. Almost make out the phantoms from which courtiers in silver-embroidered coats shrank in terror, the dark stains spreading across the walls and ceiling, the ghostly touch that caused a man to drag his nails down his cheeks in a panic as if desperate to remove his own face.

The ball quivered on the edge of becoming a riot. I glanced around sharply for the rest of the Rookery; Kessa and Bastian were conversing urgently over by the wine table, Bastian gesturing to an empty wineglass in his hand, while Ashe seemed deep in conversation with Foxglove near the buffet. Surely they must have noticed the sudden shift. I hesitated, then started to make my way toward Kessa; she was an actress, and likely had the best idea how to control a crowd if need be.

"We haven't really had the chance to talk, you and I."

It was Nightmare, her voice coiling around me like smoke.

THIRTY

I turned to find Nightmare standing far closer than I'd have liked, a glass of red wine in her hand and a smile of cruel amusement stretching her lips. Her skirts cascaded in bunched layers of vivid poison green and burnished copper, the dress exquisitely tailored to fit the dead woman she was wearing.

"Forgive me if I haven't been canceling all my other appointments to make time for the demon who's been tormenting everyone around me," I replied, wrestling my tone into something approximately civil. Much as I'd love to tell her more bluntly what I thought of her, I needed to keep her attention on me and away from those more vulnerable.

"Mmm." Her eyes narrowed in calculation. "So you truly don't remember anything?"

"I don't need to remember to know that I probably didn't like you before, either."

She chuckled at that, a rich deep sound. "Fair enough. But Madness is heartbroken, you know."

I felt an odd twinge in my chest at that.

Nightmare must have seen it in my face—or maybe in whatever patterns of energy she watched in my mind. She sucked in an excited little gasp. "Oh. *Oh.* You may not have your memories, but you still have your *feelings*, don't you? Well. This has possibilities."

I didn't like the predatory gleam in her eye. I had to try to shut this down before she pushed any further.

"You're right that I don't remember the past," I said, low and intense, "so I don't know if you're used to me standing aside and letting you play your twisted little games. But whoever I was then, I'm a different person now. I'm part of this world, and I won't let you harm it."

Whatever reaction I might have expected, it wasn't the razor-sharp grin that spread across Nightmare's face.

"Beautiful," she breathed. "But you can do better than that."

She stepped closer still, until our skirts rustled together. I forced myself not to back away. Her presence enfolded me like a thick, choking miasma of fever; the edges of my vision swarmed with sudden motion, as if horrifying images pressed and clamored to get into my brain.

"Do you know why I do this?" she asked, gesturing with her wineglass at the ballroom, the palace, the people in their finery who'd cleared a broad space around us. "What I get out of it, exactly?"

"Some vile form of entertainment, no doubt." I couldn't keep my revulsion off my face, and I didn't try very hard. She was going to tell me no matter what I said; I didn't have to be subtle.

"You never could see what Madness and Despair and I can." Her lids dropped to half hood her eyes as she gazed around her with apparent deep satisfaction. "The colors of human minds, ever changing, in the most amazing and intricate patterns. But when they're in distress—when they're full of anguish or terror..." She drew in a deep, savoring breath; my skin tingled with a faint current of energy, as if something invisible flowed into her. "It's exquisite. Addictive. Ever since I tasted it that first time, when I came to this world and possessed my first human body and partook in his dying terror, I've craved more and more."

"You deserve every curse they've called you." I clenched my hands tight on the extravagant explosions of lace at my sleeves to keep myself from doing anything rash with them. "You're a monster."

"But we're kin." Amusement danced across her lips. "If I'm a monster, that makes you one as well."

"Not like you." That much I was sure of. Whisper and my grandmother and I might be far from innocent, but Nightmare had truly earned the name of demon.

"No. Not like me," she whispered, an avid light coming into her eyes. "And that's what makes you so..." She reached out and touched my cheek, her fingers cold and hard as old bone. "Delicious."

I flinched away. "What the—"

"Your colors," she purred. "A demon's colors are so much brighter, so much more intense. But they're too static. They don't make the incredible patterns humans do. But you, ah— you have it all. The intensity of a demon, the pain of a human. And it's so easy to make you suffer."

I stepped back, my heart quickening. "Whatever you're thinking, don't try it," I warned her. "I'll defend myself."

"But you can't." A feverish light shone in her eyes. "Not without hurting your precious humans. That's the lovely irony of it, Disaster—you're one of the most powerful of all of us, but by caring for this world you make yourself utterly power-less."

She threw her arms suddenly wide, her voice ringing from the walls and the floor and the very air around us. "Behold your weakness!"

All at once, the whole palace throbbed with her power, like the beating of a massive heart.

The music twisted into something dark and wailing, an unearthly lament. The light from the chandeliers flickered and went pale and ghostly, painting the ballroom with wavering shadows. All around us, cries of horror and panic rose up, and the crowd surged into chaos.

For a moment, a cloud passed over my vision, and I could see what they saw. Dark clots of thousands of spiders unfurled from the corners and swarmed across the frescoed ceiling, many of them bigger than my hand. The windows filled with viscous black, and waterfalls of blood began pouring into the room; I gagged on the stink of death. The faces of the terrified revelers transformed as well, with gaping black empty eyes that wept dark fluid, or the rotting flesh of the dead, or the inhuman visages of monsters from someone's worst childhood dreams.

Then they were all human again, their screams piercing my ears, running for the exits or collapsing where they stood, scrambling and stumbling over each other in a blind rush to escape the invisible phantoms of their own fears.

"Leave them alone," I snarled at Nightmare. My hand dropped to my sword hilt—but violence wouldn't stop her. Even killing her would only doom some other poor wretch to become her new vessel.

"Ahhh, yes, this hurts you, doesn't it?" Her gaze remained fixed on me with awful intensity, her expression one of pure pleasure. "But I think we can hurt you more."

The people around us began dropping to the floor in graceful swooning arcs of silk and brocade. They fell heedlessly across each other in a slow expanding wave, their lids drooping shut, limbs sagging into sudden sleep. In the time it took me to draw a panicked breath, the ballroom turned to a sea of motionless bodies.

They're not dead, I told my pounding heart. *She didn't kill them. Just put them to sleep.* But by the expressions pinching their unconscious faces, their dreams were far from pleasant.

"If you intend to keep them all hostage—" I began hotly, but Nightmare laughed.

"All of them? Oh, no. I'm just clearing the stage. The scene was a bit cluttered, don't you think? I have to make certain you can see our star actors."

Something about her tone curdled my blood. I turned slowly to face the room again, almost against my will.

Some people were still standing after all: Madness, across the ballroom, who stared at me with an unnerving wistful longing—and a full dozen silver-eyed guards, who now picked their way through the sprawled sleeping bodies, converging toward one point.

Closing in on a single pale figure in a scarlet gown, lying still where she'd fallen with her sword gripped tight in her hand even in sleep.

"Don't touch her," I called, a helpless fury flooding me. There wasn't a damned thing I could do to stop them, and Nightmare knew it.

One of the guards seized Ashe's pale shock of hair and dragged her half upright, tipping her head back. Madness drifted closer to her, smoothly as if her rustling skirts somehow floated over her fallen guests, something small and silver flashing in her hand.

The bottle of quicksilver. Oh, Hells, no.

I started toward her, struggling to avoid stepping on anyone. "Madness! Don't you dare! She's my *friend*!"

Madness hesitated, bottle in hand, poised over Ashe as she sagged in the guard's grip.

"Do it!" Nightmare barked. "This will help Disaster remember you!"

Madness ducked her head, diamond crown sparkling in her pale hair. "I want to help you," she told me, an ocean of sadness in her voice. "This is for you."

She tipped a drop of shining quicksilver onto Ashe's brow.

"Perfect," Nightmare whispered. "Now the show can start."

The guard holding Ashe went suddenly reeling as she exploded into motion. He staggered back, tripping over a sleeping baron, but didn't have time to finish falling before Ashe's sword took him clean through the chest. The rest of the guards scattered—not in the alarm I'd expect at seeing one of their comrades killed, but with the more methodical retreat of those whose job is over.

"Ashe, no!" I shouted. "They're controlled! Don't kill them!"

She cast an impassive glance at me, blood dripping from Answer's bright blade. Her eyes flashed like silver mirrors.

Something in my chest snapped, the pain of it taking my breath away. I stumbled to a halt as if I'd hit a wall.

"And where are the others?" Nightmare murmured, her fingers fluttering in the air as if she were feeling around for them. "Let's see . . . there."

At the far end of the hall, Kessa lurched to her feet, suddenly awake and startled, while Bastian rose with more cautious grace and at once began checking on the fallen people around him. No silver showed in their eyes; they'd only been asleep, and Nightmare had fully awakened them.

"Ashe!" Kessa called, stretching out her hand. "Nine Hells, your eyes! What did they do to you?"

"Don't go near her!" I cried, my voice rising in panic. I could see all too clearly where this was going. "Kessa, Bastian, *run!*"

Kessa's head swiveled from Ashe to me and then back to Ashe; her eyes widened, and she grabbed Bastian's shoulder and dragged him up from where he knelt, obliviously trying to wake the sleepers on the floor. Hells take it, they weren't moving fast enough; Ashe had already turned toward them, feet shifting, sword ready.

Nightmare let out a pleased sigh. "So beautiful. But it only gets better. I'm proud of this one, Disaster. Watch, and suffer for me."

Ashe launched herself at them, sprinting across the fallen in great springing bounds, Answer flashing. Kessa stared at her in shock, lifting empty hands before her; Bastian froze, colors racing across his skin.

On the floor not far off, Foxglove rolled up onto his elbows, flintlock in hand, and took aim at Ashe.

The moment slowed and stretched as a scream built somewhere deep in my lungs, all fire and ruin, a terrible searing anguish clawing its way up toward my throat for release. I was too far away to stop them—to try to tackle Ashe, or throw myself between them, or knock the pistol from Foxglove's hand.

By my next heartbeat, either Ashe would kill Kessa and Bastian, Foxglove would kill Ashe, or very possibly both—and whoever was left alive would be broken utterly by what they'd done.

THIRTY-ONE

It was too late, Ashe closing in like death itself, Foxglove's finger tightening on the trigger.

I flung out a hand as if I could somehow stop them from across the expanse of the ballroom, the scream tearing out of me: "*No!*"

All my fear and anguish and love for them, my will to stop them, my fury at Nightmare for doing this, swelled too great for me to contain, bursting out of me in a great surge of energy.

Every lamp in the ballroom flared, the flames rearing up like angry serpents.

The palace shuddered as if someone had dropped it from a great height. With a tremendous breaking sound, a deep jagged crack opened in the floor, snaking fast as lightning from my feet toward Ashe.

And one of the great chandeliers that lit the ballroom, bright with hundreds of luminary crystals, plummeted in spectacular shattering glory to crash down between Ashe and Kessa onto the helpless sleepers below.

Anguish speared through me. I whirled on Nightmare, whose expression went from dreamy ecstasy to something very like fear.

"*You!*" I snarled. I couldn't form words big enough for my grief and fury. Thunder boomed outside, shaking the palace again. Nightmare recoiled before me, flinging her hands up between us, eyes wide.

Madness cried out, her voice ringing loud and desperate from the walls like a great broken bell, "Disaster! *No!*"

Disaster.

A great stirring and moaning ran through the ballroom, as hundreds of people awoke to a room no less transformed by nightmare than it had been in their hallucinations. Fire licked up the walls and caught in the curtains, the scent of smoke tainting the air. Some had fallen into the shallow chasm that split the room; others lay trapped and moaning in pain beneath the iron frame of the chandelier, broken, maybe dying. Shattered luminary crystals scattered everywhere, some still shining with fading gleams of fractured light.

All my doing, from a second's loss of control.

The full realization of what I'd done hit me like a bucket of ice water. I wrestled my power back inside the bounds of me where it belonged, but it was too late—the room was burning, people were screaming, dozens were hurt or worse.

And across the room, through all the chaos, the rest of the Rookery stared at me in shock. Even Ashe, staggering as Madness let go her control and the silver drained from her eyes.

They'd heard what Madness called me. They'd seen what I'd done. They knew what I was, and they were horrified.

I was, too.

I stumbled through the burning room, tripping on the cracked floor, dropped accessories, and shattered wineglasses. All around me, people pushed for the exits—terrified, coughing, weeping, helping each other walk. The smoke was thickening quickly, the flames crawling in violent orange splendor across the walls as they caught on paintings, curtains, woodwork.

I didn't spare a glance for Nightmare. No doubt she was delighted. She could go straight back to the Nine Hells in small pieces as far as I was concerned.

An elderly man struggled to get out of the knee-deep crack that bisected the ballroom floor; I grabbed his arm and helped pull him out, straining against his fragile weight. He collapsed on the edge with a twisted ankle, his face tense with pain.

"Do you need—" I began, but a younger woman swooped in and helped him to his feet, shooting me a terrified glance, and they hobbled off together.

I couldn't tell if she was frightened because I was a stranger and the room was on fire, or if she remembered I was the atheling from Morgrain, or if she'd *seen*. If she knew I was the one who'd done this.

It didn't matter. I pressed on against the urgent flow of the fleeing crowd, heading to the middle of the room, holding my cuff over my nose and mouth to breathe through the lace. My throat ached and my eyes stung, and not exclusively from the smoke.

I broke free into the empty space surrounding the shattered chandelier. Several people—Foxglove among them—strained to lift it as others dragged the injured out from beneath it; the remaining luminaries sent scattered lights dancing madly across ruined finery and sweating faces. Ashe crouched against a nearby wall, head bowed over her knees.

Bastian attended to a young man who lay unmoving and bleeding on the floor, applying potions; Kessa stood by helping him. Another guest, a middle-aged woman with a bulging embroidered satchel, seemed to be helping the wounded as well—a physician or alchemist, no doubt. A pair of women used their skirts as a sort of makeshift sling to drag an injured man off toward the ballroom doors. At least, I *hoped* he was injured. Yes, there, his arm had moved, thank the seasons.

Every cry of pain, every body lying broken on the floor, sent a stab through me like a bayonet thrust. My desperate scan of the situation didn't show me anyone lying unattended, or surrounded only by the grieving; no one had been abandoned as beyond hope, at least.

"How can I..." I cleared my throat of smoke and unshed tears. "How can I help?"

Bastian recoiled as if I'd struck him, his hands freezing on a jar of salve. Kessa huddled close to him, eyes wide as moons, her fingers flicking out from her chest in the warding sign: *avert*.

Foxglove's hand went to the pouches at his belt. "You can't. Go away."

There was nothing soft in his dark amber eyes, no trace of friendship or sympathy. Only betrayal and cold fury.

"I just want to—"

"You've done enough here." Foxglove's voice sliced across mine with unmistakable anger. "Get out."

All the strings that held me together were snapping, one after another, with a stinging pain like the lash of a severed cable.

"Fine." They had enough hands; they didn't need mine, stained as they were with blood and prone to make things worse.

I turned without another word, my chest aching, and left the ballroom.

I seized on tasks like lifelines, staving off the impact of what I'd just done with urgent action. The ballroom was still on fire, so I stopped panicked, fleeing staff and asked them the right questions to get them moving to put it out. I had no authority to give them orders, and they knew what to do better than I did—but they were too shaken by the effects of Nightmare's power, too trapped in helpless fear and lingering traces of horrible visions, to remember that they could do it.

But if there was one thing I knew, it was how to manage a crisis in a castle.

Do you have any dampening powder in your alchemical stores got a handful of servants running one way, and *Do the kitchens have fire blankets for accidents* returned satisfying gasps and sudden sprints in another. I had to resort to *How do your gardeners water the plants* because I suspected that in the Empire they used artifice, but whatever the answer was, the people I asked headed off as if they knew the answer and what to do with it.

I tried to project calm confidence the whole time. I clasped my hands behind my back to hide their trembling as I sought out anyone who might have medical skills to help the injured, startling people out of hallucinatory trances when necessary; I learned to make sure I had eye contact and that whoever I was talking to could truly hear me before I let them go. Some people were too much of a wreck to help, and them I gently directed away from the burning ballroom.

On the way to find someone who knew about the water supply for the fountains, I rounded a corner and saw Severin.

He knelt on the floor of the entry hall, graceful and careless as a child, in a shaft of golden light from one of the glowing columns. With an unguarded expression of tender concentration, he reached out and scratched beneath the chin of the ragged gray tabby cat from the gardens.

I froze. He hadn't seen me. I had no idea if he even knew what had happened in the ballroom, half the palace away. Part of me yearned to run up and tell him everything—maybe even throw my arms around him—to vomit up all my horror at what I'd done into his lap.

But he looked so peaceful, so pure, even if I knew he was plotting espionage and maybe murder with that cat. He didn't yet know how much blood I'd just washed my hands in. I wanted to fold up the way he looked right now, with a little smile dimpling his face and his ponytail falling unheeded over one shoulder, and tuck it away in my heart forever.

If I touched this moment, I would break it. I backed out of the entry hall as silently as I could and found another way around.

Finally, my body heavy with weariness and the stink of smoke clinging to my hair, I peered into the ballroom window from the cool darkness of the rain-damp garden to find the fires were out. Black smoke stained the walls and ceiling, and the beauty of the room was laid waste, with art destroyed and marble cracked and debris everywhere. But a crowd of volunteers cheered and lifted their arms in victory amid the wreckage, the hungry flames defeated.

Good. Let them find some wine bottles that hadn't been ruined and lift glasses to toast their defeat of the Demon of Disaster. As they should.

I turned away from the window, a thick miserable feeling in my throat.

The cold barrel of a pistol slid up under my chin.

I froze, face-to-face with Foxglove. Soot streaked his dove-gray coat, and mist clung silvery in his hair.

"Give me a reason not to kill you," he said.

THIRTY-TWO

I stood frozen, heart stuttering, aware of nothing more than the round metal mouth pressed up into the soft underside of my jaw. I couldn't look away from Foxglove's flat stare. There was no mercy in those eyes.

"I'm sorry," I whispered. "I didn't know until last night."

The hammer clicked back. "That's not a reason."

"Fine!" Panic pushed the truth I most feared out of my mouth in a stumbling rush. "Because if I die, I might accidentally possess someone! And you're standing *right there*, and the last thing I want is for it to be you!"

He stepped away from me in clear revulsion. His pistol stayed trained at my head, rock steady.

"So it's true," he said. "You're the Demon of Disaster."

"Yes." I tore the word out of me like one of my own organs and threw it down bloody between us.

This was everything I'd been afraid of, everything that had made me hesitate to tell them. Now he hated me, to the point where he was apparently ready to *kill* me. Part of me couldn't blame him—but a thin, hot flame of anger leaped up inside me as well. I was trying so hard, and I was so tired, and I didn't want to die here and find out what new horrors that would unleash.

Foxglove stared at me, expecting more. Pain leaked through his controlled expression; it strained the corners of his mouth, lurked in the shadows of his eyes. I'd thought him invulnerable, but I'd managed to hurt him.

I'd feel worse about that if he weren't pointing a pistol at me.

"I'm the same Ryx you've always known," I said, utterly failing to keep my voice steady. "Curse it, Foxglove, I just…I'm apparently also a demon. I didn't know."

"I'm not angry at you." His voice simmered with fury. "I'm angry at myself for having faith in you."

His words stung as if he'd struck me. "I never asked you to have faith in me."

"It was a child's mistake," he said, "thinking the Graces might have sent you. I won't make it again."

Pain, anger, and the urge to apologize for my own existence fought for control of my tongue. Anger won. "You think *you're* having a crisis of faith because I'm a demon? Try *being* the demon!"

By all Nine Hells, I was sick to death of having feelings at all.

Foxglove ignored my outburst. "The question," he said, "is what we do now. You're an enemy of humankind."

"For blood's sake, do you really think that?" I stopped myself from throwing up my hands; best not to make any sudden movements. "You're my friend! Do you really think I'm an *enemy of humankind*?"

His pistol never wavered. "I don't know. I've known you for less than a month."

Right. The knot in my chest squeezed tighter. For me, nearly friendless and starved for companionship, a few weeks was enough to care for the Rookery so much that threatening them was literally the worst thing Nightmare could do. To Foxglove, apparently I was a mere acquaintance, someone he wouldn't hesitate to shoot if he had to.

Pox rot everything. Yet again, I'd placed my trust in the

wrong person. Traitors, murderers, and the Demon of Death—though at least Whisper had turned out to be a loyal friend.

Fine. If I meant nothing to him, maybe he'd respond to logic. "If shooting demons was effective, the Dark Days would have been a lot shorter."

"I made the shot in this pistol myself. Worked it with artifice runes to scatter the target's energy, steeped it in brine, anointed it with blood, and had it blessed at the shrine of the Grace of Victory. Everything the old stories say is potent against demons, plus everything I could think of as an artificer. I never imagined the demon would be you." His eyes burned into mine, their dark amber clouded. "I recognize that it probably won't work. But if there's any chance it might...by all the Graces, if I have an opportunity to banish the Demon of Disaster, isn't it my duty to try?"

The light from the palace windows shimmered on the barrel of his pistol. His hands were trembling.

He didn't want to shoot me.

The realization washed over me in sweet relief. He didn't want to do this. Of course he didn't; here he was, talking to me, when as a former assassin he knew cursed well he should have killed me by surprise.

I met his eyes, matching all the pain in them with my own surety of this one truth. "No," I said. "That isn't who you are anymore."

His temple twitched once and was still. "How would you know?"

"You killed the assassin," I said. "Remember?"

His lips peeled back from his teeth as if my words twisted a knife in him.

"Listen, Foxglove." I lifted an empty hand. "You're still recovering from what Nightmare did to you, and her miasma is all over this place, stoking your fears. You're a sleepless wreck, you're in pain, and you're making bad decisions. Frankly, you shouldn't be trusted with a dessert fork right now, let alone a pistol." A bit of sense came back to his eyes, and I pressed my advantage. "What would Lia and Teodor say if they saw you now?"

"Don't you speak their names," he said, his voice gone cold. "You're a demon."

"Yes. I'm a demon." The words were a hard and bladed truth. "I don't like it, either, but I can't change it. And neither can you, so don't destroy yourself trying."

He let out a long, uneven breath. At last, the muzzle of his pistol dropped, slow and smooth, the hammer easing back into place.

"This isn't over." He said it like a warning—not a threat, but an omen of a danger we both faced.

"I wouldn't expect it to be."

He turned from me, averting his face as if the sight of me repulsed him. The black shadows of the garden swallowed him as he walked away.

My legs waited until he was gone to begin shaking.

I stormed off through the dark grounds, vision blurred half to blindness, vaguely in the direction of the great tree. I couldn't untangle whether I was angrier at Foxglove or at myself.

He was almost right; it was his job and that of the Rookery to protect Eruvia from strange magical threats, and I unquestionably qualified. After what had happened at the ball tonight, I could no longer pretend that I was contained and harmless, if that had ever been an accurate description in the first place.

Realizing that he had a point didn't help make it any less upsetting that my friend had pointed a pistol at me and come within a finger's twitch of killing me. My hands trembled with unspent energy, and nausea roiled my stomach.

I needed a task to focus on. Being too busy to let the full impact of everything that had happened sink in had served me well thus far, and now certainly wasn't the time to stop. But all of my most pressing goals—getting the ward key, organizing the upcoming evacuation of the palace—were tied up with the Rookery, and they'd made it pretty clear they didn't want me around at the moment. I was on my own.

Or... not quite on my own. Never truly alone.

A steady, silent call pulled at me. The inexorable draw of the earth in which my roots tangled, the spring that sourced the water in my blood: Morgrain, land that birthed and nurtured me. At its heart, a wild, fierce presence, always with me—and at the moment, not far away at all.

I became suddenly aware of a predator's gaze searing into my back.

I turned, slowly, to face my grandmother.

The wild crest of her hair and the feathery edges of her mantle roughened her silhouette, and the twin burning orange rings of her mage mark stood out from the darkness.

"So they've sent you to the shadows," she said.

"No one sent me here." I paused, feeling the weight of her skeptical gaze, and swallowed the uncomfortable knot of truth. "They just sent me away."

"It's for the best." She stepped closer, a patch of moonlight falling across her face. Seasons, she looked tired. "They can't understand us, Ryx. And your place isn't with them. It's at Gloamingard."

The name stuck in my heart like a shard of mirror glass. I missed my castle so much—the Bone Palace in its macabre beauty, the lofty green reach of the tree towers, the secret bits of Gloaming Lore carved in odd corners. Even the Black Tower, rising stark and ominous at the center of it all in a clear warning we should have heeded better.

"I have to stay with my friends." The words fell to dust in my mouth. It was a lie, and I knew it.

My grandmother grunted. "They're not your friends anymore."

After seeing the horror on their faces, the hard resolve that Foxglove turned against me, I couldn't disagree. "Nonetheless."

"Forget them." She spread her arms, her mantle hanging from them like half-folded wings. "Your family will never forsake you."

I almost laughed at the idea, except it was too bitter to laugh. "You mean my parents? Uncle Tarn, and all my cousins? Let's be honest, Grandmother. They forsook me long ago. The only one who didn't was you."

She didn't move, watching me, waiting for me to catch up with her.

Oh. That wasn't the family she meant.

"I don't want anything to do with the likes of Nightmare and Hunger," I protested.

"Nightmare gave you a place at her table, without question, even knowing you would make yourself her enemy," my grandmother said quietly. "She accepts you. Hunger accepts you. We all count you as one of us, even the ones you hate, in a way your friends never will."

In a way my blood family never had, either. Without functioning magic, I'd been an afterthought at best to them, more often an embarrassment. I might not like to admit it, but my demonic family wanted me, took me in without question, when my human family didn't.

"I can't take a side against humanity." I shook my head.

"I'm not asking you to. You and I, we're our own side, just the two of us." She held her hand out to me. "Come back to Gloamingard with me. Come home."

The words shivered down deep into my bones, my blood, the very core of my being. *Home.*

My grandmother could have commanded me. Her power infused my body, sure as the waters of Morgrain had nurtured me, and its fields had fed me. I couldn't refuse anything she demanded of me, if she willed it. But she was giving me a choice.

"Someday," I breathed, releasing the word like a messenger bird to the black, cloud-covered sky. "I have to finish this first. My friends may not want me anymore, but they still need me."

My grandmother's gaze glittered with four thousand years of skepticism. "They won't thank you for your help."

"That's all right. I don't need them to." I reached out and clasped her hand just to feel its familiar strength, its hard unyielding warmth. "Are you leaving tonight? Now?"

"Yes." She flashed a sharp grin. "I've just learned my fellow Witch Lords have called a Conclave. I wouldn't miss it for the world."

So they'd decided to do it despite Ardith's reservations. I suppressed a shudder at the idea of the Demon of Discord loose in a Conclave of Witch Lords. "Dare I ask what you plan to do there?"

"Oh, I'll improvise." Her expression sobered. "Most of all, of course, I'll protect Morgrain. You're sure you don't want to come with me? You could be my guest. Together, we could make even the Eldest tremble."

"No thank you." I wanted to urge her not to do anything too rash, too destructive; but even before she merged with Discord, my grandmother hadn't let anyone tell her what to do.

"Until we meet again, then." She squeezed my hand and let it go. The world seemed colder and lonelier with emptiness between us.

"Take care of Gloamingard for me."

"You know I will." She gave me a nod that bordered on a mocking bow. Then, in a swirl of feathers, she disappeared into the shadows.

I stood there for a long time, staring after her, as if she'd taken the best part of me with her and only the broken discards remained.

At last, I shook myself as if I were coming awake. The urgency of the situation hadn't gotten any less; I couldn't afford to stand here wrestling with my feelings in the dark like a fool. And there was one person in the palace who might still be willing to work with me.

My fellow atheling, who knew all too well what it was to be kin to monsters, and maybe a monster yourself. *Severin.*

I went to look for him, telling myself it was only to coordinate plans with him, and not to press his cool disdain for feelings like a balm to the raw wounds in my heart.

He wasn't in the entry hall where I'd seen him last. Either he was still out trailing the Zenith Society, or he'd gone back to the imperial wing; I couldn't bear the thought of facing the Rookery, so I'd have to bank on his dedication to his grievance and hope for the former.

I searched for him through the Jewel Rooms that formed the spine of the palace on the royal side, then the deserted public galleries that did the same on the Curia side, chased by the inescapable lingering scent of smoke. The lights were dimmed for the night, plunging the palace into shadow; everyone had gone to bed, exhausted from the horrifying ball and fighting the subsequent fire. I spotted only a few palace staff hurrying with the alacrity of open fear, and once a scrawny little mouse that scurried away at the sight of me across the polished marble floor. It vanished behind a statue of the Grace of Beauty in an artist's smock, her brush uplifted like a sword.

A mouse. It could be Severin's. Heart quickening, I followed in the direction it had scampered.

A line of glowing runes flared into life on the floor in front of me.

What in the Nine Hells?

Someone had laid a rune-marked rope bound with artifice wire across the wide gilded doorway I'd been about to pass through, blocking it. For a second I just stared, unable to comprehend how it had gotten there.

Then it hit me. This was a trap.

I whirled to face the long statue-lined gallery just as half a dozen people poured from a hidden servant's door to block my retreat. The Zenith Society, with Moreni at their head and Cortissa smirking in the rear, fanning out in a menacing arc. Sweet Hell of Death, this was bad.

"You're making this almost embarrassingly easy for me," Moreni said.

There was no mistaking the smooth, hostile coordination of their advance, closing in like a pack of wolves. I recognized it on an animal level, in my spine and my skin, in the electric fear that flooded my limbs with the raw energy of panic. I drew my sword, all my nerves lighting up like luminaries at sunset, and leveled the tip at Moreni's chest from across the room.

"I'll make the next part twice as hard, to compensate."

The words sounded unexpectedly confident coming out of my mouth, but it was pure bravado. I was no Ashe; I might not have the skill to beat one of them, let alone all six. Not to mention that they glittered with artifice devices, a couple of them wore pistols, and they had a Skinwitch. If they wanted to kill me, I was as good as dead.

Except that I wasn't. The thought that I might wind up looking out of Cortissa's or Moreni's eyes was enough to set my heart pounding with horror. I'd rather die in my own skin than live in theirs.

Moreni spread his hands, artifice rings sparkling on his fingers. "Oh, you're welcome to try."

Ashe's voice came to me from my training sessions with her at Castle Ilseine: *If you're outnumbered, keep moving.* I sidestepped and backed away, opening as much distance as I could, sword tip pointing at each of them in turn.

"I don't suppose you'd like to have a civilized discussion instead of resorting to violence?" I ventured.

Moreni sighed theatrically. "Normally I'd love to. But we're here on behalf of another, and they had rather specific requests."

His words set a crawling up my back. My reaction must have showed, because Cortissa's face spread into a wide grin.

"Incapacitated but alive," she sang out to her group. "And remember, with me here, *alive* is a very loose term."

Three of them drew swords, and a fourth a knife and pistol. *Pox, pox, pox.*

"This'll be quick, then," grunted the swordsman in the middle, and lunged.

I'd been practicing with Ashe, and he was a lot slower than she was. I jumped back, sucking my belly barely out of the way, and landed a light cut on his exposed sword arm. He fumbled his blade, swearing in pain.

I had no time to feel more than a brief surge of hot-blooded satisfaction. The others were closing on me, and I didn't have much more room to retreat before I hit the corner. I parried a thrust at my chest; the third blade got fouled in my layers of court skirts as its wielder cut at my legs. I flinched each time as if they'd hit, the shock jarring through me. This was too real, too full of ugly and violent intent, nothing like practice.

I was only buying time, and we all knew it. A few more seconds keeping my blood in my veins where it belonged, no more.

I parried again and again, aggressively as I could to keep them off me; their swords tore the lace dangling at my cuff and scraped my corset boning along one side. The pistol leveled at me snapped in a misfire, to more swearing.

A few more heartbeats bought, and already my arm was tiring. Now I'd let them back me into the corner, and it might prevent them from flanking me, but it kept me from opening distance, too. They had me, and they knew it; their half circle tightened, eyes calculating and hard, swords sharp and ready. Panic took over completely, and I flung up a hand.

"Wait! I'll come with you, don't—"

One of the swordswomen lunged forward, instinctively seizing the opening she'd been waiting for.

I was too slow to react. Pain erupted through my lower chest, and I couldn't breathe—only stare, in shock and agony, at the narrow blade she'd run between my ribs.

No. No, this couldn't be real. The world slipped far away, as if this were happening to someone else, everything remote and meaningless. There was only the sword stuck in my body—and then the terrible feeling of it scraping back out, streaked with blood.

My senses jumbled into a giddy, swooning mess of pain. Suddenly I was lying on the hard marble floor, struggling to breathe as I scrabbled weakly at the stone.

"I *did* say alive," Cortissa complained, somewhere in the distance.

The dizzy spark of my consciousness relaxed, its grip loosening, recoiling instinctively from the pain. My senses started to fade, my body to go numb. The fight was over; there was nothing left but to let go into blissful oblivion.

Blood and ashes. This wasn't consciousness I was slipping away from.

I was deserting my own body, instinctively abandoning my broken vessel.

Terror slammed me back into my dying shell: the struggle to breathe, the warm wetness spreading across my corset, the agony of coughing as I tried to clear blood from my throat. *No.* I couldn't let go, couldn't slip loose—this was *my* body, curse it, no matter how much of a wreck it was.

Someone roughly seized my hair, jerking my head up off the floor.

"Not so fast," Cortissa said. The horrible touch of her power crawled across my scalp, digging prickling claws into my flesh and bone.

Her voice winked out, snuffed along with my vision like a candle flame, and there was nothing.

THIRTY-THREE

THIRTY-THREE

Intense pain half woke me, and the awful squirming feeling of someone else's magic rearranging my insides with no trace of gentleness, but I couldn't move.

Pure terror lanced through my nerves—*No, not the Skinwitch, don't let her touch me*—and my power started to flare up in response. But that frightened me even more, and I crushed it down even as I struggled to cry out with a throat that wouldn't obey me.

"You're sure I can't play around while I'm at it?" Cortissa's voice sounded far too close. The cold, hard hand pressed to my ribs must be hers, and the power that knotted me back together with rough, uncaring speed. "Give me a few hours and some parts and I could make her a chimera."

Panic burned white-hot in my mind, but Cortissa's magic kept me from regaining full consciousness. I was trapped on the cusp between sleep and waking, unable to push through.

"No," Moreni said, regret in his voice, "there's no time, and we can't risk angering the lady."

"Alive and incapacitated, she said," Cortissa pressed. "There's nearly infinite leeway in that."

"Stop fooling around and finish," Moreni snapped. "They'll be here any minute."

"Fine," she sighed. "It's good enough. She's not going to die."

That was the only piece of good news I expected to get tonight. Pain still jabbed through my chest with each breath, and my whole body was horribly weak—but it had become a *this really hurts* terrible rather than a *struggling to survive* terrible.

The rest of my senses slowly faded in around the edges. My bodice felt stiff with blood. They'd laid me on something hard—a table?—and one arm dangled limply off, hanging in the air. The scent of roses nearly choked me.

I became horribly, insidiously aware that I had options.

I'd almost abandoned my body once; I knew instinctively that I could do it again. It would be so simple to drift away from this broken shell, letting go and deserting it entirely. Or I could kill them all, if I didn't mind taking the whole palace with them. I didn't have to stay here, trapped and hurting, at their mercy.

Only if I wanted to remain human.

It was far harder to accept the limits of humanity knowing they didn't need to apply to me. But once I cast them off, I could never go back.

The air grew heavy with power. Someone drew in a soft gasp.

"Here they come," Cortissa whispered.

Uh-oh. I struggled to wake up enough to move, but the moment I managed to twitch a hand, Cortissa's power flared and pushed a semiconscious fog down on me like a smothering blanket.

A door opened. Silk skirts rustled, trains dragging along the ground; there came a scuffle of movement, everyone rearranging themselves hastily. "Your Majesty," Moreni murmured, with a thickness that suggested he did so from a deep bow.

"Oh." It was Madness's breathy voice, catching with distress. "She's hurt."

An uneasy rustle. "You didn't tell us not to hurt her, Your Majesty," Cortissa said defensively. "At any rate, I've healed her, mostly."

A faint glimmer of wild hope sparked through the thick haze swaddling my mind. If it was only Madness, I could maybe talk my way out of this.

"We need her awake." That was Nightmare, sounding displeased. *Pox.*

"Awake, certainly, my lady. But…still incapacitated?" All Cortissa's cruel confidence vanished, and she took on a sickening fawning tone.

"I want to talk to her." Madness's already quiet voice went soft with sorrow. "She won't understand, but I should at least explain."

"As you command, Your Majesty." Cortissa's cold hand brushed my forehead, with a tingle of releasing magic; I suddenly found I could flinch from her touch.

I snapped my eyes open, desperate to see just how bad things were. I lay on the same table in the Rose Room that we'd gathered around for tea; the busy ceiling swarmed in a decadent splendor of golden roses in the dim, cold light of an insufficient number of luminaries. Nightmare and Madness stood by my feet; the Zenith Society clumped near my head, clearly less than fully at ease in the company of the demons whose favor they'd curried. The demons' presence held an electric edge of anticipation.

Oh, this was bad, all right.

Everything had a distant quality, like a dream, except that I was all too dreadfully aware it could still hurt me. My head felt light and fuzzy, whether from blood loss or Cortissa's magic, and pain scattered my focus; this was a terrible time not to have my full wits about me.

"You could have just invited me," I rasped. It came out as a rough whisper.

"You wouldn't have come," Nightmare said, strolling closer. The Zenith Society recoiled from her like water before spreading oil, even Moreni. "Or if you'd come, you wouldn't have let us do this to you. No, after what you did tonight, we needed you safely neutralized."

Do this to . . . Whatever that meant, the answer was no. I tried to surge upright; pain flared through my chest, and swarming sparks narrowed my vision to a tiny circle, a great rushing filling my ears. As I collapsed back onto the table, I barely heard a blurry murmur of voices—Madness telling the Zenith Society they could go.

I had to get up, had to get out of here, had to talk my way out of this or just make a break for it and run. I needed to—

Nightmare's cruel, strong fingers closed on my jaw, forcing my mouth open.

Before I realized what was happening, a heavy drop with a faint metallic taste rolled down my tongue.

Graces help me. They'd given me quicksilver.

I tried to spit it out, struggling in panic, but Nightmare held my jaw closed. She leaned down to smile into my face, her eyes alight.

"Keep suffering," she whispered. "I'm drinking up every moment."

Madness drifted closer, her wide eyes brimming with unshed tears. "I didn't want them to hurt you," she said. "All I want is to help you."

I clawed at Nightmare's hands, dragging them from my face. "Then let me go," I gasped.

"I will," Madness promised. "My beloved sister, I will. As soon as I've fixed your memory."

"*No.*" Lightning-hot fear overrode even the pain as I strove to rise. "No, I don't want—"

She caught my hand in both of hers as I tried to push her away. A gentle smile spread across her face. "I can't wait to have you back at last."

Everything fell apart into colorful pieces, like a stained glass window shattering into sand.

I was back in my grandmother's arms, in that moment of joining in the Black Tower almost twenty years ago. Red light flooded my senses, and I was afraid, so afraid, at what was happening to me——

Then nothing. Comforting black silence, a welcoming oblivion like the moment when thoughts unwind at the cusp of sleep.

"It's so clean," Madness's voice whispered in the darkness. "The severing. Now I understand why you don't remember me."

"Leave it," I begged. I'd lost track of my body, which was arguably a mercy at this point; I had no mouth with which to speak in this place, but I made the words somehow anyway, out of pure desperation. "I like who I am now. I don't want those memories."

"Shh, shh, it's all right," Madness crooned. One by one, sparks of golden light began appearing in the darkness. "I can fix it. It won't be easy, but I can do it."

Nightmare's chuckle came echoing from a great distance, somewhere far beyond Madness, beyond the growing golden lights, in another world. "Oh, I can't wait for you to remember everything you did. It'll be *delicious*."

The tiny golden stars began stretching into spiderweb-thin filaments, floating aimlessly in the darkness. Madness's power brushed against my mind like the wings of a massive dove, soft and smothering, and the ends of those threads began straining toward each other, seeking to weave together.

Terror coursed white-hot and jagged through my mind. I had to stop her, somehow. I had no illusions that I could handle the sudden return of thousands of years of demonic memory without losing myself in profound, irreversible ways. My power strained to break free, to lash out in instinctive defense—but earthquakes and storms wouldn't help me now, and that was apparently all I was good for.

Storms. A gray sea, churning with hoary and terrible waves, whipped by a screaming wind. Lightning splitting the sky again and again and again, while I laughed with childish wonder.

A seawall breaking, the ocean rushing over and through, inexorable and unanswerable, final as death. *No. No, I don't want to—*

"I'm starting to make a connection," Madness announced happily. "Not much longer, Disaster, just be patient."

"Stop," I cried out into the darkness. "This isn't—

"*Safe,*" I finished, holding up a hand and scrambling backward across the grassy hilltop, alarmed. My hand was browner than I expected, with longer and more elegant fingers. The bright-eyed girl coming up the path paused, tilting her head, a basket swinging from her hand.

"Of course it isn't safe." She laughed. "Where would the fun be in that?"

Then that fragment, too, was gone, whisked away, a glittering piece of memory falling in shards like the broken mirrors in the maze. The girl was important—something about her twisted at my heart—but I didn't know her name.

Light blazed around me. Endless light, endless power; and I was a part of it, an eddy in it, a great roiling disturbance without clear boundaries. I was power itself, immortal, unknowable—and so bored, so very bored and alone, missing my friends with a deep and abiding grief that never faded in this place where healing couldn't happen because time and space were negotiable at best.

My friends. I had to break free, to get back to the Rookery, before Madness destroyed me. They needed me; I still hadn't gotten the key—

"Can't you go faster?" Nightmare demanded. "She'll purge the effects of the mercury soon."

"I've woven a channel." Madness's voice was faint and strained with effort. "Now I need to bring the memories across."

"I'd better give her more quicksilver."

Oh, Hells, no. Not if I could stop her.

More glittering, colorful shards of memory reached for me—Whisper, swishing his tail, holding up a paw to inspect it, murmuring *This will do*—but I seized on something else: pain. The distant shadow of it beckoned, my only lifeline to the waking world.

I threw myself into it, like diving into a black pool knowing it was too shallow and I'd smash myself on the rocks at the bottom.

THIRTY-FOUR

I hit. And it hurt.

I sucked in a raw, gasping breath, opening my eyes just in time to see Nightmare leaning over me with a bead of quicksilver dangling on the end of a glass rod. I knocked it aside with a frantic swipe of my hand, sending the rod flying to shatter against the wall.

"Hush, hush," Madness murmured, stroking my clammy forehead. "Be still. Just a little longer and you'll be well again."

A knock sounded at the door.

"Your Majesty," called Bramant's muffled voice from the far side. "There's someone here to see you."

"Tell them to go away," Nightmare snapped, at the same time that Madness asked, "Who is it?"

For one brief, soaring moment, I expected him to announce the Rookery. This was some clever rescue, and I would be saved.

But the voice said, "Hunger, Your Majesty. He seems agitated."

Bloody pox. Somehow, this kept getting even worse. I lay still, pretending to lapse back into unconsciousness, and watched through my eyelashes as Madness and Nightmare exchanged a long glance over me. Madness kept stroking my head the whole time; I gritted my teeth and bore it.

"Should we tell him to go away?" Madness asked.

Nightmare let out an exasperated sigh. "Ugh, no, he'll be even more offended and won't want to reconcile with us at all. We have to talk to him. Can you pause here without undoing your work?"

Madness nodded solemnly. "I think so."

Nightmare jabbed me with a sharp finger. "Is she out again? Can we leave her alone? I suppose she doesn't look as if she could go far regardless, and she never could fix her vessels once they were broken."

"That human did say she incapacitated her," Madness recalled dreamily. I tried to stay convincingly still.

"Fine," Nightmare sighed. "Let's talk to him and get this over with."

Madness gave me a fond pat, leaning close to whisper, "We'll be back soon."

Nightmare offered me a suspicious glare; I hoped she couldn't see my eyes gleaming through my lashes.

A rustling of silk, the opening and closing of a door, and they were gone. Silence fell, and I was alone with a dubiously healed chest wound and the sickly sweet smell of decaying roses.

Shock scattered and fogged my thoughts, but I gathered them together as best I could; I didn't have much time. First, to assess the damage.

Every breath sent a sharp pain through my chest, but that didn't seem to be getting any worse, at least. I could ignore it and push through. Ginger exploration of my bloodstained bodice and the ragged gash in it found a raw, tender scar beneath. Definitely healed, but I had no idea whether it was healed enough that I didn't have to worry about it reopening if I overdid things.

I couldn't help but think of the times my grandmother had had to undo terrible damage done to livestock by unskilled or sloppy vivomancers trying to heal them. Graces only knew what Cortissa had done with her haphazard efforts. I fought back a wave of panic, closing my eyes and forcing my ragged breaths to slow to something reasonable.

I couldn't worry about that now. I had a simple job: get off this table. Without using my abdominal muscles more than I had to.

After thinking it through a moment, I gathered my courage and tried rolling onto my good side and allowing my legs to drop off the edge of the table to take my weight.

They buckled under me in a dizzy surge, and I tumbled hard to the floor.

I lay there gasping, my vision narrowing again, too stunned even to regret my choices. *Please don't let them have heard and come to investigate.* Muffled voices rose in another room—Hunger and Nightmare, arguing, it sounded like—but they didn't pause or change in response to my floundering around.

All right. Standing was too much; I'd try crawling.

The distance to the door stretched out through a haze of pain and acres of dragging ragged skirts. Luckily, by the sound of it Hunger was only getting started; Aurelio's voice kept ramping louder and higher. I wasn't even worried about them hearing me when I nudged open the door and half fell through into an empty waiting room.

It wasn't the great antechamber at the entrance to the royal wing, but a smaller one where people would wait in comfort for their private audiences with the queen. No one had lit the oil lamps set strategically about the room, and only the colder light of a few luminaries in wall niches threw long shadows in conflicting directions. Other doors led to various rooms for differently themed private meetings; one stood ajar, and I glimpsed a rather staged-looking study. Through another, closed door, the demons' argument sounded clearer now.

"You said we'd do this together." That was Aurelio's voice, with the piercing edge Hunger gave it. "Then not only do you ignore *my* plans, but you use *my* humans without permission!"

Nightmare muttered something in response that I couldn't make out.

"Disaster again! You're both *obsessed*." Hunger's voice rose, louder and louder with indignation. "If you hadn't set her off at that ball, we'd have silvered everyone in the palace by now. Never mind her! She's tainted anyway. She's not really one of us anymore."

"Oh, she is." Nightmare let out a rich chuckle. "The humanity is surface paint. Scratch it, and you'll find a demon."

I froze mid-crawl, a shudder passing through me. She could be right; how would I know?

"Evil?" The bright-eyed young woman laughed. The sound sent a shiver of pleasure through my heart. "You're not evil. I don't believe in evil, anyway."

The flicker of memory fluttered across the back of my mind and was gone. I flinched, letting out a small involuntary sound. I didn't know that woman—not in this life. But she was the same one I'd seen on a hilltop, basket swinging from her hand, one room away and four thousand years ago.

A fresh memory, leaking through. *Sweet Graces, no.*

I couldn't think about that now. I had to focus on getting out of here. I kept crawling across the room, breath coming hard, telling myself I was just staying low in case someone opened the door.

The Hall of Portraits came next, an infinite stretch of crimson struggle, the monarchs of Loreice staring down at me in contempt the whole way. My body sent me a thousand unpleasant signals that all came down to *We can't do this.* I kept forcing it onward anyway, driven by the terrifying certainty that if I wasn't gone by the time the demons were done talking, Madness would finish what she'd started, and the person I was now would cease to exist.

There were so many things, it turned out, that I was more afraid of than death.

At last I dragged myself through into the dim, echoing emptiness of the antechamber, abandoned as a broken tomb.

Or not quite abandoned. Bramant rose stiffly to his feet from a chair by the main doors, then blinked at me with silver eyes, clearly uncertain what to do.

"The queen has asked not to be disturbed," he said tentatively, as if trying out one of a few rote phrases that might activate an artifice device.

Much as I hated to do so, I'd have to hope the slack haziness of his features meant that Nightmare and Madness hadn't left him with much capacity for independent thought.

"That's all right," I said, making my tones as genteel and haughty as I could manage while crawling on the floor in a blood-soaked ballgown. "My audience is over. I'm just leaving."

"Of course, my lady." He bowed, all graciousness, and held the door open for me.

I dragged myself through it and collapsed in the cool white twilight of the Diamond Room beyond. The cold marble felt good against my cheek; my shoulders heaved as I drew in breath after painful breath, fighting off waves of dizzy weakness. The gilded door thunked politely shut behind me.

Someone made an inarticulate noise.

Pox. I lifted my head, ready to calmly explain myself to silver-eyed guards.

Severin stood there, resplendent in the elegant black-and-gold vestcoat he'd worn to the ball, eyes widening with shock.

His boots made far too much noise on the marble as he hurried to drop to his knees at my side. I wasn't sure I'd ever been so glad to see someone in my life.

"Ryx! Blood of the Eldest, are you—"

"Shh." I grabbed his hands as they reached for my wound. "It's not as bad as it looks. Cortissa did a hack job of healing me."

"I didn't know you were hurt. My animal spies—let's just say there are limits to the nuances of their reports. Curse it, I was too cautious *again*." He punched the hard marble floor, then shook out his hand.

"I wasn't cautious enough, so we're even. Were you the one who got Hunger riled up?"

He grimaced. "Yes. I ran into him before the Rookery, so he was what I had to work with. In retrospect, *make another demon angry and send him in as a distraction* is a dubious plan, but it's late and I was improvising."

"No, it was marvelous." *He* was marvelous. A loopy surge of affection that probably had as much to do with blood loss as anything washed through me. "I couldn't have rescued myself if you hadn't sent Hunger."

His mouth twitched toward something that probably wasn't a smile. "Some rescue. You're lying on the floor covered in blood."

"It's in progress." I closed my eyes a moment, gathering my strength. "Help me up."

"You can't possibly stand," he objected.

"I can if I have to."

"Mm-hmm. That's why you were crawling."

My face heated. "I was resting."

"Fine," he sighed. "We don't have time to argue about this."

I expected him to pull me up by my hand, but he slid his arms under me. With a stifled grunt, he staggered to his feet, heaving me up with him.

I grabbed on to his neck for support, sending a fresh stab of pain between my ribs. I wished I were in a situation to appreciate the warmth and closeness of being cradled against his chest, but I was too exhausted, too hurt. Too overwhelmed with fear that Madness and Nightmare would come through that door and take me back to finish erasing the tenuous barrier that made me myself—Ryxander of Morgrain, arguably human—and not simply the Demon of Disaster.

"I can walk," I hissed. "Put me down."

"I'm about to. Did you think I was going to carry you out of here like some over-muscled hero in a woodcut?" He let my legs down gently; my shoes touched the floor, and I eased my weight onto them.

"See? I told you I can—" The world seemed to tilt and float to one side. I grabbed Severin, leaning heavily on him, breath coming in short, painful gasps. "Hells take it."

"You can what?" he asked ironically, wrapping an arm around me. "Here, lean on me. I'd carry you all the way back to the Rookery quarters if I could, but frankly, my arms would fall off."

"We can't go back to the Rookery," I blurted.

He stared at me, confused. "Why not?"

"I..." He must not have talked to them yet. "*You* can go back. But I'm not sure I'm welcome there."

Recognition flickered in his eyes. I didn't have to say it: *They know.*

He shook his head as we limped into motion. "What in the Nine Hells happened at that ball after I left?" he demanded. "I've only been off stalking the Zenith Society for a couple of hours and I smelled smoke, heard screaming, thought I felt the whole palace shake—and then I find you half dead in the queen's chambers, and you say you're not welcome with the Rookery?"

"It was a terrible party," I said wearily.

He let out a long breath. "All right. I know where there's an empty guest room for Vaskandran envoys; I can take you there. And then we're going to make sure you're really healed and not actually dying, and also you'll explain everything to me properly rather than making evasive quips."

I nodded. I didn't have the energy to argue, any more than I did to explain.

It was a long, foggy, difficult struggle to the guest room on the second floor, where I collapsed on top of covers prickly with gold embroidery, barely aware of my surroundings. My pride was gone; Severin had all but dragged me here. Worst of all, flickers of disturbingly familiar images populated the haze shrouding my brain, there and gone in an instant: the scent of a flower I couldn't identify, sweet and grassy; a great city clustered with white towers in a squat round style I'd never seen before, lying far below me on a sun-splashed coast; a woman humming a slow song in the sultry summer heat. Each one came with a burden of emotion I didn't understand, and didn't want to.

"Ryx." It was Severin, his cool hand lying along the side of my face. "I'm going to get a physician."

I reached for him urgently, to keep him from leaving.

"Don't go," I croaked.

"But you need—"

"I can't be alone right now." I needed someone to remind me who I was, to anchor me to myself. My pulse hummed with the fear of falling into uneasy dreams and waking up someone else. "Please stay."

My fingers found the sharp angle of his cheekbone. He closed his eyes.

"All right." He laid his hand over mine for a moment, clasping it to his cheek, before gently removing it. "I hate to say this, because I have no idea what I'm doing and I'm frankly terrified, but we should at least take a look at your wound."

I covered the bloody hole in my bodice in panic, my cheeks burning. "It's scarred over. I already checked. Cortissa healed me; I just need some blood-restoring potions and a bit of rest to finish the job." Not that it felt as if I had any lack of blood right now, with it all on fire at the thought of stripping down in front of Severin.

"Forgive me if I'm reluctant to place my trust in a Skinwitch." He hesitated, biting his lip and staring at my bloodstained corset; finally he looked away. "Maybe a physician after all, then. Or Bastian, if you'll let me bring him here."

"He might be willing, if any of them is," I agreed reluctantly.

Severin's eyes narrowed. "That's right. You were going to tell me what happened."

"I was?"

"You were," he insisted firmly.

Hells. I wasn't ready to think about what I'd done in the ballroom yet. Much as I'd disliked getting run through, that was far easier to talk about than hurting dozens of innocent people.

I licked my dry lips. "Madness and Nightmare were trying to bring back my memories of being a demon."

He grimaced. "And, ah...I take it they didn't succeed?"

I hesitated, then shook my head. A handful of random images didn't mean anything. They could be nightmare hallucinations; they could be my imagination; and even if they *were* demonic memories, a few incomprehensible snippets without context didn't change anything.

"No," I said, with more confidence. "They didn't."

Severin sank down on the edge of the bed with a sigh. "You seem to have an impressive talent for getting yourself into trouble."

I started to laugh, then thought better of it as pain stabbed through my chest. "Severin. I'm literally the Demon of Disaster."

He put a hand to his face. "That explains an alarming number of things, now that I think about it."

"Unfortunately," I agreed, with a sinking pang.

"Like why you seem to inexplicably enjoy spending time around me." He took my hand, gently, and brushed his thumb along the back of it.

"Oh, you're not that bad," I objected. "I wouldn't call you a *disaster*."

He raised an eyebrow. "Truly?"

"Well..."

"I see I'll have to work harder."

"You do sometimes make poor life choices," I admitted, my voice going husky as my throat seemed to thicken. "Like not distancing yourself from this fool of a woman when you found out she was a demon."

He leaned on one elbow on the bed next to me, his eyes so close to mine it felt as if an invisible link humming with magical power connected us, mage mark to mage mark. "As it turns out," he said, "on average, demons seem to be genuinely more pleasant than my immediate family members."

"That's not a very high standard."

"Granted." The self-mocking smile slid off his face. "Besides, you haven't given up on me, even though I keep showing you how little I'm worth."

I almost made some joke about a demon's worth being so low I was cheaply bought, but the self-loathing tightening his face stopped me. Hells, he meant it.

"You're plenty worthy," I told him.

He shook his head fiercely. "Twice now I've bided my time too long and let you get hurt. When you fell through that door covered in blood, for a second I thought you were——" He broke off suddenly, his eyes flicking down. "I thought it was another one of Nightmare's visions."

The idea that me being hurt could be one of his nightmares—now, when he knew what I was—defied comprehension. That he could be lying here on the other side of the bed talking to me without any apparent fear made no sense at all.

"I don't…" My voice dried up into a whisper. "I don't understand why you still care about me."

For a moment, he was silent. Emotions flitted across his face, as if he were trying them on: pain, something soft and melting at the edges, and finally a semblance of his usual irony. "I never did have much sense of self-preservation."

He brushed a loose strand of hair back from my face, hesitated for half a heartbeat, then leaned in and kissed me.

It was too tender, too vulnerable, too full of gentle care. I couldn't take it, not now, when I was overflowing with desperate fear. I kissed him back with urgent passion, seizing his face in my hands.

His elbow slid out from under him and he half fell to the pillow; his lips stretched under mine in a laugh. I kept kissing him, striving to drive out the lurking shadows of ancient memories, the buried loathing I held for what I was, everything terrible that had happened since we came here. I needed this one pure, fiery moment, so I could pretend for a fleeting instant that the two of us broken souls fitted together might become inexplicably whole.

His hand trailed from my cheek down my neck, his end of the kiss becoming more fervent. I realized I couldn't breathe, and I had to pull away, gasping, my chest lighting up with pain.

"Sorry," he said immediately, sitting bolt upright. "I should have remembered. I—"

"No, no." I waved a shaky hand at him. "That was perfect."

His brows went up. "Perfect may be an exaggeration."

Seasons witness, he was beautiful. The arch of his brows, the sharp line of his cheek, the storm-ringed dark intensity of his eyes. More than anything, I wanted to catch my breath, reach out to him, and try again.

But even setting aside the small difficulty that I doubted I could sit up on my own, there was another problem as well. One that made my chest ache worse than my wound did.

"Severin," I told him, the words heavy as lead on my tongue, "we can't... We shouldn't do this."

"Certainly not while you're wounded," he agreed hastily. "I'm not that much of a scoundrel."

"No, I mean..." I swallowed. "I'm bad for you."

"Lethally dangerous," he agreed, running a fingertip along my jawline. "I might as well drink poison."

"You're not taking this seriously," I accused, frustrated. "I'm one of the Nine Demons. You can't just—"

"Kiss you?" He grinned. "I think I did."

"Curse it, Severin! There's absolutely no way this can end well, and you know it."

"I'm an adult. I think we've already established that I'm fully capable of making my own terrible decisions."

The pressure in the air seemed to shift all of a sudden. A faint scent teased my senses, somewhere in the space between smoke and ozone. A shadow fell across us both.

Behind Severin, a graceful bit of darkness flowed up into a window, flat black against the moonlit glass. Whisper arched his back, stretched, and turned his yellow eyes on me.

"This is all very sweet, but it's time to run along, human." He didn't so much as glance at Severin. "Ryx and I have things to discuss."

"You could have been more polite," I told Whisper as he leaped down onto my bed, fluid as a silk scarf sliding to the floor.

"I could have," Whisper agreed. "Yet I was not."

Something about the intensity of his narrow yellow gaze made my muscles tighten as if I braced for another blow. "This is about what Madness did to me, isn't it?"

He slinked straight up to me and stared directly into my eyes. His whiskers nearly tickled my face. It would have been funny if I weren't dreading what he'd say next.

He let out a soft hiss; I couldn't keep myself from flinching. His bushy tail swished as he paced away across the bedspread.

"This is unfortunate," he said.

A chill settled like morning dew across my entire body. "That bad, huh?"

"If you hadn't released me from my promise, I could have intervened and stopped her, rather than having to stay out of it and let her undo some of my work." Whisper began aggressively grooming his shoulder.

"Yes, well, if I hadn't released you from your promise, I'd be an amnesiac in Callamorne by now." I passed a hand across my eyes. "How bad is it?"

"It could be worse," he admitted grudgingly. "She only managed to establish the thinnest of connections to your sealed memories."

"Could you sever it again?"

He seemed to turn the idea over for a moment, watching the pattern of moonlight on the wall. At last, he sighed. "Human minds are fragile, and yours is at least partly human. I'm surprised you've held up so well through what Madness and Nightmare have done to you. My own touch may be precise, but it isn't gentle; the whole thing might unravel."

The whole thing. "You mean my mind."

"The human aspects of it, yes."

"All right, maybe we shouldn't do that." I swallowed. "So what will happen now?"

His tail lashed back and forth. "That depends," he said, "on what you remember."

"There are things…" I trailed off, my throat closing on the words, but I cleared it and tried again. "There are things I don't want to remember." I could feel the memories there now, as if I'd spent a century swallowing rocks and nails and now it all sat in a great awful mass deep within me.

"I would imagine not," Whisper agreed softly.

"I must have hurt a lot of people." My voice thinned to a bare rasp.

Whisper crossed the bed to press his forehead to mine, briefly, soft and warm and strangely reassuring. "Not deliberately," he said, "for what it's worth."

"I don't know what it's worth." I let out a long breath, ignoring the stab from my wound. "Do I have an obligation to remember the people I killed, and the harm I did? Can I make amends if I don't remember?"

"Those people have been dead for thousands of years." Whisper tilted his head. "Who would you make amends to, precisely?"

I gestured vaguely around. "The world."

"That," he said, "is a dangerous notion."

"Wanting to help the world because I hurt it?" I asked, disbelievingly. "How could that be dangerous?"

For a long moment, he was silent. At last he looked away. "You've attempted to help protect the people of this world before. It . . . ended poorly."

A sickening gulf opened in my stomach. I was sure that beyond all else, this was one thing I didn't want to remember.

"Oh," I said in a small voice.

"We can't war with each other, Ryx. Not for any reason." He sounded weary. "We're too powerful. When we use a sliver of our potential to tamper with mortals, it's bad enough. When we turn our full force against each other, it's too much for this world to withstand."

I had no desire to repeat the mistake I'd made in the ballroom tonight; I doubted very much I'd be so lucky as to avoid killing anyone if I let my power slip again. And if I loosed it on purpose, pushing it as far as it could go against an opposing demon, letting it escalate and escalate—I shuddered.

"I've learned my lesson," I said. "I have no intention of ever unleashing my demonic power again." If the Rookery needed me to unravel magic, they could release my jess and I could use it through the more controlled outlet of those human attachment points Whisper had talked about. It was strange to think of my killing touch as *safer*, but the other way—well, I didn't want to ever find out how far beyond arm's length people would have to run to be safe from me.

"Do you truly possess that kind of restraint?" Whisper asked, skeptical.

"I won't risk killing innocent bystanders again." That much I was sure of.

"Then you'd better be willing to watch your friends die," he said, with ruthless pragmatism. "Horribly and in pain."

I stared at him. *What in the Nine Hells is wrong with you*, I wanted to say. Except he was absolutely right; I'd proved it just this evening, when I unwittingly risked the lives of everyone in the palace to stop my friends from being forced to kill each other.

"Can you truly do that?" Whisper pressed.

"I don't know."

I wished I believed I'd have the luxury of never finding out.

THIRTY-FIVE

I thought for certain I'd lie awake for hours, staring at the ceiling, like I had the night before. I dreaded sleep—it would be too easy for memory to seep in through my dreams. But my body was too exhausted; I barely had time to register that Whisper was gone before my eyes drifted shut and my mind slipped off a cliff into darkness.

I woke to the sure feeling that someone was watching me.

Night still swathed the room in darkness, but Ashe had thoughtfully positioned herself in a moonbeam. She leaned against the wall, eyes bright and arms folded, staring at me. So still she might have been standing there forever, but with a kind of relaxed poise that suggested she could explode into motion in an eyeblink, like a bird taking flight.

Her fingertips rested casually on Answer's hilt. I couldn't make out the color of the gems in the monochrome light, but I didn't think they were green.

"Hey," she greeted me. "I'm going to need you to answer some questions."

I was suddenly very, very awake. I eased myself higher on my pillows, levering with my arms to avoid using my abdominal muscles, moving with slow care so I wouldn't set off the barely restrained violence implicit in every line of Ashe's body.

"That's fair," I said.

"Who are you?"

It should have been an easy question, but it stabbed me in the gut. I had to swallow before I could reply. "Who I always was."

Ashe scowled. "Ugh, I've got no patience for games *or* philosophy. Give me a real answer."

"I'm Ryx. Atheling of Morgrain, Warden of Gloomingard." *Your friend*, I wanted to add, but I didn't dare in case she contradicted me. "I've just recently learned that apparently I'm also . . ." The words tangled on my tongue, and I forced a laugh. "It's hard to say. It feels so melodramatic."

"These are dramatic times." She slid Answer slowly from its sheath, the gleaming blade catching the moonlight, and shifted her stance, stepping away from the wall and turning sideways. "Prove to me you didn't possess Ryx, and you're not just wearing her body now and pretending you were there all along. Prove you're still her."

Hells, that was a good point. I hadn't even thought of that. "Wait, let me think." I searched frantically for something that would convince her, some memory or opinion from the last month that Ashe would know but a demon wouldn't—or rather, a demon who wasn't me. "My cousin Vikal is a bit melodramatic, but I love him anyway. He has a giant riding weasel and wears purple butterflies and too much eye makeup."

"His eye makeup is fine." Her stance relaxed a little. "All right, you're you. Now convince me you're not a threat."

"Of course I'm a threat." I shook my head, chest aching from more than my wound. "You saw what I did in that ballroom. I almost destroyed the palace by accident. All I wanted was to stop you from—" I bit the rest of my sentence off. I had no idea if she'd been aware of what she did while she was silvered.

Ashe shook her head ferociously, as if casting the memory off. The tip of her sword drooped.

"I...Hells." Her fingers flicked out in the warding sign. "No matter what else happens, thanks for stopping me."

"No," I said, as much to myself as to her. "I should have found another way. I was upset, not thinking clearly—I could have killed everyone in that room. It was inexcusable."

"No one died." Ashe's eyes flicked away from mine for a moment, her voice dropping low and subdued. "Not from what you did. Bastian says one poor bastard may not ever walk again, and there were a bunch of nasty injuries, sure. But I'm the one who killed a guard, and I can tell you a lot more people would have died if you hadn't stopped me." Shadows flexed across her jaw, and the name hung unspoken between us: *Kessa*.

"Nonetheless," I said, with grim resolve, "I have to make sure it never happens again." And find out the names of everyone who'd had any kind of permanent injury and make sure they were taken care of, if we got out of here alive.

Ashe eyed me a long moment, thoughts passing like shadows across her face. "You've convinced me you don't *want* to be a threat," she said at last. "But you've done a piss-poor job of convincing me you *aren't* a threat."

"So what do we do?" I asked, spreading my hands. "I don't have any answers."

She let out a long breath. "I have one."

I tensed, eyeing her sword. She didn't *look* like she was about to attack, but I suspected that if Ashe ever decided to kill me, I wouldn't know until after I was dead.

"But I'd rather not use it unless I have to," she finished.

"Thanks?" I said dryly.

"It's like back in the Furies." Ashe gave half a shrug. "One of the things we had to deal with from time to time was human chimeras. Sometimes left over from the War of Ashes, sometimes newer ones made by rogue Skinwitches. More than a few of the Furies thought we should just kill them all."

I thought of Bastian. "That doesn't seem right."

"It wasn't," she agreed quietly. "Sure, some chimeras didn't have much human left. They were monsters with a few human parts. But others were like Bastian, as human as I am and not particularly dangerous. You...you're like the third kind."

"The third kind?" I wasn't sure I wanted to know, but I had to ask.

"The ones that were human enough, but still too dangerous." She stared out the window. "They had standing orders that meant they were murdering people even if they didn't want to, or had been modified to have killer instincts they couldn't overcome. Or they'd been changed in some way that made them deadly to everyone around them, like poison breath."

That sounded like me, all right. "And what did you do with them?"

"Me? They didn't let me decide. That's why I left the Furies." Ashe sheathed Answer, its gleaming length swallowed up by its scabbard. "If it had been up to me, I'd have watched them. Waited, and been ready to kill them if we had to, but spared them if we could."

By the heaviness in her tone, I had no doubt she'd kill me if she thought it necessary. If I had any reason to believe that my physical death would solve anything, that might even have been a relief.

"Oh," a familiar voice said, soft and shaken.

Kessa and Bastian stood in the open door. Patterns of shadow receded from Bastian's face, revealing an expression shocked enough that he must have heard some of what we were talking about. He clutched a bulging satchel, and Kessa held a basket.

Ashe grimaced. "Well, this is awkward."

For a too-long moment, we all stared at each other. Bastian and Kessa didn't come any closer to me; they stood like wary deer, ready to bolt. Kessa's hand moved to her chest as if she might make the warding sign, but she clenched her fist, stopping herself.

"Hello," I said, trying to sound as normal and soothing as possible. I probably overdid it; they didn't look reassured.

Kessa glanced between us, then squared her shoulders with an air of determination. I could almost hear her thinking, *Someone has to carry this conversation, and I can see it's not going to be any of them.*

"Severin said you were hurt and got Bastian to come see to you, since he didn't trust you to ask for help even if you were dying." She sounded far too brisk and cheerful.

"I told you to let me check whether it was safe first," Ashe muttered.

"I see." Severin appeared behind Kessa and Bastian, an edge in his voice. He kept his gaze locked on Ashe as he handed a bottle marked with the palace apothecary's seal to Bastian. "And what would you have done if you decided it wasn't?"

Ashe met his eyes unflinchingly. "What do you think, mage boy? Warn them off. I'm no scholar, but I'm not fool enough to think stabbing a demon would accomplish anything."

She was one up on Foxglove, then. And she'd looked pretty convincingly like she might stab me—but maybe that had been part of her test to find out whether I was safe.

"Anyway," I said firmly, cutting into the tension between them, "thank you. Please come in."

They did, moving with the uncertainty of guests invited to pet the war chimeras.

Bastian cleared his throat. "So. You're the Demon of Disaster."

"So it would seem." I appeared to have gotten past the point where the admission filled me with horror and progressed to it making me feel exhausted. Or perhaps my reserves of horror had simply run dry. "I apparently merged with the demon as a baby in my grandmother's rash attempt to save me from a mortal illness. So I've been a demon for as long as I can remember, but I didn't know it."

Ashe shook her head in awe. "Hell of a thing to forget to mention when you were growing up."

"*Yes*," I agreed vehemently.

"I have to admit I'm surprised." Bastian fiddled with his satchel straps, avoiding my eyes. "The stories all seem to agree that the Demon of Disaster did some, ah, well. Forgive me, but some fairly terrible things. That doesn't sound like you."

A horrible feeling sucked at my insides, like a black tide swirling down into a dark well. "I . . . I don't remember."

"And you don't need to." Severin crossed to my side, angling to put himself subtly between me and the others. "Bastian, you should know better than to pry into a lady's past."

"But . . ." Bastian protested quietly, almost in a whimper. "She's a primary source."

Kessa waved a dismissive hand. "Forget about those musty old stories. Ryx is Ryx. We *know* her. She isn't a demon."

"Hmm, hate to say it, but you're wrong there," Ashe disagreed.

"You know what I mean!" Kessa gave me a bolstering sort of smile. "Ryx is our *friend*. She's a good person. Whatever the Demon of Disaster was like thousands of years ago, it doesn't matter."

"It matters," I said sharply. "Of course it matters."

"No it doesn't," Kessa insisted. "You can't hold yourself accountable for something you don't even remember doing. You're literally a different person now."

"Am I?" My nails dug into my palms. "It's not that easy. What about Foxglove? He's a different person now than he was years ago, too. Does it matter that he killed your brother?"

Her jaw tightened. "That's different."

"Foxglove has been trying to make amends for what he's done—to balance the scales. I have to do the same, somehow."

"Or," Severin suggested, "you could forget what is literally ancient history and try living the life you've got now. Really, you have enough problems without borrowing more from the past."

The problems from my past were threatening the existence of Eruvia, but fine. He had a point. "Keeping it wholly pragmatic, then—it matters because I'm dangerous. Yes, I'm trying to do good, but things tend to twist in my hand." Like the fires that started around me in the kitchen when I was a child, or the stable roof that collapsed, or all the countless broken dishes and teacups... or the gate to the Nine Hells opening up. "Maybe I can't escape it or overcome it, and you should all stay away from me to be safe."

Just like it had always been, before the jess. My grandmother had told me long ago, when I first fell in love, *You can't ever be that close to someone. There's too much at risk.* Now, at last, I understood.

Kessa grinned. "We're the Rookery. We don't stay away from dangerous things."

Ashe let out a bark of a laugh. "Got that right."

"I've been in mortal danger almost continuously since the moment I was born," Severin said with a shrug. "One does get jaded after a while."

"We may want to take certain precautions, of course," Bastian suggested, frowning.

The fact that they were even thinking about taking me back made me want to both hug them and shake some sense into them. Not that I would do either—even with my jess working, there was too much fear still lurking in their eyes.

They hadn't forgotten what I did in the ballroom, or all the stories they knew about the Demon of Disaster. And they shouldn't.

"I'm not going to ask you to accept me back into your midst and pretend nothing's wrong," I said slowly. "I can sleep in this room while we're stuck in the palace. Tomorrow, when I'm better, I'll see if I can get the key from Madness, so we can finish our business and get out of here. And once we're free—well, we can figure out what to do then."

Ashe nodded with apparent satisfaction. "Save the drama for after the hunt, we used to say in the Furies."

Bastian stepped forward, hefting his satchel with determination. "Speaking of business, we're forgetting why we came here. You're hurt, and I need to treat you."

I laid a protective hand over the bloodstained hole in my bodice. "I'm fine. Cortissa healed me."

Bastian exchanged grim looks with Kessa. "That's what I'm afraid of."

Bastian lowered the artifice monocle he'd been using to peer at my wound. I couldn't help but notice he'd gone out of his way not to touch me, and I couldn't tell if it was because he respected my privacy—he'd shooed everyone else out, after all—or because he was terrified of me.

He let out a long sigh, a tension seeming to leave his shoulders.

"You'll be happy to know she didn't change anything. Just healed you."

My stomach flopped over with relief. "Thank the Graces." Realizing how that might sound, I hastily added, "I'm sorry, that was insensitive."

"No, no, you *should* be relieved." Bastian gave a delicate grimace. "So yes, the good news is that she really did knit you mostly back together without any, ah, creative flourishes." He rummaged in his satchel, pulling out a series of little bottles. "If you take everything I'm about to give you and sleep for around twelve hours, you'll be up again and much better by tomorrow afternoon. Of course, if you take everything I'm about to give you, you *will* sleep for twelve hours, whether you like it or not."

"And is there bad news?" I asked, bracing myself.

Bastian lined up a set of cups and started pouring different proportions of water and concentrated potions into each one. For a long moment he focused on that, without saying anything, and my stomach tightened with dread.

"Cortissa did a sloppy job," he said at last, his voice subdued. "She should be ashamed of herself. You're going to have some nasty scars, and you may find that you get short of breath during extreme exertion for the rest of your life. I'm sorry, Ryx."

At this point, that was the last thing I cared about. I waved such concerns away. "Scars I can deal with."

"Yes, well, you do have a lot going on." Bastian hesitated; fear came into his face again, and I had to suppress a wince of my own. "You know my thoughts on what makes us human," he said at last. "I won't deny it's alarming that you're a demon, but..." He let out a little self-deprecating laugh. "This is going to sound strange, but it actually gives me hope."

I blinked. "Hope? Truly?"

"I'd been thinking of the demons as forces. Probably because they're named that way. But you aren't forces; you're people." A spark kindled in his eyes. "If the demons choose to destroy us, there's not much we can do about it; we're doomed. If you're people, though, you can choose not to. You can be reasoned with." His mouth twisted wryly. "And you can make mistakes. We can use guile, persuasion, and all the hundreds of tricks and techniques humans have used when we're outmatched since time immemorial. We can *win*."

"I'm glad I could help?" A memory stirred in the back of my mind at his words: clever hands moving on a deck of cards, bright eyes full of mischief that pierced my heart. I pushed it away, suppressing a shiver.

He nudged the row of cups toward me. "Now, drink these from left to right. They'll make you sleep—and I know what you'll want to say to that, but your body really does need sleep to heal right now." He peered at me anxiously, as if he expected me to argue.

Oblivion sounded lovely, however, and after everything that had happened and my sleepless night last night, I was ready to surrender to unconsciousness. Only one thing held me back, putting an ache of cold fear in my spine.

"Will I dream?" I asked.

Bastian's brows lifted. "With these potions? You shouldn't."

"Good." I reached toward them with heady relief.

Bastian was wrong. When I slept, memory found me.

Light and fire flowed through my dreams, the only landscape eddies and swirls in the endless sea of energy around me. I used to be content here, following those drifts and currents, stirring them up into great storms simply by my own presence and watching them with fascinated awe. Now it wasn't enough; now every non-moment in this infinite and yet somehow claustrophobic place was an agony of missing my friends, missing my five senses, missing the ability to *do* things.

Missing *her*.

Then a shiver of silvery light flickered toward me: *Disaster, help, Carnage is chasing me again, she's going to hurt me—*

Anger set the currents swirling around me, rapidly growing toward a maelstrom. *Don't worry, Madness. I won't let her.*

Another time, another place: The two of us stood on a rain-lashed rocky coast, the sea whipped up into angry whitecaps, roaring in its fury. I shook the old woman's shoulders as she stared at me from wide, panicked eyes, straggly gray hair blowing unheeded across her face.

"Madness, you have to stop doing this!" I shouted at her. "You can't keep jumping hosts—you're killing them!"

She clutched her head, her wrinkled face falling into despairing lines. "I can't! They keep coming apart around me!" The wind tore her words away, but I understood them anyway, borne on the invisible energy that connected us. "They're so beautiful, but they dissolve into pieces, and then some of the pieces get stuck to me, and I'm afraid. So I look for a new one that's stable, but then *that* crumbles, too!"

"They fall apart because they're *dying!*" I had to make her understand somehow. She used to be so structured, so serene and wise, more complex and subtle than any of us; but she'd taken host after host in a cycle of wonder and panic, surely thousands of them by now, each one leaving her with meaningless residual scraps of human memory and emotion, until her own essence was hopelessly scrambled—sand made from the tiny ground-down fragments of innumerable complex and beautiful shells. "I know it's scary, but it'll pass. You have to stay in your host until everything settles, Madness, you can't just—"

Her frightened eyes were starting to glaze; I could feel the wild energy in her straining to lift up and out, to abandon the shell of the woman she'd already killed. And then she'd take another, and another, snuffing out life after life.

In desperation, I pulled her to me in a tight hug, wrapping my arms around her. "Madness, don't go! Stay in your vessel. I'll protect you. Stay here with me, and it'll be all right."

Her stolen body shook in my stolen arms, the old woman's fragile bones quaking; I stroked her hair and made shushing noises, an instinct left over from some host I'd taken myself along the way. Slowly, slowly, she stilled, her breath coming in little sobs. Another human thing, either a function of the body or an instinct of the mind that clung to us as we moved from vessel to vessel, changing us forever.

"See?" I murmured. "You just have to ride it out. It's all right."

She lifted grateful eyes to me, deep brown and brimming with tears from a nest of wrinkles. She opened her mouth to speak, but it wasn't her voice I heard.

Ryx. Ryxander!

Severin.

I struggled to wake up, desperate as if I couldn't breathe, straining against a weight as vast and powerful as the ocean. I had to flee those rainswept rocks, her drowning eyes, the memories pulling me under and flooding my soul with fathoms of unspoken grief.

I sucked in a great gasp, and my eyes flew open.

Severin bent over me in my strange bed, the moonlight throwing unfamiliar patterns across his frowning face. The dangling strands of his hair brushed my shoulder.

He snatched his reaching hand back as if I'd caught him in the act of trying to steal something, sitting down abruptly in a chair beside my bed.

"You were crying," he said.

I reached up and touched my cheeks; sure enough, they were wet. A fog enshrouded my brain—Bastian's potions, trying to push me back down into sleep.

I blinked at him, trying to muddle through what I was seeing. "Why are you here?"

"I can go." He stood at once, his chair snagging on the rug and nearly tipping over; he caught it without looking and set it right. "I know this is creepy, waking up to find someone in your room. I just—you had asked me not to leave before Whisper showed up, and then when I came in after Bastian was done, you were asleep." He shrugged, as if to shake off any implication that he might have been thoughtful. "I'm still annoyed that furry little demon had the gall to kick me out, so I thought I'd stay for a little while to spite him. But I can—"

I caught the edge of his coat, like a child. It was all I could reach. "Please stay." Consciousness formed a thin and cracking skin of ice over a deep black lake of memory, full of old rotting secrets and pale-eyed monsters I had no desire to discover. "And thank you for waking me up. I . . ." I couldn't bring myself to tell him anything about what I'd dreamed. Somehow, what fell off my potion-loosened tongue was, "I'm afraid."

He stared at me a moment, his mage mark gleaming in the darkness. At last he settled into the chair with a quiet sigh. "It must be nice to know what it's like to *not* be afraid."

"I wish I could say you'll have a chance to learn soon, but that doesn't seem to be the way things are going." I ground the heels of my hands into my eyes. "Hells, I'm tired. I need to stay awake somehow."

"Bastian told me you need sleep to heal," Severin objected. "It's only been an hour. If you were imagining I sat here all night, I get bored far too easily for that." He paused, eyeing me with a guarded expression. "What are you afraid of?"

The past. Myself. I turned my dread over critically, examining its many facets. At last, I settled on, "Becoming someone else. Losing what makes me human."

To my surprise, he let out a grunt of a laugh. "You think you're any less human than a Witch Lord?"

"I'm serious." I tried and failed to muster up a glare.

"So am I. We're athelings; we spend all our lives striving to be not quite human, and the worst of us succeed." He shook his head. "You're the first person who treated me like a fellow human being. So forgive me if I have a certain investment in believing you weren't wrong about the *fellow* part."

"You're human." The potions were weighing my eyelids down despite all my struggles to keep them open. "You're a perfectly decent one, in fact."

"Let's not go too far." He tapped the back of my hand. "Hey. You can drift off in a minute, but first—since I'm only the heir to an immortal monster and not one myself, I do need rest, unfortunately. Do you want me to stay until you're asleep, or—"

I seized his hand on a surge of terror at the idea of him leaving me alone with my dreams. At once I felt like a fool, but I couldn't bring myself to release it. "I . . . Of course you should sleep."

He glanced at a divan before the fireplace. "I could sleep over there, I suppose."

What I really wanted was for him to curl up next to me in my bed, a warm breathing presence who knew my name, who believed

I was human, reminding me with every heartbeat who I was in this life. But that would be unspeakably selfish. No matter what Severin said, I was the Demon of Disaster, and there was no way anyone I took so closely into my life could come to a good end.

But I couldn't make my fingers uncurl and let him go.

Severin's mouth twitched. "Or I guess I could drag the divan over here and fall asleep holding your hand."

He was joking. I should be sensible and laugh, and let him go to sleep. I managed a wry smile, or an approximation of one, and let go of his hand. My eyes started drifting shut almost at once, against my will.

And popped open immediately to the sound of dragging furniture.

He was really doing it. I tried to sit up, regretted it immediately, and eased back into my pillows, my little gasp lost in the much louder shuddering sound of Severin hauling the divan up beside my bed.

"There." He flashed me a grin as if he'd just done something ridiculous rather than wonderful.

"Thank you." The words came out thick and slurred, but it wasn't the potion this time. I had no strength to hold back the warm wave of emotion that rose up all the way to my eyes and made them sting.

Severin began unfastening his vestcoat, still grinning, and my breath froze, sending a stab of pain through my half-healed chest. There was nothing remotely immodest about the flowing white shirt he wore beneath it, but somehow my eyes managed to stay open after all as he flung the vestcoat over the back of the divan in a careless fall of black and gold.

"I'm just as glad, to be honest," he said. "I'm tired of having horrible nightmares every night in this cursed place. I'm willing to gamble that you can keep them away for me."

I was attempting to muster some witty retort, but he reached up to untie his ponytail and all speech fled my brain. He shook the long shining cascade of his hair loose in its full silky glory, and for a moment I forgot all about being a demon.

"Do you, uh, need a blanket," I rasped at last.

"I'll manage. But I *will* steal one of your pillows." He did, then settled himself on the divan, propped on one elbow. His hair cascaded over his shoulders in a midnight waterfall. "There. Now if we must have a night full of unspeakable dread, at least we can do it together."

A smile tugged at my lips despite myself. "I can think of no one I'd rather have by my side as I gaze into the fathomless abyss of my soul."

"So touching. I'm moved."

Only a couple of feet separated us; we stared into each other's eyes in the darkness, reading the shadows there. Severin laid his arm on my covers, fingers curling up, and I laced my hand through his.

We didn't speak another word. Just gazed at each other in the silvery darkness, pulses mingling together in the soft warmth between our fingers. I breathed in his scent along with the unfamiliar smell of the blanket and lingering woodsmoke from the fireplace.

I expected to lie awake all night. There was no way I could fall asleep with Severin so near. The sun would come up and find us still lying here, barely daring to breathe, staring into one another's eyes.

But Bastian's potions had the weight of magic behind them, and sleep crept up on me from behind when I wasn't paying attention.

I didn't dream at all.

"Up and armed! We've got a hunt on."

The door to my room banged open. Ashe burst in, murder in her eyes, Kessa and Severin on her heels.

I lurched into a sitting position before I remembered I couldn't do that; the stab of pain was less than I expected. "What? What happened?"

Severin had clearly been up for a while, his vestcoat on and his hair back in its tail; afternoon light streamed through the windows. They'd let me sleep through half the day, with everything we had to do. And by the looks on their faces, terrible things hadn't stopped happening while I was out.

Ashe prowled a vicious arc through the room, steaming with suppressed violence. Kessa drew in a breath, her eyes stricken.

"Bastian's missing," she said. "We think Cortissa grabbed him."

THIRTY-SIX

O h, Hells, no." A surge of fear and anger lifted me right out of bed and onto my feet, hanging on to the bedpost for stability. My legs took my weight; maybe there was something to this whole *rest* idea after all. "What happened? Is he all right?"

Severin grimaced. "I doubt very much that he's all right. My spies report he went off with a Zenith Society group without a fight, which is why we think it must have been Cortissa. They caught him when he was coming back from helping Foxglove work on the wards."

Ashe punched the wall, leaving a fist-sized crater in the plaster. "I shouldn't have let him wander around alone. We *know* she can control him."

Kessa put a hand on her shoulder. "We're stretched too thin with Ryx down and..." She braced herself visibly. "And with me refusing to work with Foxglove. This is my fault. I'm sorry."

We didn't have time for a guilt contest. "It doesn't matter whose fault it is," I said. "Do we know where they've got him?"

"Not their rooms." Severin showed his teeth. "It appears a dozen of the palace tomcats got in there somehow and sprayed all over the place, so they abandoned them this morning. We should hear back from my spies on where they took him soon."

So that was what he'd been talking about with that cat last night when he looked so innocent. It would have startled me into a laugh if I weren't so worried about Bastian.

"We'd better move quickly." I didn't want to think about what Cortissa might be doing to him—if they hadn't killed him already. "Come on, let's go get Foxglove."

Kessa's face tightened, but she nodded. "Whatever it takes to get Bastian back." A fury shone in her eyes like I'd never have thought her capable of. "Seasons spare Cortissa if she's done anything permanent to him, because there's no way in the Nine Hells I will."

By the time we spotted Foxglove carving away at the wards on the outer wall in a discreet corner of the palace grounds, I was out of breath, and pain jabbed my chest every time I inhaled— but that was all. Taking Cortissa's dubious help and Bastian's potions into account, I still had to suspect that demons healed even faster than vivomancers did.

Fast enough for me to run and fight, if I had to, at least for a short time. That was what mattered right now.

Foxglove looked up as we approached. His back tensed, but his hands remained steady and graceful as he cleaned his alchemical stylus and put it away.

I couldn't forget that last night, he'd been ready to kill me. He didn't so much as glance my way; his eyes locked on Kessa. Which was fair enough, given everything between them, but it only intensified the queasy mess of anger and hurt in my gut.

She stopped about ten feet from him. They stared at each other; Ashe bit her lip. I'd never seen her look so unsure. New lines of pain marked Kessa's face, and anger flickered in her eyes.

"I haven't forgiven you," she said. "But we need you."

"I wouldn't expect you to," he said quietly, rising. "And I'll always be there when you need me. For as long as I live."

Something passed between them that I wasn't privy to, private and silent and full of pain. Then Kessa reached up with careful deliberation and tugged her hat down into a businesslike angle.

"The Zenith Society has Bastian." She struck a confident pose, hands on her hips. "Time to stage a dramatic rescue." It was all fragile surface, a thin porcelain mask she'd slipped on to hide a bleeding wound.

Foxglove held her gaze. His hand dropped to his belt, his shoulders rolling as if he shrugged one burden off them and another on. "We can't allow that."

Kessa didn't look away. "Because in the Rookery," she said softly, "we stand by our own."

He bowed his head. "Thank you."

He lifted his eyes to me next, his face taut and wary. I didn't try to hide anything in my own expression; let him see my lingering anger at him. All I truly wanted was to go back to how things had been before, when the glances we shared exchanged quiet understanding, rather than bitter calculations of betrayal and guilt and fear. But it would be hard, after last night, and now wasn't the time to do that work.

"Are you with us?" he asked at last.

"I'm insulted that you feel the need to ask," I replied.

"Of course she is," Kessa said fiercely. "She's in the Rookery, too."

Foxglove let out a long breath. "So she is."

I tried not to read too much into that, but hope lifted its traitor head in me like a hungry dog.

Foxglove wasn't done. "Ryx. You stopped me from making a mistake last night—one I couldn't have come back from. Thank you."

Too many conflicting feelings snarled in my throat. "You still made a mistake."

He grimaced. "It's a bad habit."

"I made one, too. I should have told you all earlier." I shook my head so fiercely my braid whipped across my shoulders. "But that doesn't matter now. Bastian needs us."

"All right, rooks." Foxglove tugged his cuffs straight. "Let's gear up and take him back."

"I'm disappointed in you, Bastian."

Moreni's voice drifted up to the vaulted ceiling of the shrine, the soaring marble giving it a grand resonance. I lay on my belly beside Severin on the dusty boards of the choir loft, barely daring to breathe. We couldn't see Bastian from here—or any of the Zenith Society, for that matter. I yearned to peek and check whether he was all right, but I couldn't risk them spotting me. Not until we got word from Kessa that the others were in place.

"Not as disappointed as I am in you." It was Bastian's voice, weak and strained but full of resolve. My heart leaped. I gave Severin a quick relieved look.

Moreni continued as if Bastian hadn't spoken. "You were always an apt student who understood the forces of history. How can you not comprehend the simple truth that if Vaskandar has a demon, the Serene Empire needs one on our side, too?"

One of the mice in the shadowy loft skittered up to Severin, round eyes bright, whiskers twitching. He gave it a bit of cheese, and it skittered off. I pressed my palms flat against the age-smoothed wood beneath me, ready to lever myself up if it was time to move, but Severin gave a tiny shake of his head. He pointed down and held up eight fingers.

Eight of them and five of us—plus Bastian, who Cortissa could command against us. Not the best odds.

Bastian's voice floated up from below. "Protecting the Serene Empire is important, but nothing is worth siding with a demon like you've done."

Someone laughed, cruel and gleeful: it was Aurelio's voice, but I held no illusions that it was Aurelio.

"Truly?" Hunger asked, taunting. "Nothing, you say. So you won't be working with Ryx anymore, I take it?"

I stiffened. Severin put his hand over mine and gave it a quick squeeze.

Bastian remained unshaken. "Ryx is human," he said.

I pressed my forehead to the cool wooden floor and squeezed my eyes shut on the tears that threatened to leak through. They'd better not have hurt him.

"This is all very nice, but let's get to the point," Cortissa snapped. "You're wasting my time philosophizing, Moreni. You can play teacher with your little protégé later."

"Oh, very well." Moreni sighed. "I'll ask you one more time, Bastian. Where is the artifact you stole from us?"

"I truly haven't the faintest idea," Bastian said.

I itched to rush to his rescue, but Foxglove and Kessa had to scale the palace wall from the outside, disable a ward, and climb in through a window to get into position. There was no way they could be ready yet.

"Tell him the truth," Cortissa commanded. "Where is the artifact?"

"Gone," Bastian said at once, with a trace of satisfaction. "Destroyed. I'm delighted to inform you that we ripped it up into little pieces. All that remains is the core power source and its housing, which you can find in our quarters, but it won't do you any good."

"Hells take you," Moreni swore, frustration roughening his usually controlled voice. "That's going to make this harder."

"That was the idea, yes," Bastian replied.

"There," Cortissa said, with a sharp edge of impatience. "You have your information. Is it my turn now?"

Moreni let out a long sigh. "Oh, very well."

"Finally."

I exchanged alarmed glances with Severin. Cortissa's footsteps echoed on the marble. The shrine's perfect acoustics amplified Bastian's frightened gasp.

My nails dug into the floor. My job was to keep Hunger busy while Ashe drew off the Zenith Society, and Foxglove and Kessa sneaked in from the back to rescue Bastian in the ensuing chaos. If I did something rash before the others were in place, I could ruin the whole plan. *Hurry, curse it*, I wished them silently.

"Oh my love came up to meet me, and he wore a coat of gold,

"But it couldn't keep him warm against the bitter mountain cold..." Cortissa's voice floated up from below, beautiful and unearthly.

Bastian made a small, strangled noise. I didn't even realize I'd started to surge upward until I registered that Severin's hard grip on my shoulder held me down.

"Wait," he hissed. "You'll get us all killed."

"We can distract them," I whispered. "Break her concentration."

"That's an idea." Severin bit his lip, thinking. "I'll go get a bird. There's a window just down the hall." He started to crawl on his belly toward the choir loft door, which led to a narrow second-floor corridor. But then he paused and gave me a stern glance over his shoulder. *"Stay here."*

I fingered my belt knife, contemplating throwing it, and hoped he'd take my silence as assent.

"What's she doing?" came Hunger's voice, from almost directly below me.

"Finishing what she started a long time ago," Moreni replied, relaxed and amused as if this were a party entertainment. I'd never wanted to hurt a living being so badly.

"Oh my love came up to meet me, all with flowers in his hair,

"But they couldn't keep him sheltered from the deadly mountain air..."

More whimpering from Bastian. Fury expanded in me like a hot rising sun, demanding action.

"He was supposed to be a killing chimera," Moreni continued conversationally. "An assassin. He has lovely modifications for stealth, but he was stolen before she gave him any weaponry. Once he's complete, we can use him to take out the Rookery—and anyone else we want."

I crawled as silently as I could on my belly toward the narrow wooden stairs that led down from the choir loft into the temple, gritting my teeth as I dragged my aching scar across the floor. Maybe I could get them talking, stall for time—anything to get Cortissa to stop.

"Oh my love came up to meet me, for to take me as his wife,

"But the storm arose in splendor, and she stole away his life . . ."

"So those dead things, they're what, ingredients?" Hunger sounded fascinated.

"Essentially. She doesn't need them, but it's faster to use existing pieces than to make them from scratch."

My stomach turned over. *Oh, Bastian.* I was almost to the top of the stairs; if I started down them I'd be exposed, and I'd have to start talking fast if I didn't want to get shot. I'd have to hold their attention for as long as it took for Kessa and Foxglove to break into the shrinekeeper's quarters so they could come at Bastian from the other side—all without the Zenith Society deciding that stabbing me had worked pretty well last time and they should just do it again.

"Oh my love lay down in silence, with a cold unbeating heart,

"But I knelt by him and swore that we would never be apart . . ."

Muffled weeping rose up from below. Curse it, the others must be nearly in place by now, and Bastian might not have much time. We hadn't accounted for this; the plan had to change. I couldn't delay any longer.

I flung myself at the top of the stairs and began storming down them, drawing on a lifetime of watching my family make dramatic atheling entrances.

"Hunger!" I called, in the most powerful voice I could,

letting it ring through the marble arches of the shrine. "That one is mine, and you know it. How dare you?"

The shrine stretched out below me: four Graces to each side, each in their own grand alcove with a statue and an altar, with Loreice's patron the Grace of Beauty anchoring the end, stone garments swirling in an exultant dance. Colored light streamed down through stained glass windows, offering candles flickered in shadowy alcoves, and paintings of the Graces defeating the Nine Demons hung on the walls.

It was blasphemy for me to be here. But what they were doing to Bastian was a far worse offense against everything the Graces stood for.

Hunger and Moreni turned their faces up in surprise from where they stood side by side near the foot of the stairs. Several other Zenith Society members pivoted toward me, scattered in various spots around the shrine. One who'd been lounging on a bench leaped to her feet, and another two swung to face me from their posts guarding the main doors; a couple drew weapons.

Cortissa, however, maintained a serene expression of focus as she stood over Bastian, who sprawled across an offering table she'd swept clean of the candles and flowers that now scattered the floor. She held his bloody hand in hers almost tenderly, eyes half closed in concentration as colors raced in agony across his face.

"Oh my love lay down in silence, in his flowers and his gold,

"But I took his skin and made a coat to keep me from the cold..."

Hells. She hadn't stopped. On the bright side, I'd gotten everyone else's attention. I'd have to push harder to make sure I held it, and to get Cortissa's, too.

"Oh, but he isn't yours." Hunger wagged a finger at me, delighted at the opportunity for a grand scene. That much was working, at least. "He belongs to these humans, who are mine. Which means your little friend is mine, as well."

"And are these humans happy to be called your property?" Maybe I could get them quarreling. Anything to make Cortissa stop. "You think *everything* is yours, Hunger. One day, that will prove your undoing."

"But everything *is* mine." Hunger spread his arms as if to embrace this delightful idea. *Good, lecture me about it.* "And why not? We are greater than this world, Disaster. We transcend its limits. What higher purpose can it serve than our amusement?"

"Oh my love lay down in silence, on the gray unyielding stone..."

I paused a few steps from the bottom, keeping the advantage of height, mustering my answer. The people who'd drawn swords and pistols slowly lowered them as Moreni seemed content to watch us argue, a smirk pulling at his lips as if he knew I was trying to save Bastian and had no chance of success.

"But his arms still always hold me, and we'll never be alone. Ahhh, there we are."

Bastian let out a terrible, wrenching scream. The sound cut me like a knife.

The arching main doors to the shrine crashed open.

Everyone turned to look as the shuddering bang shook the air, but it was as if we moved through molasses. The blur that burst into the shrine was faster, flashing with bright metal; a crackle and sudden scent of ozone made me wonder for one fraction of a heartbeat if the Graces had struck us all down with lightning where we stood.

The two guards by the door fell, one and then the other, leaving thin trails of smoke in the air behind them. Blood soaked one's throat and the other's chest; they'd never even had the chance to draw weapons.

Ashe stood between them, a few crimson drops splashing her face like freckles, Answer unsheathed and smoking in her hand. Black crystals glittered on the wirework wrapping its pommel. Her ice-blue eyes lit with the intensity of hellfire.

"Ashe!" Aurelio gasped, and I had no doubt by the sheer

alarm in his face that it wasn't Hunger speaking. "Those were my friends! What the Hells happened to Rule Three?"

Cortissa finally looked up from Bastian, her breath hissing out in shock. Bastian himself weakly turned his head to stare, his eyes wide with something that looked an awful lot like fear.

Ashe paced forward with the murderous prowl of a stalking cat, Answer held low at her side.

"Rule Zero," she said, in a detached voice I barely recognized.

Aurelio blanched. "What?"

"Rule Zero," Ashe repeated, in that same deadly tone. "If you hurt my friends, all other rules no longer apply."

"Oh pox," I whispered.

And all Nine Hells broke loose.

THIRTY-SEVEN

Gunshots cracked the air as Ashe ducked sideways, swerving into a long, low lunge at a startled swordswoman who'd been trying to flank her. An entire flock of sparrows exploded down from the choir loft; they swooped to flutter in the face of a man with a flintlock pistol leveled at Ashe, and he threw up his arms with a cry to shield his eyes instead of firing. Moreni spun away from me and strode toward Ashe, cursing, as he pulled a ring from his finger.

"Not *her* again," Hunger exclaimed.

Before he could turn toward her, I grabbed his arm. He bared his teeth at me in a hiss.

"I thought I made it clear that you don't touch my friends." I was bluffing; with my jess sealed, anything I could do would be far more likely to hurt the Rookery than Hunger.

His eyes narrowed. "Haven't you learned not to make threats? Or do you *still* not remember?"

Something tried to claw its way up from a grave deep within my mind. *The scent of ash, the roar of the ocean, and a single unending scream.* I clenched my jaw and shook the memory off. Not now—not ever.

"You of all people should know that I don't need to unleash my full power to hurt you, Hunger."

The shrine echoed with cries of pain and the clash of steel; past Hunger's shoulder I glimpsed a bloody corpse draped across the back of a bench, gunsmoke hanging in the air, the flutter of birds. Ashe flashed into view for one moment, a blur of motion, parrying Moreni's thrown ring effortlessly out of the air on her way to skewer a man who frantically struggled to reload his pistol.

Hunger's face twisted, and suddenly his eyes softened with hurt: Aurelio.

"Ryx, don't!" he protested. "Remember that I'm in here, too. You could kill me!"

A flood of memories hit me, looking into those desperate hazel eyes. Aurelio sitting with me on the terrace at Gloamingard, unafraid of my broken magic, talking and drinking and watching the sunset. Aurelio clasping my hand, the first human being I'd touched after getting my jess. Aurelio buying me time to run when Hunger turned on me in fury on the rooftop.

Aunt Karrigan lying on the floor, her throat a bloody ruin, arrows bristling from her chest. The sickening impact of a poisoned arrow striking deep into my leg. The cold weight of chains on my wrists as a wagon took me to Alevar to be tortured to death.

I steeled myself and held his gaze. "I know."

"You wouldn't." His eyes narrowed. "You've never killed anyone on purpose in your life. And I *helped* you, remember?"

"I don't *want* to kill you," I admitted. "But you've made your choices, and you can't unmake them."

"Look, I'm sorry about giving you up to the Shrike Lord!" His words quickened with desperation. "I was angry. And you know I never wanted to—"

"Shoot me full of arrows and poison me?" I interrupted, genuinely furious now. "Murder my aunt?"

A terrible crash and a scream rose up from somewhere, but I didn't dare look away from Aurelio.

"I've learned my lesson," Aurelio insisted. "At a cost so terrible you can't even imagine it."

"Redemption isn't that easy." The words came out with more heat than I expected. "And the lives of everyone in this palace have to come first. I'm truly sorry, Aurelio."

Moreni and Cortissa backed up toward us across the shrine; Bastian stood in front of them, arms spread wide and trembling as if to protect them, Cortissa's hand laid possessively between his shoulder blades. Ashe advanced inexorably after them, splashed in too much blood for me to guess if any of it was hers. Nothing stirred in the rest of the chapel, save for a scattering of sparrows fluttering up toward the windows.

Aurelio frowned, as if the sudden silence sank in, and turned around; clashing expressions warred across his face.

"No closer," Cortissa barked at Ashe. She slapped a dagger into Bastian's hand. "Or I tell him to stab that into his eye."

Ashe paused. Moreni took advantage of her hesitation to throw a glass orb full of some bright blue potion at her; Ashe smacked it aside with the flat of Answer's blade as casually as swatting a fly. It crashed into the bloodstained offering table where Bastian had lain and exploded into flames.

"Do you need me to deal with that one for you?" Hunger asked, contempt in his voice.

"Oh, I think she'll cooperate now." Cortissa stroked Bastian's hair; he flinched. "Put the sword down, little rook."

I reached for my own sword, but Hunger tapped my shoulder. "Ah, ah! Backstabbing, Disaster? Such foul play isn't like you."

"You don't know me," I said hotly.

Ashe hadn't moved. She stared at Bastian, then Cortissa, her teeth bared in a snarl of indecision.

"Bastian," Cortissa said, her voice gone sweet as honey, "touch the tip of that knife to your open eyeball."

Bastian lifted the dagger, his hand trembling, his breath sawing rough and terrified at the air. I held my own breath, thinking furiously. I could tackle him—that would probably be more effective than going after Cortissa, and Hunger might not expect it.

"Now," Cortissa began caressingly—and staggered back, a bloody hole in her forehead, as the earsplitting bang of a gunshot echoed up to the vaulted ceiling.

Her lips worked for half a heartbeat, and she dropped limp and twitching to the floor.

Foxglove stood in the doorway to the shrinekeeper's quarters, pistol smoking in his hand, Kessa right behind him.

Bastian fell to his knees, gasping and shaking, and clutched his bloody hand to his chest. The knife clattered free across the marble. I ached to rush to him, but I didn't dare leave Hunger unattended.

Moreni drew himself up, fury contorting his arrogant features. He seized Bastian's hair in one hand, and the alarmingly complex chain of artifice amulets across his chest with the other.

"You've forced my hand," he rumbled, as an ominous glow began in every one of the amulets around his neck. The hair on my arms lifted from mere proximity to the power he was calling up. "I didn't want to use this, but *so be it*."

I started toward him, but Hunger stepped between us. "Oh, no," he said, with a vicious smile. "You distracted me from helping my humans; now that *yours* need help, you pay the price."

I glared at him, contemplating a swift knee to his crotch.

"Hey, Moreni!"

It was Severin, halfway down the stairs, grinning like he'd just stolen the last piece of cake. Moreni whirled to face him, scowling.

"Catch!" Severin called, and offered him a mocking bow.

From his back, the grizzled gray tomcat executed a glorious flying leap and latched on to Moreni's face with all four claws.

Moreni screamed and dropped his amulets, reaching desperately for the cat. Before he could lay hands on it, Answer ran him through, sprouting from his chest as if by some bloody miracle.

"Ashe!" Foxglove protested, starting forward. "We needed to question him!"

"Rule Zero," Ashe muttered, with satisfaction.

A sudden pressure fell upon us, as if the ceiling itself had collapsed. I gasped and staggered, and I wasn't the only one.

"Oh," Hunger said, his voice deadly quiet. "Oh, this was amusing enough at first, but now you've made me angry."

Every candle in the shrine suddenly shrank down to an ember. The fire licking up from the offering table went out, leaving a trail of smoke. The gray cat ran off in terror, tail bristling; the Rookery all swayed as if the ground had become unsteady beneath their feet. Foxglove grabbed the back of a bench for balance as his bad leg buckled.

"These were *mine*," Hunger hissed. "And you've broken them, and I'm quite upset about it." He lifted a hand; the air around it went dark, as if he sucked the very light into himself.

Blood of the Eldest. He was going to kill them.

"Kessa!" I shouted. "Release me!"

"*Exsolvo!*" Kessa called at once.

Aurelio whirled, eyes widening in horror. "Ryx, no!"

I hesitated. It was the face I'd called a friend for years, pleading and terrified, seeing death in my eyes. For one brief instant, my hands faltered as they lifted to grab him.

Hunger pounced and seized my arms instead, back in control. "Fool," he growled. "We'll see how *you* like it."

Pain erupted across my senses—terrible, mind-searing pain, as if he were ripping off the skin of my soul. Something vital as blood flowed out of me through my arms where he grabbed me, and his hands began to glow with a soft golden light.

I let out a cry, too surprised to even try to stop it, too shocked to protect myself. I was dimly aware of shouting and noise and movement around me, but I didn't know what any of it meant. The agony of whatever Hunger was doing to me had stripped all sense from the world. *Holy Graces have mercy.*

There was no mercy for demons. I knew what I had to do.

I clamped my own hands on Hunger's arms, so we clasped each other like old friends meeting. Teeth clenched against the pain, I *pulled*.

He let out a howl that resonated in the very stones of the palace, rattling my teeth. I dug my fingers tighter into Aurelio's arms, tearing away at Hunger even as he tore at me.

"Now it's a question of who can withstand more," I rasped at him hoarsely, through the blinding pain.

His wail only grew louder, setting the floor to trembling, knocking dust down from the ceiling. The others dropped to their knees, clutching their heads. Hunger's voice sounded in my mind, strained and wild with agony.

I'm the stronger one! You've weakened yourself with human taint— you can't take this for long!

"Oh, but you're wrong," I ground out through my teeth. "Humans are strong because we *know* pain." I pulled harder, unraveling the bright endless energy beneath my fingertips, hoping I wasn't killing Aurelio but well past the point where I had the luxury to stop if I was. "We *live* with pain. We know how to push through it. Do you?"

A hot prickle of power flowed up my arms. Hunger's cry ascended to a shriek that shattered every window in the shrine, sending stained glass showering down from above like many-colored rain. He tore away from me, wrenching his arms out of my grip, his breath coming in deep hoarse gasps. He stared at me with a fear that, at last, was his own, wild and bottomless.

"What are you?" he whispered.

"I told you," I said, advancing after him. "Human."

He cradled his arms against his chest as if they were numb and kept backing up, staring at me in uncomprehending horror. For a brief moment, Aurelio's expression flickered across his face, full of betrayal; but then it was Hunger again, shaken as if he'd entered an entirely new world full of strange new senses.

All around me, the Rookery rose back to their feet, battered and exhausted but ready to fight.

Hunger turned and ran.

Gray-gold twilight poured down through the shattered shrine windows onto utter wreckage. Shards of colored glass mixed senselessly with overturned benches and scattered offering candles. Bodies sprawled everywhere, still and bloody. A thin smoke from discharged flintlocks and snuffed altar candles hung in the air.

We all stared at each other, our eyes asking the same question: *Is it over?* My breath sounded too loud in my ears, and my hands tingled, but my chest hurt less than it had when I'd walked in. I must have gotten more energy from Hunger than he did from me, in the end.

Foxglove leaned on a marble column to support his bad leg and let out a long breath.

As if the sound had released her, Kessa ran to Bastian, who knelt on the floor holding his bloody hand.

"Are you all right?" she demanded. "What did she do to you?"

Bastian stared at Cortissa's corpse. "She's dead," he whispered. "She's really dead, this time."

Ashe flopped onto one of the intact benches and started cleaning her sword. "Good timing on that one, Foxglove."

Kessa reached for Bastian's hand. "Let me see."

He snatched it back, wincing. "Don't touch it. She only got to one finger, but the claw is dripping venom and I don't know how to stop it."

Ashe squinted at him. "Ugh. Good thing it's not your sword hand." He stared at her in disbelief, and she corrected herself, "Pen hand."

"How about you?" I asked Ashe, worried. "Don't tell me you came through all that unscathed."

"Oh, Hells, no." Ashe laughed, an edge of pain coming through. "I'm not *that* good. Nothing serious, though. Pistol ball graze, a few sword scratches, bit of a burn from something Moreni threw at me. I'm going to need some of your wound sealing and anti-infection salves, Bastian, when you get a moment."

He waved his good hand vaguely toward the scorched and bloodied offering table, without looking at it. "My satchel is over there somewhere. They...I don't know where they put it." His shoulders started trembling, and he hunched over his hand, breath coming more and more quickly.

I checked myself from starting toward him. "Bastian? What's wrong?"

He thrust his hand at Ashe, suddenly, revulsion on his face. "Here. Cut it off." A two-inch-long claw protruded from his littlest finger, wickedly sharp. "Quickly! Take the whole finger if you have to. I can't stand looking at it."

Kessa gripped his shoulder. "Bastian, maybe after we get out of here, a proper surgeon—"

"I don't want it on there one second longer." His voice had gone high and strained. "Cut it off!"

Ashe leaned closer to peer at Bastian's finger. "Yeah, I don't know what she was thinking. That'd break off in a serious fight. Kessa, can you trim this down as low as you can and bandage it for now?"

"Of course," she said, her voice surpassingly gentle as she gathered Bastian's hand carefully in hers. The look she shot Ashe was much sharper. "And then you're next."

"Speaking of next." Foxglove straightened away from the column. "I don't know where Hunger was going, but we just cut his power base out from under him. We may not have much time to finish this."

He'd assumed his usual tone of unquestioning command. I tensed, glancing at Kessa, wondering whether someone would remind him that he'd stepped down as the Rookery leader.

The moment balanced on its tipping point. Recognition flickered in Kessa's eyes; Ashe gave her a quick glance, then looked down at her own hands on Answer's shining blade.

The time for objections passed, unremarked, and Foxglove continued. "The wards are nearly ready. We can do this today if we can get that key."

"Right." I stripped my jess off and passed it to Severin. He took it with grave care. "I'm on it."

Ashe snorted. "By yourself? What are you going to do, ask for it nicely?"

"As a matter of fact," I said, "that's exactly my plan."

The gardens were nearly empty. A strong wind sighed through the leaves of the great central tree spreading above me and ruffled the green fur of the topiary animals. The faint scent of autumn came on that wind, the first touch of dry and glorious decay.

I stood beneath the tree and waited. *I'm here. I want to talk to you. Come find me.*

A gray curtain drew across the sky, softening the edges of everything. Out here, where the air was fresh, I could almost ignore the taint of fear that hung around the palace. I could pretend things were right in the world, the sun rising and setting in its usual course, the seasons turning, nothing wrong.

Except that I carried the wrongness within me. I stood in a circle of withered death on the green, immaculate lawn.

At last she came, alone like I'd asked, a pale wisp of a figure trailing acres of silver brocade like a child playing dress-up in her mother's too-long gown. Her eyes locked onto me as if I were her only anchor in a wild and drowning sea.

A child's face lifted up to mine with the same wide eyes, smiling in wonder. "I can do it on my own now, Disaster! I can do it!" She spread her hands, examining them. "Look, the colors have all faded, which is sad, but I'm still in this body! You're right, I just had to hold on and wait."

Grief dimmed my core, knowing the child she wore was dead. She didn't understand about the bright life she'd cut short, the family left broken by grief. She hadn't learned that those colorful patterns she loved had names and memories and feelings, and that once they were gone something unique and precious was lost from the world. I forced my stolen face to smile.

"That's wonderful, Madness. Now you can stay in this vessel forever."

The queen lifted a hand to my cheek, her touch light and tentative as a butterfly. "You're starting to remember."

I braced myself not to recoil from her touch, even as my flesh crawled beneath it. "Against my will, yes."

Her pale brows dipped in concern. "You're not happy."

"Of course I'm not happy." I needed to be clever, to be manipulative, to work my way around to the key—but the truth burst out instead. "Why would I enjoy remembering being a demon?"

Sadness opened bottomless wells in her eyes. "My memories with you are my best memories. I thought you'd want them back."

My breath caught in my lungs, with a twinge from my scars. Seasons have mercy. I shouldn't feel sympathy, shouldn't feel guilt—there was no good reason for this sudden urge to protect her and help her.

"It's not that I don't want to remember you," I said huskily. "It's that I don't want to remember everything else."

Madness drooped like a wilting flower. "I'm sorry. I've ruined things again. Nightmare told me you'd be happy, and that this was what you would have wanted."

"Nightmare lied." Now I was angry, a safer emotion, less fraught with sharp edges and dizzying drops. "Ever since you came through the gate together, she's been using you and manipulating you."

Madness tilted her head as if listening to something far away. "She...yes. It's different, when she thinks of me. She's never upset, like you are, and her patterns are soothing—but they're false."

"Listen." The plan faded further and further from my mind; I had to make her understand. "I may not remember much, but I know you don't want to hurt people."

A faint frown stirred her wispy brows. "I don't think it's possible to avoid hurting humans. They hurt all the time, so easily, like clouds coming and going. But I don't want to make their patterns so full of pain and sadness anymore."

Good enough to work with. "Right. And Nightmare *loves* hurting people. It's all she wants to do in the mortal realm; it's why she came here." I held her gaze, willing her to see the truth. "If you do what she tells you—if you believe her, and let her manipulate you—you'll be helping her torment them, guaranteed. Do you want that?"

"No?" She tipped her head in the other direction and repeated, more firmly, "No."

"Then you should tell her that, next time she asks you to do something to a human. Just tell her no."

A shiver of power brushed so softly at the edge of my mind, Madness's most tentative touch.

"Nightmare wants to drink up people's fear," she murmured. "Hunger wants everything to be his, to consume it all. You're a destructive energy, but you don't like to destroy things. You never did."

"No, I..." I took half a step backward without meaning to, as if I could somehow escape her invisible touch. "I don't. Sometimes I do it anyway."

"It's who you are," she said soothingly, making awkward petting motions in the air. "It's what you are. You *are* chaos and destruction. You're Disaster. It's all right."

"No, it's *not* all right." My hands clenched at my sides. "That's what I've been trying to tell you, Madness. It's what Whisper was trying to tell everyone, too, for that matter. This world doesn't belong to demons, and they—*we*—don't belong here. If we want to stay here, we *have* to stop damaging everything around us. No excuses."

"Denying our nature." Her frown deepened, as if I'd given her a difficult puzzle. "You want us to become something other than what we are."

"Humans do it all the time, every day. They make themselves *better*. Demons can do it, too." On a sudden impulse, I reached out and caught her hands. Energy tingled under my fingers, but she was strong enough to keep it to herself, and I was careful not to pull. "You can do it, Madness. All you'd have to do is learn to hold your power in check, like Whisper does."

"Like you do."

"I...need to get better at that." I grimaced. "But yes. Like I do most of the time."

"But sometimes it hurts the humans when I only look at them." Her power stirred against my mind again. "The way I'm looking at you now."

"Then don't look at them," I urged her. "Go somewhere far away from humans—an island in the sea, a lonely tower—and teach yourself not to look at them." This wasn't the plan *at all*. I was supposed to be trapping her here inside the wards, not convincing her to run away where we'd have no chance to capture her. But some long and tangled history that lay unknown beneath the glassy surface of my mind insisted that I could save her, could salvage her, and demanded that I try. "Take a hundred years if you have to. However long you need to make yourself safe for others."

A smile broke across her face, brilliant as the rising of the sun. "Like you did."

A grassy alpine meadow, stirred by wind that had come rolling all the way from the sea. The sunshine pouring over me; the fluttering of tiny yellow butterflies, so peaceful. I sat cross-legged, holding my breath, straining to contain myself inside this tiny human shell. The moment I slipped—the second my grip faltered—the wind would rise, the lightning would fall around me in its wrath, the ground would tremble and break open, the fires would kindle deep within the earth and all through the wooded slopes below me. As had already happened again and again.

I shuddered. "Yes. Like I did. But your control is better than mine, and I'll bet you could learn a lot faster."

Madness nodded, grave and determined. "That's what I'll do."

"Good." Graces help me, I'd made a mess of this. I could only hope that she'd follow through, and this would all be worth it.

"I think I should do that in here, though, or Nightmare will get lonely."

I blinked at her in confusion. She was holding something out to me—a pendant dangling a single golden key, exquisitely wrought with artifice wire and engraved with runes, sparkling with gemstones.

I didn't reach for it. "How did you—"

Madness laughed and tapped her temple. "Of course I knew."

"But if you knew—if you knew I wanted to trap you . . ."

"You didn't want to trap me." Her smile had gone warm and kind and wise; the cobwebby brush of her power wrapped around me like a blanket. "You were going to do it if you had to, but you didn't *want* to. I understand, Disaster—Ryx. They're your friends, too, and they're so fragile. More fragile than I am. You have to protect them."

"Yes," I said vaguely, still shocked. She took my hand, turned it upward, and hooked the key pendant over it, careful not to let the key itself touch me. "But . . . I can't lock you in here with

Nightmare! If you're the only one in here with her, she'll turn on you, try to hurt you—"

"Oh, don't worry." Madness closed my fingers around the pendant chain and released my hand. "Nightmare can't hurt me; she doesn't understand me. I frustrate her. She is the mirror, and I am the light."

"Still—"

"Just come visit me." She patted my head, her palm flat like a small child petting a dog. "Even if we can only talk through the wards. I miss you."

I swallowed. "I will."

"Your friends care about you," she said seriously. "They're afraid of you, but they care. I can't help you against Nightmare, because she's my sister, too, but you should keep them."

"It's up to them whether I can keep them," I said, an ache in my chest that had nothing to do with my scars. "But I can at least try to keep them safe."

Madness nodded, wisps of pale hair bobbing beside her serious face. "Go," she said. "Just don't forget me this time."

"I won't," I promised.

For an awkward moment, I thought maybe I should hug her—but no, she was a pure demon, with no human feelings all mixed up in her like I had. That wasn't what she wanted. So instead I closed my eyes and relaxed my guard for a moment and let her hesitant touch mold around the edges of my mind like a handclasp. The tickly buzz of her power flared up, then subsided into a softer hum.

At last I opened my eyes and pulled away.

"Thank you," I whispered. "I'll be back."

I strode hurriedly away before I could change my mind, so quickly the grass only had time to brown at the tips beneath my footsteps. Halfway across the great expanse of lawn, I hesitated and looked back over my shoulder.

Madness still stood there beneath the tree, forlorn in her silver gown as the shadows deepened toward twilight all around her. She lifted her hand and gave me a little wave.

"You're right, Grandmother," I whispered. "I *am* a monster."

I waved back for a good long moment.

Then I turned, holding the key carefully away from my body, and went to find the Rookery.

THIRTY-EIGHT

S he just *gave* it to you?" Kessa pushed her jaunty hat back on her forehead the better to stare at me in shock.

I didn't know how to explain to her that I felt worse about leaving Madness locked up with Nightmare than I had about the possibility of killing Aurelio. Or that I suspected Madness would give me anything I asked for, which was why I hadn't actually asked at all, in the end. Or that she was my sister. None of it made enough sense to put into words.

So I said, "Yes," and left it at that.

Foxglove picked up the key from the table where I'd laid it and gave me a long, steady stare. "I'm still not comfortable with you being a demon."

"That makes two of us."

He grunted. "Fair enough."

There was so much more I could have said, beginning with *I'm not comfortable with you having threatened to kill me* and going on through *I'm sorry I lied to you* all the way to *Please help me, what in the Nine Hells do I do about this.* But now wasn't the time.

"We've been spreading the word through the palace to be ready to evacuate, in anticipation of your stunning success." Kessa managed a semblance of her old grin. "Well, or someone's stunning success. Our backup plan involved explosions, pick-pocketing, and a supporting cast of various domestic and wild animals, and to be honest it may have been a bit overdone."

"*May* have been?" Severin muttered.

Kessa ignored him. "At any rate, the majordomo's got the housekeeping and kitchen staff helping organize everyone, and I think we should be able to get them out fairly quickly, but there are two problems."

"The first," Foxglove said, gathering himself, "is that I haven't finished altering the wards. It's close, and I've left the area around the main doors for last, so we won't have to split up to cover two locations and can start evacuating people while I complete the changes."

"Let me guess," I said heavily. "The second is Nightmare."

"All right, three problems." Foxglove started pacing, his cane clicking in time to his steps. "We've also got everyone under the effects of the quicksilver, which includes the entire royal guard."

Kessa straightened. "Oh! I've been sort of testing out how gullible the silvering makes them. If you tell them something is the queen's orders with enough confidence, and it's plausibly the sort of thing a guard might do in the normal course of their duties, they'll usually just do it. They're very suggestible. I think I can get them outside the palace, at least; I'll tell them to take up guard positions out front."

Foxglove frowned. "Excellent, but what happens after that?"

Bastian straightened from where he'd been hunched in a corner, like a crumpled leaf slowly resuming its original shape. "So far as I can tell, the silvering effect requires the sustained influence of Madness's magic." His voice started out rusty, as if he hadn't used it for a while, but gained strength as he warmed to his topic. "If we get them outside the palace and raise the wards, that should be cut off—half the point of the alterations we've been making is to keep magical energy inside. They won't be under the demons' control anymore, though they may suffer lasting effects from a prolonged time under demonic influence." His throat bobbed in a nervous swallow. "Of course, that's true of all of us."

Kessa gave her hat a tug. "Right. So we've just got to watch out for Madness or Nightmare giving them different orders before we get them out."

"Madness won't intervene." That much I was sure of. "Nightmare, on the other hand, is bound to notice that we've brought the wards down and are taking all her toys away."

"But you can take care of her, right, Ryx?" Ashe flashed me a smile that suggested she knew she was being a brat.

I stared at her. "Ashe, it's putting it lightly to say I have not come out on top in most of my interactions with Nightmare."

Bastian gave an awkward shrug. "To be fair, you did seem to deal with Hunger and Madness quite well."

On the one hand, it was nice to hear them discussing me as an asset rather than a problem. On the other hand, I could see some of them on the brink of deciding I was their friendly pet demon who would handle the other demons for them, and that was a dangerous line of thought for several reasons, not least that I couldn't actually do it.

I shook my head. "Madness *chose* to give me that key. Hunger... He picked the wrong way to challenge me, out of arrogance. All he had to do was stay out of arm's reach and I couldn't have done anything to him at all. Nightmare, on the other hand, doesn't like me *and* she's no fool. My only advantage against her is that it's hard for her to do much to me directly, but that just means she'll come after all of you."

Foxglove paused his pacing, seeming to chew that over for a moment. At last, forming the words as if he disliked the taste of them, he asked, "Can you at least hold her off while we get everyone out of the palace? If her best defense is to stay out of arm's reach, you could stand in a doorway and block her."

"You can't just throw Ryx in her path and wish her luck," Severin objected.

"No, it might work," I said. Nightmare's powers didn't seem to work well on me without a boost from Madness or quicksilver, and if I could keep her far enough away from my friends, it'd be harder for her to use them against me.

"I know it's not fair to ask you to do this." Foxglove dropped his eyes. "Not after last night. But I can't think of any other way. Your touch is the only weapon we've found that seems to so much as give them pause."

It was a risk. But everything we'd done since setting foot in this accursed place had been one long series of calculated risks.

"All right," I said. "I'll see what I can do."

It didn't take long to find Nightmare, because she came looking for me.

I'd barely set out to find her after the Rookery confirmed they were ready to start the evacuation, with everyone in position, the guards cooperating, and designated helpers for those who might have trouble moving quickly. Even Severin's animal helpers were ready to go. I'd left them in the grand entry hall by the main palace doors and only made it halfway through the Jewel Rooms on my way toward the royal wing.

Nightmare came striding toward me through the Sapphire Room in a fury, eerie blue light falling across her face, gown rustling like dead leaves blowing down a dark road. The oppressive wave of power that came with her sent me rocking on my feet, gasping for breath.

"*You*," she snarled.

Shadows swarmed at the edges of my vision, reaching for me. I planted my feet in front of the door that led onward to the

Emerald Room, steadying myself against the crushing weight of her wrath. "Nightmare."

"First you kill my humans." It took me a moment to realize she meant the Zenith Society; best not to argue with her about who, if anyone, they belonged to. "Then you do *something* to Hunger that makes him run off into the hills without even saying good-bye."

"Hunger's gone?" I interrupted. Curse it, that meant we wouldn't catch him in the wards—though I couldn't help a conflicted flash of relief that I wouldn't have to entomb Aurelio with the demons.

"Don't act surprised," Nightmare hissed. "I know you drove him off. You and Discord have been trying to split us apart because you're afraid of what we could do together."

A spark of anger drove off my caution. "No, because you're both selfish fools with no regard for—"

"*I am not done.*" The room darkened, the blue lights flickering low, the sparkle dimming from the false jewels scattered in the ceiling. "Now I've just come from Madness, asking why she let Hunger go, and she's acting even stranger than usual—a feat I wouldn't have thought possible. She told me she wouldn't play my games anymore. This is your doing, too, isn't it?"

"Did she tell you that?" A fierce warmth bloomed in my chest, driving out the crushing dread of Nightmare's presence. "I'm proud of her."

"You're poison." Disgust infused her voice. "You and Discord both. Since you debased yourselves by merging with *humans*, everything you do is tainted. I'd strip this mortal corruption from you if I could."

"But you can't." It was a genuine relief, even if I said it to keep her talking. The majordomo had thought the evacuation should only take a few minutes, but each second stretched agonizingly long with Nightmare's animosity gathering around me like the coming of night.

"Yes, I can't." Her voice took on an ominous resonance, dropping all pretense of humanity. "So instead, I'll take advantage of it. I'm going to savor your suffering all the more for what you've done."

Time to redirect *that* line of thought. I couldn't let her attention turn to my friends. All my instincts screamed to run away from her rising wrath, but instead I stepped toward her.

"You made a mistake when you forced me to remember who I was." I shaped my voice into ice and iron, willing myself to believe my own threats enough to have them ring true. "As Hunger learned. Now I know that I have nothing to fear from you."

As I said it, something white flashed in the corner of my eye: the bright tail wedges of a mockingbird flitting past, sailing over our heads near the high vaulted ceiling of the chamber, from one window to another. Severin's first signal—the palace was evacuated. For a moment, my heart lifted with hope.

But Nightmare threw back her head and laughed. "Oh, little sister. Don't lie to me about fear. I *know* your fears; I drink them up like nectar."

Deep in her eyes, purple sparks kindled and began to grow. The glittering jewels in the ceiling reflected those tiny pinpricks of violet light, as if the Sapphire Room itself stared at me with a hundred malevolent eyes.

Seasons have mercy. All those false sapphires—they were blue glass backed with tiny mirrors. She couldn't have designed a better trap on purpose, and I'd walked straight into it.

"Your mind may be demonic enough to be resistant," Nightmare hissed, the glow spreading from her eyes to surround her in a jagged purple nimbus, "but your body is still human. And your heart—your heart is *riddled* with weakness."

Whatever she was building up to, I didn't want to find out. I launched myself toward her. I couldn't pull her out of her body like I had with Hunger and Kessa, because the only other possible hosts in the palace right now were my friends, but I could hurt her enough to break her concentration.

My fingers were inches from her face when her power hit me with the roaring force of a great ocean wave crashing down on the shore. Every muscle in my body went limp at once, and I fell into soft, suffocating darkness.

possible hosts in the palace right now were my friends, but I could later gain enough to break her concentration.

My fingers went numb from her icy wind. I lowered my face with the roaring force of a great ocean wave crashing down on the shore. Everything within me gave a lurch at once, and I fell into soft, suffocating...

THIRTY-NINE

I was back in the burning ballroom, beside the great crack that ran down its center. Violent orange flames licked greedily up to the ceiling, consuming the painted Graces dancing there. All around me, human bodies sprawled in their court finery, unmoving even as the flames crept across them.

Nightmare stood before me, smiling.

"This is how I know that you're powerless against me." She spread her arms, embracing the scene of death and destruction. "This is your greatest fear—your own strength. And thus your foolish human heart curtails all of your potential, rendering you useless." Her lips curved wider. "Except, of course, as a source of satisfaction for me."

It didn't help to tell myself that the corpses all around me weren't real, that no one had died in the ballroom. I knew damned well that people had died other times.

"Having restraint doesn't make me useless," I said through my teeth. "I've accomplished plenty. You're the one who doesn't do anything but torture people for your own amusement."

"Speaking of which." Nightmare rubbed her hands. "Last time we were here, I was playing out a lovely little scene for you, but it got interrupted. Madness has refused to control humans for me anymore, but I don't need her. Your friends are quite capable of tormenting each other on their own."

Alarm spiked through my veins; Nightmare drew in a sharp, savoring breath, as if she could taste it.

"Leave them out of this," I said.

"Oh, I don't think so. Let's see." She narrowed her eyes, and the scene around us blurred and rippled.

I still stood on cracked marble in the burning ballroom, flames raging around me and bodies piled at my feet. But to my left stretched a moonlit forest, the clean scent of pine overwhelming the smell of smoke.

Bastian huddled on the forest floor, his back against a boulder, hunched over his hand. His breath came harsh and fast, and he couldn't quite muffle a whimper of pain.

It was truly him, not an illusion. I wasn't sure how I knew, but he felt more solid and real than the ballroom, the forest, or even Nightmare herself.

I started toward him instinctively. "Bastian!"

He didn't seem to hear me. He cradled his hand to his chest in horror as long claws sprouted from each finger, dripping a clear venom, and scales crept up his arm.

I whirled on Nightmare, furious. "Leave him alone."

"Shh." She lifted a finger to her lips, eyes sparkling. "We haven't even gotten to the good part yet."

The snap and crackle of people moving through dry leaves and brush spun me back toward the forest. Beyond Bastian's rock, in the distance, a party of well-armed people moved with lethal grace through the trees, scanning the darkness around them as if looking for something. Ashe's pale shock of hair shone at the front. Answer gleamed unsheathed in her hand.

She was real, too. Blood of the Eldest, this wasn't good.

"It's close," an older woman beside her snapped. "Keep your eyes out. Remember, we've got to kill this one quickly; its venom is deadly."

Bastian closed his eyes and bit his lip to stop a cry as jagged spikes burst from his shoulder, ripping through his burgundy jacket.

"Ashe, no!" I shouted, but she didn't hear me, either. I tried to move toward her, but something stopped me—an invisible and unconquerable resistance in the air, keeping me out of the scene.

"You're wondering how real this is," Nightmare said from beside me, conversationally. She was too close, her arm almost touching mine, setting my skin to prickling with revulsion. "And the answer is that it's as real as I want it to be."

Bastian's whole body shook; he doubled over as the scales crept across his face. Horns punched bloody holes in his brow and began growing in sharp, lethal curves.

I lunged at Nightmare, fury in my hands—but she vanished before I touched her. I tripped on a dead body and barely kept my feet—oh holy Graces, it was Odan. *No, don't look.*

"There's more," Nightmare whispered, her breath stirring my ear, standing on my other side now. "Look."

The other side of the ballroom had changed, too. Opposite the forest sat the drawing room of an elegant Raverran apartment, its luminaries dim and flickering with the lateness of the hour.

A boy of perhaps sixteen lay sprawled on the floor in a pool of blood, unmistakably dead. He had Kessa's black hair and sweet round face. Foxglove stood over him, head bowed, a bloody knife in his hand.

"Don't you dare," I whispered.

Nightmare only laughed.

The door flew open; Kessa stood there, face pale, eyes wide with horror. She looked from Loren's corpse to Foxglove and let out a terrible scream of rage and despair. Foxglove flinched, but didn't move.

"Kessa," he began, his voice hoarse, but he couldn't seem to continue.

There was suddenly a pistol in Kessa's hands. She raised it to point at Foxglove's chest, hands shaking. A shadow covered his face, like a mask—she couldn't see who he was.

Nightmare put her arm around my shoulders. "If somehow they manage not to kill each other, I can make them play this out again and again until they do," she murmured. "I'd be delighted to prolong the experience."

My hands trembled with the urge to draw my knife and stab at her face, but she wasn't really there. I could feel the insubstantiality of her, much as I could almost see light shining through the apartment, as if it were a scrim.

"There it is!" a voice behind me shouted. I whirled to see Ashe charging at a now unrecognizable Bastian, who let out a terrible animal howl from a muzzle full of fangs.

"No!" I screamed.

Time slowed to a horrific dreamlike crawl. Ashe leaped with agonizing slowness over a fallen log, hanging in the air for a seeming eternity. Kessa's face twisted with grief as her thumb lifted to pull back the hammer.

Nightmare grinned at me. "Which of them will kill the other first? Would you care to place a bet?" She licked her lips. "The winner gets to play Severin's father in the next act, and kill him or be dismembered."

My whole body trembled with rage. But I had to think clearly, in this frozen moment, despite the torrent of fear and anger pouring through me. This wasn't real; everything but the Rookery was illusion. I had to tear off the shroud Nightmare had cast over my mind to stop them from killing each other in the real world.

The urge to try to run toward my friends was overpowering. But Nightmare's magic only worked on me because the mirrors in the Sapphire Room amplified it.

I turned from Nightmare and ran away.

"Do you think you can escape watching so easily?" Nightmare

laughed. She still hovered beside me, ghostlike; the terrible scenes still inched toward their fatal conclusions, slow as ice melting. I wasn't opening any distance from them; my running took me nowhere, like in a bad dream. "I would never let you miss this. Your anguish is too beautiful."

She'd grown transparent around the edges, and the forest and ballroom and apartment were fading like mist in the morning sun.

"Our pain isn't yours to feed on," I growled through my teeth.

With a desperate surge of effort, straining at the fading shadows of the dream around me, I shook Nightmare's touch off and forced myself awake.

I drew in a gasp as if I hadn't been breathing. I swayed on my feet in the grand entry hall, before the rune-graved arch of the closed palace doors.

Severin curled on the floor, one lock of hair dangling over his face; Kessa stood near him, with the slack stance of a sleep-walker, her eyes closed and a pistol pointed at Foxglove. Bastian leaned against a marble column, head bowed, tears streaming down his mercifully human cheeks from between closed lids as Ashe shambled toward him, sword in hand. They'd been here the whole time; Nightmare had woven them into her illusion, and my thwarted dream-running had brought me to them after all.

There was no sign of Nightmare. Hells take her—she wasn't even in the room.

I scanned the hall, heart pounding—*hurry hurry hurry*—and spotted Bastian's satchel lying not far from him. I ran to it and rummaged in it with desperate hands.

You think unraveling my power over you will help? Nightmare's voice taunted me, echoing silently in my mind. *You can't touch*

*them without killing them. You can't save them. All you're missing is the
full dramatic effect.*

My fingers touched round frames of metal and smooth glass.
Without pausing to so much as breathe a prayer to the Graces
who'd banished me, I yanked the Verdi's Glasses from Bastian's
satchel, slapped them to my eyes, and glanced quickly around
the hall.

For a couple of fleeting seconds, I had a strange double vision,
tinted green and red. The runes around the palace doors glowed
with a steady gold light, reaching out to form a network of
power through the palace walls. Bastian's satchel was a jumble
of colors, as was a string of lights glowing like stars around Foxglove's belt. A few other glimmers shone here and there as well.

What I cared about, however, were the snaking tendrils of
glowing purple smoke that reached through a door on the far
side of the hall and wrapped around my friends. I marked their
location as my hands tingled and the lights faded, the glasses
going dead as I dissolved their magic.

I leaped to my feet, sensing Nightmare's bemusement—she
knew nothing about artifice, nothing about magical theory, and
still didn't understand—and ran toward Kessa first. Trying to recall
exactly where I'd seen the shifting purple lines of power, I jumped
in their path and waved my arms around. *Please let this work . . .*

A heady rush of power swarmed into me. Kessa let out a horrified cry and dropped the pistol, leaping back as if it were a
snake; she stumbled and fell, blinking the last of the sleep from
her eyes.

"Thank the Graces," I whispered, and never mind that a
demon did that.

I turned without a word of explanation and sprinted over to
Ashe next, who had raised her sword over Bastian's cringing
head. More wild flailing, another swelling influx of magic, and
Ashe shook herself like a wet dog and unleashed a withering
series of snarling curses.

I see what you're doing now, Nightmare's voice sounded in my head, seething with anger. *But I assure you, it won't save them. I'll simply have to come kill them myself.*

"Pox," I breathed, and ran to wake Foxglove next.

"Ryx, what's happening?" Ashe demanded, keeping Answer out as she scanned the hall.

"Nightmare's on her way here." I turned to Foxglove as he blinked awake with a shudder. "How close are you to done with the wards?"

"I…" He stared around the room, his eyes landing on Kessa. He pushed a hand over his face, took a deep breath, and reached for the tools at his belt. "I just have to do the final runes. I'll finish it now."

Bastian and Severin rose on their own even as Foxglove started across the wide hall toward the door. Nightmare must have released them, which meant she had other things on her mind, which meant—

A sense of doom came over me in a heavy cloud. Two glowing violet eyes appeared in the shadowy doorway that led to the Jewel Rooms.

"Look out!" I cried.

Nightmare stepped into the room, and all the air seemed to leave it.

Foxglove's bad leg faltered beneath him; Kessa caught his arm to steady him. They both froze at the touch, exchanging an instant's panicked, pained look. Severin let out a soft curse at the crushing dread that filled the room with Nightmare's presence, and Bastian turned a sickly sort of pale mauve.

"I'm afraid the time for nuance is past," Nightmare said, her voice full of inhuman resonance and edges, and lifted her hand.

Ashe didn't wait to see what she'd do. She leaped at Nightmare, swinging Answer in a vicious arc at her midsection.

Her sword rebounded off the air half an inch from Nightmare's skin, once and twice as she aimed the next stroke at her neck. Immediately, a crescent of purple light flashed at Ashe like a return sword stroke, opening a bloody gash along her ribs.

Ashe staggered backward, clutching her arm to the wound and cursing.

"Ashe!" Kessa cried, starting toward her at once.

Nightmare's smile spread wide. "Didn't Disaster tell you? Death severs; Hunger devours; I reflect." She glanced at the bleeding Ashe. "As for your second strike, shall I send it where it will hurt you most?"

She lifted a hand and pointed at Kessa.

"*No!*" Ashe cried, raw panic in her voice, and lunged at Nightmare. I moved, too, hoping to throw myself in the way, but I was too far.

Foxglove was closer. As another arc of scything purple light flew from Nightmare's fingertips, he pushed Kessa out of its path, blocking her with his body. Instead of hitting her in the stomach, it slashed into Foxglove's thigh. My insides lurched sickeningly at the sound of tearing flesh.

He dropped to the floor, gasping in shock and pain.

Kessa started dragging Foxglove toward the doors, cursing at him and crying, leaving a trail of blood across the marble as he struggled and failed to help her. Bastian grabbed his satchel and ran toward them both. And Nightmare—Nightmare raised her hand again, eyes fixed on the three of them.

I jumped between them, my arms spread wide. "It's me you're angry at," I challenged her. "It's me who keeps thwarting you."

"And it's you I'm trying to hurt," she snapped, swiveling around to point toward Ashe.

Severin leaped at Nightmare and grabbed her arm, forcing it up. My heart caught in my throat; they were face-to-face, far too close, and I didn't like the smile curving Nightmare's lips at all, or the way her gaze lit up with something like hunger as she met his eyes.

"Oh, it's you, my beautiful wreck," she breathed. "Come for more suffering?"

"Always," he agreed. "I don't know when to stop."

There came the horrible, too-loud cracking of bone. Nightmare let out a terrible scream and fell to her knees.

"How...?" she gasped. "You're not a Skinwitch! Your power shouldn't work on humans!"

"You, my lady, are not human," Severin said coldly. And the vicious *crack* of breaking bones came again and again, as he held her hand. My nerves cringed to hear it.

She jolted with the force of each snap, her arms twisting, her back arching, mouth wide with shock—no. Oh, holy Hells, that was a *smile*.

A shiver of magic rippled over her. Impossibly she rose to her feet, legs bent in all the wrong places.

"Oh, little one, little lovely pet," she said caressingly, her head hanging at a horrific angle. "You have made such an awful, awful mistake."

FORTY

Severin's eyes widened. He stepped back, trying to tug his hand away, but she wouldn't let go.

My insides turning to ice, I ran toward both of them. "Don't you touch him, Nightmare! Don't you—"

Snap. In a flash of violet light, Severin's wrist jerked, and he cried out in pain.

"So many ways to break you," Nightmare crooned.

Rage boiled up in me, craving release. I stumbled midstride at the overwhelming surge of power that came with it.

No. I throttled it down, without hesitation or mercy. I couldn't let my magic loose here, with my friends all around me. But by the Hells, I could rip at her energy with my bare hands until she unraveled completely.

"Let's see," Nightmare purred, "lots of bones in your lovely hands. Shall I break those? Or crack your skull and let Disaster watch you die?"

Before I could reach her, the air behind her blurred. Suddenly she flipped backward to the ground, thrown by a smear of vaguely Bastian-shaped colors, landing with a sickening crunch. A drift of pale powder rained down on her from a bag that flashed into sight for just a moment—and her dress burst into flame.

The ripple that was Bastian streaked away from her; Severin scrambled back, clutching his arm. I had to stop myself from reaching for him, without any idea whether he was braced for my touch. Fear clutched at my belly—for my injured friends, but even more, because the last thing we wanted to do was damage Nightmare's body badly enough that she decided to forsake it for another.

Lying there in her flames, Nightmare began to laugh.

Slowly, all unnatural hitches and unhealthy angles, she gathered herself, still burning, and rose.

"Oh, little humans, this has been a delightful game." Her voice was the hissing of the fire, the scrape of bone shards. "But it's time for it to end now."

Her entire body began to emit a violet glow; her eyes blazed with purple light. As the others dropped back, I stepped in front of them, ready to try to take the brunt of whatever was coming.

"Done!" Foxglove called behind me. "Out, out, *out*!"

With a terrible crunching sound, Nightmare's neck pulled straight, and an arc of violet light flew toward us.

I flung myself in front of it, heart racing, braced for pain as everyone else scrambled for the door. The light hit my chest—and dissipated into me with a shiver of harmless energy.

Thank the seasons. I could keep doing this.

Nightmare's arms jerked straight, and several more violet blades spun my way; I leaped at them, arms flung wide, and all but two splashed against me in tingling waves of magic. Behind me, Kessa let out a yelp, but it didn't sound too serious.

Nightmare's face twisted in a furious snarl. The violet glow around her intensified until I could barely make her out within it.

"Do you truly think you can protect them?" Her voice echoed with portent and power. "Do you think you can keep them safe? You're a far greater danger to them than I *ever* could be!"

The shadows in the corners writhed beneath Nightmare's dancing violet light, and at last I could make out the shapes they were trying to form. Heaps and piles of human bones, a mountain of them, an ocean—the scattered, broken skeletons of all the people I'd killed.

Holy Hells. There must be thousands of them.

I froze in front of the door. The sheer enormity of my crimes crushed the breath from my lungs as if all those bones cascaded down upon me in a landslide great enough to bury the palace.

"Ryx!" Kessa called, pain edging her voice. "Get out! We need to close the wards!"

If I stepped through that door, I carried the seeds of catastrophe with me. The violet-tinged heaps of bones stretched away in looming ghostly mounds, empty skulls staring accusingly.

"I won't blame you if you ward me in here, too, while you have the chance," I called, without looking over my shoulder. I couldn't deny the simple, practical logic of it. I was a demon, after all, and one of the most dangerous of the Nine. "Eruvia might be safer that way."

"Get out here," Foxglove growled. "Safer or not, we need you."

You know I'm right, Nightmare gloated in my mind. *You're the worst monster of us all, the greatest killer. Stay here with me and suffer for what you've done. It's no more than you deserve.*

Anger lit a clear candle flame in my chest, burning away the violet haze. I might accept that from a human, from anyone I'd wronged, but never from her.

"What would suffering accomplish?" I shook my head. "No. That's not how I atone."

Humanity needed all the help it could get; if they wanted me in this fight, I wasn't taking myself out of it. I stepped back toward the door.

A firm hand closed on my belt from behind. "I'm not leaving you this time," Severin murmured in my ear.

Nightmare let out a furious cry and unleashed all the energy she'd been building up; violet radiance coursed toward me in a massive, overwhelming wave. Severin yanked on my belt, and I toppled back through the door onto the hard stone of the palace steps.

Light blazed up around me—but it was gold, not purple. *The wards.*

Kessa stood before the doors, key uplifted and glowing; the runes that ringed the doorway blazed with golden light. All along the palace walls, they kindled—around each of the hundreds of windows, around every balcony and door, and along every edge of the roof, lines of runes blazed with a steady, powerful glow. The painstaking, intricate work of human hands and human magic, strong enough to hold back the wrath of a demon.

With a rippling blur, Bastian slammed the door shut in Nightmare's face.

Ashe collapsed to her knees on the paving stones before the palace doors; Kessa threw her arms around her with a cry. I wished I dared do the same to Severin, who cradled his wrist with a strained look and stared warily at the palace. Foxglove's gaze stayed riveted on the glowing runes around the door as well, as he pressed both hands to his wounded leg.

"Will it hold?" I whispered.

A long moment slipped by with nothing but ragged breathing from the six of us. At last, Foxglove let out a relieved sigh.

"For now," he concluded.

"Let's get you all patched up," Bastian said worriedly—or the human-shaped space where the colors of the palace blurred into strange dimensions did. "Kessa, did you get my bag?"

As she handed it to him, Severin offered Bastian a curt bow, with the stiff awkwardness of an atheling acknowledging a debt. "Thank you. If you hadn't taken Nightmare down when you did, I would have been in a very bad situation."

"I suppose being a chimera has its occasional advantages after all." The blur of Bastian-shaped colors moved toward Foxglove, satchel swinging as if in midair, but paused. "And, apparently, its disadvantages. Oh dear. I, ah, left my clothes in there. I don't suppose..."

"Here." Severin immediately began fumbling at his vestcoat fastenings one-handed.

"Let me." I waited until he nodded to be sure he was ready, then stepped in and began undoing the frogs for him, revealing a widening triangle of silky white shirt beneath. The warmth of his chest made my fingers fumble and burned away the last vestiges of the horror Nightmare had shown me from my thoughts.

"Are *you* all right?" he asked me, his voice low. "You were half dead last night."

"I'm fine—really, I mean it this time." I suppressed a shiver. "I haven't felt this good in days. I...I think I took in a lot of energy from Hunger and from Nightmare's attacks. To be honest, it's a little creepy."

I glanced up at him, braced to find revulsion on his face, and instead was shocked to find the slightest hint of pink on his cheeks as he watched my hands on his chest. *Well, now.*

With Severin's vestcoat pulled around him, Bastian could resume his normal colors as he finished salving and bandaging Foxglove's wound. Kessa did the same for Ashe, making concerned noises while Ashe sat totally rigid, her expression swinging wildly between stoic endurance, softening wistful tenderness, and winces of pain.

Severin was staring at me. Hells, he was hurt, too, and I was just standing here. "I, uh, have no idea how to treat a broken wrist," I admitted. "Do you want me to—"

"No, I'll wait," he said quickly.

"It was good of you to jump in and save Ashe," I said, partly because I knew it would annoy him to call him good and partly because it was true.

He shook his head. "I thought I had a clever idea, that was all. It just wasn't clever enough."

I gave him a skeptical look. "Trying risky clever ideas to

protect people is dangerously close to genuine heroics, Severin. You'd better watch out."

"Ugh." He put on a scowl. "I'll have to work on that."

Foxglove's voice cut across whatever I might have said. "As soon as we're able to move, we need to get out of here. The evacuees and the Empire should be waiting down the road. It may not be safe here, and we've got work to do."

The Empire was indeed waiting down the road. It turned out they had a small army encamped out of sight around a shoulder of the hill, behind an alarming array of magical seals and bristling with artifice-worked cannons, complete with a dozen Falcons. They were already handling the hundreds of shocked and harrowed people evacuated from the palace, treating any injuries and loading them into wagons to ride the rest of the way down the hill to the town below.

The officer in charge of the encampment and an escort of Falcons awaited us in the road; as soon as we came into sight, she snapped some order that brought physicians running.

"Ryx," Foxglove said to me with quiet significance as we approached, his dignity unruffled even though Bastian had to help him limp along, "You'd better wait back here. I'll explain about your power and your jess being unsealed."

We exchanged a long gaze, and I nodded. "All right."

"Do you want me to stay with you?" Severin asked, eyeing the encampment skeptically. "Castle Ilseine was bad enough; I'm not really all that eager to walk into an on-edge imperial military encampment as a Vaskandran atheling."

"You need your wrist treated." I jerked my head sternly toward the camp. "Go. I'll be fine."

I settled on a lichen-covered rock some distance from the camp as the physicians and their assistants swarmed over the others, the officer welcoming them with a respectful salute. I wrapped my arms around myself against the wind and tried not to think about questions like when I'd last eaten, or how long it might be before anyone let me know whether my injured friends would be all right, or what Madness was doing right now. My eyes pulled against my will to the palace, its windows dark and empty. The charred roof of the grand ballroom showed like a ragged wound in its poised architectural majesty.

I had a good view of the wagons they were loading with evacuees from the palace to take down the hill, and it was a relief to spot familiar faces. Councilor Altaine rode down in one of the first wagons with other members of the Curia, already deep in an animated discussion about how best to continue government operations. The majordomo helped organize his staff, checking things off in a heavy notebook cradled in his arm. I spotted Girard, who'd broken with the Zenith Society in time to avoid dying with them in the shrine, talking seriously with an officer; he didn't seem to be heading for a wagon, and a soldier stood watchfully at his side. I supposed he might be under arrest; the Graces only knew what he'd done before he decided to draw the line.

The palace guards were among the last to get sent down the hill. The silver had left their eyes, the demons' influence severed when the wards went up, but they stumbled and blinked foggily as if waking up from a long, uneasy dream. I spotted Elia among them, looking dazed, the grizzled gray tomcat cradled contentedly in her arms. Finally the last wagon rolled away, and there was nothing to distract me from worrying about my injured friends.

As the sun descended behind the hills and cold shadows crawled across my rock and all the way down to the sea, Kessa came back out of the camp at last with a tray of food and hot tea for me. Her lovely brown eyes sat in exhausted hollows as she sank down on another rock nearby.

"They'll be fine," she said wearily. "They're taking care of Bastian's finger, too. They'll have a few new scars to tell dramatic stories about, and after two injuries to the same leg Foxglove might need that cane for a while, but everyone should recover."

"Thank the Graces," I said, without thinking, then winced. I'd gone all my life swearing by the Nine Graces and cursing by the Nine Demons, but now all those ingrained habits were terribly awkward. The Graces probably *hated* me.

Kessa took a long sip from the second cup of tea she'd brought for herself. The wind teased her loose dark hair into tangles.

"I've decided to stay with the Rookery after all," she said at last.

Relief broke over me in a warm wave. "I'm so glad. It wouldn't be the same without you."

"Our past is a whole mess of mistakes, and our mistakes together killed Loren." She wrapped both hands around her teacup, shoulders hunching over it. "His death is partly my fault, partly Foxglove's fault, but mostly the Zenith Society's fault. And if our mistakes that we made together led us to save Bastian from Cortissa and all join the Rookery—well, that's the one good thing that came out of the whole mess. I shouldn't spoil it."

"Those seem like very good things," I agreed. I wished I could look at my own terrible mistakes like that—by the good that came of them. It was hard to think of anything now, but maybe I could try.

"Mind you, I haven't forgiven Foxglove." She frowned. "I don't think he *wants* me to. But he's like family. Sometimes you can keep working with someone, and even keep loving them, without entirely forgiving them."

I thought of Madness, and my grandmother for that matter. "Yes." I took a long draft of tea to soothe my aching throat.

"I'm going to tell Foxglove he's still the leader and he doesn't get to step down, and that's that." She flashed me a grin that was a shadow of her usual one, but seemed real enough. "Except of course I'm going to use this to get my way whenever I really need to, for the rest of my life."

I laughed. It felt good; the horrible pall that had hung over all of us in the palace was lifting, and it was as if I'd been stuck in a cramped position for too long and could finally stretch my legs again.

Kessa tilted her head. "What do you think you'll do now? You've had quite the journey of discovery. I can only imagine your plans may have changed."

The question pierced straight to my core. I stared at her, stricken.

She must have seen something in my face, because she hastily added, "I'd love more than anything for you to stay with the Rookery, of course. I'm sure the others would, too. I just didn't want to assume."

I had no doubt she meant it. But she was also the Rookery's spy, and figuring out the plans of the Demon of Disaster was part of her job. I couldn't even blame her.

"I wish I knew what my plans were." I started unweaving my ragged braid, to give my hands something to do. I thought about it, sliding locks of hair through my fingers, combing them out so I could braid it all up again. It was a reassuring ritual— familiar, human. "I think," I said at last, "I know a way I can be useful."

Kessa snorted. "I know about a hundred ways you can be useful."

The idea caught and blossomed, like a seed in fertile soil. "No, I think I know what I need to do. The same thing I've always done."

Her brow furrowed. "You're going back to Gloamingard Castle?"

"I don't mean acting as Warden." I tied up my braid and flipped it back over my shoulder with a new confidence. "I mean acting as a bridge between worlds. I've done this my whole life—smoothing over relations between Vaskandar and the Serene Empire, turning enmity into alliance, reconciling clashing cultures and worldviews."

Kessa's eyes widened. "You want to be an *ambassador to the Nine Hells*?"

"Or from them." I grimaced. "The point is, the demons will talk to me. And after everything that happened in the palace, it's pretty clear that's useful. I can negotiate with them, distract them, or just stand in front of them if I have to—"

I broke off. Ancient words leaped into my mind, carved into weathered stone.

I stand before the light
And hold the dark at bay
I am the guard at the gloaming

"Between the darkness and the light," I muttered, feeling a twinge in my chest that had nothing to do with my scars.

Kessa didn't seem to notice any strangeness. She nodded enthusiastically. "Yes, I love it! You know I'm always in favor of solving our problems through diplomacy when we can. You can gather information for us, get a read on their intentions, maybe feed them a bit of misinformation from time to time… Pardon me, I'm thinking more like a spy than an ambassador." She grinned sheepishly. "I can't help it."

"That too." I hesitated. "I'd love to do that as part of the Rookery, if you'll all still have me. But I'll do it regardless."

"Of *course* you can still be part of the Rookery." Kessa visibly checked herself from reaching out toward me. "I know Foxglove has rather traditional ideas about demons, but he'll come around. He already has. You'll see."

I blinked at her. *Traditional ideas about demons.*

"Kessa," I said, speaking slowly around the aching lump that sat in my throat, "it can't be the same. Even if everyone agrees to let me stay. You know that."

She struggled with that a moment, turning her teacup in both hands. I could see how badly she wanted to tell me that it didn't matter what I was; the words started to form on her lips, silently, then died there.

"I suppose not," she said at last. Determination kindled in her eyes, and she wagged a finger at me. "But that just means we build something new—something better. You, me, Foxglove, all of us. Even your pretty witch boy."

She had so much hope on her face. I couldn't bring myself to tell her that it was my nature to destroy, not build; that no matter how hard I tried, I was bound to bring everyone around me to ruin eventually. I wished I could believe with her that this was something we could do, that it would end well.

Whisper's words came back to me: *As a human, you can do more.*

"We can try, at least." Maybe that would be enough.

"We have no idea how long the wards on the palace will hold." Foxglove stirred restlessly on his divan as if it irked him that he couldn't get up and pace. The imperial embassy in the harbor town had graciously let us use this sitting room once the encampment physicians declared Ashe and Foxglove safe to be moved, and had fed us and offered us beds for the night as well. "The Falcons are adding another ring of wards around the outside and doing what they can to shore up the power sources for the existing ones on the palace, but we simply don't know what the demons are capable of. If they have some way to circumvent or destroy them, there's not much we can do. But at least we've bought some time."

"Do we have any news of where Hunger went?" I asked. He was the one that worried me most, by far, now that Nightmare was locked up. There was no way he'd stay quiet and not cause trouble.

"No," Foxglove said. "Figuring out a way to deal with him is one of our top priorities."

I had to hope we could find a way to neutralize him that would set Aurelio free, to honor everything he'd done to help us. But if we *did* free him, it would be to immediately seize him and bring him back to Morgrain for justice—and given that it would be my grandmother's justice for her murdered daughter, honestly, he might be better off where he was. Or perhaps in a Raverran prison; that might be the best mercy he could expect, and the most he deserved.

"Bet I can guess the other top priorities," Ashe said. It was strange to see her lying down instead of perched in some corner like a vulture, but Kessa sat on the arm of the couch and ran her fingers through the short tufts of Ashe's hair, so she didn't seem to mind. "Hunger's just one of them." She held up nine fingers, then folded one down.

"About that." Foxglove picked up a glass of wine Kessa had left to hand for him, stared into it for a moment, and set it down again. Something about the slow deliberation of his movements sent a thread of tension running between my shoulder blades.

At last, he lifted his amber eyes to mine and held them. "I've made a report."

The whole room went still.

I nodded, keeping my face neutral despite my racing pulse. "I understand."

"Well that's good, because I assure you I don't." Kessa stood, fists clenched. "You told them? You told our superiors she's—" She faltered.

"The Demon of Disaster?" Foxglove let out a weighty breath. "Yes, I did."

"She's our *friend*!" Kessa protested, flinging an arm in my direction as if Foxglove might have forgotten who I was. "Do you have any idea what they'll do to her?"

I checked the response gathered on my tongue because I very much wanted the answer to that question, myself.

"I don't," Foxglove said quietly. "I can guess some possibilities, though, and I'm aware most of them aren't good."

Severin threw up his hands. "Then why did you tell them? Blood and ashes, man, use some discretion!"

"We're past the point of discretion," I put in sharply. "Lots of people saw what I did in that ballroom, and heard what Madness called me. Some of them will put it together. Please don't try to defend me; Foxglove did what he had to do."

Kessa crossed her arms, clearly still angry. "So what happens now?"

This time, Foxglove did take a drink, long and weary. "We go back to Castle Ilseine. Those are our orders." He turned to me. "But you're an atheling of Morgrain. No one can give *you* orders except your grandmother. So if you don't want to come with us, I can't make you."

I understood the implications of his careful phrasing. I could run from whatever the Council of Nine and the Conclave might have planned for me; I could disappear into the hills, or go home to Gloamingard. This was my chance to escape.

Everyone stared at me. I turned the idea over in my head, but it came down to one thing: I knew what I wanted to do, and running away wasn't it.

"I can best help humanity by working *with* our governments rather than hiding from them," I said at last.

"They're not going to want to work with you," Severin warned me.

"They never have. That hasn't stopped me in the past."

Urgency infused Foxglove's voice, his eyes intent. "They *asked* me to bring you back to Castle Ilseine. If you walk through its gates with us, I don't know what's going to happen."

"Do we have any reason to believe it's a trap?" I asked.

Ashe snorted. "Do we have any reason to believe it's not?"

"No to both," Foxglove said, shaking his head. "They wouldn't tell me anything. For what it's worth, they heaped praise on us for trapping Madness and Nightmare, and they implied they wanted to honor us when we get back home. So it's possible they just want to thank you, too." His flat tone made it clear he didn't believe that for a minute.

I took a deep breath. "There's only one way to find out."

FORTY-ONE

The return carriage trip to Castle Ilseine seemed to go far too quickly, even though in reality our driver took a more leisurely pace. I had my jess back, Severin's wrist bore a splint, Foxglove could hobble around with his cane again, and Ashe was up and mobile. "A little blood loss clears the head," she said. Bastian had insisted on complete removal of all vestiges of the claw Cortissa had given him, which had meant losing the last joint of his little finger, but he seemed in fine spirits.

Almost too fine. He kept asking me questions, with his little notebook out and his pencil scratching. I wanted to help, but some of them cut too close to home.

"Do you remember anything about how the Graces banished the Nine Demons back in the Dark Days?"

A woman's scream of agony and fury. Hills crumbling to dust, and the ocean rushing in.

"I . . . I'm trying not to remember too much." Sweat prickled on my temples.

"Oh, completely understandable. Please forgive me—you're the only primary source who's talking, so I have to learn whatever I can." Bastian tapped his pencil on the edge of his notebook. "How about you? Do you remember how you were banished?"

The bright-eyed young woman standing beneath stormy skies, wind playing with her hair as she gave me the saddest, most heart-piercingly meaningful look across four thousand years.

"No," I said hoarsely, and stared out the window.

When we stopped to change horses at an Imperial Post station, Severin drew me aside in the dusty stable yard.

"You're set on this, aren't you." He sounded resigned.

"If I run, I'm throwing away any chance that I can get the Council and the Conclave to trust me," I said reasonably. "I have to show I trust them first."

Severin put his hand to his forehead. "Please tell me you don't *actually* trust them."

"Well, no, but I have to make the gesture."

"That's something, anyway." He blew out a frustrated breath; his eyes strayed north, pulling toward Alevar like a lodestone. "I've been thinking about what I'll do."

That sounded ominous. Suddenly all I could think of was how much I didn't want him to leave. "Oh?"

"Not only am I my brother's heir, I'm the one who made him a Witch Lord in the first place. While I think duty as a concept is overrated, I do have responsibilities to my domain, which I can't ignore in a time of apocalypse." He sighed dramatically, as if the duties of an atheling were an annoying guest coming for tea. "My brother, as you know, is a bludgeoning instrument, diplomatically speaking. It's often been my job to mitigate damage he leaves behind him, and I'm forced to recognize that's not going to change."

My heart plunged, but I tried not to show it. "I understand if you need to go home. I'd want to go back to Morgrain, too, after almost losing it."

"What? No." His mouth twisted bitterly. "Even if my brother would take me back, I'm well rid of him. No, I was thinking I'd stick with you."

Relief washed over me. "I'm sure the Rookery will be glad

to hear it. We're going to need all the help we can get against Hunger."

"I didn't say the Rookery. I said *you*." His dark eyes wouldn't let go of mine. "If you stay with the Rookery, so will I. If you run, I'll run with you."

The moment went crystal clear: a horse blowing as busy grooms worked on harnessing it, the dust hanging in the sunlight, the whisper of the wind that ruffled trees in the distance before stirring Severin's hair. I could only stare at him as if I'd never seen him before.

"I could tell you it's because you're planning to do the same thing I need to do," he said. "Trying to build relationships that will keep our neighbors from backstabbing or sacrificing our domains, or demons from eating them—and that's true." He glanced away, the light catching scars on his temple. "But I'd be lying if I told you that was my only motivation."

For no cursed good reason, my eyes stung, and I was suddenly fighting back tears.

"You realize," I said, "that sticking to me is like tying yourself to a boulder and then pushing it off a cliff. I'm the—"

"Warden of Gloamingard, I know," he interrupted me. "Dreadful place. Too many bones, too dusty, could use some fresh paint—"

"Hey! Don't you say anything nasty about Gloamingard." I scowled at him even as my heart leaped.

"—but I'll follow you there if I have to," he finished, with a mock-aggrieved sigh. "Because you clearly need someone to keep you out of trouble, and I can't count on the Rookery to do it."

"Well, thank you, but I'm not sure you're going to have much luck keeping me out of trouble. I sort of have to seek it out to make this 'Ambassador to the Hells' idea work."

"Then you can keep *me* out of trouble." He grinned. "You're the only one who seems willing to try."

For his own sake, I should tell him to leave and never see me again. I should push him away, like my grandmother had done to protect Rillim when that spark bloomed between us, years ago. There was no way that anything between us could end well; he knew it, and I knew it.

Instead, I murmured, "Hard to keep you out of trouble when there's already so much trouble in you."

Somehow, the space between us had narrowed. His shadow cut off the rosy fingers of afternoon light that held us apart, and then I was tasting the road dust on the warmth of his lips. It was only a brief kiss, with people bustling around us in the busy stable yard—stolen quickly, full of anxious promise.

It was a kiss that said, *This is an absolutely terrible idea, but let's give it a try anyway.*

Castle Ilseine appeared on its hill at last, blunt and squat and practical, lined with cannons and runework, the weathered stones of an older keep rising up inside it and the sleek tower of the courier lamp spire spiking up above everything. The dark brooding stretch of forest to the north sank hooks in my heart and yanked: Morgrain.

The road split, and for one wild moment I wanted to yell at the driver to stop the coach so that I could jump out and run for that line of woods like a child running to her mother's arms. I could feel it tickling at my senses, the distant leaves murmuring my name as the wind rustled them.

But I'd already made my choice. If helping humanity against the demons was how I could best atone for what I'd done as one, well, I couldn't accomplish much skulking in my castle alone with my grandmother. Maybe, just maybe, if I could get the Serene Empire and the Witch Lords to listen to me, I could go home soon enough bearing terms for negotiation.

The sun had slipped below the hills and the sky softened into twilight by the time our carriage passed through the dark throat of the entry arch into the open central courtyard of the castle. Foxglove's family waited anxiously for him, and he climbed down first to meet them; Lia kissed him soundly, and Teodor wrapped his arms around him in a fierce hug. Foxglove returned their embraces slowly, hesitantly, like a man with too many aches to move with confidence.

I looked away, my own eyes stinging with foolish jealous longing, only to land on Kessa helping Ashe down from the carriage with a tender care that Ashe seemed to take great pleasure in gruffly brushing off. Bastian was already talking with a young scholarly Falcon stationed at the castle, excitedly comparing notes.

Of course they all had people waiting for them. They had human connections, because they were human.

I was the last one in the carriage, and I could hardly just sit here. I clambered for the open door—only to find Severin waiting at the foot of the carriage steps for me, hand extended, the shadow of a smile tugging at his lips.

He didn't have anyone here, either. Except me.

I returned his smile, sadness and all, and reached for his hand as I started down the narrow carriage steps.

"Excuse me," said a smooth, oddly familiar voice. "Exalted Ryxander?"

A tall, broad-shouldered, graceful man with spectacles and a neat brown ponytail stood respectfully by, his hands clasped behind his back. Everything about him defied categorization. He had Raverran features and accent but used my proper Vaskandran title; he held himself with the precise bearing of a soldier but wore no uniform; and he spoke with deferential respect but radiated the understated assurance of someone entirely comfortable in their own power. I'd never seen him before in my life.

"Yes?" I asked cautiously, climbing down from the carriage on my own as Severin let his extended hand drop casually to his side. I could feel the wariness coming off him.

The stranger offered a deep, controlled bow. "If you'll come with me, please, my lady."

Cold certainty coiled in my belly like a snake. This was it. If a trap waited at Castle Ilseine for me, this man was the baited hook.

Severin drew himself up and gave the stranger his best arrogant stare. "And who are you, to issue such an impertinent summons to an Exalted Atheling of Vaskandar?"

The stranger bowed again. "My name is Gaetano, and naturally for an atheling there can be no summons, only a respectful request." There was something familiar about that name, too. "Perhaps this will help clarify matters." He drew a shimmering object from his sleeve and showed me, swift and discreet: a stiff square of paper bearing a seal in opalescent blue alchemical wax, the kind that melted if the wrong person tampered with it. I squinted at the seal—the winged horse of Raverra rearing in a circle of nine stars.

The imperial seal, which only the doge and the Council of Nine could use, or those they directly designated. Holy Hells.

My mouth dry, I offered him a respectful nod. "Of course I accept your invitation."

Severin gave me an alarmed look, but his voice remained light and casual. "Shall I accompany you, then?"

"Forgive me, Exalted Severin of Alevar." Gaetano offered Severin yet another bow. "The invitation is for Exalted Ryxander alone."

That didn't bode well. Severin caught my eyes and gave a tiny shake of his head. *Don't trust him. Don't go.*

"Let the others know where I've gone," I told him lightly. Foxglove was occupied with his family, Kessa and Ashe with each other, and Bastian with the heady excitement of exchanging information; Gaetano's presence was so smoothly unobtrusive that I wasn't at all certain anyone would notice that I'd left, let alone who I'd gone with.

Severin gave a slow nod. "If you're sure."

I wasn't. "I am."

Gaetano turned with the precise swivel of a cage door closing. "Then if you'll follow me, Exalted Atheling."

To my surprise, Gaetano led me to the old keep at the heart of the fortress that was the Rookery headquarters. I followed him up the central winding stairs, past the levels I knew and had lived in for three weeks, all the way to the top floor, which I'd never seen and understood was kept locked. Foxglove had told me it was reserved for his superiors on the rare occasions when they visited the Rookery in person.

Oh. Oh pox. Now I remembered where I'd heard his name. Lady Cornaro's personal aide. Of course he had access to her chambers.

Gaetano paused on a broad landing, almost a simple anteroom, before an unassuming door at the very top of the central tower. Luminaries on the stairs had kindled awake at sunset, and their cold light picked out every detail in the rough old stonework but turned the windows to a mass of black and twilight purple. Gaetano opened the door and bowed, gesturing me through it.

No luminaries shone within; I blinked at the shadows, trying to adjust to the dimmer light. I could vaguely make out the indistinct bulks of furniture, the paler squares of windows, and a pair of figures waiting for me.

If this was a trap, it wasn't the sort of trap you could decline to spring. Hesitantly, my nerves taut as an overtuned string, I stepped into the room.

"Don't be alarmed," said a woman's voice, deep and rich with power. And at once I was very alarmed indeed.

A rune-scribed circle blazed into glowing life on the floor around me.

FORTY-TWO

My nerves tingled with the urge to flee, but I stood still as a spooked deer, wondering if the next thing I'd feel was a pistol ball through my heart.

"Apologies for the inconvenience, Exalted Atheling." Gaetano executed another flawless bow and slipped past my glowing circle to enter the room. "A simple security precaution; I'm sure you understand."

He touched the wall and luminaries flickered to life all around the room, bathing it in a warm golden glow.

A regal woman in her eighties occupied a chair by the fireplace as if it were a throne. Elegant gold pins held most of her white hair up, Raverran style; she wore an exquisitely cut jacket, brocade waistcoat, and tall boots rather than a gown. An obsidian and wirework brooch and an intricate artifice necklace suggested she was well protected even without Gaetano moving to stand attentively at her side. No mage mark graced her hazel eyes, but an aura of a different kind of power hung about her.

Just far enough away to be clearly not part of her entourage, the second figure I'd spotted in the shadows leaned against the mantel: a man in his thirties or forties, silver just beginning to touch his loose tumble of dark hair. He wore a short, plain vestcoat, with a serviceable-looking sword on one hip and a pistol on the other, and he would have been easy to overlook—almost too easy—if I didn't know the significance of the necklace of crow feathers and talons hanging on his chest. An emissary of the Crow Lord, then—one of the most influential of the nineteen Witch Lords, and the ultimate authority behind the Rookery on the Vaskandran side.

Apparently Foxglove's report had prompted a response from the very top.

I swallowed to wet my throat. "I understand."

Gaetano gestured toward the Vaskandran man. "This is Verinath, of the Crow Lord's Heartguard."

Blood of the Eldest, he was taking this seriously. The Heartguard were the Crow Lord's most trusted agents. He might equally be here to negotiate with the Crow Lord's full authority or to kill me with the backing of his full power. My skin prickled.

"I'm honored." I offered Verinath a respectful nod.

He returned it, more deeply; his fingers flicked subtly out from his chest in the warding sign. "Exalted. The Crow Lord would have come himself, but he's at the Conclave."

With my grandmother. Sweet seasons, that was bound to be a debacle. I tried to keep my expression polite and attentive.

Gaetano inclined himself toward the lady. "And may I present Lady Lucaria Cornaro, of the Council of Nine."

Holy Hells. I managed a bow, of the depth and duration I'd offer a Witch Lord. "Your—ah—Excellency? Forgive me, I don't know the correct address; I never expected to meet one of the Council of Nine."

She waved off all consideration of titles with a curt motion of her hand, her eyes fixed on me with piercing intensity. "And I never expected to meet one of the Nine Demons."

Something about the tone of her voice turned my blood thick and cold as slush. This wasn't going to be a mere polite exchange of greetings. They'd trapped me in a warding circle for a reason.

"You will doubtless be pleased to know that Foxglove made heroic efforts to convince us that you should be allowed to continue working with the Rookery." Lady Cornaro's even tone gave no hint as to whether she had in fact been convinced. "His report sparked quite a debate in the Council over what should be done with a nominally cooperative demon."

"I suspect your name has already come up at the Conclave as well," Verinath put in dryly.

This was my one chance to convince them to work with me. Possibly my one chance to convince them not to throw me in an artifice-sealed coffin and toss me in the ocean, too, but one thing at a time.

I took a deep breath. "There's a lot I can do to help. When we were in the palace, I distracted the demons and gathered information about their plans, but there's more." I had to think how to phrase this so they wouldn't reject the idea out of hand. "Some of the demons, like Hunger, will always be a problem and likely can't coexist peacefully with humankind. But there are others who I think can."

Verinath lifted a skeptical eyebrow. "Like you?"

Ouch. "Certainly. But some of the others as well. I think there's hope that we could work out some kind of terms that would let them stay in this world if they don't cause problems for humanity, and I'd be happy to help facilitate negotiations."

Lady Cornaro's eyes narrowed. "You realize that entering into agreements with demons is an axiomatically terrible idea."

"I know." They weren't going for this; their faces remained closed and wary. I pushed on, desperate. "A couple of weeks ago I'd have told you that anyone who made a deal with a demon was a fool at best and more likely flat-out evil, and deserved whatever ill fate they got. Now...well, I have no choice but to believe otherwise."

"I don't think you understand your situation." Lady Cornaro pressed her fingertips together. "Given the treachery of the

Zenith Society, the idea of working with *any* demon is even less popular than you might imagine. Currently, the Council is largely divided between those who wish to destroy or banish you, and those who wish to bring you back to Raverra to study you."

The whole world seemed to sink a few inches, as if another chasm had opened beneath my feet.

Verinath straightened away from the hearth, uncrossing his arms. "Stop right there. Exalted Ryxander is still an atheling of Vaskandar. You can't drag her back to Raverra and stick her in some research laboratory, even if she *is* a demon. I don't have to send a bird home for instructions to tell you the Witch Lords won't stand for that." His eyes flicked to me, and he gave me a sort of apologetic nod. "Killing her is another matter entirely. Sorry, Exalted, but you understand."

"I do." And I did, but I also wished very much I could sit down and put my face in my hands instead of standing in my glowing ward circle like a prisoner. I wished I had a cup of tea. I wished I could somehow make them understand about Madness, confused and earnest and horrifically dangerous, but ultimately teachable; or all my grandmother's difficult and mercurial complexities; or Whisper, elusive and untouchable and very much best left alone.

"It's too early to say what the Conclave will decide about you," Verinath said seriously, "but with two out of the Nine Demons tied to Morgrain, there are bound to be alliances forming already against your domain."

I drove my fingers up into the hair at my temples. "They need to leave Morgrain out of this."

Verinath's brows rose. "It's where the gate is. The Lady of Owls is a demon. It's impossible to leave it out."

"Listen to me." I took half a step forward. Sparks flew up from the warding circle at once, and my skin prickled with proximity to the barrier; I fell back, frustrated. "If you pick a fight with the wrong demon, this world is going to slide into chaos and darkness and we'll have lost our best chance of preventing a second round of the Dark Days. Even if you want to banish all of them eventually—" I swallowed. "All of *us*, that is—it's irrational to start with the ones who will leave humanity well enough alone if we leave them alone. We *have* to prioritize the ones who will cause the most damage if they're not stopped. And with Nightmare imprisoned, right now that's Hunger."

They regarded me for a long moment, then exchanged glances with each other.

"Foxglove seems to have been right about her priorities, anyway," Verinath said. "Morgrain and Eruvia, but not herself."

"Let's see if he was right about the rest." Lady Cornaro turned to me, her eyes narrowing. "You can provide us with assessments of the other demons' capabilities and intentions, strengths and weaknesses, methods and goals?"

"To the best of my ability. I'm not a mind reader—that's Madness."

"And you're resistant to their powers, and willing to use your own to help us trap or banish them?"

The sky blackened with ash, turning day to night. An endless shuddering within the tortured earth. The thunder of the ocean claiming the land with its devouring darkness.

"I...I can't use mine." I shivered. "My lady, I'm the Demon of Disaster. I can't ever use mine. Only what I can do as a human, and no more."

Verinath grimaced. "Point taken."

Best to be completely honest. I pressed ahead. "I also may not always be willing to help with every plan against every demon. My grandmother is—well, she's my grandmother. And if you're foolish enough to try something against the Demon of Death, I won't be part of that. But I'll be straightforward with you about it, and I won't ever side with demons against humanity."

"Honest, too," Verinath muttered. "Maybe too honest for your own good."

Lady Cornaro leaned forward. "Understand this. We don't control what the Council or the Conclave will do. The Crow Lord and I are just one member of each. What we *do* control is the Rookery."

"And the Rookery seems to want us to protect you." Verinath shook his head, as if this were sheer folly.

"For now, I'm going to give the Rookery the task of watching you." Lady Cornaro's eyes suddenly flicked to the window, where a mockingbird sat on the windowsill; she leveled a glare at it, and it fluttered away, startled.

Severin. My heart warmed. I wasn't alone.

"Let me be clear that this isn't for your sake," Lady Cornaro continued, her voice stern. "You're a demon. I cannot in good conscience consider you an ally."

Her words cut like knives, but I nodded. "That's fair."

"It will be the Rookery's job to keep us informed of your actions, assess how much of a threat you pose, and neutralize you if necessary." She performed a delicate shrug. "If you find yourself willing and able to help them in their missions in the meantime, that's your own business. I of course can't tell you what to do or not to do, since you're foreign royalty."

A traitor bubble of hope started rising beneath my rib cage. No matter how she dressed it up in cautionary words, she'd found a way to let me keep working with the Rookery even if the Council of Nine and the Conclave didn't want my help.

"I understand." I stopped myself from adding *Thank you.* She seemed to want to keep her own hands as clean of me as possible, and I couldn't blame her; I could only imagine that her political opponents would seize any hint that she'd made a deal with a demon and run with it.

Verinath met my gaze almost defiantly. "Understand also that we don't trust you. The Rookery may say nice things about you, but we can't forget that you're a demon."

I grimaced. "Yes, well, me either."

To my surprise, Verinath grinned. "Luckily, trust is a luxury, not a necessity. We're facing demons again, after four thousand years; we need all the help we can get. Just don't make us regret this."

"I'll try not to." I wished I could promise more, but given my record, I didn't dare.

"Good." Lady Cornaro gestured graciously toward the door. "Now Gaetano will release you from the circle, and you had better reassure your friends that you're all right. I believe half the Rookery is currently plastered to the outside of that door."

It was well past midnight when I finally stumbled back to my room, exhausted but happier than I'd been in what seemed like an age. I'd stayed up drinking tea and talking with Severin and the Rookery in their sitting room, the others mostly a bit drunk—or a lot drunk, in Kessa's case—basking in the sheer relief of everyone being alive and free. Certainly, most of them had been awkward around me from time to time, with fear creeping into their eyes at odd moments or grimacing pauses after they reflexively cursed by the Nine Demons; but everyone seemed determined to accept me, and that was good enough.

My own room felt welcoming and familiar, even though I'd only lived here for three weeks. It might not be home, but it was a place I belonged. A place that was mine, and that wanted me.

I hummed as I pulled off my boots, got into my nightshirt, and undid my braid. Even the ugly mass of scar over my ribs didn't bother me. Two of the four demons I'd released were bound now, at least for a time; all we had to do was find Hunger and deal with him, and then sort things out somehow with my grandmother. It had gone from an impossible task to a merely daunting one—and I had the best friends I could hope for to help me do it.

The air in the room changed subtly, coming alive like a storm ready to unleash its lightning. My heart missed a beat, then kept going a little faster than before.

I turned around to find Whisper standing in my window, yellow eyes glowing, back arched, tail bushy.

"There's a problem," he said.

Bloody pox, that couldn't be good. I sank down on the edge of my bed. "Whisper, we have so many problems already. I don't want any new problems."

"You've got them." His tail lashed. "Three more of them, to be precise."

"Three?" For a moment, I was confused. Then it hit me. "Oh, no. No, no, no."

"Yes." He almost spat the words. "Hunger took advantage of your grandmother's absence from Gloamingard, as she's off wreaking havoc at the Conclave. He got into the Black Tower somehow and opened the gate. He's let the others through out of pure spite."

Memories churned in the blackest depths of my mind, threatening to resurface. Corruption, Carnage, and Despair—three of the very worst of us, the ones not even the other demons had wanted to see loose in this world.

All Nine Demons had come through now. The Dark Days were upon us once more.

The story continues in . . .

THE BONE CHAMBER

Book Three of Rooks and Ruin

Coming in 2022!

ACKNOWLEDGMENTS

To put it mildly, 2020 was a hard year in which to write a book. I absolutely couldn't have done it without the help and support of my wonderful husband, Jesse King, and my children, Maya and Kyra. They did everything from providing emotional support to wrangling our new puppy, Lupa (who, let the record show, was *not* a helper but is very cute), and they were endlessly understanding. Thank you so much for everything.

This book has come a long way from its messy first draft, and it would still be languishing far short of its potential if it weren't for a few amazing people. First and foremost, my editor, Nivia Evans, insightful and relentless in the best possible way, who pushed me to make it better...and then better than that. And also my trusty beta readers who have stayed with me through the decades, Deva Fagan and Natsuko Toyofuku, who helped me realize key things about structure, character, and more. I wish I could bake each of you a whole cake. Thank you.

The entire Orbit team is always wonderful, both extremely competent *and* a pleasure to work with, and I'm so lucky to have them on my side. In the US, thanks to my managing editor, Bryn A. McDonald, and my copyeditor, the eagle-eyed Kelley Frodel, for helping this book across the finish line. I'm deeply grateful for the publicity efforts of Ellen Wright, the marketing work of Laura Fitzgerald and Paola Crespo, and the marketing design of

Stephanie Hess. And I remain frankly in awe of the breathtaking cover sorcery of the astounding Lisa Marie Pompilio and the art of Mike Heath—reader, when I first saw this gorgeous cover, I *screamed*. Thank you all!

In the UK, thanks as always to my wonderful editor, Emily Byron, who has guided me true through all my journeys to Eruvia. My gratitude goes out to Jenni Hill, Joanna Kramer, and Tom Webster for helping edit and produce the UK edition, and Nick Evans for adapting the cover. And my deepest appreciation for the marketing efforts of Maddy Hall and the sheer publicity power of Nazia Khatun. One of the strange things about being a traditionally published author is that all these amazing and talented people work on your book, and you often don't get to meet them or even know who they all are, so I'm sure I've missed people. But I'm deeply grateful to every single person at Orbit on either side of the Atlantic who had a hand in this book, and I'm awed and humbled by all you've done.

You wouldn't be reading this book without my amazing agent, Naomi Davis, who not only opens magic doors for me but always has my back. And it would have been immeasurably rougher facing down deadlines during a global pandemic without the support and sympathy of the writers of the Bunker, as well as my own cheering squad of LARPer friends who endured my daily writing updates. Thank you all for being there for me!

And finally, thank you, my wonderful readers, for letting my story and characters into your head for a while. This book is for you.

extras

orbitbooks.net

extras

about the author

Melissa Caruso was born on the summer solstice and went to school in an old mansion with a secret door, but despite this auspicious beginning has yet to develop any known superpowers. Melissa has spent her whole life creating imaginary worlds and, in addition to writing, is also an avid LARPer and tabletop gamer.

She graduated with honors in creative writing from Brown University and has an MFA in fiction from the University of Massachusetts Amherst. Melissa's first novel, *The Tethered Mage*, was shortlisted for a Gemmell Morningstar Award for best fantasy debut.

Find out more about Melissa Caruso and other Orbit authors by registering for the free monthly newsletter at orbitbooks.net

if you enjoyed

THE QUICKSILVER COURT

look out for

THE MASK
OF MIRRORS

Rook & Rose: Book One

by

M. A. Carrick

Nightmares are creeping through the city of dreams...

Renata Virdaux is a con artist who has come to the sparkling city of Nadeẓra — the city of dreams — with one goal: to trick her way into a noble house and secure her fortune and her sister's future.

But as she's drawn into the aristocratic world of House Traementis, she realises her masquerade is just one of many surrounding her. And as corrupted magic begins to weave its way through Nadeẓra, the poisonous feuds of its aristocrats and the shadowy dangers of its impoverished underbelly become tangled — with Ren at their heart.

1

The Mask of Mirrors

Isla Traementis, the Pearls: Suilun 1

After fifteen years of handling the Traementis house charters, Donaia Traementis knew that a deal which looked too good to be true probably was. The proposal currently on her desk stretched the boundaries of belief.

"He could at least try to make it look legitimate," she muttered. Did Mettore Indestor think her an utter fool?

He thinks you desperate. And he's right.

She burrowed her stockinged toes under the great lump of a hound sleeping beneath her desk and pressed cold fingers to her brow. She'd removed her gloves to avoid ink stains and left the hearth in her study unlit to save the cost of fuel. Besides Meatball, the only warmth was from the beeswax candles—an expense she couldn't scrimp on unless she wanted to lose what eyesight she had left.

Adjusting her spectacles, she scanned the proposal again, scratching angry notes between the lines.

She remembered a time when House Traementis had been as powerful as the Indestor family. They had held a seat in the Cinquerat, the five-person council that ruled Nadežra, and charters that allowed them to conduct trade, contract mercenaries, control guilds. Every variety of wealth, power, and prestige in Nadežra had been theirs. Now, despite Donaia's best efforts and her late husband's before her, it had come to this: scrabbling at one Dusk Road trade charter as though she could milk enough blood from that stone to pay off all the Traementis debts.

Debts almost entirely owned by Mettore Indestor.

"And you expect me to trust my caravan to guards you provide?" she growled at the proposal, her pen nib digging in hard enough to tear the paper. "Ha! Who's going to protect it from them? Will they even wait for bandits, or just sack the wagons themselves?"

Leaving Donaia with the loss, a pack of angry investors, and debts she could no longer cover. Then Mettore would swoop in like one of his thrice-damned hawks to swallow whole what remained of House Traementis.

Try as she might, though, she couldn't see another option. She couldn't send the caravan out unguarded—Vraszenian bandits were a legitimate concern—but the Indestor family held the Caerulet seat in the Cinquerat, which gave Mettore authority over military and mercenary affairs. Nobody would risk working with a house Indestor had a grudge against—not when it would mean losing a charter, or worse.

Meatball's head rose with a sudden whine. A moment later a knock came at the study door, followed by Donaia's majordomo. Colbrin knew better than to interrupt her when she was wrestling with business, which meant he judged this interruption important.

He bowed and handed her a card. "Alta Renata Viraudax?" Donaia asked, shoving Meatball's wet snout out of her lap when he sniffed at the card. She flipped it as if the back would provide some clue to the visitor's purpose. Viraudax wasn't a local noble house. Some traveler to Nadežra?

"A young woman, Era Traementis," her majordomo said. "Well-mannered. Well-dressed. She said it concerned an important private matter."

The card fluttered to the floor. Donaia's duties as head of House Traementis kept her from having much of a social life, but the same could not be said for her son, and lately Leato had been behaving more and more like his father. Ninat take him—if her son had racked up some gambling debt with a foreign visitor...

Colbrin retrieved the card before the dog could eat it, and handed it back to her. "Should I tell her you are not at home?"

"No. Show her in." If her son's dive into the seedier side of Nadežra had resulted in trouble, she would at least rectify his errors before stringing him up.

Somehow. With money she didn't have.

She could start by not conducting the meeting in a freezing study. "Wait," she said before Colbrin could leave. "Show her to the salon. And bring tea."

Donaia cleaned the ink from her pen and made a futile attempt to brush away the brindled dog hairs matting her surcoat. Giving that up as a lost cause, she tugged on her gloves and straightened the papers on her desk, collecting herself by collecting her surroundings. Looking down at her clothing—the faded blue surcoat over trousers and house scuffs—she weighed the value of changing over the cost of making a potential problem wait.

Everything is a tallied cost these days, she thought grimly.

"Meatball. Stay," she commanded when the hound would have followed, and headed directly to the salon.

The young woman waiting there could not have fit the setting more perfectly if she had planned it. Her rose-gold underdress and cream surcoat harmonized beautifully with the gold-shot peach silk of the couch and chairs, and the thick curl trailing from her upswept hair echoed the rich wood of the wall paneling. The curl should have looked like an accident, an errant strand slipping loose—but everything else about the visitor was so elegant it was clearly a deliberate touch of style.

She was studying the row of books on their glass-fronted shelf. When Donaia closed the door, she turned and dipped low. "Era Traementis. Thank you for seeing me."

Her curtsy was as Seterin as her clipped accent, one hand sweeping elegantly up to the opposite shoulder. Donaia's misgivings deepened at the sight of her. Close to her son's age, and beautiful as a portrait by Creciasto, with fine-boned features and flawless skin. Easy to imagine Leato losing his head over a hand of cards with such a girl. And her ensemble did nothing to comfort Donaia's fears—the richly embroidered brocade, the sleeves an elegant fall of sheer silk. Here was someone who could afford to bet and lose a fortune.

That sort was more likely to forgive or forget a debt than come collecting...unless the debt was meant as leverage for something else.

"Alta Renata. I hope you will forgive my informality." She brushed a hand down her simple attire. "I did not expect visitors, but it sounded like your matter was of some urgency. Please, do be seated."

The young woman lowered herself into the chair as lightly as mist on the river. Seeing her, it was easy to understand why the people of Nadežra looked to Seteris as the source of all that was stylish and elegant. Fashion was born in Seteris. By the time it traveled south to Seteris's protectorate, Seste Ligante, then farther south still, across the sea to Nadežra, it was old and stale, and Seteris had moved on.

Most Seterin visitors behaved as though Nadežra was nothing more than Seste Ligante's backwater colonial foothold on the Vraszenian continent and merely setting foot on the streets would foul them with the mud of the River Dežera. But Renata's delicacy looked like hesitation, not condescension. She said, "Not urgent, no—I do apologize if I gave that impression. I confess, I'm not certain how to even begin this conversation."

She paused, hazel eyes searching Donaia's face. "You don't recognize my family name, do you?"

That had an ominous sound. Seteris might be on the other side of the sea, but the truly powerful families could influence trade anywhere in the known world. If House Traementis had somehow crossed one of them...

Donaia kept her fear from her face and her voice. "I am afraid I haven't had many dealings with the great houses of Seteris."

A soft breath flowed out of the girl. "As I suspected. I thought she might have written to you at least once, but apparently not. I . . . am Letilia's daughter."

She could have announced she was descended from the Vraszenian goddess Ažerais herself, and it wouldn't have taken Donaia more by surprise.

Disbelief clashed with relief and apprehension both: not a creditor, not an offended daughter of some foreign power. Family—after a fashion.

Lost for words, Donaia reassessed the young woman sitting across from her. Straight back, straight shoulders, straight neck, and the same fine, narrow nose that made everyone in Nadežra hail Letilia Traementis as the great beauty of her day.

Yes, she could be Letilia's daughter. Donaia's niece by marriage.

"Letilia never wrote after she left." It was the only consideration the spoiled brat had ever shown her family. The first several years, every day they'd expected a letter telling them she was stranded in Seteris, begging for funds. Instead they never heard from her again.

Dread sank into Donaia's bones. "Is Letilia here?"

The door swung open, and for one dreadful instant Donaia expected a familiar squall of petulance and privilege to sweep inside. But it was only Colbrin, bearing a tray. To her dismay, Donaia saw two pots on it, one short and rounded for tea, the other taller. Of course: He'd heard their guest's Seterin accent, and naturally assumed Donaia would also want to serve coffee.

We haven't yet fallen so far that I can't afford proper hospitality. But Donaia's voice was still sharp as he set the tray between the two of them. "Thank you, Colbrin. That will be all."

"No," Renata said as the majordomo bowed and departed. "No, Mother is happily ensconced in Seteris."

It seemed luck hadn't *entirely* abandoned House Traementis. "Tea?" Donaia said, a little too bright with relief. "Or would you prefer coffee?"

"Coffee, thank you." Renata accepted the cup and saucer with a graceful hand. Everything about her was graceful—but not the artificial, forced elegance Donaia remembered Letilia practicing so assiduously.

Renata sipped the coffee and made a small, appreciative noise. "I must admit, I was wondering if I would even be able to find coffee here."

Ah. *There* was the echo of Letilia, the little sneer that took what should be a compliment and transformed it into an insult.

We have wooden floors and chairs with backs, too. Donaia swallowed down the snappish response. But the bitter taste in her mouth nudged her into pouring coffee for herself, even though she disliked it. She wouldn't let this girl make her feel like a delta rustic simply because Donaia had lived all her life in Nadežra.

"So you are here, but Letilia is not. May I ask why?"

The girl's chin dropped, and she rotated her coffee cup as though its precise alignment against the saucer were vitally important. "I've spent days imagining how best to approach you, but—well." There was a ripple of nervousness in her laugh. "There's no way to say this without first admitting I'm Letilia's daughter...and yet by admitting that, I know I've already gotten off on the wrong foot. Still, there's nothing for it."

Renata inhaled like someone preparing for battle, then met Donaia's gaze. "I'm here to see if I can possibly reconcile my mother with her family."

It took all Donaia's self-control not to laugh. Reconcile? She would sooner reconcile with the drugs that had overtaken her husband Gianco's good sense in his final years. If Gianco's darker comments were to be believed, Letilia had done as much to destroy House Traementis as aža had.

Fortunately, custom and law offered her a more dispassionate response. "Letilia is no part of this family. My husband's father struck her name from our register after she left."

At least Renata was smart enough not to be surprised. "I can hardly blame my gra—your father-in-law," she said. "I've only my mother's version of the tale, but I also know *her*. I can guess the part she played in that estrangement."

Donaia could just imagine what poison Letilia's version had contained. "It is more than estrangement," she said brusquely, rising to her feet. "I am sorry you crossed the sea for nothing, but I'm afraid that what you're asking for is impossible. Even if I believed that your mother wanted to reconcile—which I do not—I have no interest in doing so."

A treacherous worm within her whispered, *Even if that might offer a new business opportunity? Some way out of Indestor's trap?*

Even then. Donaia would burn Traementis Manor to the ground before she accepted help from Letilia's hand.

The salon door opened again. But this time, the interruption wasn't her majordomo.

"Mother, Egliadas has invited me to go sailing on the river." Leato was tugging on his gloves, as if he couldn't be bothered to finish dressing before leaving his rooms. But he stopped, one hand still caught in the tight cuff, when he saw their visitor.

Renata rose like a flower bud unfurling, and Donaia cursed silently. Why, today of all days, had Leato chosen to wake early? Not that fourth sun was early by most people's standards, but for him midmorning might as well be dawn.

Reflex forced the courtesies out of her mouth, even though she wanted nothing more than to hurry the girl away. "Leato, you recall stories of your aunt Letilia? This is her daughter, Alta Renata Viraudax of Seteris. Alta Renata, my son and heir, Leato Traementis."

Leato captured Renata's hand before she could touch it to her shoulder again and kissed her gloved fingertips. When she saw them together, Donaia's heart sank like a stone. She was used to thinking of her son as an adolescent scamp, or an intermittent source of headaches. But he was a man grown, with beauty to match Renata's: his hair like antique gold, fashionably mussed on top; his ivory skin and finely carved features, the hallmark of House Traementis; the elegant cut of his waistcoat and fitted tailoring of the full-skirted coat over it in the platinum shimmer of delta grasses in autumn.

And the two of them were smiling at one another like the sun had just risen in the salon.

"Letilia's daughter?" Leato said, releasing Renata's hand before the touch could grow awkward. "I thought she hated us."

Donaia bit down the impulse to chide him. It would sound like she was defending Renata, which was the last thing she wanted to do.

The girl's smile was brief and rueful. "I may have inherited her nose, but I've tried not to inherit *everything* else."

"You mean, not her personality? I'll offer thanks to Katus." Leato winced. "I'm sorry, I shouldn't insult your mother—"

"No insult taken," Renata said dryly. "I'm sure the stories you know of her are dreadful, and with good cause."

They had the river's current beneath them and were flowing onward; Donaia had to stop it before they went too far. When Leato asked what brought Renata to the city, Donaia lunged in, social grace be damned. "She just—"

But Renata spoke over her, as smooth as silk. "I was hoping to meet your grandfather and father. Foolish of me, really; since Mother hasn't been in contact, I didn't know they'd both passed away until I arrived. And now I understand she's no longer in the register, so there's no bond between us—I'm just a stranger, intruding."

"Oh, not at all!" Leato turned to his mother for confirmation.

For the first time, Donaia felt a touch of gratitude toward Renata. Leato had never known Letilia; he hadn't even been born when she ran away. He'd heard the tales, but no doubt he marked at least some of them as exaggeration. If Renata had mentioned a reconciliation outright, he probably would have supported her.

"We're touched by your visit," Donaia said, offering the girl a courteous nod. "I'm only sorry the others never had a chance to meet you."

"Your visit?" Leato scoffed. "No, this can't be all. You're my cousin, after all—oh, not under the law, I know. But blood counts for a lot here."

"We're Nadežran, Leato, not Vraszenian," Donaia said reprovingly, lest Renata think they'd been completely swallowed by delta ways.

He went on as though he hadn't heard her. "My long-lost cousin shows up from across the sea, greets us for a few minutes, then vanishes? Unacceptable. Giuna hasn't even met you—she's my younger sister. Why don't you stay with us for a few days?"

Donaia couldn't stop a muffled sound from escaping her. However much he seemed determined to ignore them, Leato knew about House Traementis's financial troubles. A houseguest was the last thing they could afford.

But Renata demurred with a light shake of her head. "No, no—I couldn't impose like that. I'll be in Nadežra for some time, though. Perhaps you'll allow me the chance to show I'm not my mother."

Preparatory to pushing for reconciliation, no doubt. But although Renata was older and more self-possessed, something about her downcast gaze reminded Donaia of Giuna. She could all too easily imagine Giuna seeking Letilia out in Seteris with the same impossible dream.

If House Traementis could afford the sea passage, which they could not. And if Donaia would allow her to go, which she would not. But if that impossible situation happened...she bristled at the thought of Letilia rebuffing Giuna entirely, treating her with such cold hostility that she refused to see the girl at all.

So Donaia said, as warmly as she could, "Of course we know you aren't your mother. And you shouldn't be forced to carry the burden of her past." She let a smile crack her mask. "I'm certain from the caterpillars dancing on my son's brow that he'd like to know more about you, and I imagine Giuna would feel the same."

"Thank you," Renata said with a curtsy. "But not now, I think. My apologies, Altan Leato." Her words silenced his protest before he could voice it, and with faultless formality. "My maid intends to fit me for a new dress this afternoon, and she'll stick me with pins if I'm late."

That was as unlike Letilia as it was possible to be. Not the concern for her clothing—Letilia was the same, only with less tasteful results—but the graceful withdrawal, cooperating with Donaia's wish to get her out of the house.

Leato did manage to get one more question out, though. "Where can we reach you?"

"On the Isla Prišta, Via Brelkoja, number four," Renata said. Donaia's lips tightened. For a stay of a few weeks, even a month or two, a hotel would have sufficed. Renting a house suggested the girl intended to remain for quite some time.

But that was a matter for later. Donaia reached for the bell. "Colbrin will see you out."

"No need," Leato said, offering Renata his hand. When she glanced at Donaia instead of taking it, Leato said, "Mother, you won't begrudge me a few moments of gossip with my new cousin?"

That was Leato, always asking for forgiveness rather than permission. But Renata's minute smile silently promised not to encourage him. At Donaia's forbearing nod, she accepted his escort from the room.

Once they were gone, Donaia rang for Colbrin. "I'll be in my study. No more interruptions barring flood or fire, please."

Colbrin's acknowledgment trailed after her as she went upstairs. When she entered the room, Meatball roused with a whine-snap of a yawn and a hopeful look, but settled again once he realized no treats were forthcoming.

The space seemed chillier than when she'd left it, and darker. She thought of Alta Renata's fine manners and finer clothes. Of course Letilia's daughter would be dressed in designs so new they hadn't yet made their way from Seteris to Nadežra. Of course she would have enough wealth to rent a house in Westbridge for herself alone and think nothing of it. Hadn't Gianco always said that Letilia took House Traementis's luck with her when she left?

In a fit of pique, Donaia lit the hearthfire, and damn the cost. Once its warmth was blazing through the study, she returned to her desk. She buried her toes under the dog again, mentally composing her message as she sharpened her nib and filled her ink tray.

House Traementis might be neck-deep in debt and sinking, but they still had the rights granted by their ennoblement charter. And Donaia wasn't such a fool that she would bite a hook before examining it from all sides first.

Bending her head, Donaia began penning a letter to Commander Cercel of the Vigil.

Renata expected Leato Traementis to see her out the front door, but he escorted her all the way to the bottom of the steps, and kept her hand even when they stopped. "I hope you're not too offended by Mother's reserve," he said. A breeze ruffled his burnished hair and carried the scent of caramel and almonds to her nose. A rich scent, matching his clothes and his carriage, and the thin lines of gold paint limning his eyelashes. "A lot of dead branches have been pruned from the Traementis register since my father—and your mother— were children. Now there's only Mother, Giuna, and myself. She gets protective."

"I take no offense at all," Renata said, smiling up at him. "I'm not so much of a fool that I expect to be welcomed with open arms. And I'm willing to be patient."

The breeze sharpened, and she shivered. Leato stepped between her and the wind. "You'd think Nadežra would be warmer than Seteris, wouldn't you?" he said with a sympathetic grimace. "It's all the water. We almost never get snow here, but the winters are so damp, the cold cuts right to your bones."

"I should have thought to wear a cloak. But since I can't pluck one from thin air, I hope you won't take offense if I hurry home."

"Of course not. Let me get you a sedan chair." Leato raised a hand to catch the eye of some men idling on the far side of the square and paid the bearers before Renata could even reach for her purse. "To soothe any lingering sting," he said with a smile.

She thanked him with another curtsy. "I hope I'll see you soon."

"As do I." Leato helped her into the sedan chair and closed the door once her skirts were safely out of the way.

As the bearers headed for the narrow exit from the square,

Renata drew the curtains shut. Traementis Manor was in the Pearls, a cluster of islets strung along the Upper Bank of the River Dežera. The river here ran pure and clear thanks to the numinat that protected the East Channel, and the narrow streets and bridges were clean; whichever families held the charters to keep the streets clear of refuse wouldn't dream of letting it accumulate near the houses of the rich and powerful.

But the rocky wedge that broke the Dežera into east and west channels was a different matter. For all that it held two of Nadežra's major institutions—the Charterhouse in Dawngate, which was the seat of government, and the Aerie in Duskgate, home to the Vigil, which maintained order—the Old Island was also crowded with the poor and the shabby-genteel. Anyone riding in a sedan chair was just asking for beggars to crowd at their windows.

Which still made it better than half of the Lower Bank, where a sedan chair risked being knocked to the ground and the passenger robbed.

Luckily, her rented house was on Isla Prišta in Westbridge—technically on the Lower Bank, and far from a fashionable district, but it was a respectable neighborhood on the rise. In fact, the buildings on the Via Brelkoja were so newly renovated the mortar hadn't had time to moss over in the damp air. The freshly painted door to number four opened just as Renata's foot touched the first step.

Tess made a severe-looking sight in the crisp grey-and-white surcoat and underskirt of a Nadežran housemaid, but her copper Ganllechyn curls and freckles were a warm beacon welcoming Renata home. She bobbed a curtsy and murmured a lilting "alta" as Renata passed across the threshold, accepting the gloves and purse Renata held out.

"Downstairs," Ren murmured as the door snicked shut, sinking them into the dimness of the front hall.

Tess nodded, swallowing her question before she could speak it. Together they headed into the half-sunken chambers of the cellar, which held the service rooms. Only once they were safely in the kitchen did Tess say, "Well? How did it go?"

Ren let her posture drop and her voice relax into the throaty tones of her natural accent. "For me, as well as I could hope. Donaia refused reconciliation out of hand—"

"Thank the Mother," Tess breathed. If Donaia contacted Letilia, their entire plan would fall apart before it started.

Ren nodded. "Faced with the prospect of talking to her former sister-in-law, she barely even noticed me getting my foot in the door."

"That's a start, then. Here, off with this, and wrap up before you take a chill." Tess passed Ren a thick cloak of rough-spun wool lined with raw fleece, then turned her around like a dressmaker's doll so she could remove the beautifully embroidered surcoat.

"I saw the sedan chair," Tess said as she tugged at the side ties. "You didn't take that all the way from Isla Traementis, did you? If you're going to be riding about in chairs, I'll have to revise the budget. And here I'd had my eye on a lovely bit of lace at the remnants stall." Tess sighed mournfully, like she was saying farewell to a sweetheart. "I'll just have to tat some myself."

"In your endless spare time?" Ren said sardonically. The surcoat came loose, and she swung the cloak around her shoulders in its place. "Anyway, the son paid for the chair." She dropped onto the kitchen bench and eased her shoes off with a silent curse. Fashionable shoes were *not* comfortable. The hardest part of this con was going to be pretending her feet didn't hurt all day long.

Although choking down coffee ran a close second.

"Did he, now?" Tess settled on the bench next to Ren, close enough that they could share warmth beneath the cloak. Apart from the kitchen and the front salon, protective sheets still covered the furniture in every other room. The hearths were cold, their meals were simple, and they slept together on a kitchen floor pallet so they would only have to heat one room of the house.

Because she was not Alta Renata Viraudax, daughter of Letilia Traementis. She was Arenza Lenskaya, half-Vraszenian river rat, and even with a forged letter of credit to help, pretending to be a Seterin noblewoman wasn't cheap.

Pulling out a thumbnail blade, Tess began ripping the seams of Ren's beautiful surcoat, preparatory to alteration. "Was it just idle flirtation?"

The speculative uptick in Tess's question said she didn't believe any flirtation Ren encountered was idle. But whether Leato's flirtation had been idle or not, Ren had lines she would not cross, and whoring herself out was one of them.

It would have been the easier route. Dress herself up fine enough to catch the eye of some delta gentry son, or even a noble, and marry her way into money. She wouldn't be the first person in Nadežra to do it.

But she'd spent five years in Ganllech—five years as a maid under Letilia's thumb, listening to her complain about her dreadful family and how much she dreamed of life in Seteris, the promised land she'd never managed to reach. So when Ren and Tess found themselves back in Nadežra, Ren had been resolved. No whoring, and no killing. Instead she set her sights on a higher target: use what she'd learned to gain acceptance into House Traementis as their long-lost kin... with all the wealth and social benefit that brought.

"Leato is friendly," she allowed, picking up the far end of the dress and starting on the seam with her own knife. Tess didn't trust her to sew anything more complicated than a hem, but ripping stitches? That, she was qualified for. "And he helped shame Donaia into agreeing to see me again. But *she* is every bit as bad as Letilia claimed. You should have seen what she wore. Ratty old clothes, covered in dog hair. Like it's a moral flaw to let a single centira slip through her fingers."

"But the son isn't so bad?" Tess rocked on the bench, nudging Ren's hip with her own. "Maybe he's a bastard."

Ren snorted. "Not likely. Donaia would give him the moon if he asked, and he looks as Traementis as I." Only he didn't need makeup to achieve the effect.

Her hands trembled as she worked. Those five years in Ganllech were also five years out of practice. And all her previous cons had been short touches—never anything on this scale. When she got caught before, the hawks slung her in jail for a few days.

If she got caught now, impersonating a noblewoman...

Tess laid a hand over Ren's, stopping her before she could nick herself with the knife. "It's never too late to do something else."

Ren managed a smile. "Buy piles of fabric, then run away and set up as dressmakers? You, anyway. I would be your tailor's dummy."

"You'd model and sell them," Tess said stoutly. "If you want."

Tess would be happy in that life. But Ren wanted more.

This city *owed* her more. It had taken everything: her mother, her childhood, Sedge. The rich cuffs of Nadežra got whatever they wanted, then squabbled over what their rivals had, grinding everyone else underfoot. In all her days among the Fingers, Ren had never been able to take more than the smallest shreds from the hems of their cloaks.

But now, thanks to Letilia, she was in a position to take more.

The Traementis made the perfect target. Small enough these days that only Donaia stood any chance of spotting Renata as an imposter, and isolated enough that they would be grateful for any addition to their register. In the glory days of their power and graft, they'd been notorious for their insular ways, refusing to aid their fellow nobles in times of need. Since they lost their seat in the Cinquerat, everyone else had gladly returned the favor.

Ren put down the knife and squeezed Tess's hand. "No. It is nerves only, and they will pass. We go forward."

"Forward it is." Tess squeezed back, then returned to work. "Next we're to make a splash somewhere public, yes? I'll need to know where and when if I'm to outfit you proper." The sides of the surcoat parted, and she started on the bandeau at the top of the bodice. "The sleeves are the key, have you noticed? Everyone is so on about their sleeves. But I've a thought for that...if you're ready for Alta Renata to set fashion instead of following."

Ren glanced sideways, her wariness only half-feigned. "What have you in mind?"

"Hmm. Stand up, and off with the rest of it." Once she had Ren stripped to her chemise, Tess played with different gathers and drapes until Ren's arms started to ache from being held out for so long. But she didn't complain. Tess's eye for fashion, her knack for imbuing, and her ability to rework the pieces of three outfits into nine were as vital to this con as Ren's skill at manipulation.

She closed her eyes and cast her thoughts over what she knew about the city. Where could she go, what could she do, to attract the kind of admiration that would help her gain the foothold she needed?

A slow smile spread across her face.

"Tess," she said, "I have the perfect idea. And you will love it."

The Aerie and Isla Traementis: Suilun 1

"Serrado! Get in here. I have a job for you."

Commander Cercel's voice cut sharply through the din of the Aerie. Waving at his constables to take their prisoner to the stockade, Captain Grey Serrado turned and threaded his way through the chaos to his commander's office. He ignored the sidelong smirks and snide whispers of his fellow officers: Unlike them, he didn't have the luxury of lounging about drinking coffee, managing his constables from the comfort of the Aerie.

"Commander Cercel?" He snapped the heels of his boots together and gave her his crispest salute—a salute he'd perfected during hours of standing at attention in the sun, the rain, the wind, while other lieutenants were at mess or in the barracks. Cercel wasn't the stickler for discipline his previous superiors had been, but she was the reason he wore a captain's double-lined hexagram pin, and he didn't want to reflect badly on her.

She was studying a letter, but when she brought her head up to reply, her eyes widened. "What does the *other* guy look like?"

Taking the casual question as permission to drop into rest, Grey spared a glance for his uniform. His patrol slops were spattered with muck from heel to shoulder, and blood was drying on the knuckles of his leather gloves. Some of the canal mud on his boots had flaked off when he saluted, powdering Cercel's carpet with the filth of the Kingfisher slums.

"Dazed but breathing. Ranieri's taking him to the stockade now." Her question invited banter, but the door to her office was open, and it wouldn't do him any good to be marked as a smart-ass.

She responded to his businesslike answer with an equally brisk nod. "Well, get cleaned up. I've received a letter from one of the noble houses, requesting Vigil assistance. I'm sending you."

Grey's jaw tensed as he waited for several gut responses to subside. It was possible the request was a legitimate call for aid. "What crime has been committed?"

Cercel's level gaze said, *You know better than that.* "One of the noble houses has requested Vigil assistance," she repeated, enunciating each word with cut-glass clarity. "I'm sure they wouldn't do that without good cause."

No doubt whoever sent the letter thought the cause was good. People from the great houses always did.

But Grey had a desk full of real problems. "More children have gone missing. That's eleven verified this month."

They'd had this conversation several times over the past few weeks. Cercel sighed. "We haven't had any reports—"

"Because they're all river rats so far. Who's going to care enough to report that? But the man I just brought in might know something about it; he's been promising Kingfisher kids good pay for an unspecified job. I got him on defacing public property, but he'll be free again by tonight." Pissing in public wasn't an offense the Vigil usually cracked down on, unless it suited them. "Am I to assume this noble's 'good cause' takes precedence over finding out what's happening to those kids?"

Cercel breathed out hard through her nose, and he tensed. Had he pushed her patience too far?

No. "Your man is on his way to the stockade," she said. "Have Kaineto process him—you're always complaining he's as slow as river mud. By the time you get back, he'll be ready to talk. Meanwhile, send Ranieri to ask questions around Kingfisher, see if he can find any of the man's associates." She set the letter aside and drew another from her stack, a clear prelude to dismissing him. "You know the deal, Serrado."

The first few times, he'd played dense to make her spell it out in unambiguous terms. The last thing he could afford back then was to mistake a senior officer's meaning.

But they were past those games now. As long as he knuckled under and did whatever this noble wanted of him, Cercel wouldn't question him using Vigil time and resources for his own investigations.

"Yes, Commander." He saluted and heel-knocked another layer of delta silt onto her carpet. "Which house has called for aid?"

"Traementis."

If he'd been less careful of his manners, he would have thrown her a dirty look. *She could have* led *with that*. But Cercel wanted him to understand that answering these calls was part of his duty, and made him bend his neck before she revealed the silver lining. "Understood. I'll head to the Pearls at once."

Her final command followed him out of the office. "Don't you dare show up at Era Traementis's door looking like that!"

Groaning, Grey changed his path. He snagged a pitcher of water and a messenger, sending the latter to Ranieri with the new orders.

There was a bathing room in the Aerie, but he didn't want to waste time on that. A sniff test sent every piece of his patrol uniform into the laundry bag; aside from the coffee, that was one of the few perks of his rank he didn't mind taking shameless advantage of. If he was wading through canals for the job, the least the Vigil could do was ensure he didn't smell like one. A quick pitcher bath in his tiny office took care of the scents still clinging to his skin and hair before he shrugged into his dress vigils.

He had to admit the force's tailors were good. The tan breeches were Liganti-cut, snug as they could be around his thighs and hips without impeding movement. Both the brocade waistcoat and the coat of sapphire wool were tailored like a second skin, before the latter flared to full skirts that kissed the tops of his polished, knee-high boots. On his patrol slops, the diving hawk across the back of his shoulders was mere patchwork; here it was embroidered in golds and browns.

Grey didn't have much use for vanity, but he did love his dress vigils. They were an inarguable reminder that he'd climbed to a place few Vraszenians could even imagine reaching. His brother, Kolya, had been so proud the day Grey came home in them.

The sudden trembling of his hands stabbed his collar pin into his thumb. Grey swallowed a curse and sucked the blood from the puncture, using a tiny hand mirror to make sure he hadn't gotten any on his collar. Luckily, it was clean, and he managed to finish dressing himself without further injury.

Once outside, he set off east from Duskgate with long, ground-eating strides. He could have taken a sedan chair and told the bearers to bill the Vigil; other officers did, knowing all the while that no such bill would ever be paid. But along with stiffing the bearers, that meant they didn't see the city around them the way Grey did.

Not that most of them would. They were Liganti, or mixed enough in ancestry that they could claim the name; to them, Nadežra was an outpost of Seste Ligante, half tamed by the Liganti general Kaius Sifigno, who restyled himself Kaius Rex after conquering Vraszan two centuries past. Others called him the Tyrant, and when he died, the Vraszenian clans took back the rest of their conquered land. But every push to reclaim their holy city failed, until exhaustion on both sides led to the signing of the Accords. Those established Nadežra as an independent city-state—under the rule of its Liganti elite.

It was an uneasy balance at best, made less easy still by Vraszenian radical groups like the Stadnem Anduske, who wouldn't settle for anything less than the city back in Vraszenian hands. And every time they pushed, the Cinquerat pushed back even harder.

The busy markets of Suncross at the heart of the Old Island parted for Grey's bright blue coat and the tawny embroidered hawk;

but not without glares. To the high and mighty, the Vigil was a tool; to the common Nadežran, the Vigil was the tool of the high and mighty. Not all of them—Grey wasn't the only hawk who cared about common folk—but enough that he couldn't blame people for their hostility. And some of the worst glares came from Vraszenians, who looked at him and saw a slip-knot: a man who had betrayed his people, siding with the invaders' descendants.

Grey was used to the glares. He kept an eye out for trouble as he passed market stalls on the stoops of decaying townhouses, and a bawdy puppet show where the only children in the crowd were the pickpockets. They trickled away like water before he could mark their faces. A few beggars eyed him warily, but Grey had no grudge against them; the more dangerous elements wouldn't come out until evening, when the feckless sons and daughters of the delta gentry prowled the streets in search of amusement. A pattern-reader had set up on a corner near the Charterhouse, ready to bilk people in exchange for a pretty lie. He gave her a wide berth, leather glove creaking into a fist as he resisted the urge to drag her back to the Aerie for graft.

Once he'd passed under the decaying bulk of the Dawngate and across the Sunrise Bridge, he turned north into the narrow islets of the Pearls, clogged with sedan chairs. Two elderly ladies impressed with their own importance blocked the Becchia Bridge entirely, squabbling like gulls over which one should yield. Grey marked the house sigil painted onto each chair's door in case complaints came to the Aerie later.

His shoulders itched as he crossed the lines of the complex mosaic in the center of Traementis Plaza. It was no mere tilework, but a numinat: geometric Liganti magic meant to keep the ground dry and solid, against the river's determination to sink everything into the mud. Useful... but the Tyrant had twisted numinatria into a weapon during his conquest, and mosaics like this one amounted to emblems of ongoing Liganti control.

On the steps of Traementis Manor, Grey gave his uniform a final smoothing and sounded the bell. Within moments, Colbrin opened the door and favored Grey with a rare smile.

"Young Master Serrado. How pleasant to see you; it's been far too long. I'm afraid Altan Leato is not here to receive you—"

"It's 'Captain' now," Grey said, touching the hexagram pin at his throat. The smile he dredged up felt tired from disuse. "And I'm not here for Leato. Era Traementis requested assistance from the Vigil."

"Ah, yes." Colbrin bowed him inside. "If you'll wait in the salon, I'll inform Era Traementis that you're here."

Grey wasn't surprised when Colbrin returned in a few moments and summoned him to the study. Whatever Donaia had written to the Vigil for, it was business, not a social call.

That room was much darker, with little in the way of bright silks to warm the space—but warmth came in many shapes. Donaia's grizzled wolfhound scrambled up from his place by her desk, claws ticking on wood as he trotted over for a greeting. "Hello, old man," Grey said, giving him a good tousling and a few barrel thumps on the side.

"Meatball. Heel." The dog returned to Donaia's side, looking up as she crossed the room to greet Grey.

"Era Traementis," Grey said, bowing over her hand. "I'm told you have need of assistance."

The silver threads lacing through her hair were gaining ground against the auburn, and she looked tired. "Yes. I need you to look into someone—a visitor to the city, recently arrived from Seteris. Renata Viraudax."

"Has she committed some crime against House Traementis?"

"No," Donaia said. "*She* hasn't."

Her words piqued his curiosity. "Era?"

A muscle tightened in Donaia's jaw. "My husband once had a sister named Letilia—Lecilla, really, but she was obsessed with Seteris and their high culture, so she badgered their father into changing it in the register. Twenty-three years ago, she decided she would rather be in Seteris than here . . . so she stole some money and jewelry and ran away."

Donaia gestured Grey to a chair in front of the hearth. The warmth of the fire enveloped him as he sat down. "Renata Viraudax is Letilia's daughter. She claims to be trying to mend bridges, but I have my doubts. I want you to find out what she's really doing in Nadežra."

As much as Grey loathed the right of the nobility to commandeer the Vigil for private use, he couldn't help feeling sympathy. When he was younger and less aware of the differences that made it impossible, he'd sometimes wished Donaia Traementis was his mother. She was stern, but fair. She loved her children, and was fiercely protective of her family. Unlike some, she never gave Leato and Giuna reason to doubt her love for them.

This Viraudax woman's mother had hurt her family, and the Traementis had a well-earned reputation for avenging their own.

"What can you tell me about her?" he asked. "Has she given you any reason to doubt her sincerity? Apart from being her mother's daughter."

Donaia's fingers drummed briefly against the arm of the chair, and her gaze settled on a corner of the fireplace and stayed there long enough that Grey knew she was struggling with some thought. He kept his silence.

Finally she said, "You and my son are friends, and moreover you aren't a fool. It can't have escaped your notice that House Traementis is not what it once was, in wealth, power, or numbers. We have many enemies eager to see us fall. Now this young woman shows up and tries to insinuate herself among us? Perhaps I'm jumping at shadows...but I must consider the possibility that this is a gambit intended to destroy us entirely." She gave a bitter laugh. "I can't even be certain this girl *is* Letilia's daughter."

She must be worried, if she was admitting so much. Yes, Grey had suspected—would have suspected even if Vigil gossip didn't sometimes speculate—that House Traementis was struggling more than they let on. But he never joined in the gossip, and he never asked Leato.

Leato...who was always in fashion, and according to that same gossip spent half his time frequenting aža parlours and gambling dens. *Does Leato know?* Grey swallowed the question. It wasn't his business, and it wasn't the business Donaia had called him for.

"That last shouldn't be too hard to determine," he said. "I assume you know where she's staying?" He paused when Donaia's lips flattened, but she only nodded. "Then talk to her. If she's truly Letilia's daughter, she should know details an imposter wouldn't easily be able to discover. If she gives you vague answers or takes offense, then you'll know something is wrong."

Grey paused again, wondering how much Donaia would let him pry. "You said you had enemies she might be working for. It would help me to know who they are and what they might want." At her sharply indrawn breath, he raised a hand in pledge. "I promise I'll say nothing of it—not even to Leato."

In a tone so dry it burned, Donaia began ticking possibilities off on her fingers. "Quientis took our seat in the Cinquerat. Kaineto are only delta gentry, but have made a point of blocking our attempts to contract out our charters. Essunta, likewise. Simendis, Destaelio, Novrus, Cleoter—Indestor—I'm afraid it's a crowded field."

That was the entire Cinquerat and others besides...but she'd only stumbled over one name.

"Indestor," Grey said. The house that held Caerulet, the military seat in the Cinquerat. The house in charge of the Vigil.

The house that would not look kindly upon being investigated by one of its own.

"Era Traementis...did you ask for any officer, or did you specifically request me?"

"You're Leato's friend," Donaia said, holding his gaze. "Far better to ask a friend for help than to confess our troubles to an enemy."

That startled a chuckle from Grey. At Donaia's furrowed brow, he said, "My brother was fond of a Vraszenian saying. 'A family covered in the same dirt washes in the same water.'"

And Kolya would have given Grey a good scolding for not jumping to help Donaia right away. She might not be kin, but she'd hired a young Vraszenian carpenter with a scrawny kid brother when nobody else would, and paid him the same as a Nadežran.

He stood and bowed with a fist to his shoulder. "I'll see what I can discover for you. Tell me where to find this Renata Viraudax."

his flattened but she only nodded. "Then talk to her, Frank, truly I really, daughter, he should know details an imposter wouldn't easily be able to discover. If she takes you vague answers or tales of time, then you'll know something is wrong."

Grey paused again, wondering how much Toones would let him pry. "You said you had enemies, did me, if he looking for, it would help me to know whether they are and what they might want." A bit sharply and now harshly, he raised a hand to pledge, "I promise I'll say nothing of it—not even to Camp."

In a tone so dry it burned, Toones began making possibilities off on her fingers. "Chapmans took up rent in the Chiquero at Kainote only daily gently, but I have made a point of blocking out all mob to control our own barters. Besting likewise. Simoedo, Dematilo, Shayne, Cuotor—Jubilusto—in that I'd…" crowded in, "If."

"That was the entire Chapman and others besides, I but she'd only stumbled over one name.

"Indeed," Grey said. "The house that held Caerule, the primary seat in the Chiquero." The house in charge of the Vigil."The house that would not look kindly upon being investigated by one of its own."

"Tre Faustino, sir," did you ask for any offense, or did you specifically inquire after?"

"You're Caru's friend," Toones said, holding his gaze. "That bet ter to ask a friend for help than to confess our trouble to an enemy. That landed a chuckle from Grey. At Donata's furrowed brow, he said, "My brother was fond of my exasperation giving. A family for certain he'd cover dirt wandered to the step notion.

And so boy would have given Grey a good scolding for not jumping to help Donata right away, she might've not been in, but she'd hired a young Vizentian carpenter with an unruly kid, brother, whom nobody else would, and paid him the exact old take run.

He stood and bowed with a fist to his shoulder. "I'll see what I can discover for you. Tell me where to find the Arcana, Vizentino."

Enter the monthly

Orbit sweepstakes at

www.orbitloot.com

With a different prize every month,
from advance copies of books by
your favourite authors to exclusive
merchandise packs,
**we think you'll find something
you love.**

orbit

facebook.com/OrbitBooksUK

@orbitbooks_uk

@OrbitBooks

www.orbitbooks.net